Praise for *New York Times* bestselling author Lori Foster

"A standout story of friends, lovers, and even a very cute puppy."

—*Booklist*, starred review,
on *Sisters of Summer's End*

"A bubbly summer escape, and beyond that, a heartwarming look at the healing power of family."
—*Entertainment Weekly* on *Cooper's Charm*

"Brimming with heart, heat and humor."
—Jill Shalvis, *New York Times* bestselling author,
on *Worth the Wait*

"A beautifully matched pair find each other despite their misgivings (and their baggage) in a steamy romance laced with mystery and suspense that is a pure delight."

—*Library Journal* on *Cooper's Charm*

"Foster fills her scenes with plenty of banter and sizzling chemistry, ensuring longtime fans will feel right at home in this new series."
—*Publishers Weekly* on *Driven to Distraction*

"A sexy, heartwarming, down-home tale that features two captivating love stories... A funny and engaging addition to the series that skillfully walks the line between romance and women's fiction."
—*Library Journal* on *Sisters of Summer's End*

"Full of healing, hope and, most importantly, love... An absolute delight."
—Maisey Yates, *New York Times* bestselling author,
on *Cooper's Charm*

"Storytelling at its best! Lori Foster should be on everyone's auto-buy list."
—#1 *New York Times* bestselling author
Sherrilyn Kenyon on *No Limits*

"Foster's fans will savor this."
—*Publishers Weekly* on *Sisters of Summer's End*

LORI FOSTER

Sisters of Summer's End

ISBN-13: 978-1-335-01497-9

Sisters of Summer's End

First published in 2019. This edition published in 2020.

Recycling programs for this product may not exist in your area.

HQN
22 Adelaide St. West, 40th Floor
Toronto, Ontario M5H 4E3, Canada
www.Harlequin.com

Printed in U.S.A.

CONTENTS

SISTERS OF SUMMER'S END

Lori Foster

To all my readers,

Thank you for *everything*—
for the positive reviews you've posted,
for visiting my Facebook page with comments
and most especially for purchasing my books.

I'm convinced I have the nicest, smartest
and most considerate readers in the world. :-)

I hope my stories never disappoint you!

Lori Foster

CHAPTER ONE

AFTER DROPPING HER son off at school, Joy Lee returned to Cooper's Charm, the RV resort where she worked and lived. It was backtracking since she had an appointment near the school later this morning, but it wouldn't do to show up a half hour early.

Actually, nothing in the small town of Woodbine, Ohio, was too far away. In fifteen minutes she could drive to the school, the park, the grocery...or visit the new owner of the drive-in, who she'd be meeting today.

Hopefully Mr. Nakirk would continue to work with her. As the recreation director of the park, she and the past owner had put together various events with a lot of success. Halloween was coming up and she didn't want to have to completely restructure a tried-and-true camper favorite.

Coming through the grand entry of the resort, Joy couldn't help but admire the beauty of it. She'd been seeing the same gorgeous scenery for six years now, yet it never failed to soothe her.

She'd found peace here, a kind of peace she hadn't known existed. Now she couldn't imagine living anywhere else.

Large trees, currently wearing their fall colors, lined the property and served to add privacy to the costlier campsites.

A wooden walk bridge divided a pond from the large lake. Wooden cabins were scattered about, with plenty of lots for RVs and level, grassy areas for campers who preferred a tent. Even the playgrounds were well maintained, colorful and attractive.

Deciding a cup of coffee wouldn't hurt, Joy headed for Summer's End, the camp store. Maris Kennedy, a woman close to her own age, always had coffee ready. She also worked nonstop and treated everyone like a friend.

When Joy came into the camp store, Maris was busy wiping down the tops of the dining booths. She glanced up and said, "Hey."

In so many ways, Joy admired Maris. For one thing, the woman never seemed to tire. She opened early, kept it open late and rarely slowed down throughout the day. During the busiest season, Maris employed part-time help, but she handled the bulk of the responsibility herself.

Maris apparently preferred it that way.

Another admirable thing? Maris *always* managed to look fantastic with her dark blond hair in a high ponytail and a shirt at least a size too large over her jeans.

Unfair, but Maris was so incredibly nice, and she took such great care of all the employees, Joy forgave her the perfection. "Good morning."

"Is it?" Maris turned her gaze to the window. "Ah, sunshine. Better than rain and clouds, right? Coffee?"

Joy hated to pull her away from her task. "Yes, but I could—"

"I'll get it." Toting her little carrier of cleaning supplies, Maris headed to the kitchen. Joy heard her wash her hands, and then a moment later she reappeared with two cups. "I just made a fresh pot."

Of course she had. Smiling, Joy shook her head.

The café in Summer's End offered a menu of sandwiches, soups and daily specials. Positioned on the walls behind the seating area, packed shelves held basic grocery necessities and emergency items, as well as things like pool floats, sunscreen and fishing tackle. Campers didn't have to leave the park once they arrived, and if they didn't want to make use of the grills, Maris always had something to eat.

Joy took a sip of the coffee, fixed just the way she liked it, and sighed.

Instead of moving on to another chore, Maris stood there with her own coffee. "I'm wondering something."

"Oh?" She and Maris were friendly; Maris was too nice for anyone *not* to be friendly with her. But Joy wouldn't say they were close.

Sadly, it had become Joy's habit to keep some measure of distance from everyone.

"How the hell do you always look so put together?"

Surprised by the question, Joy looked down at her cotton skirt and button-up sweater. "It's a casual skirt." At least five years old, like the majority of her wardrobe. She'd updated only a few pieces since moving to the park.

"Yeah, but everything you wear looks like it came from a fashion magazine. Always, no matter what, you're styled head to toe. There are days I can barely get my hair into a ponytail, and yet you never have a wrinkle."

Feeling suddenly self-conscious, as well as amused by the irony, Joy laughed.

"Why's that funny?" Maris asked, looking genuinely curious.

It wasn't like Maris to linger, so Joy hastily explained, "I was literally just thinking how great you always look. Especially your ponytail! No matter what's going on, you... glow."

"Me?" Maris snorted. *"Glow?"*

Even more embarrassed and feeling completely out of her element, Joy continued. "You don't need makeup or anything. You always look fresh, even when you've been working all day. There's an energy about you." A wholesomeness that few other women could pull off. It was probably attitude as much as appearance that was responsible for that vibe. Maris personified friendliness, but she owned the space around her in a way Joy could never manage. "Believe me, the natural look works for you."

When Maris laughed, it made her even prettier, but before Joy could say so, she asked, "So what are you up to today?"

Hmm. Had Maris just deflected? Maybe she was as uncomfortable with compliments as Joy. "Meeting the new owner of the drive-in."

"That's right. I heard it changed hands."

"Very recently," Joy confirmed.

"Heard the new guy was a gorgeous hunk, too."

"You...what?" Joy sputtered. *A gorgeous hunk?* Definitely not what she'd hoped for, although it absolutely wouldn't matter. A man's appeal meant nothing to her—

and good thing, since the guys at the park were all very handsome in varying ways. "Who told you that?"

"I'm like a bartender, you know?" Maris bobbed her eyebrows. "Everyone talks to me. You should try it sometime."

Generally the small town shared everything about everything. If a squirrel dropped a nut, someone announced it and the gossip spread like wildfire—though Joy was usually the last to hear it since she didn't cultivate those close relationships. Maybe she *should* chat with Maris more, if for no other reason than to keep up on current affairs in Woodbine. "I don't know about the hunk part since I haven't met him yet, but it's not an issue. My only interest is—"

"In recreation for the park, I know." Maris rolled her eyes in a playful way. "But there are all kinds of recreation, and I'm thinking you should try the kind that involves a man."

A nervous laugh trickled out. Since when was Maris Kennedy interested in her lack of a love life? Joy's next thought was whether or not the lack was that obvious.

Did she seem...lonely? Or, oh God, *needy*?

No, Maris more than anyone else at the park understood that a woman didn't need a man to complete her. Joy's life was already full, thank you very much.

To keep things friendly, Joy said with a smile, "Jack gets all my free time. I don't even know when I'd fit in a date." Just to clarify, she added, "Not that anyone is asking."

"Hello," Maris said. "You realize you have a big old blinking *not available* sign on you, right? Guys would—" she pinched the air "—if you'd give them just a teeny tiny bit of encouragement."

"But I don't want to encourage anyone. I mean, not for that reason."

"Why not? Jack's in school now, so don't tell me you can't eke out an hour or two."

"Hmm. Well, I guess technically I could..." Joy sat at the counter and finished with, "But I won't."

"Spoilsport." Maris joined her, taking the stool to her left.

Well, that was new. Sure, Maris conversed with Joy, but usually while she worked. She didn't sit down and join her.

She didn't focus on her.

Unsure what was going on, Joy said, "I don't mean to hold you up..."

"Already got through my routine, so I was ready for a break."

Curious, she asked, "What type of routine?"

"Coffee first—that's as much for me as it is for anyone who might drop in. Then I turn on the oven so I can make cookies from the dough I prepared the night before."

"Wow."

"I dust again, make sure all the chrome shines. Face up the shelves so they look orderly." Maris looked around her store with obvious pride. "There's always food stuff to prep, too. Soup to get in the pot, tea to make. Oh, and I have to put money back in the cash register. I like to take inventory each evening before I head home, so I know what I need to replace the next day. That means sometimes I have to restock the hot dogs or condiments."

Joy shook her head. "I have no idea how you do it all."

"Listen to who's talking, Super Mom."

"I'm not—"

"Yup, you are. I see plenty of moms here at the park, but you make it look effortless."

"Oh. Well, thank you." What else did someone say in this situation? Joy had no idea. Before moving to Woodbine, she hadn't had any friends like Maris. Her social group had been superficial, not down-to-earth. They talked about the latest high-end fashions and the next important social function. None of her so-called friends would have ever owned a wonderful little camp store like Summer's End—and none of them would have ever ended up as a single mom. Losing them hadn't been a hardship.

Other things had been hard. So very, very hard.

Like finding herself alone.

Over the years she'd adjusted, but now she shied away from getting too personal with anyone. Life felt safer that way.

"So." As if she'd been privy to her innermost thoughts, Maris gave her a direct smile—one filled with warmth and sincerity. "I'm just saying if you ever want to go out, or even if you just want some time to yourself, let me know. I'd be happy to help."

Touched by the offer, Joy laid a hand to her heart. After all her effort to keep real friendship at bay, Maris still reached out to her. It meant a lot and made Joy rethink some of her choices.

Honestly, since turning thirty, it had played on her mind, anyway. Perhaps she should begin to open up a little.

Jack certainly had. Then again, her son was one of the most personable, engaging, adorable people…and maybe she was just a tiny bit influenced by the incredible love she had for him.

Jack liked Maris a lot, and vice versa.

That didn't explain why Maris was suddenly so keen on Joy dating. "So…what's going on?"

Maris lifted her brows. "What do you mean?"

Ha! That innocent look didn't cut it. "You're up to something. We've known each other five years now and you've never asked me about dating."

"Sure I did. You just didn't answer much, so I let it go."

Ouch. That could be true.

"Gawd, don't look guilty," Maris said. "Here's the thing. You were quiet, I was swamped, so we let it go, right? But know what? I'm thirty-one now. Freaking *thirty-one*."

"Oh my God," Joy said, amazed that their thoughts seemed to be on the same track. "I'm thirty now, so I know exactly what you mean."

"Yesterday," Maris said, "this lady came in with three kids, one of them a newborn. She and her husband were frazzled and happy, and they said it was their first vacation after buying their house. Guess how old that woman was."

Joy said, "Um…thirty-ish?"

"Twenty-nine. Two years *younger* than me."

"Younger than us," Joy corrected.

"Right, but you have a kid. A *great* kid." Maris propped her head on her hand. "My point is, I can't do the whole family and home thing—but you can. Heck, you're already halfway there."

Family? Joy almost choked, since her family didn't want anything to do with her. She knew that wasn't what Maris meant, though. "You can't do it…why?"

"It's not my thing." Maris shrugged that off with haste. "You're great at being a mom. Heck, you're great at everything you do. So the least *I* can do is lend a hand, and maybe give you a push."

After all that, Maris smiled, as if she'd explained everything to her satisfaction and Joy should be jumping on board.

When Joy just blinked at her, Maris said, "Consider this your push."

It was almost laughable, but also very sweet. Joy said with feeling, "Thank you so much. Even though I don't have any hot prospects, I appreciate the offer."

"That's what friends are for, right?"

Joy had no real idea, but she nodded, anyway. "The same from me. If I can do anything for you, please just let me know."

"Great. Know what you can do? After you meet with the new owner, let me know if he's as gorgeous as everyone says he is. I'm dying of curiosity."

"Right, okay. Sure." Wondering if she'd misread this entire conversation, Joy offered, "If you want, I could mention you to him...?"

Maris blinked at her, then laughed. "We're talking about *you*, not me, but thanks." She nodded at the coffee. "Good?"

After another, more cautious sip, Joy sighed. "Mmm. Of course. You make the best coffee."

"True story." Maris suddenly sniffed the air. "Be right back."

So much for Maris's break. "Whatever that is smells delicious." Through the last five years, Joy had taught herself to cook by trial and error, but she didn't come close to Maris's skill in the kitchen. From full-blown formal dinners to the soup of the day, Maris worked magic.

Less than a minute later, Maris returned with a plateful of warm chocolate chip cookies. "Fresh from the oven. Want one?"

"I wish I could, but if I don't get going, I'll be late." Joy prided herself on her professionalism. Showing up tardy for an appointment was unthinkable.

"We stay too damn busy, don't we? We should carve out more time to visit." Maris wrapped two in a napkin. "For the road, then."

Joy's mouth already watered. "They won't last five minutes. Thank you." Smiling, she stood and slipped her purse strap over her shoulder. Hesitating, she said, "This was nice. Us talking more, I mean."

"Right?" Moving the cookies under a covered dome, Maris remarked, "We need to do it more often."

Surprised by the idea, Joy nodded. "That would be terrific."

She loved her role of recreation director at the park, and she appreciated all the wonderful people. She thought she did a good job—and yet, she'd never truly fit in. This morning, for a few minutes, Maris had been much more like a friend than an acquaintance. She didn't know if it was seeing the other couple with the three kids, or because Maris was suddenly more aware of her age.

Whatever the reason, Joy liked it. She liked it a lot.

TWENTY MINUTES LATER, cold and miserable, Joy peeked in the small door window of the concession stand at the drive-in.

How had things changed so quickly?

The meager overhang barely shielded her from the pounding rain of the pop-up storm. Not that it mattered since she was already soaked to the skin.

If you could see me now, Maris...

There wasn't anything fashionable about her drowned-rat appearance. Joy couldn't remember a time when she'd been more of a wreck.

Freak rainstorms could do that to people.

Instead of knocking, she peeked inside again. People didn't usually catch her off guard like this, but for once, she felt totally flummoxed.

Royce Nakirk was everything Maris said he'd be—and more.

He stood over six feet tall, his body very...*fit*, and his dark hair reflected the blue of the concession lights.

Didn't matter. Men, attractive men in their prime, held no significance to her.

She was a mother.

A dedicated employee.

A once-burned, never-again divorcée.

My, oh my, the gossips hadn't exaggerated.

Joy wanted elderly Mr. Ostenbery back. She could deal with him. She could charm and bargain and coerce him without noticing his thighs. Or his shoulders.

Or his...butt.

All she'd ever noticed on Ostenbery was the impressive size of his nose and his genuine smile and kindness.

But this new owner was a different animal. Denim companies should pay him to wear their jeans. The way his T-shirt fit his body—snug in the shoulders, loose over a flat midsection—caused her ovaries to twitch. Until this moment, she'd forgotten she had ovaries.

Mother.

Employee.

Divorcée.

The mantra marched through her brain without much effect. She wondered what Maris would say when she told her about this.

Would she tell her?

Yes. It might be fun to share her shock. No doubt Maris would have some witty comment to contribute.

With his back to her, the owner squatted to rinse a cloth in a bucket of soapy water.

Biting her lip, Joy let her gaze track over him.

Stop it, she silently demanded, and she wasn't sure if she spoke to herself or the new, much too young and attractive owner.

When he turned, she saw his intent concentration as he scrubbed at a corner of the counter.

Joy almost envied the counter. How long had it been since she'd garnered that much concentration from anyone? Five years? Closer to six?

Scowling, he glanced at the clock, a jolting reminder that she was already fifteen minutes late.

Joy shoved wet hair away from her face and straightened her sodden clothes. No chance now for a good first impression. If the day hadn't dawned with sunshine and clear skies, she wouldn't have left her umbrella behind. The weather had held long enough for her to almost arrive at the drive-in—and *then* the black clouds had rolled in, tumbling one over the other as if racing for a finish line. A deluge split the skies, flooding a crossroad so she'd had to drive around, making her late.

The irony, of course, was that she could have walked through the woods and arrived at the drive-in within five minutes. Driving meant going around the long way, but she'd considered walking too informal. Her skirt and cute flats, which Maris had admired earlier, wouldn't have survived the woods.

Now it didn't matter, since the look was ruined, anyway.

Before she made things worse, Joy stepped to the side of the little window and gave a brisk knock.

It opened exactly two heartbeats later, making her think Mr. Nakirk must have reached it in one long stride.

Dark eyes went over her in a nanosecond and his frown deepened. He rubbed his mouth—then his gaze pinned her. "Joy Lee?"

Rain blew against her back but she barely felt it as she tried to summon professional confidence. If looking at him through a window had been disturbing, it was nothing compared to seeing him face-to-face.

He waited.

"Yes." Fashioning her frozen lips into a smile, she lifted her chin. "I'm sorry I'm late." Good. That sounded formal and sincere. She cleared her throat. "A road was closed and I had to take a detour." Pretty sure her lips were still smiling, but she turned it up a bit, anyway.

He looked at her mouth and nodded. "Come in." Belatedly, he stepped back, making room for her. "Wait on the mat. The floor can be slippery when wet. I'll get you a towel."

"Thank you." So he wouldn't belabor her tardiness? She appreciated his restraint.

After watching him disappear into a room behind the concession stand, Joy glanced around the interior. She couldn't help noticing that the counter was spotless. The glass fronts of the candy cases sparkled, and even the black-and-white tiled floor shone. Admiring the fresh new appearance, she looked up...and found the same old stained ceiling tiles there.

"Next on the list," he said as he walked back in, startling her. He had an orange striped beach towel in one hand, a utility towel in the other. He stepped into her spreading puddle.

This close, he was taller than she'd realized. At five-nine, few men made her feel small but she had to tip her head back to meet Royce's inscrutable gaze. *And*...her thoughts fled once again. "Pardon?"

His mouth twitched. "I haven't heard that expression since my grandmother passed a decade ago."

Ohhh, he mentioned his grandmother. How sweet was that?

No, wait. Joy prided herself on her professionalism, on making a good appearance.

She did not lose her poise over a man's butt or his mention of a grandmother.

But his eyes…they were incredibly dark, framed by short, dense, ebony lashes. In a less welcoming face, she'd have labeled his eyes sinister, but the only thing deadly about this man was his bold appeal.

"Pardon," he said, as if explaining. "It's something Nana used to say. Most people aren't that polite anymore."

He called his grandmother Nana—and why would that make him more appealing?

Joy cleared her throat. "I see." Ah, yes, way to bowl him over with scintillating conversation.

He pointed up. "I meant the ceiling. I'll be replacing the tiles when I can, probably sometime over the winter so it's done before the next season." He held the beach towel out to her.

Making sure not to touch him, she accepted it, and noticed that his hands were large, his wrists thick, his forearms sprinkled with dark hair.

What is wrong *with you? So the man has hands. Most men do.* It was no reason for her temperature to spike.

She could probably blame her new distraction on Maris. If she hadn't steered the conversation toward hooking up, maybe Joy wouldn't be thinking about it now.

While she patted at her face, trying to look delicate instead of desperate, he dropped the utility towel into the puddle and moved it around with his foot.

Rain continued to drip from her hair, her clothes, even the tip of her nose. Her brain scrambled for conversation, a way to ease the awkward moment.

His nearness made that impossible.

"Well." Joy plucked at her clinging sweater. Maybe if she didn't look at him, it'd be easier for her brain to function. "I hope you've been properly welcomed to Woodbine."

"I've only met a few people."

Enough to make an impact, she thought.

"Mostly I've been stuck in here all week, trying to get it spick-and-span before movie night on Friday."

"Mr. Ostenbery was a wonderful person, but not a stickler for organization."

"Or cleanliness," he said with a smile.

For a second, Joy stared, caught in that smile, before regaining her wits. "You've done a great job. Everything shines."

The drive-in ran on Friday and Saturday nights, from March until the end of October, but Mr. Ostenbery had often hosted other events during off-hours. Joy hoped to continue that practice, and maybe even add to it.

Suddenly Royce flagged a hand toward her face. "You're washing away. Did you want to use the restroom? I can put on coffee while you do that."

She looked at the towel where she'd patted her face and saw it smudged with makeup. Oh good Lord. Cold and embarrassment nearly took out her knees. "Yes, if you don't mind."

"In fact—" He ducked back behind the counter, snagged a folded T-shirt from a stack, and offered it to her. "You look...chilled."

Apparently being faced with a sodden woman in ruined makeup didn't faze him. She accepted the navy blue shirt with the drive-in's logo on the front. "You want me to change?"

"I want you to be comfortable. Doesn't seem possible

while you're shivering." He pushed aside the half door that allowed her behind the concession stand. "This way."

As they walked, Joy gave herself a pep talk. Never mind that she hadn't had sex for nearly six years. Forget that he was a specimen with a capital *S*, for *Sexy*. Disregard that she was sometimes lonely.

She would cease daydreaming about his jeans, and that fine backside in his jeans, and she wouldn't notice anything else about his body. Or his face. Or even that deep voice.

She would concentrate only on the purpose of this meeting.

"Right here," he said, pushing open yet another door to show her the most sanitary business restroom she had ever seen. The white porcelain toilet and sink shone, as did the floor and wall tiles. "There's a dryer around the corner if you need it. For your skirt, I mean."

That surprised her enough that she almost slipped on her own trail of water. "You have a dryer here?"

"I brought in a small stack unit for convenience. The mop head and cleaning towels get laundered regularly."

The positives were adding up. Joy mentally tallied them: butt. Nana. Neat freak.

Oh, and those sinfully dark eyes.

Poise, she reminded herself. *Professionalism*. "I'll only be a minute."

Accepting that, he turned away. "I'll go get the coffee started."

And… She watched him walk away, already forgetting her lecture.

When he glanced back to say, "Take your time," she knew that he knew she'd been staring.

Mortified, Joy quickly closed the door, muttering to herself about decorum. One glance in the mirror and her heart almost gave out.

Her pathetic attempts at smiling couldn't have had any impact at all, not when mascara created comical black stripes down her cheeks. Add her long, light brown hair plastered to her skull, throat and chest, and she was hideous.

The worst, though, was her sweater.

Opaque, yes, but through the soft material her chilled nipples seemed to beg for attention. *Look at me, look at me.*

She couldn't really blame them, not with a man like that standing around as if such a thing happened every day. She'd certainly never seen anyone like him before. Even in a Photoshopped magazine ad, the men weren't so...perfectly *manly.*

It was indecent.

Her nipples were indecent.

Her standing in front of a mirror carrying on a private, one-sided discussion about her nipples was indecent.

In an attempt to recover, her lungs grabbed a deep breath. *Being a good mother is your number one focus. Period. You don't care about attracting men.*

No, she didn't. So what did it matter if she looked like a murdered body washed up on the shore? It didn't.

As of right now, her hormones were going back in hibernation.

And yet, she frantically scrubbed her face and fretted over her hair.

ROYCE POURED HIMSELF a cup of coffee and tried to quit glancing at the clock. *What was she doing in there?*

Changing her shirt and removing the tracks from her face shouldn't have taken twenty minutes. He rubbed the back of his neck and tried not to think about her tall, trim body in wet clothes, but yeah, he may as well tell himself to stop breathing. Pretty sure that image would stick with him for a while.

Funny thing, how a woman nearly drowned in rain and ruined makeup could still look so classy. She had a calm deportment that defied circumstances.

Gifting her with the shirt had been an act of self-preservation, to make it easier for him to refocus on the important stuff.

Not that breasts weren't important. They just weren't important right now.

For several reasons, this meeting had to be his priority. One, he'd just taken over the run-down drive-in and, for some ridiculous reason, he wanted to hear her opinion on his improvements. Two, he needed to first be accepted to the small, intimate town. Working with her would be a start. Three…damn, he'd forgotten three the second he'd opened that door.

He couldn't tell the true color of her hair, not with the wet hanks clinging to her face, but there was no mistaking the green of her eyes. Not just green, but a light green with shades of amber, all ringed in blue.

Pretty eyes. Startled eyes. Joy Lee had stared at him as if he'd somehow surprised her.

She'd sure as hell surprised him.

From everything Ostenbery had told him, he'd expected a polite but formal businesswoman. Maybe she was…usually.

But not today.

Not with the way she'd looked at him.

Damned if he hadn't looked back.

A foolish move since he had zip for free time. Only a month remained of the season for the drive-in, but he planned to make the most of it, to send it off with a bang so that when he reopened in the spring, the locals would remember. Plus he had some ideas for off-season activities, if he could get Joy Lee on board.

First, she'd have to emerge from the bathroom.

He drank more coffee, stewing over the impressions Ostenbery had given. Though the retiree hadn't mentioned Joy's age, his descriptions of her had led Royce to expect someone older. Someone not so attractive.

Someone austere and aloof.

Instead, Joy Lee had openly gazed at him while her face and throat flushed pink.

Focus, he told himself. After far too long taking care of others, this was his turn and he wouldn't get derailed by wet clothes clinging to a sweet body, or bold, mesmerizing eyes.

With that in mind, Royce strode to the door and called back, "You okay in there?"

Her head poked out, not from the bathroom but from his utility room. "Yes, sorry. You said I could use the dryer, so..." She smoothed back a long hank of still-damp hair.

Royce realized he was doing it again, allowing his brain to go down paths it shouldn't. At least this time he had good reason for staring.

She stood there in the logo T-shirt, knotted at the side so it'd fit her waist, with the beach towel tied like a toga skirt around her. The colors clashed, but that was the least of the fashion disasters.

Yet somehow, on her, the hodgepodge outfit looked like a trendy statement.

When she laced her fingers together and smiled, he felt it like a kick. Luckily, a kick was just what he needed to get back on track.

Royce cleared his throat. "I pulled some chairs up to the

counter for us." The building had a small break room, but it felt too isolated for this meeting.

He gestured for her to precede him, then wished he hadn't as she moved past, slim legs parting the overlap of the towel, giving him a glimpse of calf and thigh.

Calf and thigh? he repeated to his libido. This wasn't the 1700s. A man could see legs—gorgeous legs, not-so-gorgeous legs, young legs and old legs, plus a whole lot more—any damn time he wanted. Just because they were *her* legs didn't make them special.

Sure, the past year had been...rough. No sex, no dating. Nothing but all-consuming responsibility, focused around sickness, culminating in the inevitable end of life.

But legs?

Royce followed her, doing his utmost to keep his gaze on the back of her head and not anywhere else.

Being here in Woodbine, rebuilding the drive-in to what it could be, was *his* turn and he wouldn't let pretty green eyes and shapely legs muddle his plans.

Keeping that in mind, Royce got down to the task of building a business relationship, and absolutely, one hundred percent, nothing else.

As Royce parked at the entrance to the RV park three days later, he paused just to enjoy the view. Fall painted the landscape a breathtaking pallet of hues, from bright orange honey locusts, red maples and the purple sweetgum trees, to the softer yellow of aspen trees. The pale blue skies, interrupted by only a few fluffy clouds, met the darker surface of the rippling lake.

As a kid, every tree was a challenge to climb. Now, as an adult, he took in the colors and understood how others would see them—and why his mother had been so single-minded in her pursuit to catch the image.

Dispelling the pang of that memory, he inhaled the crisp scent in the air and glanced around at the plentiful fall flowers.

Without meaning to, he searched the various people moseying around the grounds. Most of them were likely campers, but the second he saw the slender woman, a long, patterned skirt drifting around her legs as she walked, he knew it was Joy.

He'd done his utmost not to dwell on her, but still a tension fell over him that had nothing to do with stress and everything to do with awareness. A gentle breeze teased her long, fawn-colored hair and she looked like a woman with a purpose, striding toward the back of the grounds where she disappeared into a building.

Would he run into her? Would he get close enough to see those remarkable eyes again? It seemed likely, and damned if he didn't hope he would.

Goals, Royce reminded himself, starting down the slanted drive from the extra parking area to the park itself. He was here for an appointment with Cooper Cochran, the park owner, not to indulge a juvenile infatuation.

A few campfires burned outside RVs and tents, the wood smoke scenting the air. People waved to him as he passed, friendly in the extreme. The play areas were still and empty, but Cooper had explained that with school back in session, weekdays were naturally quieter now. Weekends, though, the park would fill, especially toward the end of the month when Joy helped facilitate a site-by-site Halloween event. Guests decorated their campers, kids wore costumes, people handed out candy and the lodge hosted a "friendly" haunted house, appropriate for kids of all ages.

The evening would end at the drive-in with campers getting discounted tickets and a free bag of popcorn. According to Joy, that got the kids settled before dark, when mishaps could happen if they were still out going door-to-door for candy.

His visit to the park today was just to get to know another businessman, since he and Cooper were neighbors of sorts, with the drive-in just through the woods that bordered the property. If it weren't for the tall trees, campers would be able to catch a free movie every weekend, minus sound.

Suddenly Joy came around the corner only a few yards away from him. She had her arms loaded down with more boxes, a large scarecrow under one arm and her sunglasses were slipping.

Royce stepped into her path. "Joy."

She stopped so abruptly the uppermost box toppled, spilling fall decorations around her feet. Glasses askew, she blinked at him. "Royce."

"Here." He reached for the remaining load she still held, setting everything aside while squatting down to collect the things she'd dropped. "Sorry if I startled you."

"You didn't," she said a little breathlessly. Pushing her glasses atop her head, she looked him over in that same intent way she had at their first meeting.

"Just throwing things at me, huh?" Trying to ignore the charge of her nearness, Royce replaced everything as neatly as he could, although he had no idea how she'd gotten it all in the boxes in the first place.

Her lips parted. Soft lips. Naked lips.

He was thinking things he shouldn't when she suddenly rushed into explanations.

"I'm running late and I'm afraid my mind was elsewhere…" She trailed off and then knelt, too, quickly rearranging things. "What are you doing here?"

She smelled nice, Royce thought, her scent subtle but

sexy. Stirring. Maybe it was the October sunshine on her skin, or the warmth of her hair. He breathed her in before explaining, "I'm meeting Coop in the camp store. I'm a little early yet. Let me help you carry this stuff."

As they both reached for the same box, their hands bumped.

She jerked back to her feet. "Oh no." A nervous laugh. "That's okay. Really."

Why she was nervous Royce couldn't guess. He watched her, trying to figure her out—trying to figure himself out, too. He had no business lingering here, deliberately running into her and then prolonging his time with her.

Yet there was a pull, opposite of what he told himself he should be doing. Business, that was number one. Building a relationship in the community. Establishing himself and, therefore, the drive-in needed to be his goal.

So why was it so hard to look away from her? Seeing the flush on her face, he had to assume she felt it, too.

Like him, did she find it equally alarming and exhilarating?

Without taking his gaze off her, he slowly stood with two boxes in his hands as a natural barrier so he didn't do something really dumb. Like step up against her.

Breaking the spell, Royce asked, "Where to?"

After a deep inhalation, she forced a bright smile and snagged up the scarecrow. "This way."

Following her through the grounds, Royce continued to admire...well, the area, sure. It really was a well-laid-out, nicely tended park. But he also admired Joy. The sway of her hips. The flow of her hair. How everyone greeted her with smiles.

That is, everyone except the guy who pulled up on a golf cart, a toolbox beside him on the seat. Shoving sunglasses to the top of head, he frowned at Joy. "Hon, I told you I'd get this stuff for you. Don't you need to go?"

Royce remembered her saying she was running late. He waited, unsure who the young man might be, but assumed he worked for the park.

"I'm leaving as soon as I drop this stuff off at the lodge." She gestured back to him. "Royce is helping."

The man eyed him. "Royce, as in the new owner of the drive-in?"

"One and the same." Juggling the boxes in one arm, Royce reached out a hand. "Royce Nakirk. Nice to meet you."

"Daron Hardy, handyman extraordinaire, or so I'm told." He accepted the handshake. "You going to do a horror night for Halloween? Something really scary that'd make a sexy lady friend want to cuddle?"

Royce glanced at Joy.

She gasped, then quickly denied, "Not me!" as if that idea were the most absurd thing she'd ever heard.

Daron grinned. "Could be you, hon. You fit the bill." To Royce, he said, "Sadly, Joy gives me the cold shoulder. To hear her tell it, there's only one guy in her life."

Well, shit. Royce automatically looked at her hands, though he already knew she didn't wear a ring. Not married...but that didn't guarantee she wasn't involved in some other way.

Not liking that idea at all, he gave his attention to Daron. "We'll have a double dose of kid-friendly flicks that night, but leading up to it we're playing movies that'd probably work for you." He mentioned the latest blood-and-gore movie that'd hit the big screen.

"I'll take what I can get." Back to Joy, Daron asked,

"So you'll be there Halloween weekend for the kids' flick, right? If Jack can stay awake long enough?"

Jack? Royce watched her get more flustered. "Yes, we're planning to attend that weekend, along with many of the families from the park." She adjusted her purse strap. "Speaking of Jack, maybe I'll need your help, after all, or I really might be late." She strode around to the back of the golf cart. "Drop this stuff off for me, okay?"

"Sure thing."

Royce watched the younger man, and realized he had no real interest in Joy. He was friendly in a flirting way, but he wasn't at all serious about it.

Already walking away, Joy said over her shoulder, "Royce, thank you for your help. Just give the boxes to Daron. He'll take care of it." She practically jogged away, her skirt dancing around her calves as she headed toward a parking area.

Daron cleared his throat in an exaggerated way, drawing Royce's attention. "Seriously, dude, you're wasting your time."

"How's that?" Pretending he hadn't just been watching her, Royce unloaded the boxes onto the rear-facing seat, then secured the scarecrow there.

"Joy doesn't date. Her whole focus is on Jack."

"And Jack is…?" he asked, trying to sound casual.

Judging by Daron's wide grin, he wasn't fooled. "Her five-year-old son. Cute kid. A little shy."

Royce forgot that he wasn't interested in a relationship. He wasn't even interested in dating. He felt like he'd just taken one in the gut. "She's a mother?"

"Head to toe."

"But…single?" His brain stuck on that fact, regardless of how Royce tried to block it.

"Always has been, far as I know."

Royce looked back and saw her driving out of the park in a small yellow Ford hatchback. It took a strong woman to raise a kid alone. He knew that firsthand.

"Again, fair warning," Daron said. "Joy assigns all men to the 'casual friendship' zone. In all the time she's been here, plenty have tried to get past it with no luck."

Royce shot him a look. "You?"

Laughing, Daron tugged off his hat to run a hand through messy brown hair, then jammed it back on his head. "Not me, no. I could say I don't play where I work, but truth is, she's a mom through and through. She's also a really nice person, a hell of a hard worker and she's never given me a single hint of interest. Fact, most times she treats me like a bigger version of Jack."

Huh. From what Royce could tell, Daron was a mid-twenties, fit, decent-looking *man*—but Joy saw him as a kid? Fascinating.

She sure as hell hadn't looked at *him* that way. Royce was rusty, no doubt about it, but he figured he could still pick up on sexual tension. "So she's going somewhere to get her son?"

"Kindergarten. If you're into lost causes, she'll be back in half an hour."

He wouldn't mind seeing her again, but it wasn't the reason for his visit. "Actually, I'm meeting with Coop, and now *I'm* late." But only by two minutes. "Hope I'll see you Halloween night, if not before."

CHAPTER TWO

IT WAS COWARDLY, Joy knew, but she didn't trust this new version of herself. So instead of heading directly back to the park, she took Jack to a restaurant for fried chicken and biscuits.

Even though he was thin, Jack was a bottomless pit and he finished off two legs and a biscuit while Joy nibbled on a wing.

Her thoughts refused to veer long from Royce.

Now that he knew she was a mother, what would he think?

It didn't matter, but still…

"What's wrong, Mom?"

Joy gazed at her son's big brown eyes and smiled. "Nothing. I just have a busy day yet ahead."

Warily, he eyed her around a third piece of chicken. "Will I get to play?"

Unable to resist, Joy stroked his fair hair. "We play every night, don't we?"

"Could I play longer?"

Oh, that wheedling tone. Jack was at the age where he negotiated everything. She loved each new facet of his growth, watching him expand his horizons. He was still shy, but kindergarten had helped him to make friends. And thank God for that because while the summer had provided constant entertainment, the park would now be incredibly quiet until spring. If it weren't for school, he'd spend all his days without peers.

For the thousandth time, Joy questioned her decision in moving to the Cooper's Charm resort. At the time, she'd been desperate for work that would accommodate a baby and allow her to be both caregiver and breadwinner.

Because there was no one else.

Cooper Cochran hadn't owned the park long when she'd shown up largely pregnant with a nonexistent résumé and promises that she'd be perfect for the job, vowing that she'd work harder than anyone else possibly could. At that time, promises and determination were all she had to offer. She'd felt so fragile, so utterly alone, that when he hired her, she'd broken down into tears.

Badly needing a positive focus, and grateful for his confidence, she'd thrown herself into the job, going above and beyond the requirements, and in that process, she'd found a new love: organizing recreational activities for kids and adults alike. Jack had grown up with the other employees as family—more so than her real family would ever be. She, however, still kept others at a distance.

Trust, once broken, instilled a very real fear.

"Tell you what," Joy said, leaning an elbow on the table and smiling at him. "We'll grab an ice cream at the camp store first, then play for an hour if you promise to help me with some of my work afterward." On her strict budget, ice creams were a treat, but she needed to see Maris, anyway. Jack didn't know that, and she'd found he was really great at sorting craft items, as long as she gave very clear instructions. He liked helping out, plus it kept him busy—and close.

"Deal!"

The way Jack's face lit up had Joy grinning, too. With their frugal lifestyle, it wasn't often he got to eat out and have ice cream. She'd grown up the opposite, indulged to a ridiculous degree. Rarely were there meals at home, and if she'd chosen a diet of jelly beans and milk shakes, no one would have denied her.

Only in hindsight had Joy realized it was lack of interest, not an excess of love, that had motivated her parents. The hard truth was forced on her at twenty-four, and in some ways, it felt like her life truly began after that moment.

Now, without her family's influence, she lived on a shoestring budget—and it didn't matter. Her life couldn't be happier. She had Jack, so she had everything she really needed. She'd give her son the more important things in life, like her attention, guidance, protection and supervision. And yes, unconditional love.

And if occasionally, when in her bed alone, she felt an undefined yearning…well, that didn't matter, either. She wouldn't let it.

Cupping her son's face, Joy put a smooch on his forehead. "You are the most perfect little boy I could ever imagine."

"Mom," he complained, wiggling away as his dark eyes

quickly scanned the room, ensuring no one had witnessed her affection. He didn't mind hugs, cuddles and kisses, but only when they were alone.

Hiding her smile, Joy cleared away their mess, and within minutes they were headed back to the park. Of course, with Jack buckled up in the back seat with a picture book, her thoughts returned to Royce.

The morning after their first meeting, she'd given her report to Maris, who'd been suitably interested and impressed. But as far as Joy knew, Maris hadn't met him in person yet—unless the introductions had happened earlier today, after Joy left for the school.

Would Maris be as impressed with his looks as Joy had been?

Somehow Joy doubted Maris would lie awake at night thinking about him. And for sure, Maris wouldn't have let his presence at the park chase her away.

Or more accurately, Joy had let her attraction for him get in the way of her responsibilities.

Since she'd be seeing him more all through October, she had to figure out how to keep her physical reactions to him in check.

Or you could just grab one more indulgence?

Oh no. Definitely *no.* Royce hadn't shown any particular interest, and when would it be possible, anyway? Ruthlessly, Joy snuffed that idea.

But after she parked and she and Jack headed for Summer's End, she spotted Cooper Cochran standing near the scuba shack, at the edge of the boat ramp. Two others stood to his left on the shore, their wet suits rolled down to their waists.

One of them was Baxter, the scuba instructor. Joy had seen him and his very fine physique a great many times.

She took in the sight of him the same way she admired art—with an eye of appreciation, but nothing more. *He* didn't keep her awake at night.

However, the other man was… Royce.

Seeing him like that, chest bare, dark hair slicked back, sun glinting off his wide shoulders, caused a very different sort of appreciation. Her heart raced, her stomach seemed to take flight and she couldn't breathe.

She forgot her resolve. She forgot everything.

Good God, she felt…*alive*.

"WELL?" COOP ASKED HIM.

Now that they'd peeled down the wet suits, Royce felt goose bumps assault his torso. "Other than freezing my balls off, it was awesome. I haven't done this since college. I'd love to visit again, longer next time." He'd forgotten how good it felt to just relax. After the endless obligation, he'd been elbow-deep in the effort to restart his life. Fun and recreation hadn't factored in.

It still couldn't, not in any significant way. But the occasional swim? Losing his worries while exploring the bottom of the lake—a lake that had once been a quarry so it still offered a unique underwater landscape? That he could manage.

"You're a natural." Baxter set his gear aside, tossed Royce a towel and used one himself. "The water is colder now than in the summer, but clearer, too, since we don't have any swimmers churning it up."

It wasn't the water that bothered Royce. The wet suit had insulated him from that. But the chilly October air? An altogether different matter. The fins made it tough to walk, so going into the shack to change wouldn't have made sense.

If he did this again—and he hoped to—he'd be better pre-pared for exiting the lake.

Coop took Royce's mask and tank. "The season ends for guests after Halloween, but Baxter still dives as long as there isn't ice."

While briskly drying, Baxter shrugged. "Some men jog. I dive."

Royce looked out over the rippling surface of the lake. A bird skimmed low, squawking, and in the distance a large, silver fish jumped. Something about the combo of sun and water and sand filled him with peace. "If you don't mind, I'll join you a few more times before winter lands."

"I'd be glad for the company," Baxter said.

"Thanks." As Royce turned, he roughly ran the towel over his head. The sun warmed his shoulders, but the sharp breeze cut over him.

The park was a thing of beauty this time of year. He gazed around the empty beach and foamy shoreline—then paused when he noticed Joy some distance to his left, stand-ing by the entrance to the camp store, a small boy hold-ing her hand.

She seemed surprised to see him, almost frozen...and then he remembered he was shirtless. Joy wasn't staring at his face.

Her gaze was on his body.

The sight of her chased away much of his chill. In fact, as he watched her, he forgot about everything, including the two men standing with him.

"You've met Joy, right?"

Drawing his gaze from her, Royce glanced at Coop. It wouldn't do to give the wrong impression. "Yeah, she came by the drive-in the other day." He snagged his T-shirt from the picnic table and pulled it on. The wet suit, rolled down to his hips, would have to stay in place for now. All he wore under it was his boxers, but he sat to remove the fins.

When he glanced up again, he saw Joy and the boy darting into the store.

It had been a hell of a long time since he enjoyed a woman's attention. Too damn long. Yet he couldn't deny what he felt: pleasure that she looked at him, pride that she appeared to like what she saw and, worse, an almost instinctive urge to reciprocate her interest.

"That's Jack."

Hearing the fondness in those two words, Royce turned to Coop. "Her son?"

"Good kid," Baxter said as he stripped off his suit without a care. Of course he'd thought ahead and worn compression shorts underneath. "Friendly but shy with strangers."

"Joy's protective of him." Coop moved around to the other side of the table. "We all are."

A warning? Royce wasn't sure how to take that.

While he was trying to decide on a reply, Coop said, "No one's around. You're good to go."

Royce realized that Coop had his back to him while he kept watch for anyone who might come along. Joy and her son were nowhere to be seen.

"Might take me a minute. I'm not as practiced as Baxter." He struggled out of the wet suit and quickly drew on his jeans. As he zipped up, he said, "Thanks." The T-shirt stuck to damp places on his body, so he shoved his arms into his flannel shirt before sitting down to pull on his socks and shoes.

Was it his imagination or had the temp dropped ten degrees?

Baxter clapped him on the shoulder. "Have Maris pour you a cup of coffee and I'll store the gear."

Not wanting to start off on the wrong foot, Royce shook his head. "I'll help."

Baxter offered a friendly smile. "Not this time."

"For today only," Coop explained, "you're a guest." He indicated the open door of the camp store that Joy and Jack had entered. "Next time you can learn the ropes."

"Ask Maris to pour me one, too," Baxter said, already striding off with the tanks and fins. "I'll join you in a few."

Royce looked at Summer's End. Sunshine bathed the entry, shielding the doorway like a yellow curtain so that he couldn't see anyone inside. The faint strains of country music drifted out, along with the low drone of conversation. And, damn it, he couldn't deny the jolt of…excitement? Anticipation?

He wanted to see Joy again.

With another absent, "Thanks," for the men, he started forward.

The unwelcome, heated interest intensified as he neared. Everything else faded away; he no longer heard the squawking of gulls, the constant washing on the shoreline or the rustling of drying leaves in the trees. The closer he got, the deeper he breathed and the warmer he felt.

And then he heard her voice.

"What do you mean?" A nervous denial. "I wasn't staring."

"Give it up," another woman said. "You were eyeballing the new guy big-time. Your face is still hot, too." He heard a laugh that was both soft and husky. "It's not a crime to admire a nice bod, you know."

Flattered, Royce looked down at himself and gave a mental shrug. Yes, he'd stayed fit, mostly through strenuous physical labor. As a mobile sawmiller, he'd been able to tailor his hours to make a living wage while also meeting his other obligations.

Joy's pause sounded loud in Royce's ears.

Yes, he'd picked up on her scrutiny, but it had been so long since he'd done the whole man/woman thing, he liked having her awareness verified by someone else.

Suddenly Joy groaned. "All right, so I stared." In a lower voice, she added, "I thought he'd be gone by now, so I hadn't expected to see him, and then he came out of the lake half-naked..."

"And lookin' fine," the other woman said with humorous admiration. "I'm glad to know you still have a pulse. And before you get offended—"

"I wouldn't," Joy said, her tone tinged with self-directed disgust. "I know I come off as cold."

"Not cold at all. You're one of the nicest, most considerate people I know. But around men, you're always disinterested. Maybe even oblivious. God knows plenty of campers have tried to get your attention."

Joy dismissed that. "Not seriously."

"Come on." The other woman guffawed. "I get that your big focus is on Jack, and he's a sweetheart because of it. But every single guy—and some of the not-so-single guys— do their best to get your attention, and they all fail." Her voice went lower, soft with understanding. "I've been trying to tell you, Joy. You're allowed to have some fun, too."

Stopped just outside the doorway, Royce paused. So he was expected to be fun? Hell, fun had been absent for so long he wasn't sure he'd recognize it anymore. But now, finally, he was close to having a new life.

This was no time to lose sight of his end game.

"I know what you've been telling me," Joy said. "And

I've explained that I can't get involved. Between my job and being a single mom, I have zilch for free time."

"I'm not saying you have to get involved. Offer him a night. An afternoon. Hell, I'll watch Jack for you right now and you could—"

Joy laughed while shushing the other woman at the same time. "You don't even know if he'd be willing."

The woman gave a soft snort. "Oh, he'd be willing. Men are *always* willing."

Not necessarily true, Royce knew. He had a stretch of celibacy to prove it. But was he ready now? He couldn't deny the way his cock jumped at the idea, though as a grown man, he made decisions with his brain. Still, other parts of his body rallied persuasions, ganging up against better sense and—

"Who are you?"

He'd been so enthralled by the women's conversation Royce hadn't noticed the little fair-haired boy approaching until he spoke.

Silence swelled around him until it picked up a pulse beat. Or maybe that was his own guilty conscience now drumming in his head. Listening in equaled eavesdropping...and he only just realized he was doing it.

In his defense, he'd been so surprised that he hadn't even thought about it. Instinct alone had kept him standing there, taking it all in.

Avoiding looking toward Joy, Royce turned his attention down to the kid. Chocolate ice cream dripped over the small pale hand gripping a cone. It also smudged the boy's mouth, and even the tip of his button nose.

Grinning, he held out his hand. "I'm Royce Nakirk, a neighbor of sorts since I own the drive-in."

Big brown eyes rounded comically wide as they stared at

Royce's hand. Though he felt the women watching, no one said a word. Finally Jack shoved the cone into his left hand and held out his very sticky right hand. "I'm Jack Lee."

Royce took one step in the door, snagged a few napkins from the first booth and then knelt down. "Nice to meet you, Jack." He took the boy's hand—melted ice cream and all—and gave it two careful pumps. That done, he asked, "Mind if I mop up a bit?"

Narrow shoulders rolled in a shrug…and Jack thrust his face up for Royce to clean.

Nonplussed, Royce's grin widened more. He'd meant to tend his own hand, but he wasn't a novice at this sort of thing—although his experience wasn't with kids.

He carefully wiped the boy's mouth and chin.

Suddenly Joy was there, protectively close to her son as she took over, efficiently swabbing his face and hands.

Jack was quick to say, "I'm not done yet." Then to Royce, "She usually cleans me up when I'm done." And back to his mother, with firm insistence, "I'm *not* done, Mom, okay?"

Fighting a laugh, Royce said, "I'm sure your mother will understand that I interrupted things." He looked up at Joy, saw something like panic in her eyes and smiled. *Yes*, he wanted to say. *I heard every word*.

But that would only get him in deeper, and he figured he was already mired ass-deep in feelings he didn't recognize.

"See, Mom," Jack said. "I saw him standin' there and that's why I'm not done." Again to Royce, "Ain't that right?"

The kid was a charmer with his blatant honesty. Royce gave a solemn nod. "Exactly right."

"*Isn't*, not *ain't*." Joy's face softened. "And I'm not rushing you, but if you want time to swing we need to get going soon."

Royce, *still* on one knee, watched Jack jam as much

of the cone in his mouth as he could, determined to get every bite.

Instead of getting annoyed as ice cream dripped down his shirt, Joy stroked the boy's hair. "Jack," she said softly. "You'll have Mr. Nakirk thinking you're without any manners at all."

That tone reeked of affection, as did the gentle touch, and it took Royce a moment to refocus.

Coming back to his feet, he looked past Joy—a necessary break from her impact—and asked the woman behind the counter, "Do you have coffee?"

"Do I have coffee," she scoffed. "Only the best coffee in town. Grab a seat and I'll bring you a cup."

"Thank you. One for Baxter, as well, please. He'll be joining me shortly." This woman he could deal with. She was pretty in a more practical way, with dark blond hair held back in a bouncy ponytail, and brown eyes that weren't at all as innocent as Jack's, yet held an all-business mien when she met his gaze.

As Royce moved around Joy, Jack fell into step behind him. Mouth full, he asked, "Do you get to watch movies every night? Do you pick the movies? Do you have a favorite?"

Because her son followed him, Joy did, as well...though she held back a few steps.

"At the drive-in, you mean?" Royce chose a booth in the middle of the store. "Since I run it, I'm usually working when they play. And we only have movies on the weekend, though I wouldn't mind changing that a little, maybe in the future. I pick them, but I base it on what's popular because it's not about what I want to see, right? It's what will bring in an audience."

Jack took all that in, chewed it over in his head and

nodded. "I'd like to own a drive-in." Taking the position across from Royce, he balanced his knees on the seat and his elbows on the tabletop. "When my windows are open, I can hear the movies. Sometimes moaning, sometimes screaming."

Lifting his brows, Royce wondered exactly which movies the boy had heard. A horror flick...or something else? "Is that right?"

He nodded and grinned. "Since I can't see it, I make up my own movies to go with the moans."

Royce choked. "Fascinating."

"Jack." Joy tried to interject while still not getting too close. "Mr. Nakirk is expecting a guest. Let's move to another booth."

"Not a guest," the kid argued. "Just Baxter, and he likes me, too."

Too? The boy didn't lack for self-confidence, something Royce considered a good thing. "I'm pretty sure everyone around here likes you," Royce said.

"Of course we do." The other woman reappeared with two cups of coffee, a coffeepot, creamer and sugar on a tray. "What's not to like, right?"

"Agreed." Royce waited until she'd set everything down, making sure it was all out of Jack's way. "I'm Royce—"

"Nakirk, new owner of the drive-in." She winked. "Listening in goes both ways." After drying her hands on an apron skirt, she held one out. "Maris Kennedy. I run Summer's End."

Her hand was warm, small but strong. "It's nice to meet you." As they each pulled away, he looked around. "Seems you have quite the business going here."

Maris took it upon herself to nudge Jack over so she could sit beside him. "I have all the staples campers might need, basic food stuff, camping items and even a few things for the lake. Plus I run the café. With the end of the season, I won't prepare daily specials anymore, but if you're ever in a pinch, let me know. I often throw together lunch or dinner for everyone who works here."

That didn't include Royce, since he wasn't a camp worker. "I wouldn't want to impose."

"No imposition. Coop supplies me with what I need to keep the coffee going for employees—or friends." Maris smiled at him, putting emphasis on how she said *friend*s... as if she expected him to be more?

When her gaze slanted to Joy, he caught her meaning. The lady was a matchmaker, and oddly enough, Royce didn't mind.

Now that Maris sat, only Joy remained standing—and it felt awkward. "Thank you," Royce said. "I appreciate the warm welcome." So far, everyone at Cooper's Charm had proven to be friendly and easy to like.

Standing, Royce turned to Joy. "Why don't you sit with us?" *Next to me.* He gestured at the booth seat.

Their gazes held a moment before she forced a smile.

Royce knew she would refuse. Maybe, like him, she was wary of the attraction. He couldn't blame her. At least on his end, it felt out of place and somewhat disconcerting.

"Jack and I should get going."

Accepting that, Royce retreated back to his seat.

"But I'd rather talk to Mr. Nakirk," Jack announced.

The way both Maris and Joy stared at the boy, this must be an unusual request.

"We're going to the playground to swing," Joy reminded him.

Jack grabbed more napkins now that he'd finished his

ice cream. They quickly shredded against his sticky little hands. "We can swing anytime."

Without planning it, Royce heard himself say, "You can visit with me anytime, too. I'll be back to the park off and on, and I don't live that far away."

"I can?" Jack bounced. "Can I see how the popcorn machine works?"

"Jack," Joy said firmly, her tone a mix of reprimand and exasperation. "It's definitely rude to invite yourself over."

Maris chuckled.

Royce wondered what Joy objected to most, her impetuous son or the idea of visiting him without the excuse of business.

Or maybe she didn't like for her son to get too close to men. He gave that brief thought, but given how Coop and Baxter reacted, Jack didn't lack for male figures in his life.

It would be different, though, for a man who wasn't a coworker. The other men in the park would be a constant in Jack's life.

But a man interested in *her*? That would be a risk for a dedicated mom.

Hoping he didn't overstep, Royce offered, "I'd be happy to show him around. Maybe that'd be a good field trip for his class?"

Jack cheered, almost toppling the pot of coffee. Royce caught it. "Careful."

Abashed, Jack bit his lip. "Sorry."

"I like your enthusiasm, but we don't want anyone to get burned, right?" He glanced up at Joy—and caught her staring, her expression almost dazed.

Had she expected him to snap at Jack? Hell, he liked kids being kids. That's how it should be.

Whatever Joy had been thinking, she shook it off. "Jack, we really do need to go."

"You're the only one who doesn't have brown eyes, Mom. Did you know that? But Mr. Nakirk's eyes are really dark." He leaned over the tabletop, this time with more caution, to closely study Royce. "They're maybe even black."

Grinning at the near nose-to-nose scrutiny, Maris patted Jack's back and left the booth. "I have to get back to work." With a touch to Joy's shoulder, she whispered, "Sit, drink the coffee. I'll bring Baxter another," before she walked away.

It occurred to Royce that he was enjoying himself. *Again.* Joy's son was pure entertainment with his frank, inquisitive manner. He was so close now Royce felt his breath.

"Jack," she said again, sliding into the booth. "That's enough."

To let Joy know she shouldn't fret so much, Royce flashed her a smile, then took Jack by the chin and did his own scrutiny.

"Your eyes are pretty dark, too. But you're right. They're not as dark as mine." He turned Jack's face this way and that to study him. "I got my grandmother's eyes. Looks like you got your mother's...ears."

Mouth dropping open, Jack clapped both hands on his ears to feel them, then scrambled over to examine his mother's. Despite his sticky fingers being in her hair, Joy laughed, and that made Jack suspicious.

He shot Royce a look. "You serious?" Again, he felt his ears.

"Cross my heart."

Baxter stepped through the open front door, spotted Royce with Joy and hesitated. Instead of joining them, he went to the counter to speak with Maris.

Damn. Was everyone at the park trying to push them together?

Joy turned to follow his gaze, spotted Baxter and apologized. "I'm sorry. We've interrupted your—"

"My what?" Royce sat back, wanting her to stay a little longer. "My visit was to get to know everyone, and I did." He smiled at Jack. "Including this character."

Frowning slightly, Jack still felt his ears.

Joy let out a slow breath. "I saw you in the water with Baxter."

Hoping she wouldn't be embarrassed, he nodded. "I know."

"Were you cold?" Jack asked. "Mom said I can't swim because it's too cold."

"Your mom is right. Even I won't go in too many more times."

Jack fidgeted. "If you can't swim, do you think you'd want to swing?"

Immediately, Joy was on her feet again. "He has a meeting with Baxter, sweetie. Come on. Time for us to go."

Well, damn. Now that Jack had mentioned it, Royce kind of wanted to swing. He definitely wanted to visit more with Joy. And he hated seeing the disappointment in Jack's eyes.

He got to his feet, saying, "Next time, okay?"

"You mean it?" Jack scrambled out. "You might be too big for the slide. Mom says she is."

Joy rolled her eyes and laughed.

Leaning in, Jack said, sotto voce, "I think she'd fit, but she's chicken."

"Challenged by my own son?" She tickled his ribs. "I'll show you who's chicken!"

Jack squealed with laughter, and that brought Baxter from the counter. "I hope I didn't break up your visit?"

"Jack and I are off for the swings." She clasped her son's hand, silencing his arguments with a firm, "We've lingered too long already, especially since I still have a lot to get done."

"Anything I can help with?" Royce offered, before he could think it over.

Taken by surprise, she shook her head. "Camp stuff. But thank you."

Inspiration struck, and Royce again knelt down. "Jack, it was nice meeting you."

"I don't want to go yet."

His mouth twitched. It was nice to be liked. "Your mom is the boss, though."

"I guess."

"But I was wondering, since you seem like an expert on swings, maybe you could give me some pointers on the old playground equipment at the drive-in. What do you think?"

"Pointers?"

"On what needs to be replaced, what I should add, what rambunctious little boys like most. That sort of thing."

His whole face lit up and he turned to Joy in a rush. "Can I, Mom? Can I?"

Flushed—likely because she saw through his ploy—Joy waffled. "Um…"

"I'd enjoy seeing you both." Royce felt it necessary to offer that dose of honesty. Yes, he wanted to see her. Against all logic and in direct opposition to his plans, he wanted that a lot. But he'd also like to visit more with Jack.

For whatever reason, the boy had taken to him.

To let her off the hook for now, Royce said, "Not tonight. Seems we're all busy. But maybe over the weekend? That is, if your mom has the time?"

Baxter contributed to the cause, saying, "Good idea. Jack is the foremost swing set expert in town."

"I… Okay." Taking two steps back, Joy nodded. "I don't have my calendar with me, so I can't check my schedule—"

"No problem." From behind the counter, Maris said, "I can give him your number. And, Royce, you could leave yours. That way one of you—" she lifted her brows at Royce "—can check in with the other to see what works."

"Fine by me." Royce saw Joy's expression and knew she wasn't quite as eager as Maris. It didn't insult him. Given what he'd heard, this was a big step for her.

And he respected that Jack was her number one priority.

"Well, then." With that vague response and a harried expression directed at Maris, Joy turned to go, prodding a reluctant Jack to follow.

The boy waved and said, "I'll see ya, Mr. Nakirk."

Once they were gone, Maris shook her head. "He never got past Mr."

"I noticed." Baxter sipped his coffee. "Took Joy a month to let Jack call me by name, and only after she knew for sure I had nothing but friendship in mind for her."

"You," Maris said to Royce, striding toward the booth with a plate of cookies, "are different."

"Am I?" Just that morning, Royce would have said he wasn't. The idea of inserting himself into a woman's life, into her son's life, would have been roundly rejected.

But now… Well, now he felt an invisible pull, a need to know her better, to befriend Jack. The things he'd heard, the way he felt when she was near, how much he enjoyed talking with her, even just watching her…it wouldn't go away.

Royce wasn't one to fight a losing battle, and that's what it would be if he tried to resist her. Add in Jack, and he knew he had to pursue things, at least to see where it took him.

He had a better understanding than some exactly how it would be for a single mother, and for a lone boy. Maybe Jack reminded him of himself—though Royce was pretty sure he hadn't been as cute and precocious at that age. Whatever the reasons, he already looked forward to seeing Joy again.

When Maris offered a cookie, he gladly took one. "Will you tell me more about Joy? Jack, too?"

"I'll tell you anything she wouldn't mind you knowing."

Royce laughed at that diplomatic reply. "Spoken like a true friend."

"I'm working on it." Propping a hip against a booth top, Maris shrugged. "Given how I pushed her today..." She grinned, clearly unconcerned. "I might be back at square one, but Joy is the forgiving sort, and she deserves a night off, so here's her number." She took a slip of paper from her apron pocket, then held it out of reach. "Just be sure you don't abuse it."

"I get it." Royce gave her a level look. "I wouldn't pressure her if she's not interested." Besides, he wasn't sure he wanted to move too fast, anyway. He wasn't one hundred percent sure of anything—except that he did want to see her.

"She's interested," Maris assured him. "I could tell. She's just out of practice."

That made two of them, then...yet some things a man never forgot. "Thanks." Royce tucked the paper into his back pocket.

Satisfied, Maris asked, "You guys need anything else?"

Baxter shook his head. "Ridley and I are heading out for dinner tonight."

"And I need to get going soon."

"Then I better get to my chores. Put the plate and cups on the counter when you finish, and give a yell if you need me."

Once Maris disappeared into the back room, Baxter shook his head. "If you think Joy works hard, she's got nothing on Maris."

Royce knew Coop and Baxter were both married, but he wasn't sure about Maris. "Don't misunderstand—I'm not personally interested—but she's single? Maris, I mean?" He looked around the store again. "She runs this alone?"

"Sunup to sundown, yeah." Baxter finished off his coffee. "Now that we're heading into the off-season, she'll do any repairs and upkeep that's needed."

"I thought that was Daron's job."

"Ha! Yeah, it is, but those two butt heads a lot. It's pretty damned amusing actually. He'll do what he can to help, but he flirts with her the whole time so Maris will do what she can to keep him away. If you're around enough, you'll see what I mean."

That gave Royce another idea. He was good with his hands, and he wouldn't mind pitching in around the park. For one thing, it'd give him an excuse to be around more, which meant he'd have opportunities to see Joy. Plus it'd help shore up his standing in the community, since the entire town seemed curtained around the resort. But mostly, he'd enjoy repaying Maris's kindness.

Things were coming together nicely. Not quite as he'd expected, but each day his optimism grew.

SMILING, MARIS LOCKED UP behind everyone and began her evening routine that included starting the dishwasher, a thorough cleaning of the seating area and switching out the entry rug, which had collected dirt from shoes during the day.

She lived for her routines, morning and night. They reminded her that she alone guided her future, and because of that, she'd never again have reason for shame.

Growing up, there'd been no order to anything, no planning, no...pride.

Maris had plans. As soon as she'd gained her independence, she'd set up goals and never, not once, had she veered from them.

Tonight, though, she smiled because of Joy.

How had she known Joy so long and yet never known certain things about her—like her sense of humor, her modesty over her appearance...and her willingness to expand their friendship?

Maybe, like Maris, age had inspired that last part.

Damn it, her routines were starting to feel tired, but today, chatting with Joy had renewed her.

No, she couldn't get involved with anyone—that'd definitely put a kink in her goals. But Joy? There was absolutely no reason for Joy to avoid dating, and every reason for her to finally have some fun.

Maris planned to encourage her in every way she could, and she'd start with Royce.

CHAPTER THREE

HOURS LATER, JOY peeked in on Jack and saw he was finally asleep. Meeting Royce had gotten him so hyped that she'd had a difficult time getting him to wind down.

It wasn't like her son to get so familiar so quickly. He was generally a shy boy, at least until he knew someone well. Before kindergarten, he'd often hidden behind her when they met new people. Yes, he'd come out of his shell some since the interactions at school, but not like he had today.

She thought of how Royce had knelt down to talk to him, how earnest Jack had been in meeting him almost eye to eye. And *how* Royce had spoken, not like he humored a little kid, but in a more respectful way.

He'd won her son over with very little effort.

Resting a hand over her heart, Joy stood in the doorway, looking at Jack's small body curled under his favorite Ninja Turtle blanket. The few toys he owned were scattered about. Luckily, Jack didn't ask for a lot, because she didn't have much to spend on indulgences.

However, she'd given him everything she knew he needed, including love, security, affection, guidance and boundaries.

But had she cheated him out of a father figure? Had she let her own insecurity about involvement negatively affect her son?

Jack had always chased after Coop, Baxter and Daron, but she'd been careful not to let him get too close. She'd feared for his disappointment.

And her own.

The ringing of her cell phone in the other room startled her. No one called her after nine p.m.

Leaving the door open a tiny bit, as was her habit, she hurried down the hall and to the small living room. There on the desk, her phone buzzed.

For only a heartbeat, she warred with herself before snatching it up and saying a soft, "Hello?"

"Joy? It's Royce. Am I calling too late?"

She eased out the desk chair and sank into it. "No." Dumb. *Say something else.* "I was just about to shower." *No. Not that.* Catching her breath, she rushed on, explaining, "I mean, Jack is asleep now, so—"

"I understand."

He'd sounded amused…and now he was silent.

She briefly closed her eyes. Damn it, she was an intelligent adult, a divorced woman, a single mother. She could carry on a coherent conversation. "How was your day?" *Gawd, so bland and clichéd.*

"Good. Yours?"

"Jack was excited. He enjoyed meeting you." That, at least, was sincere.

"I enjoyed meeting him, too. He's a smart kid. Cute."

Smiling, Joy said, "Once we got home, he stayed in front of the mirror for ten minutes studying his ears. Then he tried drawing them a dozen times. He's not yet satisfied that he's got it right."

Royce laughed. "Does he have any features that resemble family members?" He paused, then asked lightly, "His dad, maybe?"

Shadows filled their apartment over the rec center. Only the glow from her laptop screen and a small light over the stove lit the interior. Floodlights from outside, stationed around the park, filtered in through the windows.

Joy always made their home dim and quiet in the evening when it was time for Jack to sleep. Her chair squeaked as she sat back and curled her feet beneath her. "Actually, he does look a little like his father, at least from what I can remember. I haven't seen Vaughn since…well, six months before Jack was born actually."

Silence stretched out. "He knew you were pregnant?"

"He'd already talked of divorce. Finding out I was pregnant only shored up his arguments to leave."

Royce gave a low curse. "I didn't realize. I'm sorry if I overstepped."

"You didn't. It's fine." What wasn't fine was her talking about her ex to a…what? Prospective date? Joy shook her head, hating how pathetic that seemed. "I should apologize for saying so much. It's just that Jack rarely asks about his father. I'd prefer that you not mention it when he's around."

"No problem." After a second or two, Royce asked, "You're divorced now?"

"Yes. We were already having issues—" what an un-derstatement "—when I found out I was pregnant. Vaughn walked out the day I told him, and I haven't seen him since the divorce became final shortly after that."

"How old were you?"

If Royce had sounded too sympathetic, it would have bothered her, but he seemed only politely curious. "I was a very immature, very dependent twenty-four." That made her laugh a little. She knew a lot of people, Daron among them, who'd been far more mature at a much younger age. "Nothing makes you grow up like becoming responsible for someone else."

"A hard truth."

He sounded like he understood something about that. "Have you ever been married?"

"No." Then he asked, "How long were you with him?"

Had he just changed the subject to get it off him? Joy considered pressing him—did he disapprove of marriage, or had some woman broken his heart? There were so many things she wanted to know about Royce, but this was nice, just talking to him, and she didn't want to chase him off. Chatting on the phone instead of looking at him made it easier for her.

Oh, she had a vivid image of him in her head, but her imagination didn't quite replicate his potent impact on her senses.

"Vaughn and I were together for a year. My parents de-tested him. Actually, *detest* might not be a strong enough word."

"I suppose that made you want him more?"

Why was she telling him all this? She never discussed Vaughn with anyone. Not since the last big blowup with her parents.

Not since they'd disowned her.

She put her head back and closed her eyes. "Like I said, I was immature."

"It's human nature. Don't beat yourself up over it."

Too late for that. Following his lead on topic changes, she prompted, "Did you want to get together this weekend? Jack's talked about it a lot."

"That's part of why I called."

Did she hear a hesitation? Would he back out now? Jack would be crushed. She never should have—

"I was thinking maybe I could take you both to lunch Saturday. Afterward we could stop at the drive-in so I could show Jack around. That'd still give me time to get you both home and get back before sunset when I need to prep for the showing."

Like a teenager being asked out on her first date, Joy felt exhilarated, excited—and so disappointed that she had to refuse. "That sounds wonderful, Royce, but until the season officially ends, I do activities from afternoon to evening here with the campers. This Saturday we have fall crafts."

Without missing a beat, he asked, "Sunday works better for me, anyway, since the drive-in is closed that day. What do you think?"

She bit her lip to suppress the smile, then cleared her throat. "Sunday we're free." Perfect. She sounded calm and mature and not like a woman whose toes had just curled in anticipation. "It's a school night so I'd have to be back early."

"Done." She heard his smile, too, when he asked, "Any chance I can get in on that afternoon craft action?"

Laughing, Joy hugged herself and savored the new freedom of flirting. "Oh, I think that can be arranged."

"Perfect." His voice went a little deeper. "Fair warning,

though. If at all possible, and with due respect to your son, I plan to steal a kiss before I go."

More than her toes curled over that statement. "Oh, um…"

"Good night, Joy."

"LOOKING FOR SOMEONE?"

Startled, Joy ducked her head to hide her guilty face. "Hmm?" She *had* been watching the door, wondering if Royce would really show, and when. She hadn't even heard Maris come in from the back entrance.

Maris openly laughed at her in that easy, friendly way she had. "I'm on to you now. That particular expression has something to do with Royce, doesn't it? Is he coming by today?"

Straightening, Joy stared at her in wonder. How could Maris read the situation so easily? Joy had known her for a while now, and never before had she read her mind.

Of course, never before had Joy been infatuated with a man. Plus Maris was usually too busy working to waste time wondering about anyone else.

In the past week, something had shifted in their friendship. Whatever it was, Joy enjoyed it.

"I was only putting out craft supplies." She gestured at the bins on the round table filled with glue and markers and yarn. "Just that. Nothing telling or obvious. So how did you know?"

Setting aside a tray filled with cookies, Maris crossed her arms and leaned on the wall. "I'm a woman. You're a woman. That gives us some common ground." She shrugged. "Call it female intuition."

"But we're nothing alike."

At that, Maris's brows rose up. "You don't think so?"

Hoping Maris didn't take that as an insult, Joy glanced around to ensure they weren't overheard. Luckily none of the kids had shown up yet. Jack sat alone coloring at a smaller table toward the back, and everything was ready for afternoon crafts.

Drawing a breath, Joy stepped closer to Maris. "I didn't mean that how it sounded."

"It's all right. I get it. You're always polished, while I'm something of a mess and it doesn't bother me."

"We already discussed this. You're beautiful."

"And you're generous with compliments, but come on." Maris nodded at Joy's long skirt and ballet flats. "I can't even remember the last time I dressed up."

Joy stared at her, surprised yet again. "That's not at all what I meant. My wardrobe is just what I have left from... Never mind." Once, long ago, she'd thought clothes mattered. Now, she wore what she had because investing in the newest fashions wasn't feasible. Was it the same for Maris? Somehow she didn't think so. "It's just... I admire you, you know."

Maris snorted. "I can't imagine why."

"Are you serious? I have a hundred reasons!" And Joy didn't mind listing them for her. "You're so confident and self-assured. You always know what you're doing and why. You accomplish more in a day than most people do in a week. You're completely self-reliant. Plus my compliments were honest, not generous. You look *amazing* in jeans— and no makeup. That's just unfair, because you're right, makeup is a pain. If I had your flawless skin or dark eyelashes, I wouldn't wear it, either."

Maris blinked at that outpouring of compliments. "Thank you. I admire you, too." With a laugh, she wrinkled her nose. "Though I have to say, this conversation is a little embarrassing."

Right. People didn't walk around detailing attributes. They met, became friends, and it was all more natural.

Twisting her mouth, Joy pointed out, "That's another way we're different, I guess. I'm…awkward." That wasn't precisely the right word, so she shook her head and tried again. "Awkward on the inside, I mean. I tell myself to be confident, but you just *are*. You always seem to know the right thing to say or do to put other people at ease. You're so together and take-charge, but also comfortable and friendly."

Maris took her hands. Joy realized that Maris's were work-worn, her fingers a little roughened from all the dish-washing and cooking she did.

"I think we're both misunderstanding. I've never seen you look or act awkward. What I meant is that the flattery embarrasses me because I'm not used to getting compliments like that. Compliments that matter."

Joy searched her face and saw the truth. "You mean, compliments for something other than looks?"

Maris nodded. "It shows what a nice person you are that you see beyond the surface. Especially since my look is usually some shade of permanent determination and stubborn will."

"It's a good look," Joy promised her with a laugh. *Much better than deep-rooted insecurity.* Honestly, Maris looked like the woman Joy wanted to be.

Maris grinned. "You're those things, too."

"I want that to be true, for myself and Jack." It was important for Jack to know she'd always take care of him. Her confidence was as much for him as for herself. She did what she could to ensure he'd never have the same worries she'd had. "I work at it, but it seems so effortless for you."

Laughing, Maris reached for a cookie. "I've been working for as long as I can remember. The day I turned eighteen, finding a job was my top priority. By now it's second nature for me—still difficult, but part of my life."

Shame hit Joy, thick enough to make her throat tight. She didn't know what type of childhood Maris had, but it was surely different from her own. Joy knew she'd been given far more advantages than most, so what right did she have to complain? "I'm sorry."

A smile teased over Maris's mouth. "Don't be. I've enjoyed talking to you. We need to do this more often."

When? They both stayed busy, but Joy vowed she'd make time—if Maris could. "I'd like that."

"Maybe we should start our own little club where we drink coffee, eat cookies and praise each other."

Oddly enough, that sounded like a very good time. "Count me in."

"But someone also has to share fun stories that involve a hunk. Since I'm out—" she tapped Joy's shoulder "—you're it."

It? Wondering what that meant, Joy asked, "Why are you out?"

"I don't date," Maris stated. "Never have."

"You say that like it's part of your religion or something." Joy crossed her arms. "Why can't you date?"

Maris choked on a laugh, quickly covered her mouth and shook her head. "It's not that I can't, it's that I don't."

True. Joy couldn't recall a time where Maris did anything other than...work. "Okay, but *why*?"

"Let's just say I have other priorities. Financial security tops the list. Independence is right behind it."

Joy couldn't help but wonder about Maris's background—and why those two things were so important. "Doesn't everyone want to be secure?"

"Sure, I guess. But since I've personally felt the bite of dependence, I'll do what I can to never end up there again." She pointed her half-eaten cookie at Joy. "And no, I'm not talking about any of that right now, so stop deferring. You're it and that's that."

Giving up, Joy said, "Fine," and then she felt a small thrill when she thought of Royce. "What do I have to do?"

"Something…" Maris gave it thought, then grinned. "Something *scintillating.*"

"Um…okay. Define that."

Maris rolled a shoulder. "If Royce shows up, steal a kiss." She quickly clarified, "Not a peck. Those don't count. Make it something substantial, something with *tongues.*"

At that, Joy outright laughed. Royce had said he wouldn't leave without kissing, so… "I might be able to make that happen."

"Perfect." Maris nodded toward the door and whispered, "Make it hot and wild, and then you can tell me all about it. I'll get some vicarious thrills, since I'm not getting anything else." As she backed up, she thrust a fist in the air and said, "To the Summer's End club!" then turned and ducked through the back door again, no doubt returning to the camp store.

Everyone working at the park would be happy to lend her a hand now and then, but Maris delegated only the most insubstantial tasks to others. Anything of importance she handled herself.

When it came to her livelihood, Maris considered nearly everything important.

Laughing, Joy glanced to the entrance and found Royce

walking in with Daron. Jack spotted him right off and with a happy cheer he raced over. Daron said something, ruffled Jack's hair and left again.

Probably chasing Maris, if Joy had to guess. Why Maris didn't orchestrate her own wild night, she didn't know. It seemed obvious to her that Daron was anxious, willing and able.

With a hand to her son's back, Royce crossed the room. His dark gaze moved over her, lingering a heartbeat on her fitted sweater before meeting her eyes. "Hey."

She'd taken extra care today with her appearance, wearing a little more mascara, choosing clothes that flattered her figure. She'd wanted him to notice—and he did. "You made it."

Those dark eyes zeroed in on her mouth. "Daron walked me in." He glanced around. "He said you live here, too?"

"Upstairs," Jack said. "We have to go outside to get in. Wanna see?"

Unprepared to take Royce through her meager home, Joy stalled.

"Someday soon," Royce said, saving her from having to come up with an excuse. "Right now your mom is busy, so I figured we'd lend her a hand."

"She doesn't need help. Mom's organized." He looked up at her. "Aren't you, Mom? Everyone says so."

Joy laughed. "I try." She smoothed down Jack's hair. In many ways it reminded her of Daron's. His hair, too, was often unruly. "Why don't you get your picture to show Mr. Nakirk and I'll make coffee for the parents."

As Jack ran off, Royce walked with her to the nook designated as a kitchen area. "Do a lot of adults accompany the kids?"

"More so toward evening, but I always try to be prepared with coffee, regular for afternoons, decaf later on. The kids get juice, and Maris brought over cookies." She went about coffee prep while Jack skidded to a halt with his picture in his hands.

"Let's see." Royce knelt down, took the artwork when Jack shyly offered it, then he fell silent. Joy was just starting to worry when he said, "Wow."

"You like it?" Jack anxiously shifted from one foot to the other. "It's not done yet."

"I... Of course I like it." More silence as he studied the picture.

Curious, Joy set aside foam cups and came to look over Royce's shoulder.

Jack had drawn the big screen of the drive-in, a row of cars and a large man—hands on hips—smiling widely.

"It's terrific, Jack." Joy nudged Royce. "Don't you think so?"

"I think it's better than terrific." He lowered the picture. "How old are you again?"

One hand lifted, fingers spread. "Five, but I'll be six soon."

Royce shook his head in wonder. "This is phenomenal for a kid your age. You've got perspective in here, and the dimensions are good. And I knew it was me." He lowered the paper. "It is me, right?"

Jack nodded, then he, too, looked at the picture. "What's perspect...?"

"Perspective. It means you've shown things in a way that I feel like I'm standing right here, behind the row of cars."

"But you're there." Jack pointed to the figure in the drawing.

"Right. You drew me there, but if someone else was

looking on…" He gave up and glanced at Joy. "How do you explain perspective to a kid?"

Joy knelt down beside him. "It's like looking at a photograph. Everything is where it should be and it's all sized right for positioning."

Pursing his mouth, Jack studied the picture once more. "It's not a photograph."

"It's better." Royce dropped to his behind and crossed his ankles, holding the paper against his knees. "Do you think I could keep it?"

A smile beamed across Jack's face. "Sure."

"Will you sign it for me?" Royce glanced back to Joy. "Can he sign his name?"

She nodded. Jack was smart, but more than that, he received loads of attention from her. All that one-on-one helped him to grasp things more quickly. "Jack, try to put it smaller in the bottom corner, okay?" She touched the paper. "Down here."

"Okay." He turned and ran off again.

Royce faced her. "Do you realize how talented he is?"

"He's my son. I think he's brilliant at everything."

Amused, Royce reached out and touched her hair, drifting his fingers from her ear down to the ends that lay against her back. For only a moment, his hand rested there, warm and firm against her, before he withdrew. "That might be, but he's also artistic with natural skill. Few kids would have included that many details, or been able to add depth."

She leaned in, liking this nearness to him. He smelled really nice, sort of dark and spicy, and she could feel the warmth of his body.

So that Jack wouldn't hear, she whispered, "He drew you a little short and thick."

Royce laughed. "He's five." Standing again, he caught her elbow and helped her up, and then didn't let her go. A glance at Jack showed him hunched over the paper, his lip caught in his teeth as he painstakingly added his name.

When his gaze came back to her, Joy's heart tripped.

Royce looked at her mouth. "Have you thought about it?"

"What?" she asked, knowing exactly what he meant.

"Me, kissing you." He drew closer and his hand slid to her back, his fingers dancing little circles over her spine. "Not here. Not now. But at some point before the afternoon ends, I'll have your mouth."

Her breath thickened and a sweet ache pooled low in her stomach. Such a tease. Well, two could play that game.

She put a hand on his biceps and lowered her voice. "I have." Her attention now snagged on *his* mouth. "A lot. So you should know my expectations are high."

"Good." Coming closer still, he breathed near her ear, "Always demand the best, Joy. Even from me."

Sensation washed over her—and then he stepped away, turning as Jack came up to them.

"All set?"

Paying no attention to adult antics, Jack held up the picture. "I messed up the *J*."

Royce examined it critically. "You know what? I think that gives it character. I wouldn't change a thing." To Joy, he asked, "Is there someplace safe I can put this until I'm ready to go?"

Still a little breathless, Joy indicated the corkboard where a lot of artwork got shared. "You could pin it there."

He looked down at Jack. "What do you think?"

Jack tried to look humble. "If you want to."

They went over to the board together. Royce bent his head to listen as Jack talked. Two males, one under four feet tall, his body narrow, his movements frenetic, and the other more than six feet of calm, carved strength.

It was a dangerous thing, seeing them together, liking how they looked as they interacted. It'd be so easy to get caught up in the emotions of seeing her son so happy, knowing he enjoyed the attention and praise.

It was dangerous for Jack. Dangerous for her.

Her instinct, always, was to protect Jack from possible hurt and disappointment.

And yes, she wanted to protect herself, as well.

They had a good life right now, and it unnerved her to think of rocking the boat, changing the dynamic of the peaceful, contented existence she'd so carefully created. Yet Jack deserved more.

She did, too.

A kiss, the wild night Maris encouraged or more… Joy didn't know yet, but for now, she was open to all possibilities.

ROYCE STOOD BACK, talking to a man who'd brought three kids—a daughter and two sons—to take part in the fun. Seven other kids were there, too, creating a small, boisterous crowd. Most were rowdier than Jack, definitely louder, but Joy handled them with the skill of a veteran grade school teacher. The noise level alone was enough to make his brain vibrate, yet she took it in stride.

She praised some crazy-looking results, because most of these kids didn't have Jack's artistic bent. She gave directions on others, and assisted with some. Things that should have looked like miniature scarecrows turned out to be the stuff of nightmares.

Even sitting among other kids, Jack managed to be by himself. When it came to art, he was too contained, not at all the animated kid at the camp store the other day. Did Joy notice it, the way he created his own little world? Royce would have loved to see him run around the table once, knock over the glue or shout for attention. Instead, he kept his head down and worked.

Crazy, but at only five, the kid had an artist's soul. Every ounce of concentration was on his task.

Maybe someday he'd show Jack his mother's work. Royce inhaled a deep breath, let it out slowly and accepted that he wasn't ready for that yet. But soon.

At two p.m., Joy wrapped up the activities, promising the kids she had more fun lined up for them after dinner. Parents began to filter in to collect their children, scary scarecrows, falls wreaths and all. Jack looked up, saw things were ending and went back to work with renewed purpose.

Excusing himself from the camper, Royce strolled over to Jack. Around them, chaos ensued...but Jack either didn't notice, or he didn't care. His scarecrow, made from a toilet paper roller, *looked* like a damned scarecrow.

To the side of him, he'd also created a fall wreath. Both were colorful, neat and meticulously assembled.

Royce eyed the small chair, decided it wouldn't hold him and instead leaned over with one hand flat on the table. "Jack."

Brown eyes flashed up. "I'm almost done."

"I wasn't rushing you, but will it bother you for me to watch?"

"I don't care." He was already back to work, gluing a few more pieces of straw around the scarecrow's neck. When he finished, he held it up and scowled. "I got stuff crooked."

"It's a scarecrow. Things are supposed to be crooked." The kid took himself far too seriously. "And actually, it's pretty amazing. See the mouth? You drew on stitches."

"It looks like the one Mom put up there." He pointed to the front of the room where Halloween decorations clustered around the art supplies. Sure enough, a small, smiling scarecrow sat with fake, light-up jack-o'-lanterns.

"But most kids wouldn't have noticed that." On his fall wreath, he'd not only made some lopsided leaves to go on it, but he'd drawn the veins in the leaves. His eye for detail went well beyond his age, even beyond the average adult's comprehension of art.

"When can we come to the drive-in?" With the scarecrow finished, Jack half crawled up into his seat and tilted toward Royce. "Could we go tonight? Will you play a movie for me? Can I get popcorn?"

Now here was the lively kid he remembered. "Pretty sure your mom wasn't planning any outings tonight." From what he understood of her schedule, they'd overlap; she'd still be working with kids when he'd be at the drive-in, starting the first movie.

"I'll ask her."

"She's been working, right? How about we help her clean up instead, and then when she's ready to visit, she'll let us both know."

It took some doing, but Royce convinced Jack to pitch in. Joy finished saying goodbye to all the guests, reminding them of the next activity planned, and after getting the last kid out, she closed the door. Her gaze sought Royce.

He liked the flush on her cheeks and the anticipation in her eyes. If ever a woman deserved to be thoroughly kissed, she did. Royce banked his smile and asked, "What can I do to help?"

She looked around. "If you don't mind, you could gather up the foam cups and put them in the trash."

"Sure thing."

Going to Jack's seat, she picked up his fall wreath. "Jack, this is wonderful."

Jack shook his head at Royce. "She always says that."

"She's your mom and she loves you. But I don't always say it, right? Heck, I barely know you, and I also think it's terrific."

Laughing, Jack began gathering up crayons.

Joy bent to kiss his cheek. "Thank you for helping, honey." She collected scattered paper scraps and headed to the kitchen.

The quiet, empty kitchen.

While doing his own share of picking up, Royce watched Jack. He was busy sorting crayons by colors, putting them in individual bins. It amused him, because the boy was *such* a little artist, right down to the need for color coordination.

Knowing he wouldn't get a better chance, Royce casually joined Joy in the kitchen. She had her back to him as she emptied the coffee grounds from the maker and rinsed it all in the sink.

After putting his own handful of trash in the bin, Royce came up behind her and nuzzled against her ear. She went perfectly still, her hands remaining in the sink.

With one hand, he moved her hair away from her neck, then brushed his lips over the sensitive skin there. "Jack is busy sorting, so we probably have one minute…and I don't want to waste it." He grazed his teeth over the soft skin along the column of her throat, followed by his tongue.

She melted back into him. "Royce."

Damn, that was a turn-on. He'd missed hearing a woman whisper his name so softly.

He had a few things to discuss with her, parameters that they needed to establish, but first…

When he reached around to gently clasp her chin, she

hurriedly dried her hands and turned toward him. Her attention skipped to the door, and when she didn't see Jack, she met his gaze. Voice low and cautious, she said, "He switches gears pretty quickly so we should probably—"

Royce kissed her midsentence. No way in hell would he miss this scant opportunity.

Her lips softened, fitting to his. Keeping things slow and easy, the way a first kiss should be, he tilted his head and traced her bottom lip with his tongue, lightly kissed her upper lip, the corner of her mouth.

God, she tasted good, smelled good—all soft and womanly—and he had to concentrate to keep from moving too fast. More than anything, he wanted to crush her close, take her mouth with his tongue and press his hips to hers so he could feel every inch of her.

Instead, he forced his hands to stay on neutral ground and reminded himself that her son was nearby.

Joy wasn't quite as restrained. Hands fisting in the material of his shirt, she pulled him closer until her breasts met his chest.

With a low sound of hunger, she opened her lips and deepened the kiss—exactly the way he'd wanted to.

CHAPTER FOUR

HONEST TO GOD, Joy's urgency took Royce off guard—for about two seconds, after which he was right there with her. He tunneled his fingers into her silky brown hair and wondered how a woman this combustible had turned men away.

It had been far too long for him, too, and he couldn't get enough, kissing her deeper, hotter, their tongues stroking, heat spiking. He pressed a hand down her back, urging her hips in, aware of her accelerated breathing.

Whatever the reason, he was damned glad she'd chosen him now that she'd stopped denying herself.

Of course, that reminded him of the here and now. She wasn't only a woman, but a mother, too, and if Jack busted them she might not want to chance it again.

Smoothing his hand over her hair and shoulder, Royce eased up on the kiss by small degrees until he raised his head.

Her amazing eyes were more gold than green now, her cheeks flushed and her long hair mussed. "God, you're beautiful."

She smiled, and given that her lips were damp and full from kissing, it was an especially sexy look.

Because he badly wanted to kiss her again, it seemed prudent to take a step back. As he did so, Royce leaned away and glanced into the other room. Jack was stacking the bins, meaning he'd finish any minute.

"I enjoyed that."

Joy's husky voice drew him back around. "So did I, believe me."

Running his fingers over her hair, he tried to return it to some order. "If Jack wasn't nearby, I wouldn't have stopped."

"I wouldn't have, either," she said. "Thank you for understanding. He's never seen me with a man, other than in a friendly, distant way."

Royce finished with her hair and moved his fingers to her cheek, drawn by her softness. He wanted to touch her all over. Hopefully he'd get a chance soon. "You know I heard you talking to Maris."

Her gaze skittered away. "Yes."

"I'm sorry. I should have left, or walked on in and announced myself, but you took me by surprise. A nice surprise." Tilting up her chin, he brought her gaze back to his. "To say I'm flattered would be the understatement of the year."

Uncertainty sobered her expression. "But?"

"No buts. I just want to make sure we're on the same page."

Stepping out of reach, she leaned back on the counter and waited.

He wished he had more time to work into this conversation, but knowing a five-year-old loomed nearby, he was pressing his luck already. "You said you weren't interested in a relationship."

"I'm not. I have little enough free time as it is."

Nodding, Royce said, "I understand. I suspect I have more time than you, but I'm still working on the drive-in, and once that's done, I have a ton of renovations to do to my house."

"So we're in the same predicament." With a nod of satisfaction, she clarified, "Interested, but unavailable for anything too time-consuming."

It wasn't the time, as much as the emotional commitment, that concerned Royce. The past few years had drained him to where he felt he had nothing left to give. Not anything meaningful.

Not what Joy and her son deserved.

After being so focused on a single purpose, he'd looked forward to regaining his autonomy, having the power to do what he wanted to do, when he wanted to do it, with no one to answer to. But along with anticipating the future, he'd also grieved and dealt with guilt. Those things combined had compelled him to start over in a new place, away from harsh, sometimes heartrending memories.

He needed to be there for himself again, before he could be there for anyone else.

So he gave Joy a small smile and asked directly, "Does that still work for you?"

"Perfectly." Her chin lifted a notch, but other than that, she showed no reaction. "Where did you buy your house?"

He didn't mind veering off topic, but planned to circle

right back. "Next door to the drive-in. It's convenient and the price was right." Right meaning *cheap*.

The house had "good bones," and since he was more than adequate with his hands, he'd eventually enjoy working on it. For now, though, his priority was the drive-in.

"Nice. I know that neighborhood. It's quiet. Most of the people who live there are older."

He hadn't met the neighbors yet, so he couldn't comment on that. "I want to see you, Joy. You and Jack. If things progress to sex, I'm all in. If not, I can handle that, too." He'd still enjoy her company, even without added benefits—though he was definitely rooting for more. "Like you, I'm not looking for anything too involved."

That pretty smile came again, this time almost mocking. "If I get a vote, things will definitely lead to sex." Her gaze skipped over him. "After all, the idea of sex is what first drew me to you."

Talk about conflicting emotions. What she said, and how she said it, made Royce burn with interest. And yet, it also insulted him. Could she not simply enjoy his company, as well?

"It's been a while since I was attracted to a man that way. The tricky part," she continued, "will be the when and where, but we can work that out later."

Royce rubbed the back of his neck. She might have been discussing her work schedule, for all the emotion she put into saying that. "Good to know." At least she'd agreed to sex. He'd work on the rest when and however he could.

Jack called out, "Mom?"

"Just a second, honey." Joy stared up at Royce. "I think a noncommittal relationship based on convenience works best for both of us. I have no expectations, and you shouldn't, either."

Damn. This blunt acceptance wasn't at all how he'd planned things to go, but since he'd brought it up, all he could do was nod.

"Good. We'll still see you tomorrow?" One eyebrow lifted. "I don't want to tell Jack if we're not getting together."

"We are." Royce studied her face, but whatever she felt, she wasn't showing it. "I could come by and get you both at five, if that works."

"Perfect."

Jack ran into the kitchen, carrying four markers. "These are dried up, and we're running out of red."

Joy said, "Maybe we'll have time to buy some new markers tomorrow, before Mr. Nakirk picks us up."

Eyes widening, the boy spun around to face Royce. "You're picking us up? Where are we going?" He jumped in excitement. "Will I get to see the drive-in?"

Jack had paint-stained fingers, a smudge of marker on his cheek and dried glue on his chin. At least, Royce hoped it was glue. "I'd planned on dinner and a trip to the drive-in. But if you need art supplies, I know the perfect place." He turned to Joy. "I'd be happy to show you both. Maybe make it four instead, to give us time?"

He knew he shouldn't push, definitely not in front of Jack, but the less enthusiastic she seemed, the more determined he felt.

Although she'd been plenty enthusiastic about that kiss.

Because Jack stood there, his gaze ping-ponging back and forth between them, or maybe to make a point, Joy stuck out her hand and said, "Sounds like a deal. Thank you."

Royce had no choice but to shake her hand like a business associate.

Jack whooped. At least *he* was happy about the plans.

Bending down, Royce shook his hand next. With the boy trailing him, a gigantic smile on his face, Royce retrieved the picture Jack had done for him, said his goodbyes and went out the door to make the walk up to the parking area.

From a distance, he watched Joy and Jack leave the lodge, circle around and go up a flight of outside stairs. Seconds later, they disappeared inside.

Wind whistled over the park. It would only get colder, and going up those stairs in snow or ice wouldn't be ideal, especially at night. If he put some thought into it, he might be able to think of a way to enclose them.

That would be overstepping in a big way and Royce didn't want to do that, but...he'd think on it.

On the drive home, he kept glancing at the painting on the passenger seat. Things had ended a little awkwardly, but overall, he felt good about how the visit had gone. He'd met a few more people from the area, he and Joy had sketched the groundwork of a plan, Jack was happy—and even better, he hadn't thought about his past even once.

He did *now*, of course, but then, he never escaped it for long.

Glancing at the artwork again, Royce smiled. Irony was a son of a bitch. The first woman he'd really wanted in far too long, and her son was a guaranteed kick of nostalgia.

JOY FELT A bit like a third wheel.

Several steps ahead of her, Royce listened as Jack exclaimed with enthusiasm over everything at the drive-in. He *loved* the popcorn machine. He especially *loved* the T-shirt Royce gave him, and he was horribly disappointed that the projection room didn't, in fact, have a projector. Instead, everything was computerized.

Her son was a different boy around Royce, and she'd watched him change right before her eyes.

They'd started their "date" with a lot of promise. Since Jack was playing in his room, he hadn't heard Royce knock. The second she'd opened the door, Royce had looked beyond her, saw they had a moment alone and bent to her mouth before she could even finish greeting him.

It was crazy how he affected her, but there at the top of her outdoor stairs where anyone walking by might have seen—and of course someone did—she'd leaned into him, her hands on his shoulders, her lips parted.

At least, that had been her response until the loud "Whoop" interrupted. She'd almost jumped away, but Royce's arm around her kept her from too much movement. With far more calm than she could muster, he'd glanced down, then called, "Hi, Maris."

"My bad. Didn't mean to interrupt." Grinning, she waved to them both, instructed, "Carry on," and strode away.

Snickering, Joy hid her face in his shoulder. "She's going to grill me later."

"Then I better give you something good to talk about." He'd nudged up her face and treated her to a slow, thorough kiss that left her breathing hard and hungry for more.

Lifting his mouth, he whispered, "Damn. Remind me not to start things I can't finish."

"I won't," she said, touching her fingertips to her tingling lips. "That was too nice."

"Nice?" He gave a mock frown. "If Jack wasn't bearing down on us, I'd try to earn higher praise."

Yes, she, too, heard her son's rapidly approaching footsteps, but still managed to say, "Hmm, how about scorching? Bone-melting?"

He leaned down to whisper, "My bone did not melt," and seconds later, as she stifled a laugh, and resisted looking at his lap, Jack joined them.

Chaos reigned as Jack jumped around, asking questions in rapid-fire succession, and thankfully oblivious to the steam in the air.

Joy took that moment to slip away for their jackets, and to calm her racing heart.

The trip to the art supply store was an eye-opener. Yes, she'd known Jack enjoyed drawing, but his face as he looked around at new and unfamiliar medium made her heart swell. Like a kid on Christmas morning, he took it in with wide, awestruck, *hungry* eyes.

Royce clearly had some knowledge of art himself, given how he schooled Jack on various canvases, different types of acrylic paint versus oil, chalks, special textured papers and even self-drying clay with a variety of modeling tools.

In contrast to the rambunctious way Jack had greeted Royce, he moved through the store with near-reverence. Using infinite care, he'd feathered a touch along the bristles of a paintbrush, studied a set of soft chalks and examined the grain on a canvas.

While he'd been involved looking at the clay, Royce had quietly asked her, "Would you mind if I got him a few basics?"

Knowing she couldn't ask Jack to leave empty-handed, not when this was obviously his world, she said, "That's kind, but I can do it."

"You could," Royce acknowledged, "but I really want to."

Something in his solemn expression swayed her. There was sadness in that dark gaze, and though she couldn't begin to guess why, Joy knew it had something to do with art.

"All right, thank you. Just don't go overboard."

At that point, Royce had looked almost as eager as Jack. Together, the two of them chose a sketchbook, a set of paintbrushes and a very fine box of watercolors with a pallet.

It was a bit much, but she didn't have the heart to deny Jack…or Royce.

Of course her heart lifted at seeing them together. Royce was just so… Damn him, he was perfect. *With Jack*.

Patient, attentive, encouraging. He would make an incredible—

No, she firmly told her heart. *No, don't you dare even think it.*

It wasn't what Royce wanted.

It wasn't even what she wanted.

But God, she was such a mom. Royce's affection for her son did more to chip away at her reserve than flowers or gifts ever could.

Dinner had been the unique experience of watching her son and Royce further bond, mostly without her. He'd chosen a kid-friendly place to eat, but in the end, it hadn't mattered. Jack had carried that box of paint tubes in with him, almost like a favorite toy. Instead of playing any of the available games while they waited for their pizza, he'd asked questions. Endless questions.

And Royce had answered.

That is, until she joined in, asking, "Are you an artist, Royce?" He certainly knew a lot about it.

Mysterious shadows stole the easy smile from his face. "My mother was."

Was?

Before she could ask anything more, he promptly changed the subject to primary colors, explaining to Jack how to create his own secondary color shades and the impact white or black had on watercolors.

Her takeaway on their scintillating conversation? Don't be afraid of experimenting with color, but always go easy with black because it could muddy hues.

Also: anything too personal was off-limits.

So far, when it came to reengaging with a man, she scored a big fat zero. He preferred her five-year-old son's company to her own.

Oh, Royce was attentive. He kept a hand to her back as they left the restaurant…while Jack ran around to hold his free hand, instead of hers.

He ensured her comfort in his car, a newer Renegade… and then talked cars with Jack, explaining that he also had an ancient Chevy truck.

All in all, she was content to see Jack having such a great time.

As they toured the interior of the drive-in, Royce alternately answered Jack's questions, while also asking her about opportunities for holding events once the season ended. Possibilities included a classic car show, a Christmas bazaar and, as a goodwill gesture, a light show, since the main road brought drivers past the drive-in.

After they finished going through the concession, Royce asked Jack, "You know what's next?"

Still clutching that box of paint, Jack bounced on the balls of his feet and asked, "What?"

"Playground equipment." Around Jack's cheers, he said, "Let's go out and you can try it all while I talk with your mom. Then you can give me some recommendations."

When Jack raced away, Joy warned, "Slow down, please."

Jack reduced his run to a jog, going out the door ahead

of them, but it didn't seem important when Royce looped his arm around her and urged her forward.

Near her ear, he said, "Hi."

After spending nearly three hours together, that was so ridiculous she laughed as they stepped into the brisk fall air. At almost seven o'clock, the sun slid low in the sky, prompting some of the security lights to flicker on.

Jack had already reached the gym equipment; he was close enough for her to see, but not for him to overhear.

With their shoes crunching on the gravel lot, the squeaking of Jack's swing cutting the quiet, she and Royce walked together.

It felt…intimate. His hand on her hip. The dusky sky. Her son so happy.

Intimate, like a budding relationship.

But it wasn't and she'd have to keep that foremost in her mind. Royce had made it perfectly clear that he was no more prepared for commitment than she was. Last night, she'd reminded herself that it was for the best. All she really wanted from Royce, all she needed, was the escape of sex. Hot, mind-blowing, satisfying sex.

Today, however, she had some doubts. Royce wasn't acting like a man anxious to get her naked, but he was very natural as a role model to her son.

"Not even a hello, huh?" His hand at her hip squeezed her closer and he lightly nipped her earlobe, touched it with his tongue, then kissed her behind her ear. "I'll have to think of a way to soften you up."

Oh, she was plenty soft. If the breath caressing her skin hadn't done it, the feel of his mouth and the huskiness of his words would have. She'd gone years not even holding a man's hand, and now Royce had kissed her, touched her, lightly bit her ear…

She stopped and looked up at him. The dim light left secrets in his ebony eyes and that particular tilt to his mouth stirred her need. Thinking back on that earlier kiss... God, she wanted more.

If they were alone, she'd be all over him.

The swing squeaked—not that she'd forgotten Jack. Never that. But with her son so close, what did he want from her?

Ridiculously breathless, she whispered, "Hello, Royce."

"Yeah, that's better." Catching a long lock of her hair, he slowly eased his fingers along the length of it, letting his knuckles brush her shoulder, then her upper chest. "You seem pensive. Did Jack and I bore you today?"

She looked toward her son. He'd scampered off the swing and was climbing the ladder for the slide. "I haven't seen him this excited in a long time. He really enjoys your company." The second she said it, she feared it'd scare Royce off. A boy looking up to him, adoring him, probably reeked of a trap. It was certainly scary in her mind.

What if Jack got too attached? It would be awful to see him hurt when things inevitably ended.

Shaking her head, she said, "I'm sorry, I didn't mean..." Words failed her. How to explain? She was so damn rusty when it came to conversing with interested men.

Hugging her arms around her upper body, Joy warded off the evening chill, and gave it another attempt. "You were wonderful with him today, but I don't want him to get the wrong impression." There. That was frank but not unkind.

For a moment, they stood there in silence.

"Royce?" she whispered. "We were both up front about what this is—what it *will* be." And what it wouldn't.

"Right." He shoved his hands into the pockets of his jacket. "You asked me about my understanding of art."

Something in his tone wrenched at her heart. "It seemed like a difficult topic for you." She knew all about that. There were so many things she didn't discuss with others. "If I overstepped—"

"It's not that." His expression guarded, Royce stared toward Jack. "I don't particularly like talking about it, not yet, but…"

Unwilling to press him, Joy waited.

"I told you my mother was an artist." He popped his neck as if loosening tension. His jaw flexed. "A very successful artist actually. It's how she supported us. Even after she got dementia and would sometimes forget me, she remembered her love of art."

Joy didn't know much about dementia, but for his own mother not to recognize him? That would be wretched for anyone. Had Royce been her caregiver? Did he have siblings who had helped? A father?

He'd made it clear that he didn't want to get into a lengthy discussion, so rather than ask questions, she whispered, "I'm sorry."

Royce nodded his thanks. "To the day she died, she wanted to paint. Anything and everything." His mouth quirked. "She even painted the sheets in her room when she was too sick to get out of bed."

Feeling her heart break for him, Joy lightly pressed her hand to his solid chest, offering comfort. Beneath her palm, his heartbeat thumped steadily. "You feel an affinity to Jack because of that?"

He shrugged. "I recognized his talent." He glanced at her, a quirky smile in place. "I'm sure you did, too."

"I…" Guilt burned Joy's face. "Honestly, before Jack, I knew zip about kids. I wasn't the girl who babysat or wanted to hold other people's babies. I don't think I'd ever held a baby until Jack was born."

The quirk turned into an understanding smile. "Must have been a shocker when you found out you were pregnant."

"That's putting it mildly. I was scared out of my wits." Scared, and entirely alone. She started them walking again. The wind blew and she shivered. "All I know of kids is based on Jack. I've always appreciated his art and thought he was talented, but I didn't realize..."

Royce put his arm around her shoulders, hugging her closer. "Without any comparison, how could you know?"

"I've seen his art compared to other kids' at the camp. I noticed he has a fascination with color, and a singular concentration when he works."

"There's that, yes. Plus he also picks up on details most kids his age would miss. Eyelashes on eyes, four fingers and a thumb on hands. A neck instead of a head just sitting on shoulders." With laughter in his tone, Royce said, "Necks constitute a recall awareness of what he's seen. That's a lot of talent in a five-year-old."

"I'll make sure to carve out more time for him to paint. Unfortunately, I'm not artistic. Crafty, yes, but nothing that's really creative." She got most of her ideas from Pinterest and Facebook.

"What I know," Royce said, "I learned from Mom trying to teach me, and watching her create. Where most people had a dining room, we had an art studio." He glanced down at her. "Windows on two walls gave that room the ideal light."

"Well, you saw my home. We don't have a dining room to convert, or any available space." The eat-in kitchen was just big enough for a table and four chairs. "But I think for

Christmas I'll get him an easel, and maybe you could suggest more supplies."

At the mention of the holidays, he grew quiet again. Joy wanted to smack herself. Of course that would be difficult for him if he'd only recently lost his mother.

She was about to overstep again, wondering if he had any other family, when he stopped walking.

His gaze sharpened. "Jack? Where are you going?"

Joy looked up in alarm. Jack had left the lighted area and was peering into the woods that bordered the property between the drive-in and the park. "Jack!" She hurried forward, aware of Royce right behind her.

"Something's in there," Jack said, going to his hands and knees. "I hear it crying."

"Back up," Joy ordered in her most stern, no-nonsense tone that demanded immediate attention. He could be hearing a feral cat, an enraged raccoon or... *"Right this instant."*

Surprised by her vehemence, Jack stood and took a step back—and the brush moved. Just as she and Royce reached him, they heard a whimper.

And something half crawled out.

"It's a dog," Jack yelled as he tried to wiggle free of Joy's hold.

"A puppy," Royce corrected. "You need to be real quiet so we don't scare it, okay?"

In an eager whisper, Jack said, "You gotta get it, Mr. Nakirk."

The light didn't quite carry this far, and all Joy could make out was pale yellow fur and floppy ears framing big dark eyes.

Royce knelt down and held out his hand. "C'mon, boy. I won't hurt you."

The dog limped forward.

"It's hurt," Jack cried, his whole body vibrating with tension and worry.

Joy hugged him closer, saying, "Shh."

"Can we keep him?"

Keep him? In their tiny apartment? Not possible. Jack had been asking for a dog forever, but hopefully she could appease him with art supplies for now.

At least those didn't shed fur, pee in the corner or require walks.

"He's not ours, honey."

"But he could be. *Please*, Mom?"

Joy patted his shoulder and said again, "Shh. You don't want to scare the poor thing."

The dog finally got close enough for Royce to touch it. "That's a good boy," he crooned, his voice soft and low as he stroked the puppy's head and over his back, urging him closer. "What do we have here, huh? Some brambles? Yeah, that's got to hurt, doesn't it, buddy?"

Unfair that Royce was good with her son *and* so incredibly kind to animals. How was she supposed to resist that?

Damn it, obviously she couldn't. "What can I do?" she asked. "Is he hurt?"

"It's too dark out here to tell." Carefully, Royce lifted the animal into his arms. The poor thing licked his chin in a show of gratitude, then looked worriedly at Joy and Jack.

She felt horribly helpless against his appeal, and desperate to somehow assist. "Why don't we take him into the drive-in so we can better see?"

"Good idea. Lead the way," Royce said, and when Jack started to run, he added, "*Calmly.* The little guy is already shaking."

Jack immediately slowed, but still got to the door first.

He held it open, his bottom lip caught in his teeth as he watched Royce carry in the dog.

"It's bleeding," Jack breathed, his eyes round with worry.

"Just a little. I think that might be an old wound." Sending Joy a meaningful look, Royce asked, "Would you mind getting a few towels by the dryer, and maybe a wet one so we can see what we're dealing with?"

"I'll be right back." Seconds later, she returned to see both Royce and Jack sitting on the floor across from one another, legs folded yoga-style. Royce still held the dog, softly whispering to it.

It had its face hidden under Royce's chin, and Jack was carefully pulling burrs from its fur.

"Right here, between us," he said to Joy, and then to Jack, "Remember, slow and quiet, okay?"

Eyes wide and unblinking, Jack nodded.

Joy arranged the towels, but held on to the wet cloth. She saw dirt and brambles in the dog's fur, but also a nasty nick on its front leg, close to its paw, with what looked like both dried and fresh blood.

Royce gently set the dog before him, all the while stroking it and speaking in soft, soothing tones. His large hands moved with care as he untangled pieces of a sticker bush from the dog's scruff and tail. Jack had gotten many of the burrs, but Royce also dislodged a nasty thorn in his hip. The dog whimpered constantly, then snuffled and licked where the thorn had been.

As quietly as she could, Joy gathered up the discarded brambles and burrs and took them to the garbage can, before returning to sit beside Jack.

When Royce glanced at her, she knew without words and handed him the wet hand towel. He tried to swab around the bloody area, to see the source of the wound, but the dog yipped and tried to lurch away, burrowing against Jack.

With tears welling in his eyes, Jack helplessly cuddled the dog.

"Easy, easy now. I know it hurts." For only a second, Royce seemed undecided. Then he let out a breath. "I need to run him to a vet. Do you know anyone?"

Joy shook her head. "Phoenix might, though. She and Coop have Sugar. I'll call her."

Sunday evening, of course, no vets were open. But Phoenix did know of an animal hospital that was open for emergencies and she shared the number. Fifteen minutes later, they were all ready to go.

Royce wrapped the dog in a towel and stood. "It's getting late. I should probably run you home first—"

"But I want to go, too," Jack said, almost at the same time that Joy said, "We can stay and help."

Searching her gaze, Royce asked, "You're sure?"

"Positive." It wasn't like he could drive while holding the dog, and she wasn't sure the animal would come to her.

Being more familiar with Phoenix's directions, Joy drove and Royce sat in back with Jack, the puppy wrapped in towels on his lap.

Yes, this was definitely the strangest date she could have imagined.

Funny thing, though. As Joy pulled into the hospital, she knew she didn't want to be anywhere else.

CHAPTER FIVE

Two hours later, Royce unlocked the front door to his small, messy house, reached in to flip on a light switch and then stepped back for Joy and Jack to enter.

Several things went through his mind. It was probably near, maybe even past, Jack's bedtime. He wished he'd tidied up the house more. And apparently he now had a dog.

The pup, which the vet guessed was a three-month-old Lab mix, slept in a box padded with the towels. After meds that made him loopy, his front leg was shaved around the injury, stitched and wrapped, and he'd been treated for several nasty things Royce didn't want to think about.

Stepping around Joy, he headed for the kitchen. "You can leave your coats on the couch. Turn on more lights if you want."

He heard her quietly talking to Jack. Shoes dropped—at least he thought they were shoes—and then Jack slid into the kitchen in his socks.

Royce leaned out of the kitchen to see her laying their jackets over the arm of the couch. The shoes were set neatly by the front door.

At least his couch and chair were new, though the only end table was part of a folding tray set. No rugs. Temporary blinds on the windows. A small TV hanging on the wall.

Not exactly high style.

It wasn't a great first impression, but he hadn't had time for more than the barest necessities for comfort.

When Joy headed toward him, he said, "Sorry it's so barren. I have a lot I need to do yet. Tables, stuff for the windows, rugs… It's just that—"

"You've been busy with the drive-in. It's understandable, Royce. We all have to prioritize." As she walked, she took in the crown molding, the original hardwood floors, the glass doorknobs and the telephone nook. "Besides, your house is really nice. It has a lot of character."

Exactly what he'd thought before making an offer and buying it.

"It's way bigger than our apartment." Jack spotted his picture on the refrigerator and darted forward. "This is mine!"

The pup didn't stir. Royce hoped the poor little thing wouldn't be sick when he woke up. He set the box in the corner, to the side of the refrigerator, before turning to Jack. "I plan to frame it in my office, but haven't had a chance yet."

"You have your own office, too?" Joy smiled. "Now I'm jealous."

"The office is a converted third bedroom, that's all. The

second bedroom is empty and I only have a bed in the master." Realizing Joy still held two bags, he took a big step forward and relieved her of them. "Sorry."

"Please, stop apologizing." Tipping her head, she studied him as he put them on the counter. "I'm glad we could help. After all, you've taken on the hardest part of things."

Right. A dog. Definitely not what he'd intended, but what else could he do? Jack had nearly cried when the vet explained the wound on the pup's leg. Somehow, probably on an old fence, the dog had been cut deep enough to cause a lot of pain. Untended, he might have lost the leg—and eventually died.

Joy had looked devastated at the news. Clearly her small apartment couldn't accommodate a puppy that would grow into a large dog.

After assuring Jack that the vet would make it okay, the boy had looked at him like he was Superman. With glassy eyes, Jack had said, "Good thing you got him, huh?"

Yeah. Good thing.

Rubbing the back of his neck, Royce looked at the dog, then at his kitchen. The vet claimed the pup would probably be groggy through the night.

So what would he do with him in the morning? There'd be follow-up appointments, and Royce had entire days where he'd planned to be at the drive-in working.

They were able to buy dog dishes, food, a collar and leash from the hospital, but tomorrow he'd get a real carrier and probably do some repairs to the fence around the backyard.

"What is it?" Joy asked. "Anything I can do?"

He shook his head. "The backyard… I was going to tear down the old chain-link fence, but now, I suppose I should keep it. That is, if it can be made safe." The fence was another thing he hadn't yet tackled.

On his knees next to the dog, Jack whispered, "He sure is pretty." Very lightly, he stroked the dog's ear. "He'll need a name."

Shit. Royce loved animals, but a dog was the very last thing he'd planned—right up there with a kid who tugged at his heart, and a woman who made him forget he *had* plans.

Joy touched his arm. In fact, she touched him often. Recently in commiseration when he explained about his mother, and now, to draw his attention.

Both times that he'd kissed her, she'd clutched at his shoulders as if she felt the same, hotly sexual things he did.

He wanted her. Goddamn, he wanted her bad.

Yet today, much of his attention had gone to Jack. Such an engaging kid. Joy thought her son reminded him of his mother.

Actually, Jack reminded him too much of himself when he was a kid—minus the talent.

Quietly, so her son wouldn't overhear, Joy said, "If you need me to help with the puppy, just let me know." She stared up at him, green eyes tired but still beautiful. "The park is pet-friendly, and once Jack is in school, my mornings are flexible."

The urge to kiss her pulsed inside him. Her upturned face, the sincerity in her eyes, the sweetness in her offer, all drew him. Hell, everything about her drew him, including her dedication to her son.

Of course, accepting her help would only complicate things more and Royce knew he was already in too deep. Enjoying her company was one thing, but the rest of it...

He shook his head, but then heard himself say, "Appreciate it. I'll let you know." Damn it, not a good idea.

Withdrawing, she laced her fingers together and glanced around. "You'll put him here, in the kitchen?"

"Just until I get you and Jack home. Then I'll probably bring him into the bedroom with me. If he wakes up and needs anything, I want to know."

A heart-wrenching softness entered Joy's gaze. "You're a very nice man, Royce Nakirk."

"The nicest," Jack echoed, proving he'd been listening to them.

Hiding a smile, Joy went to the counter and began unloading the bags. "I'll wash the dog dishes for you. Why don't you take the tags off the leash and collar?"

That would make more sense than wallowing in indecision.

It was a unique experience, stepping around a kid in his own kitchen, working together with a sexy woman. He finished before Joy, so he located a few unpacked boxes to block the kitchen in case the dog woke while he drove them home. He wouldn't be more than a few minutes, but still, he didn't want to take any chances.

Once he was done, Royce caught Jack eyeing fruit in the bowl. "You getting hungry again, bud?"

Jack's eyebrows went up and he said candidly, "That apple looks really good."

Grinning, Royce checked with Joy first and got her nod.

By the time they had everything ready to go, including food and water in the dog dishes on the floor, Jack had finished an apple and a banana and was starting to yawn.

"I've kept you too long."

"Actually, I've enjoyed it." She smiled as Jack leaned on the box, watching the dog with that same intent expression he usually reserved for art. "And so has he. Thank you for such a nice day."

"And for the art stuff," Jack added. "I'll paint you another picture when I get home."

"It's your bedtime, Jack. But you can paint him something tomorrow, okay?"

"Mo-om," he complained, making the word into two syllables.

"We need to go, now. Get your jacket and shoes back on, please. And no complaining."

Like a boy sent to the gallows, Jack slowly rose and dragged across the kitchen to the living room.

It was all Royce could do not to laugh—until he realized he had her alone again.

He drew her against him. "Today didn't go quite as planned."

"Fair warning, Royce. Things that involve kids never do."

Her hair, light brown, long and silky, always drew his fingers. "Today was nice, but will I ever get to see you alone?" They had arrangements to make, and sooner would be preferable to later. He cupped his hand around her neck, using his thumb to tip up her chin. "I want to do more than sneak a kiss or two."

She drew in a shuddering breath and nodded. "Me, too." Her tongue licked over her lips; she took a peek at her son, then went on tiptoes to kiss him firm and quick. "Text me your upcoming schedule. We'll work it out."

Before he could register that heated promise, she slipped away. When he came out of the kitchen, he saw why. Jack was slumped on the couch, all but asleep, one shoe on and the other in his hand.

While she tended to Jack, Royce finished blocking the kitchen doorway. Tomorrow they'd compare schedules.

After sealing away his feelings for so long, there were

now many things he wanted, many things he craved—all with her.

Only her.

With any luck, they'd finally be able to make it happen.

"NOTHING HAS WORKED OUT."

At that sorrowful voice, Daron looked up from his phone to where Maris and Joy were whispering at the counter.

Sitting toward the back of the camp store, Daron gave the women their privacy. Or at least he'd tried to. Joy sat with an elbow on the counter, her head propped on one hand. Maris, as usual, bustled around. Busy. Always busy.

The woman never slowed down—not for anyone or anything.

Although…she did pause now and then to whisper with Joy.

He studied her high ponytail and sun-kissed cheekbones, those soft, full lips that always flattened when he got too close. Her long-sleeved T-shirt and well-worn jeans shouldn't have been sexy, yet the way they fit kept his gaze glued to her, imagining the body underneath.

That is, until Maris slanted suspicious brown eyes his way.

Quickly, Daron pretended to text, even smiled as if he'd read something amusing.

Truthfully, he had zero amusement right now. None.

Instead, he had frustration, with a capital *F*.

Aware of Maris, always aware of her, he knew when she shifted closer to Joy. "What does that mean? Haven't you two…sealed the deal yet?"

"Not even close," Joy lamented.

Sealed the deal? Knowing that had to be a euphemism

for sex, Daron went still, his gaze blindly on his phone screen.

"You've been over to see Royce a lot this week."

"It's that puppy," Joy said.

"Uh-huh. So a big gorgeous guy has nothing to do with it?"

Joy laughed. "Well, that's a bonus, sure. But I'm worried that Jack is getting too attached."

"To Royce or the dog?"

"Both," Joy lamented.

"And you, hon? Are you getting a little attached, too?"

Daron blinked. Maris had never used such a sweet, understanding voice with him.

"Don't be silly." And even to him, Joy sounded defensive. "I've only been seeing him a little more than a week."

"That's long enough," Maris argued. "Definitely long enough to get better acquainted. Like *naked* acquainted."

It was all Daron could do not to frown at her. Far as he knew, Maris didn't have sex, most especially not with him. He was pretty sure...not with *anyone*.

He'd have noticed something like that, right? Another guy hanging around, making moves? Or Maris wearing that look—the look of a woman satisfied?

No, Maris worked from sunup to sundown, leaving no time for *naked* acquaintances.

If she'd let him, Daron could work around her schedule. Instead, she was pushing Joy to have all the fun?

Maris continued, saying, "I thought the whole plan here was to enjoy Royce."

Laughing, Joy replied, "So you could live vicariously, yes, I remember."

Scowling, Daron wondered why Maris wouldn't just sign

on for the real deal. Give him a sign, any encouragement at all, and he'd be there in a heartbeat.

"It's just that things haven't worked out. Royce has to be at the drive-in every Friday and Saturday, and I need to be here doing crafts. During the week would be better, but then Jack missed school two days for his cold, and Royce had one catastrophe after another with the pup. Did I tell you he named that sweet little dog Chaos?"

With a grin, Maris asked, "Should I ask why?"

"You can probably guess. After surviving outside, the dog is used to going anywhere he wants. Royce is trying to house-train him, but Chaos isn't catching on too quickly to the concept. Worse, he likes eating shoes. Royce thought he had it covered by closing the closet, but while he was in the shower the dog figured out how to slide it open. Royce lost a favorite pair of sneakers."

Maris's husky laugh made Daron draw a shaky breath. Before he accidentally sent a gibberish text to some unsuspecting contact, he deleted the meaningless letters he'd put on the screen and opened Facebook instead.

"Sounds to me like you both deserve to get laid," Maris stated. "Sort of as a reward for surviving all that."

Daron stared blindly at his newsfeed. Ha! Like *Maris* was a proponent of sexual activity? Not likely, not when she happily said no to his every suggestion. Every damn time he tried to get closer, she pushed him farther away.

He'd tried just spending time with her, being helpful, chatting as she did now with Joy—but she rejected that, too. Hell, she rejected that *more*, as if letting him close would be worse than casual sex.

And yet, he couldn't stop trying. Sure, he covered it now by joking more about sex, but if she'd only give him a little leeway, he felt sure they'd be a good fit.

In more ways than one.

Really, he'd turned into a masochist, trying to sweet-talk her even as she insulted him with a scathing look. Other women didn't disdain him.

But unfortunately, he didn't want other women. Not anymore.

Not for a while now.

"Tell you what," Maris said. "Sundays are my slower days, and those work for you and Royce, right? Let me watch Jack for you then. He likes hanging out here and he's never any trouble—"

"Maris." Joy touched her forearm, momentarily keeping her in place. "I couldn't do that. If you get any time to relax, you should take it for yourself."

"Pfft." Maris slipped away to remove cookies from the oven.

The woman was forever baking.

Speaking louder from the kitchen, she said, "Jack can visit while I do a few chores. He has a favorite coloring spot, you know, right by a window so hc can see the lake. I'll even print out some neat coloring pages for him." She came back around the corner, a slight frown in place. "That is…unless you're uncomfortable leaving him with me?"

"Of course not!" Joy protested. "You're always terrific with Jack."

"Well, I know you're protective," Maris said, without her usual conviction, "so I'll understand if you'd rather find someone else."

"It's not that, I promise." Joy drew a finger around the top of her coffee cup. "You and I have gotten closer lately." She hesitated. "We're better friends now, right?"

"Good friends, definitely. I wouldn't live vicariously through just anyone."

When Joy laughed, Maris glanced at Daron again, almost like a dare.

Daron didn't look away. He held her gaze until she frowned.

Teasing her, he slowly smiled…and got to his feet.

"So," Maris said quickly. "I'll watch Jack on Sunday."

"But I don't want to take advantage of our new friendship, and what would we do with the dog? If Royce leaves him alone, he might destroy the whole house."

Before Maris could speak, Daron plopped down next to Joy and said, "How about I contribute to the cause?"

As if she'd just remembered him, Joy jumped. She looked at him with caution, maybe trying to decide how much he'd heard. "How would you do that?"

"I'll stick around Sunday, too, and keep an eye on Chaos. I'm good with animals," he added, before Maris could refuse him. "Better than good actually. My uncle used to train dogs, and when I was a kid, I sometimes helped."

"That sounds like fun," Joy said. "I love animals, but my family never had pets when I was growing up, and then I had Jack and, considering where I live, up a flight of stairs, a dog never seemed like a good idea. Jack adores that puppy, though, so I'm sure he'd enjoy visiting with you both." She turned back to Maris. "If you're positive you don't mind?"

Put on the spot, Maris said, somewhat through her teeth, "I'm already looking forward to it."

"Me, too." Daron couldn't quite remove the triumph from his tone. For once, he'd managed to outmaneuver her, and it was for a good cause. "I'll check out the dog's temperament and then teach Jack some simple commands to practice with him."

"I think Royce would appreciate the pointers, too. Right

now, he can't leave Chaos alone for a minute. The dog goes with him everywhere, even the grocery store."

"Then that's decided." To keep from pushing his luck, Daron stood again. "In fact, I was heading out to see Royce. I'll talk to him about the dog."

Maris folded her arms and gave him a look. "Why are you seeing him?"

"What's that?" Damn it, he hadn't expected her to ask.

"You and Royce. What's up with that?" After a meaningful glance at the clock, she tucked in her chin to make her expression stern. "It's Friday. You're usually finishing up work so you can be on your way to a hot date."

Not as true as she might think, but then, he'd allowed her to go on believing it rather than have her know that he spent most of his free nights thinking about her.

After a second of mental scrambling, Daron came up with a truth. "With the campers thinning out, I have less to do so I already finished." And like a glutton for punishment, he'd gravitated to Maris, though he hadn't realized that she and Joy would have such a fascinating conversation.

It struck him funny then.

He'd known Joy as long as he'd known Maris. Both women had been off-limits, in part because he worked with them, but mostly because they both made it clear they weren't interested.

No problem with Joy. He'd been more than happy to go the platonic route with her.

But Maris? Everything she did and said sizzled with underlying emotions and he wanted her. Maris wanted him, too—he felt it in his bones—but for whatever reason she *did* refuse him.

And he would never pressure any woman, so he'd turned

his attention to joking instead—and annoyed her in the process.

Getting back to her question, Daron rolled a shoulder. "Royce had asked about a few tools to borrow. I'll go through the maintenance building to see what I can find, then take the stuff over to him."

"I need to get going, too." Joy slid off the stool and gathered up her purse. "It's time for me to get Jack from school." She paused, smiling at Maris, then at him. "Thank you both. Really. If I can ever return the favor, please let me know."

She already had, by giving him the opportunity to spend time with Maris under different, better circumstances. With Jack around, Maris couldn't give him hell—and he couldn't come on to her. Not overtly, anyway.

They'd be forced into neutral ground, and that had to be a good thing. "You're welcome, hon. Anytime."

The second Joy walked through the doorway, Daron felt it. A ratcheting up of awareness. Throbbing sexual tension.

His own heavier heartbeat.

He was now alone with Maris.

Neither of them spoke. He still stared at the door, giving himself a moment to think.

After he managed to plaster on a smile, he turned to her.

Ugh…not good. Her crossed arms tightened and her eyes narrowed. Over the years he'd learned to read Maris's many moods, and this one proclaimed he was in the doghouse.

"Problem?" Maybe if he played dumb…

"You *know* what the problem is."

Yeah, he did. Pretending an exaggerated wince, he leaned on the counter. "Well, two things can be true, right? Yes, I manipulated that situation just a bit so I could visit with you." Preferably without her scowling at him the entire time.

"Daron…" She made his name an exasperated groan.

"But." He let that sink in, because he did have a caveat. "I like Joy, too, you know. You don't have exclusive interest in seeing her loosen up a little."

Miraculously, her expression softened. She even dropped her arms as she sighed. "Okay, so you're also her friend."

"And you know Joy, so you know that took some doing. Friendly, yes. She always is. But accepting me as a real friend? She's…cautious." That seemed like as good a word as any.

"Same," Maris said. "She's only recently opened up to me."

"About sex." Daron nodded as if that made perfect sense. "Maybe we should be thanking Royce for creating the change in circumstances."

Her lips lifted into a grin. "Maybe."

"I like seeing her happier. Plus Royce is a great guy. Jack sure adores him."

"Whoa." Leaning down, Maris crossed her arms on the counter. "Don't get ahead of yourself."

The words hit his brain but he didn't quite follow, not with Maris that much closer to him, her breasts sitting on her crossed arms, plumped up in an impossible-to-ignore way. What his brain did was conjure an image of her in that exact posture, but maybe with a low-cut sweater on instead of her usual, no-nonsense crew neck top. Something that would show some cleavage.

Or more.

Naked would be good, too. If he ever got her to say yes, he'd reenact this exact scenario, just to feed his muse.

God, he had it bad when his imagination with Maris was better than reality with anyone else.

To cover for his male-brain deficiency, he said, "What does that mean?"

"Joy doesn't want to get locked down with anyone, and from what she's said, neither does Royce. She just wants to live a little again."

Of all the… Daron snorted. "Yeah, right."

"She deserves to enjoy herself," Maris stated with conviction. "Not only as a mother, but as a woman."

"Couldn't agree more. Every woman deserves that." He knew she'd caught his point when her gaze shifted away. "But I also overheard the two of you talking."

In clear complaint, Maris muttered, "There's an awful lot of that going on lately."

Daron grinned. "Maybe if there weren't so many fascinating discussions happening to catch our attention, the men wouldn't stop to listen."

She gave him that one, saying, "It has been fascinating, hasn't it? The change in Joy is incredible. I nudged her, yes, but she was already headed in the right direction."

From what he'd heard, Maris was doing more than nudging, but Joy didn't seem to mind. "They're already involved. If they're saying they aren't, they're just fooling themselves."

Maris rolled her eyes. "I know you're the expert on detached relationships—"

"Wait, what?" Daron was far from detached when it came to her.

"But you can't speak for Joy or Royce."

He let the first part of that go and said instead, "Have you *seen* them together?"

She shrugged. "You know, women can…" Her mouth closed.

Oh, but he knew what she'd been about to say, so he finished for her. "Women can enjoy sex for the sake of sex. I'm aware."

"Of course you are."

The fact that she laughed after saying it didn't take the sting from the words. "More importantly," he asked, "are *you* aware of it? Because from what I can tell, you haven't—"

She smashed her fingers over his mouth, then lowered her voice in another warning. "Don't pretend you know me, Daron."

Yeah…so. Her hand on his lips smelled like fresh sugar cookies, and just the fact that she touched him, touched his *mouth*, caused his balls to clench. He considered options for all of a split second, then for another second he tried to talk himself out of it—to no avail. He gave in and prodded the seam of her first two fingers with the tip of his tongue.

Her eyes flared, warmed, and she snatched her hand away. "Did you just *lick* me?"

That kind of talk wasn't helping his balls to relax. "Yeah." Shit. That sounded like a feral growl so he cleared his throat and tried again, striving for indifference. "You touched, I reacted."

For the first time in forever, deep pink washed her face.

A blush. On Maris? Oh, now that was interesting.

She looked him over, calculating…something. "So you're saying if I touch you again—" she reached out one finger to lightly prod his shoulder "—I can expect…what?" Proving she had a torturous mean streak, she whispered, "Another lick?"

Full. Blown. Boner.

That's what she could expect. He resisted the urge to clear his throat again. "I aim to please."

"Wonderful. Then please be on your way so I can get back to work."

Such a cruel, cruel woman. Daron caught her hand before she'd completely straightened. "Maris."

She gave him a look so sultry he felt singed. "Daron?"

Of its own accord, his thumb drifted over the smooth, sugar-scented skin of her wrist. "Gotta admit, I like it when you tease me."

She gave a playful shrug. "It's payback, because you're always teasing me."

"Flirting, more than teasing. It's a habit now."

"A bad habit," she pointed out.

"Oh, I dunno." She wasn't pulling away, so Daron slid his hand up her forearm in a featherlight caress, until he reached her upper arm just above her elbow. The cotton T-shirt was soft, but not like her skin. "I can't believe anything with you is bad, although I know I'd enjoy it more if you were just a little more receptive."

"But then, would I enjoy it?"

Such a loaded question. He looked into her eyes and made a heated promise. "I'd make damn sure you did."

Her lips parted. Better still, her gaze dropped to his mouth. Daron held his breath.

"You're younger than me."

Not at all what he'd expected. "A couple years," he said, dismissing the age difference. "It's nothing."

"Six years," she countered. "With a decade of conflicting perspective added in."

"Perspective?" He'd rather talk about licking, but since she brought it up... "What do you mean?"

"Outlook. Attitude." She came closer, her words going breathless. "Priorities."

What did she know of his priorities? He was about to ask when she closed the space between them, putting her mouth to his.

Oh, hell, yeah. Daron nearly groaned aloud. After wanting her so long, a single kiss equaled a massive accomplishment. She wanted to talk about priorities? She'd been a priority to him for longer than he wanted to remember.

Now that she finally wanted him, too, he wasn't about to let her get away.

Catching the back of her neck under the fall of her ponytail, Daron kept her close while they fell into a hot, open-mouthed, hungry kiss.

God, she tasted good, even better than he'd ever imagined. And this close, various scents filled his head. Sugar, yes. Maris was forever baking for the camp store customers and the employees. Feminine warmth, too, because damn it all, that warmth had a fragrance and it intoxicated him.

In contrast, he picked up the scents of lemons from her shampoo, and something floral in her lotion. All combined, it equaled Maris, a fantasy come to life.

He wanted closer. He wanted every part of her against every part of him.

Damn the counter between them.

And damn the open front door that meant anyone could walk in.

Knowing he had to do this right, that he had to consider Maris and all the things that mattered most to her, Daron lightly cupped her shoulders and started a slow retreat.

A nip to her bottom lip. A lick to her upper. A kiss to the corner of her mouth and then her chin.

She wouldn't want to be caught making out over the

counter where she served customers. More than anyone he knew, Maris lived and breathed her work. She had a reputation and never, not in a million years, would he want it to feel tarnished because she got busted fooling around with him at work.

It was one of the harder things he'd done in the last decade, but he gradually ended the kiss.

"Mmm," she murmured, eyes still closed, body slightly swaying and her breath heavy. "That was perfect."

Perfect. Yeah, exactly the description he would use, because *she* was perfect. "We should try this again," he suggested, his voice low and deep. "Maybe in a place where we're guaranteed some privacy."

Smiling, she slowly opened her heavy eyes. Through kiss-dampened lips, she whispered, "Maybe."

He needed no more encouragement than that. "Maris—"

"But not tonight." She licked her lips, and managed to clear her gaze. "Not even this weekend."

Well, hell. How long did he have to wait? "What are we talking here?"

Drifting her fingertips through his hair—something she'd never done before—she wore a look of barely banked curiosity.

Daron had the urge to smooth his hair back down. He rarely did more than a quick combing of his unruly mop, followed by smashing on a ball cap.

Given her touch, he was glad he'd skipped the hat today.

"A few things, Daron."

Anything. Trying not to sound that anxious, he replied, "Yeah?"

"You're tempting."

Hell, yeah. He lifted his brows, waiting.

"But I've been focused on…other things for most of my

life. I have a set of rules I follow, and they don't include getting involved with someone like you."

He wasn't cut out for too many rules. "What do you mean, someone like me?" Was she still hung up on the age thing? Ridiculous. He was twenty-five, not eighteen.

She glanced toward the open door, making him aware of voices approaching. "Customers are coming."

"Now wait a minute! You can't leave me hanging." Were they going to happen or not?

"I'm sorry. Really." She touched his hand in a gesture of sincerity. "Rule number one is never ignore the job, and I'm about to have customers."

For a woman like Maris, would he ever come first?

"Let me think about things and I'll get back to you." After patting his hand, she retreated to put Joy's coffee cup away and wipe off the counter.

Was he really going to feel insulted? He'd been aware of her for years. He'd wanted her forever. She knew that, and damn it, she wanted him, too.

And yet, after that kiss, she needed more time to think?

Yes, apparently he felt insulted. Straightening away, Daron waited until she got close again, then said, "You do that."

His indignation only made her grin. "Relax. We'll both still be here Monday. We'll talk then."

Why did he have his doubts? "If you say so."

Now she outright laughed. As two campers strolled in, she leaned closer to say, "We promised Joy we'd watch Jack on Sunday, along with a rowdy puppy, so whatever you're thinking or feeling, put a lid on it for now."

Call him easy, but he liked this new casual vibe on her. "How am I supposed to do that?"

She winked. "Let the anticipation build. That's what I plan to do."

With that parting remark, she greeted the campers, and happily took their orders for hamburgers.

She seemed unaffected, while he was anything but.

Walking out, Daron had to wonder how his ingenious plan to infiltrate her space with a kid and a dog as allies had somehow morphed into one more way for Maris to torture him.

CHAPTER SIX

IT WAS AWKWARD, Joy thought, having others know her intentions for Royce. Maris was one thing; she'd enjoyed having a woman to talk to, to share her most intimate thoughts.

But Daron? He was everything she wasn't—carefree, openly sexual, free.

Even thinking it gave her a twinge, because it seemed like she resented Jack when nothing could be further from the truth. It gave her pangs to think of leaving him with Maris even for an evening. An early evening. She'd literally only be gone a few hours.

Stolen time with Royce... Did *he* know what she intended?

Joy hoped so, because she intended sex, *tonight*, while the opportunity presented itself.

If she had to wait any longer, she just might go nuts.

Skipping ahead of her, Jack occasionally stopped to pick up rocks that caught his eye. One streaked with pink, another smooth as a robin's egg, another coal black.

How had she never noticed his artistic eye?

"Look at this one, Mom!" He held up a dirt-streaked hand with the small rock displayed on his palm.

Joy looked, but to her, it was just a rock, like all the others in the gravel lanes. "Very nice."

He lifted it toward the sun to study it, and then asked, "How far do you think I can throw it?"

She grinned. Being a little boy took precedence over art, apparently. "We'll go down on the shore and see. But we have to make it quick."

When he started to run ahead, she cautioned, "Don't get your feet wet!"

At a slower pace, Joy followed, enjoying the feel of the sun on her face and the scent of fall in the air. It was a day for new experiences, fresh excitement, and she couldn't keep the smile off her face.

She'd arrived a few minutes early so she'd have a chance to talk to Maris before Royce got there with Chaos. Maris had her number, and Joy trusted her to call if she needed to, but…for her own peace of mind, she wanted to go over things again.

A dark sedan caught her eye. Sleek, shiny, obviously expensive and parked where it shouldn't be, blocking in the golf carts used only by employees.

As a single mom living off an RV resort's employment, pricey transportation had no relevance to her.

But she'd come from money, and she knew money when she saw it.

The new model Bentley would cost more than most people made in an entire year. More than some people's houses.

Dread throbbed like a live thing inside her, making her mouth dry and her stomach churn.

Daron, who'd been standing in the camp store doorway, spotted her and strode out. He looked grim and that bothered her even more.

She knew. Of course she did. Time away hadn't made her dumb, but God, it had numbed her to the hurt—a hurt that came washing back with the force of a tsunami.

Jack. She sought him out on the shore, watching him use all his might to throw that rock out into the cold lake. He was her world and she wouldn't let anyone, *anyone*, hurt him.

When Daron reached her, she grasped his hands. "Jack. Can you watch him for me? I don't want him…" *To face whatever I'm about to face. To meet the people who don't love him.*

The people who didn't want him.

Daron nodded. "You got it, hon." He hesitated. "You know who it is?"

"No." She inhaled deeply through her nose, drawing in calming purpose. "Not specifically." But she had a good guess, and she knew whoever it was would only bring heartache.

Daron worriedly searched her gaze. "She says she's your mother."

Worst suspicions confirmed.

For a second, Joy had to close her eyes. What could have brought her here now? How had her mother even found her? No, Joy didn't keep her location a secret, but neither had she been in touch with her family, not in six long years.

Not since they'd disowned her.

What if her father had died? He was ten years older than her mother, but last she knew he'd been in good health.

He'd allowed her mother's decision, but Joy couldn't say that he'd actively participated in it. He never really did. All her life, her father had been busy. Busy with work, busy with socializing. Busy managing his fortune.

He was kind to her, and he'd sometimes enjoyed showing her off. She couldn't recall him ever forgetting a birthday... and yet, they hadn't been close. After the last big blowup with her mother, she'd seen sympathy in her dad's eyes.

Well. There'd be no sympathy from her mother, so she may as well quit stalling. Joy worked up a strained smile. "Guess I should see what she wants."

He didn't let her go. Instead, he drew her into a tight hug, surprising her with the unfamiliar gesture. It took her a second, and then Joy returned the embrace, drawing strength from his friendship.

"Thank you," she whispered as she pulled back.

He nodded. "It's what friends do. Remember that, okay?" With one last reassuring look, he headed off for Jack.

Grateful, so very, very grateful, Joy got her feet moving and walked, as gracefully and unhurried as she could manage, into Summer's End.

Maris caught her eye the second she entered. She, too, wore a false smile. "There you are." Circling out from behind the counter, she said, "Your mother has come to visit."

Joy nodded, not yet looking in that direction. Unable to make herself do it.

"Coffee? A cola?" Maris got closer and whispered, "What can I do?"

How? Joy wondered. How did these amazing people know this was difficult for her? Was it intuition, her mother's cold persona or did they simply know her well enough, despite her lack of sharing in the past, to see it for what it was?

Honestly, the tension in the air was as thick as soup.

Maybe it was just that hard to miss.

"A cola," she said to Maris, meeting her eyes and managing a wan smile to let her know it was okay. "Thank you."

"You bet." Maris's long ponytail bounced as she headed off to get the drink.

Girding herself, Joy turned and there in a booth was her mother. The set of Cara Vivien Reed's mouth showed her disdain. Back ramrod straight, she sat slightly forward as if afraid that resting against the plastic seat might somehow infest her. She looked the same as she had so long ago, the same disapproving manner and impeccable appearance. She'd be sixty now, but she hadn't aged a day.

That was a perk of the wealthy: the best dieticians and cooks, yoga instructors, personal cosmetologists and stylists to provide an ever youthful appearance.

The one thing that had changed? Her mother looked... tired. It only showed a little, but Joy saw it just the same.

Standing in the aisle, just behind Cara's shoulder, was a suited man who likely served as driver and bodyguard. He was new to Joy, yet the position was familiar. Her mother had always traveled with security.

So pretentious.

Never in her entire life had Joy known her mother to actually *need* protection. So much of what she did was for effect, from the house with more rooms than they could ever use, to the designer clothing that didn't look at all comfortable and the jewelry specifically created for her, to the fake friends she chose and the family she...thrust aside.

A fatherless grandson, regardless of how passé that

thinking might be, didn't fit the illusion of perfection through privileged wealth.

Feeling contrary, Joy smiled at the driver and asked, "Would you like something to drink? Maris makes the best coffee ever. Or a cola?"

Startled that she would speak to him, the man shifted his alert stance. "No, ma'am. Thank you."

Ignoring that, Joy turned and said to Maris, "Another cola, okay? It had to have been a long drive to get here. Just put it on my tab."

Her mother tipped her chin. "Are you deliberately wasting my time?"

Joy replied, "Yes?" and then accepted two drinks from Maris.

"Mrs. Reed," Maris said with absurd deference, "are you sure you wouldn't like something?"

She eyed the plain glass and plastic straw. "No, thank you."

To Joy, Maris whispered darkly, "Maybe I should go get one of the guys?"

"I'm fine, I'm promise. This is nothing new." She hesitated, then admitted, "I'm glad you're here, though. That's enough."

With a crooked smirk, Maris said, "It's my place. I'm *always* here, and just so you know, I've thrown out bigger guys than that dude."

Joy chuckled at the visual that leaped to mind. "I believe it."

"You, however, would have to tangle with your mother." Leaning in closer, Maris whispered, "I'm not getting anywhere near that one."

Understanding that sentiment only too well, Joy nodded. "Let's hope it doesn't come to that."

Maris winked and headed back to the counter, which meant Joy couldn't stall any longer. Drawing a breath, she approached the booth, again without haste, and handed the cola to the driver. He had no choice except to take it, his gaze skirting down to her mother.

Cara gave him a small nod and dismissed him.

How had she ever belonged to that world? Joy shook her head with a small laugh and took the liberty of sitting across from her mother. Elbows on the table, her chin in her hands, she said, "You've caught me at a bad time. I have an appointment in just a few minutes." *An appointment with a big, gorgeous, kind man who will hopefully take me to bed today.* "Is there a reason you've called?"

"Your grandmother Reed passed away."

Shock swept away Joy's feigned indifference. She searched her mother's stern expression. "You're serious?"

"Your father's mother. And of course I'm serious. It's hardly a joking matter."

Grams. Throat going tight, Joy thought of the bold, irreverent and sometimes silly grandma she'd adored. Not long after she'd gotten pregnant with Jack, Grams had suffered a severe stroke and it changed everything. Joy had still visited her, but it wasn't easy, not with nurses always around her and the acrimony in her family. Grams was just as smart, just as caring, but she had so much difficulty expressing herself that visits almost seemed to frustrate her. After her family disowned her… Joy never went back.

Oh, she'd wanted to. She'd thought about her grandmother many times, but she'd been too busy surviving, too determined to find a way to support herself and her baby. Too busy putting distance between herself and her mother.

Suddenly those excuses didn't suffice.

Guilt was a terrible thing, but Joy swallowed it back, determined not to let her mother see her pain. "When?"

"A few months ago."

Her mouth nearly dropped open. *Months?* And no one had cared enough to tell her? That said a lot. Too much, really—none of it a surprise.

As if her mother had read her mind, she gave a slight, defensive shrug. "Since you walked away from your family, I wouldn't be here now except that it appears your grandmother left you an inheritance."

Joy reacted to the first part of that statement with a gasp of outrage. "You *told* me to leave. You said I wasn't your daughter anymore."

"Well, you didn't exactly fight to stay, did you?"

Of all the... Had her mother wanted her to beg? Why would she bother when she knew her mother so well? Cara Reed never retreated.

Arching one carefully drawn brow in censure, her mother pushed a crisp business card forward. "There are papers to sign, of course. You need to meet us at the attorney's office Monday morning. The date and time are noted, as a reminder."

Staring at the linen card without touching it, Joy's thoughts scrambled. Jack had school on Monday. Any attorney her grandmother used would be at least two hours from here, closer to where her parents lived.

They'd have to reschedule.

However, she'd discuss that with the lawyer, not her mother. The real dilemma was figuring out what timing would work for her. She'd need the better part of the day just for traveling back and forth. And if the meeting took too long? She wouldn't be back in time to get Jack. Yet taking Jack with her was not an option.

She didn't know how she'd work it out, but she wasn't about to share the difficulty of her circumstances with her mother. Even now, after delivering that awful news, she knew Cara watched her for signs of weakness.

"Have your...*circumstances* changed?"

Stumped by the abrupt question, Joy lifted her gaze to her mother. Her circumstances seemed pretty clear. After all, her mother had found where she lived. "What do you mean?"

Brows beetling, Cara clarified, "The child."

Dear God. Her mother didn't even know that she'd birthed a son—*her grandson*. Yet she thought...what? That Joy had at some point changed her mind about having him? That she'd left her family and everything familiar just to be difficult?

No, she'd done that for Jack, and she'd do it all again in a heartbeat.

"If you count being a mother a change of circumstances, then yes."

Her mother sucked in a breath, her expression unreadable.

"You knew that's what I always intended." Joy's hands tightened of their own accord, now fisted on the booth top. How dare her mother come here and disrupt her peace? Rage pressed against her composure. Resentment boiled up, churning with hurt.

And then Joy felt it, felt *him*, and she shifted in her seat to see the door.

Royce stood there, taking up a lot of space, his direct gaze calmly evaluating the situation.

Joy saw the moment he made up his mind. The intent showed clearly in his dark shark eyes, in his purposeful stride as he came to her.

Was this good or bad?

She frantically tried to decide. Yes, his presence helped to order her emotions, but as Joy hurriedly stood to greet him, she badly wished him away from the venom her mother would spew.

"Royce," she said, trying to keep her tone light despite her anxiety. "I can join you in just a—"

"Who," her mother's sharp voice demanded, "is this?"

Joy closed her eyes. She wasn't in time. Keeping her back to her mother, she tried to think. "No," she whispered, telling herself not to engage.

Undeterred, her mother stood, too. "Is this the man you allowed to use you? The one who ruined your life?" Each question cut a little deeper. "The one who left you saddled with a—"

Whirling to face her, Joy snapped, "*Don't say it.* Don't you *dare* say it." Nostrils burning with her fast breaths, her eyes glazing with furious tears, she pointed at her mother. Her hand shook as scalding rage burned through her.

She would not allow *anyone* to insult her son.

Joy had gladly stayed away from all of them to protect Jack. To insulate him from their poison. She would not tolerate her mother showing up so many years later with the same hateful agenda.

Royce moved closer. She felt the heat of his body along her back. Not a bodyguard, certainly.

But something so much better.

Royce offered silent support, and the generous gesture meant the world to her.

Drawing a slow breath, Joy lowered her arm…and lifted her chin. "No one ruined my life. To the contrary, I love the life I have now."

"So." Her mother breathed harder, too, her narrowed

gaze going over Royce. "Is he the father, or just another mistake about to happen?"

Royce shifted—and released a short, soft laugh of pure amusement.

Laughing? He was laughing at her mother's taunt?

True, it was absurd, but…he wasn't insulted?

He laughed again, more a snicker that he couldn't control, and that somehow zapped the tension from Joy's body.

Somewhere behind her, Joy heard Maris's not-so-subtle "Ha!" and suddenly everything was easier.

She could relax her shoulders. She could draw a deep, smooth breath.

These fun, quirky, supportive people were in her life. People who accepted her, faults and all, instead of judging her.

Blinking back tears of appreciation, Joy picked up the card from the tabletop. While her mother glared, she said, "Thank you for bringing this to me. I'll get in touch with the attorney."

The dismissal hung there in the air.

There'd been no polite greeting for her. No introductions to her friends. Joy wasn't about to gift Cara with a nice farewell.

Her mother left no room for anything nice.

Like a bad actor in an absurd performance, Cara overplayed her lines, ruining the impact of the delivery. Now if Joy could just get her away from the park before she met Jack, the visit could be chalked up as a blip in her otherwise wonderful day.

Not really tragic.

Not *too* devastating.

It felt good to know she'd grown beyond her mother's realm.

After grabbing her clutch purse, her mother glanced around the room. "This is exactly what I warned you about. I told you this is where you'd end up, but you didn't listen." Her attention went over Joy, and she shook her head. "I should have known better than to think you'd changed."

With a gentle smile, Joy said, "I certainly knew you hadn't."

The dig hit home, and Cara reacted as if she'd been slapped. For only a single heartbeat, Joy saw hurt in her eyes.

Then, with a lot of indignant fanfare, her mother departed, the poor bodyguard hurrying ahead to lead the way as if he feared some heinous danger lurked between the camp store and the lakeshore.

No, the only thing out there was...

Crap. Joy pushed past Royce and rushed to ensure her son wasn't anywhere near. She wouldn't allow her mother to see him, to possibly slight him in some way.

She paused in the doorway, frantically searching, but she didn't see Jack anywhere.

Royce put his hand to her back. "Daron took him over to the scuba shack with Chaos. They're playing."

Ah, so Daron had known there was trouble and he'd been a true friend by removing her son from the scene. Relief and gratitude made her knees weak.

Suddenly depleted, Joy dropped a shoulder against the door frame and released an exhausted breath. "She still knows how to suck the oxygen out of a room."

His hand smoothed up and down her spine. "You held your own."

Barely, and now of course Royce would want an explanation.

An explanation beyond what he'd just witnessed.

What could she say? That after nearly six years of separation, her mother wanted to reinforce her disappointment in her only daughter? Clearly, she could have called. She could have sent someone else to give her the news of her grandmother's passing.

But no, then she would have lost the opportunity to spit her scorn one more time.

Joy felt...not disappointment. That had died a few years back. But embarrassment? Yes, she felt that in spades.

Most people had normal families that were a little quirky sometimes. They had a member or two with eccentricities, a relative who tended to say the wrong thing, another who arrived late to every event.

Hers was more in the range of abnormally detached, superficial and spiteful.

Trying to push through her humiliation, Joy spun to face Royce. The concern in his dark eyes tested her resolve. It invited her to confide in him, lean on him.

But that would be a breach of their agreement.

Companionship, with hopefully some side benefits of a sexual nature. That's what they each wanted. Despite the scene he'd happened into, emotional support wasn't part of the deal. He was not her rock.

And she stood on her own now, damn it.

"Well." Shoulders back and a painful smile in place, Joy asked, "I hope you're not in a hurry. I need to talk to Jack before we go—" she badly needed to hug him "—but I'll only be a minute."

With his gaze unnervingly intense, Royce searched her face. "You're okay?"

"Of course." She tried a carefree laugh, and succeeded more than otherwise. "That nonsense with my mother is nothing new, believe me. It's fine." I'm *fine*.

"Joy," he said in soft exasperation, as if he knew she lied not only to him but herself, as well.

"Really, Royce. It's nothing at all—"

He bent and touched his mouth to hers in the sweetest, least demanding kiss ever. His warm lips lightly caressed, reassured. Lingered, but only for a moment, lasting just long enough to silence her. Still very close, his tone rough but gentle, he asked, "That was your mother, right?"

Unfortunately. "Yes."

With a hand cupped to her neck, he stroked his thumb over the line of her jaw. "She thought I might be Jack's father?"

"She was fishing. Or maybe she just wanted to be nasty and found an excuse." Joy shrugged to show that it didn't matter. "I hope you weren't offended."

"It caught me off guard." His fingers tunneled into her hair at the back of her head in a brief massage. "Sorry I laughed."

"Don't be. I'm not." His amusement had saved her from escalating the scene. "It was exactly the right response to her nonsense."

His touch and tone gentled even more. "I thought your mother knew Jack's father and disapproved of him."

Joy understood how he'd gotten that impression. "Mother knew *of* him." To keep this as short and succinct as possible, Joy said, "Vaughn had a rather colorful reputation and my parents learned of it through their friends. Everyone was scandalized that Joy Reed, the princess of Cara and Wallace Reed, would lower herself to associating with a bartender." Her mouth twisted. "That was his job when I hooked up with him, but he never kept any job long. My parents were furious when I refused to stop dating him, and doubly so when I married him. They were certain he was only after my money, and in hindsight, that was probably true."

Royce frowned slightly. "Despite him being their son-in-law, they refused to ever meet him in person?"

Joy shrugged. "We got married at a justice of the peace. The whole relationship was doomed from the beginning. My parents continued to ensure I had money, but they didn't subsidize anything Vaughn wanted." Remembering his reaction when she told him no money would be coming for his extravagant indulgences, she huffed a short laugh. "Rightfully so, as it turns out. When Vaughn didn't have unlimited funds, he tired of me pretty quickly."

"He sounds like a prick."

Joy stole her own small kiss this time. "Rest assured, Royce, you're not like him in any way."

"I take it you and your mother are still at odds?"

Covering her mouth, Joy laughed and shook her head. "Truthfully, Mother despises me."

"That can't be true."

"I disappointed her one time too many." Glancing at the door to ensure Jack remained out of hearing range, Joy added, "Marrying Vaughn was bad enough, but when he left me pregnant, she wanted me to wash my hands of… well, everything that had to do with him."

Royce went still as understanding dawned. "She didn't want you to have Jack?"

"She was quite clear that if I wanted my family's support after the divorce, if I planned to stay with them while I re-grouped, I had to do so without any connection to Vaughn."

"That wasn't her decision to make."

Oh, how Joy agreed. "When I refused, she disowned me and I moved out." That massive blowup felt like an eon ago. She'd changed a lot since making her own way.

She liked the person she was now much more than she liked who she used to be. At least for that, she could thank her mother.

"They've never met Jack, and I'd prefer to keep it that way."

"Got it." After a brief hug, Royce stepped away. "I'll go get him for you. I need to check on Chaos, anyway."

"Thank you."

The second he was gone, Joy's gaze skipped over to Maris. She bustled around as always, refilling napkins and straws in their dispensers, but she met Joy's gaze.

"That was wild," Maris remarked casually.

Putting a hand to her throbbing temple, Joy said, "I'm sorry that happened here."

Abruptly she stopped, her gaze direct. "I'm sorry it happened at all. It shouldn't have."

"No, but that's never stopped my mother." She came up to the counter, but didn't sit. Instead, she picked up a stack of paper napkins and helped to fill another dispenser. "My mother and I aren't close."

"No shit."

How amazing that Maris could make her laugh even now. Truly a blessing in a friendship. Smiling, Joy explained, "She doesn't like it when anyone goes against her wishes."

"And you did?"

A hard truth to share, but with Maris, sharing seemed easy. "I had Jack, so yes."

Maris scowled, dropping the box of straws and jamming her hands on her hips. "That's why she was so hateful? Seriously? She resents her own grandson?"

"He's not her grandson." The denial came out harsher

than Joy meant it to. Rubbing her temples, she said, "I'm sorry."

"Hey, I get it. You probably wish it was true."

Joy dropped her hands, knowing there was no way to escape the tension, or the embarrassment. "Jack is mine, so by blood he's also related to my parents, but they've never met him, have never even asked about him." *They don't care about him any more than they care about me.*

Maris shrugged. "Their loss."

It amazed Joy that Maris could always be so pragmatic. It *was* their loss. If she thought about it long enough, she could almost feel sorry for them.

Almost.

"After my divorce, I stupidly wanted to go home." It dawned on her that her apartment with Vaughn had never felt like home, not really. "I thought I could stay with my parents awhile, figure out what I wanted to do." It wasn't easy, but Joy met Maris's gaze—and was glad she had when she saw only the usual acceptance. No judgment, no pity. "It seemed the easy way out of my predicament, you know? Suddenly single, no job and a baby on the way."

"That's what family is supposed to do, lend a hand when you need it."

Maybe for family who hadn't burned bridges, but Joy had. Looking back, she knew she'd torched that bridge completely. "I was spoiled rotten without realizing it. I'd never worked. Even while married to Vaughn, we'd lived out of accounts my parents had set up for me." When she'd returned to them, her pride damaged and fear of the future a live thing inside her, she'd wanted more than a hand. She'd wanted them to make it okay for her.

Their solution had been…unacceptable.

It still hurt Joy's heart to remember. "We had a big argument about me being pregnant…and it ended with my mother disowning me. I left and I haven't been back."

Maris thought about that while finishing a chore. "Striking out on your own must've taken a lot of guts."

Leave it to Maris to see the best in her. It's how she treated everyone. "Honestly, it was the best decision I've ever made," Joy said. "If I hadn't left, I never would have learned to take care of myself. I'd still be dependent on them." She wouldn't have Jack, wouldn't be at the park…

"And we wouldn't be friends," Maris said, almost as if she'd read Joy's mind.

"Another upside," Joy agreed with a smile…that quickly dimmed. "Apparently Mother hasn't kept up with my life at all. She didn't know if I'd had a son or daughter."

Picking up the now-empty cardboard containers, Maris took them to the recycle can. "So basically, she disowned you and her grandchild?" She shook her head. "You might have been a little spoiled, but what she did seems downright mean."

It *felt* mean, especially for her mother to seek her out only to continue the antagonism.

She and Maris settled onto stools, knees touching. It wasn't planned, but it just happened. Sort of like their growing friendship. "I'm glad she's not a part of my life anymore, because that means she's not a part of Jack's life, either, and as you just saw, that's a good thing."

Rather than remark on that, Maris asked, "Was it horrible growing up with her for your mother?"

"Not at all. In fact, I was pampered. I had stuff before I even thought to ask for it." More stuff than she ever needed. More than she could even use. The truth of that shamed her. "Everything except love."

"Are you *sure* they don't love you?"

"Did that look like love to you?"

Maris shrugged. "When someone doesn't care, they rarely show strong emotion. She found out where you live, right? She could have sent a letter. Or even just called the park and left a message."

Huh. Maris had a valid point. Had Joy misread the situation? "If they loved me, they didn't tell me so very often."

"Saying it doesn't always mean much." A crooked smile put a dimple in Maris's cheek. It wasn't her usual smile, full of wit, warmth or sarcasm, depending on where she aimed it. Combined with her downcast eyes, this expression was…poignant. "My parents told me all the time how much they loved me, but they didn't do much else."

Confused by what that meant, Joy put her hand over Maris's, giving her fingers a squeeze. "I'm sorry."

"Not sure which is worse, you know? An empty belly or an empty heart."

An empty belly? Dear God, what had Maris gone through? Her expression closed off, keeping Joy from asking too many questions, but she didn't release Maris's hand. Not because Joy needed it, but because, for once, she sensed that Maris did. "I think being hungry would be a terrible thing."

"It was." Deliberately lightening her expression, Maris nodded at the tray of fresh cookies. "Maybe that's why I enjoy baking so much."

"Maybe." In that moment, Joy saw Maris in a whole new way. Possibilities opened up, reasons for her workaholic attitude and stringent lifestyle. She was a strong woman, a survivor and a valuable friend.

For so many reasons, Joy considered her a good influence in Jack's life. Daron was, too—as well as Coop and Baxter, Phoenix and her sister, Ridley…

The park sign took on new meaning for her: Cooper's Charm: A Good Place to Get Away. It should also say *The best people in the world work here.*

"So." Pulling her hand free, Maris said, "What I want to know is, how did you turn out to be such a sweet person? Because seriously, Joy, you were way too nice to her."

Just that easily, Maris broke the melancholy and returned to her usual self. In one respect, Joy was relieved. It hurt her to see her friend hurting.

But in another…well, she hoped that one day Maris would trust her enough to share everything—the good, the bad and the unfortunate, past disappointments and future goals.

For now, Joy had one little secret she could share. Hopefully Maris wouldn't see it as an unwelcome obligation.

There was only one way to find out. "You're on Jack's emergency contact list," she blurted.

Blinking, Maris leaned back, eyes widening. "Come again?"

"I don't expect there to be an emergency," Joy rushed to say, "but I felt that if something happened to me, if Jack got sick and they couldn't reach me, or…or whatever."

"You named *me*?"

Joy rather liked the astonished look on Maris's face. It reflected surprise, but not in an unpleasant way. More like she'd been given a gift. "The school needed a contact. You're it."

"You… I mean, I…" Laughing, Maris shook her head and started over. "Okay, first, wow, I'm flattered."

"You are?" Relieved, Joy let out a breath and smiled.

"Seriously, insanely flattered. I thought you might not want to leave the squirt with me, since I don't have kids of my own."

"You're good with him," Joy promised. "He treats you like an aunt."

"An aunt, huh? Hey, I like that." Boasting, Maris said, "I'm an honorary aunt," she said, tasting the words and then nodding. "Cool beans."

Laughter bubbled up. "You don't mind? Being on the emergency list, I mean?"

"I'm seriously honored, but when did that happen?"

With a wince, Joy admitted, "The beginning of the school year." Joy rushed into explanations. "I should have told you, I know that, but it never seemed like a good time and then I guess I just put it out of my mind. Even without discussing it, I knew if the school ever called you, you would go. I've always…" Joy shrugged. "I've always trusted you—whether I told you so or not."

Pleasure put color in Maris's face. Softly, without humor to detract from the sincerity, she whispered, "Thank you." She even leaned in for a brisk hug before setting Joy away from her. "Really. That means a lot."

"Thank *you*," Joy laughed. "I hope nothing comes of it, but I feel better knowing there's backup for Jack."

"Hey, we're part of a club now, right? I'm here for you."

Well, then… "I want to be here for you, too. If you ever need me to help, or to fill in for you, I'm a quick learner. You'd just need to tell me what to do."

Appearing bemused by the offer, Maris nodded. "I might take you up on that someday."

Joy grinned. Who knew being needed could feel so good?

On some level, she realized now why Maris was so happy about being her backup. They'd just forged a new bond in their friendship, something far more substantial than compliments and conversation, and it filled her with warmth.

Right now, though, she had other things to discuss. "My mother said that one of my grandmothers had passed and left something to me, so I need to make arrangements to sort that out."

"That's why she tracked you down today?"

"So she says, but to be honest, I don't trust her." Knowing her grandmother, the inheritance could be anything from family photos to substantial funds. Whatever it was, her mother probably knew all about it. "I don't think she'll return, but if you see her again, or my father or a lawyer—anyone other than our friends here in the park—"

Proving she understood, Maris said, "I won't let them anywhere near Jack. Daron or I will have eyes on him every second."

The added reassurance helped. "Thank you."

A clatter had both women swiveling toward the door. Jack stormed in, laughing silly, with Chaos hot on his heels. The dog still had bandages around one leg, but he already looked healthier, his pale yellow fur silkier now that it was free of burrs, his ribs no longer visible.

"I won," Jack said, dropping onto his butt on the floor, legs out, for Chaos to scramble over him. The pup frantically licked his face while Jack laughed some more and attempted to dodge him. In a quick turnabout, Chaos shifted and tried to chew on Jack's sneaker.

Jack found that hilarious, too. His carefree laughter proved contagious and soon Joy and Maris were chuckling, as well.

Royce and Daron came in right behind Jack. Even amid all the hilarity, they couldn't disguise their concern. It wasn't Joy's intent to ever make Royce worry over her.

She'd need to explain that to him, but she put that on hold as she pulled Jack aside and gave him a list of rules.

"I want you to listen to Maris and Daron."

He nodded, anxious to rejoin the dog.

"Stay right with them," she emphasized. Better than any single person, Joy understood how quickly a boy his age could run off. "And don't get too rowdy in the camp store, especially when customers come in."

"Okay, Mom."

"Remember to be polite."

Grinning, he said, "I *know*, Mom. Don't worry," with all the drama of a little boy who just wanted to play.

"Most of all," she added, pretending to be stern, "have fun."

When Jack threw his small, strong arms around her waist, she drew him closer, one hand in his fair, silky hair. She clutched him a little too tightly. A little too desperately.

Until that day the doctor had placed Jack in her arms, she hadn't known real love, couldn't even have comprehended the scope of an emotion so powerful and deep.

Leading up to his birth, she'd fretted over so many things, and she'd felt sorry for herself.

But the second she'd held her baby boy, her focus had narrowed to razor-sharp intent. She'd both wept and smiled, felt vulnerable and yet infused with iron determination. She'd stopped thinking of Vaughn, because she knew Jack was better off without him in his life. And she quit grieving the separation from her parents, determined instead that she'd pour all the love she had on Jack so that he'd never, ever feel unwanted or unworthy.

Motherhood, she'd learned, was a constant battle of emotions.

Today was no exception.

"I love you." Joy smoothed down his hair.

"Me, too," he said by rote, grinning up at her. "Daron's going to teach Chaos and me some dog tricks."

Daron clipped the leash onto Chaos's collar and lifted the squirming bundle into his arms. "We'll be right here, Joy. No reason to fret."

"I know." She did. Truly. Otherwise, she wouldn't go, but already Jack was excited and she…well, she knew they each deserved the fun planned for today.

Royce stood back, giving her all the time she needed. If it hadn't been for her mother's visit, she wouldn't feel so edgy about going. Trust, she reminded herself. She trusted these people completely.

Hoping she looked confident, Joy smiled at Royce. "Ready?"

CHAPTER SEVEN

THEY WERE ONLY in the car two minutes when Royce said, "You don't have to do this, you know."

Lost in thoughts of her mother, the attorney and the idea of an inheritance, Joy replied, "Hmm?" And then it occurred to her, and her eyes widened.

What if Royce had changed his mind about wanting her?

No, she told herself. That couldn't be it. He was here, so that said something. Yet she still sounded cautious as she asked, "What, exactly, don't I have to do?"

He shot her a look. "Pretend none of that happened."

"None of what?"

"Your mother, her attitude. The way you reacted to her." He lifted one shoulder. "All of it."

"Actually, I can." When he gave her another look, she

clarified. "I can pretend it didn't happen. You should do the same." After all, she'd gotten pretty darned good at pretending she didn't have a family, that they hadn't hurt her, that she was just fine and dandy on her own.

Actually, she *was* fine on her own, no pretending there.

Unfortunately, Royce didn't let it go. "You don't want to talk about it?"

She already had, with Maris.

Maris was a friend. She made a good confidante, was supportive without being sappy, funny without being dismissive. Most importantly, Maris hadn't stressed up front that there were boundaries—as Royce had.

To be considerate, though, she'd be careful about unloading on Maris too many times. She didn't want to be a buzzkill, not when she and Maris could have so much fun just visiting. And once she found out more about Maris's upbringing, she'd be better able to return the favors if, when, Maris needed anything.

So far, though, Maris was a rock of independence.

"Joy?" Royce prompted.

He missed the turn toward his house. In fact, they should have been there already. Surprised, she finally took note of their surroundings. The road he remained on would take them into town. "Where are we going?"

"Dinner. It's a quiet place, so we'll have some privacy."

Joy stared at him. That had to be a joke. For what *she* wanted, no restaurant could provide enough privacy. "I thought we'd go to your house?"

He slowly inhaled, as if bracing himself. "We can go there if that's what you want."

"Good."

A muscle ticked in his jaw and his hands flexed on the

steering wheel, gripping, releasing. Gripping again. Following a few seconds of silence, he stated, "After dinner."

Of all the… Here she was, giving herself a pep talk, all prepared to forge ahead, and he wanted to spend their time on food? Well, he wasn't the only one here, and what she wanted mattered, too. He wasn't the inconsiderate sort, so maybe he didn't know her preference.

Should she tell him? How exactly should she word that request? *I'd rather we go to your house, get naked and have sex until we're both exhausted.*

No, she couldn't say that. She'd never been overly outspoken and here, now, didn't feel like the right time to start.

But in her head, she could almost hear Maris telling her to speak up. Unfortunately, she wasn't Maris, not by a long shot. Maris wouldn't need someone prodding her to take a stand.

In honor of her new friendship, Joy decided the least she could do was give it a try.

"So… I'm not hungry." Oh great. That was miles away from bold. She quickly added, "I mean, are you actually hungry?"

Rather than answer, he said, "You can admit you're upset, honey. I'll understand."

Joy blinked at him. He would understand.

Okay, sure, that was nice of him. But nice wasn't what she wanted right now.

She wanted him. As a man.

Why had she assumed this would be easy? Actually, she knew why. She thought Royce would jump at the chance to get physical, that he'd somehow take charge of the situation and all she'd have to do was go along.

It wasn't working out that way, so apparently she had to steer things in the right direction. "I appreciate the concern.

I really do. But the situation with my mother isn't new and I'd rather not dwell on it."

He shot her an appraising look. "Are you sure?"

Frustration sharpened her tongue and she asked, "Should I remind you what this—" Joy gestured back and forth between them "—is about?"

He was silent a moment as he drove, and then he nodded. "Yeah. Why don't you?"

Huh. Joy hadn't expected that. "Well…" She screwed up her nerve, tamped down her modesty and stated, "Today, it's about sex."

"What?" He shot another look, this one almost comical because he looked so surprised. Oh, he kept driving, but he didn't blink; he even took a few seconds to inhale. "You said sex?"

Did he have to sound so unsure? "Us. Today. At least, that's what I'm hoping." Embarrassment put her tongue on the fast track, and she started rambling. "I realize things went off the rails a little bit today. I was surprised that my mother dropped in so unexpectedly." Mild definition of her reaction. "I'll have plenty of time to think about it later, I promise, but right now we have a limited opportunity. Who knows how many times Maris and Daron will work together to make this happen?"

"Wait." He lifted a hand. "You're saying…?"

"Sex." She repeated again, and it was easier this time. "Us. Today."

"Right. Believe me, I'm with you on that part. But did you say that Maris and Daron know that's what you have on the agenda?"

After Joy explained, Royce gave a short, gruff laugh. "It makes sense now, the way Daron offered to watch the dog, how insistent he was about it." Pulling up to a stop sign, Royce turned toward her. His gaze had warmed, and his mouth curled in the slightest smile. "So you made these arrangements, huh?"

Do not blush. Do not blush. "Yes." She'd even bought condoms, though she was hoping he had his own. She'd taken extra care with her appearance, too. "So what do you think? Could we skip food for now?" If they delayed, she had the awful feeling they'd miss the opportunity.

Royce glanced in the rearview mirror, drove forward and made a U-turn. "I'm thirty."

Unsure what that meant, but relieved that he'd turned around, Joy said, "We're the same age, then."

"I had a bitch of a year before coming here. Actually, more than a year, though the last year was the worst. It wore on me, to the point I feel fifty most of the time."

Again, she didn't know why he mentioned it, but she also felt older than thirty, mostly because she'd been in permanent mom-mode with her sexuality on ice. "I understand." She just hoped this wasn't his way of edging out of a sexual relationship.

"The thing is, around you, I feel like a horny high school kid."

A big grin of relief made her "Oh good" sound silly. She laughed, only a little embarrassed. "I mean, because I feel the same."

"Good to know."

Briefly, she wondered what had happened in his life to make the past so difficult. Because he'd been clear about those damned boundaries, she didn't ask.

Royce reached for her hand and held it on his thigh. "Don't ever think I'm disinterested, okay? If it ever seems that way, check me on it."

"Same here." Before meeting Royce, she might have

thought about sex every now and then, in an abstract, peripheral way featuring blurry, imaginary men.

With Royce, her thoughts were very specific, very direct and detailed. All about him.

"We both have a lot going on right now, and honestly, I'm out of practice. But for the immediate future, consider me an automatic *yes* anytime there's opportunity, okay?"

That "immediate future" qualifier didn't bother her in the least—because it went both ways. "Same from me."

"Yeah?" Grinning, he pulled into a deli. "How much time do we have?"

Joy didn't know what to think. "I told Maris I'd be back by eight."

"Perfect." He parked and removed his seat belt. "Give me two minutes to grab some ready-made sandwiches—for *later*." Leaning across the seat he took her mouth in a firm, warm kiss that held loads of sensual promise. "Be right back."

HOLDING THE BAG of food in one arm, Royce unlocked the front door, then stepped back for Joy to enter.

With her expression a mix of shyness and anticipation, she silently stepped over the threshold.

Joy might be thirty years old, but this was new for her.

Hell, it was new for him, too—because it was Joy, and he not only wanted her, he admired everything about her. It was a different combo for him.

Prior to his mom's illness, he'd enjoyed bachelorhood and the freedom from commitments. He'd set his own hours, leaving plenty of room for travel. His mother's illness had altered his life drastically and there'd been no room to cultivate relationships with women. Never had he even been tempted to try.

It had been easier and less complicated to just get through each day, to do what had to be done, focus on the necessary stuff and keep his mind free of anything else.

Now here was Joy, and she drew him in in ways no one else had—before or after his move. If ever a woman deserved patience and finesse, she did, but the urge to rush her straight to the bedroom punched a wild beat in his heart. He wanted to touch and taste her everywhere.

Hell, he'd been thinking about it since he met her.

She was here in his house with him now because she wanted him, too, enough that she'd taken the initiative and arranged it with her friends.

Knowing that created lust so powerful he had trouble breathing as he closed the door again behind them.

"I'm amazed at everything you've accomplished."

Flipping on a few lights, Royce asked, "How's that?"

"All the remodeling at the drive-in, getting to know the community, and you're even unpacked and organized here. When I moved in at the park with Jack, I lived out of boxes for a long time. I think he was a year old before I finally got everything set up the way I wanted."

"You were younger and had a baby to take care of." He couldn't imagine what that must have been like for her, especially after seeing her mother firsthand. "This place..." Royce glanced around at the very underwhelming interior of his home. "It's orderly, but it's not even close to what it'll be after I put in some work. I have ideas—a ton of them— but they'll have to happen later."

She stripped off her coat and put it with her purse on the sofa. "Jack and I have distracted you."

Royce gave a low laugh. "Jack's entertaining. But you?" He let his gaze skim over her. Joy had a way of making a plain skirt and sweater ultrafeminine yet still professional. He'd love to see her in jeans.

Naked would be even better. Soon. Very soon.

"You are most definitely distracting," he managed to say. "In all the best ways."

She smiled and smoothed her hands down her skirt. "Good."

Reminding himself that he couldn't rush her, Royce said, "I'll put this stuff away," and headed for the kitchen.

Joy followed, but paused in the wide doorway, still looking around at his house, specifically his bare walls. "Do you own any of your mother's art?"

He had everything his mother had completed after she became ill, as well as gifts she'd given him throughout the years. It added up to a sizable collection. "Some," he said noncommittally. For now he kept the art in storage, where it would stay until he could emotionally tackle it.

"You said she was…ill?" She wasn't sure how to categorize dementia.

Royce inhaled and held a breath. Right, they were both out of practice, but Joy couldn't seriously expect him to talk about his deceased mother right now?

Given her concerned gaze, she did.

Aware of her tracking his every movement, Royce took his time storing the food in the fridge. "The dementia came with a lot of complications," he said, in a way that didn't invite more questions.

"I'm sorry."

Nodding, Royce killed time by carefully arranging the sandwiches on the middle shelf, the colas on the bottom, the potato salad on top.

But to what end? Not like he'd start wanting Joy less. Not like they had all night.

"Did Chaos do this?"

Closing the fridge, he looked at the bottom of the kitchen door frame where deep gouges in the white paint exposed the wood. "Yeah, first time I tried to leave him behind." To keep his hands off her, Royce braced them behind him on the counter. "Poor dog went nuts. I think he felt abandoned all over again."

When he'd found Chaos loose in the house, two different shoes destroyed and a screen knocked out of a window, he'd been both exasperated and apologetic. The dog couldn't help his fear, and Royce hadn't meant to add to his anxiety.

For the next hour he'd played with Chaos in the yard, hoping his attention would reassure the dog, and that the play would help to wind him down. He'd also vowed not to leave Chaos behind again—not if he could help it.

Nodding at the scratched-up linoleum, Royce said, "He tried to dig his way out, I guess. Once I was here, he went crazy loving on me, then wouldn't leave my side."

"Poor baby," she said, full of sympathy.

To lighten the mood, Royce grinned and asked, "Me or the dog?"

Her smile matched his. "Both?"

He accepted that with a laugh. "Even while I showered, Chaos kept his nose stuck in past the curtain. At least when I can see him, he's not getting into trouble."

"I'm glad he has you." Moving closer, her gaze on his chest, Joy said, "Someone else might have given up on him already, especially when he does so much damage."

"It's not that bad. I think by the time I start remodeling here he'll be more secure." The house felt strangely quiet without Chaos racing around from one end to another, yapping at shadows and sliding across the hardwood floors, or sometimes just chasing his own tail. "It'd be great if Daron could teach him some commands before then."

Smiling, she turned those beautiful eyes up to him.

And there went the last of his restraint. She was close enough now that he couldn't keep his hands off her. Catching her shoulders, he drew her into his body. God, she was soft, and curved just right. With her height, she fit against him perfectly.

His voice rasped as he said, "I don't want to talk about the dog—" *or my mother* "—anymore."

Her palms settled against his chest. "Okay."

"Joy." He looked from her eyes, now heavy with need, to her slightly parted lips. "I'm about to implode here."

Nodding, she inhaled a deep breath. "Me, too."

"Good." Perfect, even. Sliding his hands down her back, he paused here and there to stroke, to absorb the shape of her—the dip of her waist, the rise of her hip. When his hands opened on her backside, she pressed her face into his neck.

Patience, he told himself again...but he was already too far gone. "If I start this here, we won't make it to the bedroom."

"Honestly, here works for me."

He choked on a laugh. His first time with her would *not* be up against a counter. "Let's be a little more conventional this first time, okay?" Stepping her back, he caught her hand and headed down the hall to his bedroom.

Unfortunately, he hadn't even come close to making his bed. Chaos had pulled one corner of the blanket off on the floor. Royce's pillow still wore the indent of his head, and the other pillow...well, it was pretty obvious Chaos had slept curled up on it.

Shit.

"The dog fur—" he started to explain.

"I don't care."

He turned to see her stripping off her long cardigan and stepping out of her shoes. She didn't wear nylons or tights, and her bare feet looked so cute that it stalled his brain for a second until it registered that she was undressing.

His cock thickened. Soon, very soon, he'd have this woman and he didn't quite know how he'd managed it. Beauty, brains, compassion—and she wanted him enough to make arrangements. Despite him being obtuse. Despite the obviously painful visit from her mother.

All together, that said a lot. Joy claimed she wanted this and nothing more. Well, then, he'd make *this* as good as he could.

That meant he had to lay some groundwork to ensure her pleasure. If she got her clothes off first, he was a goner.

"Slow," he murmured, hauling her close and taking her mouth in a deep, thorough kiss. Her lips immediately opened, an invitation to his tongue. No finesse, but she didn't seem to mind, not with the way she pushed closer, how she clutched at him and sucked on his tongue.

God, there was so much he wanted, *needed*, to do with her, but he felt her hands on the hem of his sweatshirt and knew he couldn't wait. "Let me." He moved back far enough to jerk it off over his head.

Joy inhaled, her gaze stroking every inch of his upper body. The way she whispered, *"Wow,"* so breathlessly made him even harder.

Wearing an expression of fascination, she reached out to touch him, molding her palm across the front of his shoulder, then trailing her fingertips down to his pec, over his left nipple, down to his waist—and the snap of his jeans.

She really was in a hurry, and much as he wanted to accommodate her, he knew she needed to catch up.

Lifting her hand away, Royce kissed her fingers. "Your turn." He finished easing her cardigan down her arms and tossed it toward a chair. With both hands, he brushed her long hair behind her shoulders—and then had to linger on it a moment. Thick, silky, golden brown, her hair had factored into his fantasies a lot lately.

None of those fantasies were as stirring as the reality of having her here, in his bedroom, hearing the quickness of her breath and seeing the thrust of her nipples through her shirt and bra.

He skimmed his hands down her narrow waist and hips, then up again. She held herself so still he thought conversation might help and asked, "Do you always wear skirts?"

She swallowed, nodded. "Usually."

Slowly, he pulled up the shirt, revealing first the smooth skin of her midriff, then the lacy edging on her bra, and finally the fullness of her breasts.

Right there, with the shirt held under her chin, the material bunched in his hands, Royce paused to soak up the sight of her. Until this moment, he hadn't realized that she'd be so lushly built. Her white bra was both sturdy and pretty, supporting breasts that would fill his large hands.

Joy didn't play up her figure in any way. Hell, she probably played it down in an effort to shore up that persona of a mother, only a mother.

Before he took her home, she'd have no doubts about being a woman.

"Royce," she whispered, her hands fluttering at her sides.

His gaze sought hers. The flush in her cheeks and the trembling of her lips showed equal parts embarrassment and urgency. "You're incredible."

She gave a slight shake of her head. "I'm just…me."

Pressing a gentle kiss to her lips, he said, "There's no 'just' to it." Slowly, he eased the shirt up and over her head, while reminding himself that she hadn't undressed in front of a man in a very long time. Much as he wanted to visually devour her, he'd have to save that for later.

As he tackled the side zipper of her long tan skirt, he kissed her, along the column of her neck, the sensitive spot where it joined her shoulder, up to her jaw and ear.

The skirt dropped to her feet. Before he could steal a look at her, she stepped out of it and against him, her hands on his chest again, her mouth on his.

Now when he held her bottom, only silky material separated his hands from her warm, pliable flesh. He didn't mean to rush. In fact, he was telling himself not to do that when he pressed one hand inside her panties, the other into her bra. She sure as hell wasn't complaining—and so he stopped thinking.

Just stopped.

Instead, he gave in to instinct, touching and tasting, licking and fondling. Like a man starved, and maybe he was, he greedily explored every inch of her available to him.

The softness of her combined with the scents of her hair, her sex, her excitement, made him hard enough to hurt.

He loved the way she lightly dragged the tips of her nails over his back with just enough pressure for him to feel it, to know she was turned on. He didn't think she was aware of it, that she did it deliberately to turn him on. No, she was wrapped up in her own innate response, soft, mewling moans escaping her. When he opened her bra to free both breasts and bent to draw one stiffened nipple into his mouth, she speared her fingers into his hair and held him close.

"Royce," she whispered on a shuddering breath.

Suddenly they were both busy, him stripping away her bra and panties, her attacking the zipper on his jeans.

Again, he took over. It was that or risk injury, a thought that pushed him even more. Joy wanted him, probably not as much as he wanted her, but close. It was there in the heat of her mouth on his skin, the broken way she breathed.

He kicked off his shoes and shucked his jeans and boxers in record time. For a single heartbeat they looked at each other, and what he saw in her gaze, the same sharp hunger he felt, had him reaching for her, then tumbling with her to the bed.

He kissed her hard, each of his hands filled with her breasts, his erection burning against her belly.

Protection. Belatedly, it sank into his head and he levered up to his forearms. Her eyes were heavy, her lips wet and her hair tumbled around his pillow. Damn, he didn't want to leave her, not even for a second, but... "I need to get a rubber."

She licked puffy lips, swollen from his kiss. "I brought some, but I forgot my purse in the other room."

God love her. "You bought rubbers," he repeated, a little awed that someone so sweet, so sexy, could also be so practical.

"Are you laughing at me?"

"No, I'm—" *Loving you.* Shit. He shook his head.

"What?" she whispered, her hand to his jaw.

True, he loved things *about* her, but it couldn't go any farther than that. He wouldn't let it.

"You impress me, that's all." Another kiss, because he couldn't resist her mouth. "Thank you, but I have it covered."

He left her long enough to snag the box from the closet.

He fished out a condom and tossed the rest of the box on Chaos's pillow.

"You bought them, too?"

He grinned, wondering if she'd gotten hers from the same small, family-run pharmacy. If so, he imagined a little speculation going around.

"As soon as I knew I wanted you. Seriously, I wasn't making assumptions, but neither would I ever take chances."

She tucked back her hair. "So that whole box...is for me?"

Deadpan, teasing, he said, "I don't think we'll use them all today."

She grinned. "Well, if we do, I also have a box, but I only brought three with me."

Three? She had more faith in his stamina than he did.

Joy watched him intently as he ripped the packet open with his teeth, then rolled it on.

The short interruption returned a modicum of control to him, so when he came back down beside her, he took the time to touch her again, to leisurely lick her nipples until she squirmed.

He trapped her legs with one of his own, and then drifted his fingers up the inside of her knee, along the warm velvet length of her thigh.

Just as he reached the slick softness between her legs, she arched her back, silently asking for more. Drawing in her nipple, he caught it with his teeth and lightly tugged... as he pressed the tip of his finger into her.

Wet. And so damned hot.

Tight, too, tight enough to make him ache.

He worked his finger deeper, loving the rough groan she gave, the impatient shifting of her hips. To make it easier on her, he slid his finger out, and worked two back in, stretching her a little, preparing her, all while reveling in the new rush of wetness.

"Now," she demanded, suddenly tangling her fingers in his hair and drawing his mouth up to hers. "Right now."

Not a problem. Royce kneed her slender thighs apart and settled into the cradle of her body. As her legs went around him, he positioned himself, and entered her with one firm, steady thrust.

Her head back, her eyes staring into his, Joy gasped... and the gasp turned into a vibrating moan of pleasure.

Thank God. Knowing he wouldn't last, Royce braced on one elbow and concentrated on her, on what she needed, how she reacted to what he did, if she liked it easier.

Or harder.

Her hair tangled around her and she strained against him, matching the roll of his hips, reaching desperately for a climax.

Scooping his free arm under her hips, he levered her up so he could go deeper, so that with each thrust and withdraw he slid against her clit—and it was enough.

Her teeth clenched and her eyes squeezed tight.

The climax came on her so quickly it stunned him. Her pleasure was raw and real, and so fucking hot he felt his own release gathering in unstoppable force.

She clenched around him, her hold on him tight.

And perfect.

Tucking his face into her throat, he struggled to hold back until he felt her begin to soften, the tension easing from her limbs.

And then he let himself go, one hand clasping her ass to keep the contact just *there*, driving hard and fast while looking at her, her bouncing breasts, yes, but also her face, her slight smile, those amazing green eyes and the complete satisfaction in her expression.

He put his head back and gave in with a guttural growl as he pumped into her. It had been so long since he'd felt this bone-melting pleasure.

Actually, he was pretty sure he'd never felt anything like this.

Great sex, yes. But…more. So much more.

Dodging the thought of that, Royce rested against her a moment, both of them spent, both struggling for breath.

"Wow," she whispered again, making him smile.

Smiling, he moved to his side. For a heartbeat they were separated and he didn't like it, so he slung an exhausted arm around her and dragged her close.

She snuggled in, draping one slim leg over his and resting a hand over his heartbeat. Long before him, she recovered and began toying with his chest hair. Normally that might have tickled, but at the moment he wasn't feeling much.

Except satisfaction.

Maybe a little confusion.

With a bit of alarm creeping in.

If he had any sense, if he was half as dedicated to his plans as he professed, he'd be running as fast as he could. Instead, he put a kiss to the top of her head and wondered where they went from here.

He had jackola to offer a woman like her. A struggling business under rehab? He had faith in the drive-in, but since he'd bought it just as the season was closing, he wouldn't be able to measure its success until the spring. His house was in desperate need of repairs. Eventually it'd be nice, but now? He ran a hand over his face, knowing it was underwhelming at best.

His bank account was strained from his mother's illness, and he'd recently taken in a troubled pooch who wouldn't let him out of his sight, and enjoyed eating shoes.

A man his age should have had more to recommend him.

Almost as if she'd read his thoughts, Joy opened her hand over his sweaty shoulder. "That was pretty amazing."

Right. Good sex. That was enough to build on, right? Did he *want* to build more? He wasn't yet sure.

Not yet opening his eyes, still trying to reground himself, he teased, "Braggart."

Laughing, she lightly swatted his chest…and went back to exploring him. "I meant you. Or maybe us." She nuzzled her nose to his throat. "Together."

His cock stirred. So did his heart.

He couldn't deny it, this wasn't just great sex.

It could be more…if he let it.

And if Joy wanted it.

He got one eye open. "Are you hinting that we should do this again?"

"Would you be up for it?"

The slow smile crept in on him. "Joy Lee, is that a double entendre?"

She quirked a supercilious brow. "Yes?"

This playful mood of hers could be his undoing. She made it too damn easy to be comfortable with her—before sex, during and after. If he said that to her, she might see it as an insult. She couldn't know that comfort had long been missing in his life.

Yes, she turned him on, more than any other woman he'd known, and if it was just the chemistry, he could get past that. Explore it, enjoy it and move on.

It'd be a hell of a lot harder to dismiss everything else she made him feel.

Taking her to her back, he said, "For your information, I'm half-up already, and—" leaning around her, he glanced at the clock "—we have plenty of time yet."

"Plus we have all those condoms." Grinning, she looped her arms around his neck. "So my vote is that we make the most of it. Who knows when we'll get a chance to be alone like this again?"

It was a strange thing to be turned on, wary and regretful all at once. Here he was thinking about the future, and she wasn't even sure they'd have a next time.

He wanted her. Again. Now and tomorrow, too.

But even if he managed to remember that he was supposed to get his act together, to reestablish who he was and what he wanted before committing to anyone else, after today *she* might not think it was worth the trouble to align their schedules.

Then what?

She didn't exactly sound ready to jump through hoops for him. *Who knows when we'll get a chance to be alone like this again?*

She could make it happen. *They* could make it happen— if it mattered enough. But did it?

God knew Joy had more than her fair share of responsibilities already, one of them a five-year-old boy who she would never shortchange.

So where did that leave him?

"Royce?" She turned somber, concerned, as she traced a fingertip over his chin. "Is something wrong?"

He didn't know how to answer that, so instead he kissed her, thoroughly and lazily, enjoying the way she curled into *him*, how she wanted *him*.

For now, that'd have to be enough.

"I need to get rid of the spent condom," he said against

her lips before sitting up. "And I heard your stomach growl. Think I can convince you to eat before you have your way with me again?"

Green eyes glimmering, she smiled. "Depends. Can we eat here in bed?"

With the dog hair? If she didn't mind, he didn't, either. "I'll be back in three. Stay naked."

Stretching out, she said, "I will if you do."

To Royce, to a man who'd mapped out his future with specific details, that sounded like one hell of a plan.

CHAPTER EIGHT

It surprised Daron how much fun he had. Sure, he always knew he liked kids and animals, but it was different enjoying them with Maris.

How had he overlooked her maternal streak?

The endless cookies, the quick effort to serve—not only her guests but her friends... Actually, anyone and everyone who came within her realm. Maris lived to make others comfortable.

Did anyone do the same for her?

He wouldn't exactly call her a homebody. Overall, he'd describe her as goal-oriented, a planner and sharp businessperson who understood how to continually advance her own personal agenda, whatever that might be.

Financial security, sure. But it was more than that. She'd

taken Summer's End from a place to get a few necessities or a cup of coffee, to the central hangout for everyone who worked at or visited the park.

It frustrated Daron that Maris's mantra was all about hard work.

Back to work.

Stuff to get done.

Things to do.

Work.

She always sang the same refrain.

Yet yesterday, during major lulls in business, she'd joined in during his not-so-successful attempts at showing the dog a few commands.

Chaos was aptly named because the frisky little pooch couldn't seem to focus on any one thing for more than a heartbeat. The puppy raced, full speed, from Jack to Daron, occasionally tripping over his own feet, playfully tugging at shoelaces, demanding attention, turning circles, chasing his tail, attacking a rogue leaf that dared blow past him, barking at the shoreline and so on.

The little dude seemed hell-bent on soaking up as much attention as he could, while he could get it. It'd take time, patience and consistency to train the dog, and it'd be easier after a long walk that wore him down a little.

But during his efforts to accomplish that, Daron had heard Maris laugh. Repeatedly. Like, *real* laughs. Robust and rich. Free-spirited.

Damn, it was sexy.

She was sexy.

Clever, too, because once Royce and Joy showed up, both of them pretty damn mellow and smiling, Maris closed up shop and left with them, thwarting Daron's plan to see her alone.

He'd wanted to get another kiss—actually, he wanted much more than a kiss, but he liked to keep his expectations reasonable.

Regardless of how she'd ended the night, he'd had a great time.

Chaos had, too. The dog had finally worn down a little right before Royce returned. Royce might not have known the fun they had, given the way the pup carried on when reunited. Clearly, Chaos loved Royce, and once he saw him, he remembered it, going berserk with happiness, his barks high-pitched, fast and frantic.

Until Royce cuddled the squirming little furball up close and spoke softly to him. Then finally Chaos had quieted down.

Maybe Chaos thought he'd been abandoned. Again.

He was a heartbreaker for sure.

Much like Maris.

One way or another, Daron knew he'd get the dog to trust him enough for basic training.

And as for Maris…well, if she just trusted enough to give him another kiss, he'd count it as a win.

For now.

POKING HER HEAD around the camp store door the next morning, Joy spotted Maris behind the counter, a cup of steaming coffee held in both hands close to her face. Eyes closed, she inhaled the steam.

"Knock, knock."

Cocking one eye open, Maris saw her and quickly took a big gulp. "Come in and tell me everything!"

Broom in hand, Joy moved the doorstop out to keep the door open. "I refuse to sit and gab when I know you have a routine. So I'm going to pitch in—" it was the only thing she could think of to show Maris how much she appreciated her "—and we can talk while we both stay busy."

Maris eyed her, eyed her coffee cup and asked, "Do I look like I'm busy?"

"I know you." Joy began sweeping away the fallen leaves from the stoop. "You might slow down long enough to inhale that coffee, but it'll be a short-lived pause. Once I get these leaves cleared up, I'll get them in the trash and then you can tell me what to do inside."

Maris laughed. "Got it all planned out, huh?"

Putting her nose in the air, Joy teased, "You're not the only hard worker."

"Fine. Knock yourself out. But at least give me the big scoop. How'd it go last night?"

Joy couldn't hold back the smile that felt like it came from the inside out. She'd never really had anyone to talk to about stuff like…well, anything, really. But definitely not sex.

Since she hadn't had sex in forever, that one was easy to skip. But even back when she had been sexually active, there'd been no one close enough to share with.

She wanted to dish now. She wanted to somehow explain everything Royce had made her feel, but was that done between grown women? She didn't know.

"Uh-oh," Maris said. "Are you hesitating because he let you down?"

"No! Definitely not." In fact, the opposite was true. Royce had exceeded her wildest expectations.

"My God, you're blushing!" Maris said. "Stop teasing and tell me, did you get lucky or not?"

Laughing, Joy gave up on her uncertainty. If there was a standard decorum on the issue, Maris clearly didn't follow it, or care about it. "Oh, indeed I did. Very, very lucky."

Grinning, Joy lowered her voice when she admitted, "Three times!"

Maris gave a long whistle. *"Three?"*

"Well, three for me, two for him."

Laughing, Maris hurried around the counter and grabbed her up for a big hug, even danced around with her in a circle, then she thrust her back the length of her arms. "He was good?"

"Oh, Maris." Leaning her weight on the broom, Joy sighed. "He was absolutely *perfect*. Honest to God, I didn't even know it could be that..."

"Orgasmic?"

"Yes." He'd pushed her over the edge *three* times. It didn't get much more orgasmic than that.

"Explosive?"

So explosive. Joy happily nodded.

"Made your toes tingle, huh?"

The giddy laugh erupted. "He made *everything* tingle."

Maris grinned with her. "And how about you? Did you rock his world?"

Ugh, a sobering thought. Joy covered her face with one hand. "Sad to say, I have no idea."

"Are you telling me he was a quiet comer?"

"What?" Quickly Joy peered around to make sure no one else was around to hear that. Her face went hot when she said, "I don't mean that at all. He, ah, he..."

"Got his?"

Joy hadn't laughed this much in forever. "Yes, he did. And he seemed really satisfied. But what do I know? I haven't been with anyone since I got pregnant with Jack."

Maris whistled again, this time with surprise.

Joy gave her a playful shove. "How about you? When was the last time you—?"

"You know those triple chocolate cookies I make?"

Unsure what that had to do with anything, Joy nodded. "What about them?"

"I call them 'chocolate orgasms,' because that's as close as I've gotten in forever."

Joy started snickering, and when Maris joined her, the humor escalated and they ended up roaring together like two loons.

Coop poked his head in the door, said, "Um…never mind," and started to leave again.

"Wait!" Wiping her eyes, Maris called him back. "What did you need? Coffee? Danish?"

He looked back and forth between them. "Did you spike the coffee?"

"Nope."

"Then I'll take two to go." Propping a shoulder in the doorway, he asked, "You have any cookies this morning?"

And Joy absolutely choked on her hilarity.

Doing some snickering of her own, Maris brought him the coffees in foam cups, along with a plastic bag of oatmeal cookies.

Coop took it all, but paused to smile at them. "Whatever's up with you two, I like it." His gaze strayed to Joy's face. "It's nice to see you laughing. Both of you." He lifted one coffee in a toast. "Thanks, hon."

"Anytime. Give Phoenix my love."

"Will do."

After he left, they both drew some deep breaths to regain control.

"Ah." Maris slid into a booth and beckoned for Joy to join her. "My face hurts now from laughing."

"Mine, too. And I've ruined my makeup."

Grabbing a napkin, Maris leaned over the booth and

carefully touched it to the corner of her right eye. "There. Good as new."

They looked at each other and grinned.

"I read *Cosmo*," Joy admitted. "You know, to see if I could bring myself up to speed."

"Yeah? How'd that work out for you?"

Joy wrinkled her nose. "I think I'm thirty going on fifty or something, because none of it sounded right to me. Nothing that would happen naturally, and I'm not up for forcing a situation just to make it erotic."

Maris agreed. "I read this magazine article once that talked about all the ways to drive your boyfriend insane with lust. It pissed me off." Wearing a frown, she said, "If I ever get around to having sex, he's the one who'll be working at it, not me."

"Last night," Joy said, "it was mutual."

"Mutual work, mutual payoff?"

"There was no work." Joy knew she could have been happy exploring Royce's body for an entire day. An entire week.

Maybe longer?

She shook her head, dismissing thoughts of the future and concentrating instead on what they'd experienced.

It fascinated her, the things that made Royce grit his teeth. The touch that caused a groan. How his eyes blazed dark fire when he watched her come.

"It was more than I'd ever expected." Leaning in, Joy confessed, "We laughed a lot. Isn't that nuts?"

"Depends on your timing, I guess."

"We joked around and ate cold sandwiches in bed, and then had sex again." Joy remembered something important, and grabbed Maris's hand. "Did you know he lets Chaos sleep with him? Isn't that the sweetest?"

Mouth twitching, Maris nodded. "He's a good guy, but now I'm glad Daron butted in and insisted on keeping the dog. Otherwise, I might not be getting this fascinating report right now."

Two more customers came in, and while Maris tended to them, Joy finished clearing the walkway. She really hadn't meant to sit down on the job.

She was just about done when the campers left.

Maris looked at her face, at the smile Joy couldn't suppress, and she shook her head. "So tell me this. Was he good enough to make you start thinking about more than just the horizontal mambo?"

Joy caught a golden leaf tipped in red that rolled in on the breeze and swept it back outside with a few insistent brushes of the broom. Phoenix, the park's groundskeeper and Coop's wife, had her hands full with all the leaves this time of year.

Leaning on the broom again, Joy decided to be honest. "You know, I could. It'd be so, so easy. But it's not my decision to make. Not alone, anyway. Royce was pretty up front about things. Whatever he had going on before he moved here, he's not looking to get tied down again."

"You're not a rope, Joy. He'd be lucky to have you."

Having such a loyal friend was a real ego boost, but when it came down to it, a single mother of a rambunctious little boy screamed commitment, and Royce didn't want that. "Thanks. I don't want to get ahead of myself, though. I'd rather just enjoy the moment."

"I know what you mean since I'm not looking for commitment, either." Maris put her nose in the air and said, "I'm married to this store."

Joy laughed at that sentiment. She couldn't seem to stop laughing, or thinking about Royce, or wanting him. Again.

But how would that work?

"So did you two make any new plans?" Maris asked.

Joy shook her head, and since she didn't see anything else to sweep, she headed into the kitchen. "No new plans."

"Well, why not?" Maris followed after her.

The kitchen was disgustingly pristine, not a single pan out of place, the sink scrubbed clean. "Yesterday, Royce wanted to take me to dinner."

"So?"

"He didn't realize that I preferred to go to his house, get him naked and have my way with him."

Maris grinned. "Had to explain it to him, huh?"

"I brazenly laid out my intentions once. Shouldn't I give him a chance to do the same? I mean, if he wants to see me again?"

"He'll want to see you again."

Joy wished she could be as confident about that as Maris seemed to be. "Until he says so, we can't know that for sure." Though they had joked about all the condoms and how they shouldn't go to waste, so she was hopeful. "Now give me something to do."

Giving in with a toss of her hands, Maris opened a few cabinets, found cleaning supplies and led the way back to the seating area. "The napkin holders need to be polished."

Joy jumped on it. This, at least, was something she could do for Maris.

They collected all the metal holders and sat at a booth together again. Maris poured her a coffee, and refilled her own.

A few minutes into it, Joy said, "This morning I made arrangements to meet the attorney. My appointment is on the Monday after Halloween here at the park." They celebrated separately from the night of the community, using the entire weekend for decorations and parties, and letting the kids "trick or treat" on Saturday evening.

"So not this week, but next?"

Joy nodded, feeling pretty damn anxious about it. "It's going to be awful."

Worried, Maris set aside her cloth. "Why don't I go with you?"

This time, Joy's smile was of appreciation. Under no circumstances would she subject a friend to her family's scrutiny. She adored Maris for her casual vibe, her workaholic manner and indifference to impressions, yet those things would make Maris a prime target for Joy's mother.

"Thank you, really, but it's something I should do alone."

Maris snorted, but kept her gaze on the polishing cloth. "I met your mother, remember? You should *not* face her again by yourself." She seemed to give that another thought and added, "No offense."

"None taken."

Glancing up, Maris said, "If you won't let me be your wingman—or wingsister or whatever—maybe you should take Royce."

Wingsister. Now, didn't that sound amazing? She'd never had a sibling to share the good times and the bad. If someone had offered her a choice, she'd have happily taken Maris as her sister.

But the suggestion of Royce around her family... Good God, no. Joy couldn't imagine anything that'd scare Royce off quicker than being invited into her mother's drama. "I'll be fine, I promise. I'll drive straight there after I drop Jack off to school, and I should be home before he finishes for the day." She dusted off her hands. "Done."

She could tell that Maris didn't buy her nonchalance, but being a true friend, she didn't pressure her.

"It's so quiet here this time of year." Maris peered out the window. "I love the bustle of the summer, the work that keeps me jumping."

Joy nodded. "Then we roll into fall and it gets so chilly." Through the window she saw little foamy caps on the lake, stirred by a brisk breeze. The waves repeatedly lapped at the shoreline, leaving a darker line in the sand. The blue sky was easily visible through now-barren trees. All together, Joy thought it was beautiful.

"And quiet." Propping her chin on a fist, Maris sighed.

"Not a fan of the quiet?" Joy guessed.

"You have to feel it, too. The big…lulls. Too much time to think."

"Keeping busy is better," Joy agreed. Another idea hit her. "Will you shop with me? I mean, for clothes and stuff. Girl shopping. We could have lunch and each buy a cute new top."

"That might be fun." Gesturing at her own body, Maris asked, "But do you ever see me wearing *cute*?"

No, she didn't. "You could totally pull it off."

"No, *you* pull it off." Maris grinned. "But hey, I could use a new coat and maybe some boots, so let's do this."

"Today?" Joy asked.

"How about tomorrow instead. *But*," she said with emphasis, "if anything comes up with Royce, he gets priority, and I want your word that you won't hesitate to let me know if you want me to watch the squirt again."

Joy thought of the times she'd had to take Jack out when he was sick because he needed medicine, and she had no one to watch over him. All the times she'd gone without sleep so she could get things done around Jack's schedule, and the times she'd been running late for work because Jack had skinned his knee and needed coddling.

She wouldn't overly impose on Maris, but the idea that she could rely on someone else almost overwhelmed her.

It felt good, not being alone. So damn good.

"Hey," Maris said. "Don't go getting weepy on me. Jack isn't any trouble, I've told you that, and it's not like I have anything else going on."

Words weren't sufficient, but for now, they were all Joy had. "Thank you."

"It's my pleasure."

"But speaking of your lack of a social life…"

Maris groaned.

Ignoring those theatrics, Joy asked, "How'd it go with you and Daron?"

"Nothing *goes* with us."

"You keep doing that," Joy accused.

"Doing what?"

"Putting emphasis on different words." Usually in a way to play down the truth. Maris thought she wasn't *cute*, when in fact she was extremely pretty—and yes, with her ponytail and smile, very cute. She thought there was nothing between her and Daron, when anyone with eyes could see the truth.

They were totally into each other.

"I only do that when it's *necessary*," Maris said with a cheeky grin, letting Joy know she'd done it again on purpose.

"Know what?" Joy sat back and folded her arms. She'd gladly accepted advice from Maris, but it was time for her to share some of her own. "I think you're trying to convince yourself that you don't like Daron, and it's a lost cause because you and Daron—"

"Joy—"

"Set off sparks. I think you know it, and what's more, I think you *like* it."

"Joy," Maris said again, this time a little more urgently.

"I think you like him. A lot." Judging by the look on Maris's face, Joy knew she'd hit the nail on the head. "Admit it."

Instead, Maris said, "Now who's doing all the emphasizing?"

"You want him. And you know what? I think you should give it a shot."

"Hell, yeah," Daron said from right behind her, making her jump. "I second that."

Glancing back, Joy saw that Daron had his arms folded on the back of the booth, meaning he'd been there long enough to get comfortable.

Feeling her face heat, Joy asked, "What is it with all the eavesdropping going on around here?"

"Not my fault if you two get so busy talking you don't notice anything, even the sound of the tractor pulling up out front."

"The tractor?" Joy asked.

"Yeah, weather is supposed to turn nasty so Phoenix and I are putting in double time to get the leaves up first." He turned puppy-dog eyes on Maris. "I was hoping for a few cookies to sustain me for a long morning of work."

Given the way Daron grinned, and how Maris glared at him, Joy decided she'd done enough for one day. She mouthed a silent, *Sorry*, to Maris, then said, "See if she has any chocolate—"

"Joy!" Maris's face went red.

Brows up, Daron studied each of them in turn. "Chocolate...what?"

"Maris will explain—or not," Joy said with a wink before sidling out the door.

From outside, she heard Daron say in a low, sexy voice, "I'm intrigued, Maris."

Whatever Maris replied was lost on Joy, but still she started grinning again, and by the time she reached the lodge, she was laughing. Her life had taken many twists and turns, not always for the better.

This, though, having friends, laughing over coffee, teasing the resident stud, was definitely an improvement over isolating herself. Especially since, for the time being at least, she had a stud of her own.

She hoped Royce would call.

And if he didn't? Well, she just might chase him down again.

MARIS WASN'T SURE what to say to Daron with him giving her that particular look, a look that said too many things, showed too many things—like interest and humor and... hope?

Was it possible he really wanted her? Or, as one of the few women to turn him down, was she just a challenge? It didn't feel that way. It felt...genuine. And scary.

God, she was a coward. But what did she know of relationships with men? Especially a man like Daron, a guy who could have his selection of women.

And yet, he seemed to want her.

He watched her with complete attention, his gaze fixed on hers. "You skipped out on me last night."

Yup, she had—but she wouldn't admit it. "How could I skip out on you, when I wasn't with you in the first place?" She headed around him for the kitchen. Putting a half wall and a counter between them made sense to her self-preservation. "I have brownies, oatmeal cookies, cranberry scones or shortbread."

"One of each would be great."

Jumping, Maris turned—and there he was, right behind her, standing too close and looking far too tempting. What was it about his disheveled appearance that turned heads, including her own? He hadn't shaved today and the light brown scruff made her fingertips twitch with the urge to feel his jaw. Brisk wind had tossed around his always-unruly hair. His sweatshirt looked older than him, fitting over his broad shoulders and then dropping loosely around his torso.

And yet, all together, it equaled some seriously hot appeal.

"I like when you look at me like that," he murmured.

A rude sound escaped before she could stop it. "You like when any woman looks at you."

"Well…" He rubbed the back of his neck as if the truth made him uneasy. "Yeah, sure. I mean, being noticed is nice. But no one else is you."

Barely resisting an eye roll, Maris made to step around him.

He stepped, too, blocking her, and when she glared he immediately held up his hands. "I get it," he said. "Tell me to get lost and quit trying, and I'll respect that, I swear." In a rush, as if he feared she might take him up on it, he added, "But there's something between us. You know it. That kiss the other day proved it."

"Pfft. That kiss was an experiment," Maris lied.

He looked insulted, and maybe a little hurt. "The results were so bad you don't want to try it again?"

Damn it, now she felt guilty for giving him that impression. "That's not what I said."

"No, you didn't. You said to let the anticipation build, and I have. I'm about to combust with anticipation."

Damn it, so was she, but she had to stick to her guns. Didn't she?

Determined, Maris stared up at him. "I also said I had rules." So many rules. It was past time she remembered them.

Daron nodded. "Right, rules that we'd discuss—but then you dodged out instead." He held out his arms, which raised the hem of his baggy sweatshirt, giving her a peek at his low-hanging jeans, and a downy line of hair leading from his navel into the top waistband of colorful boxers.

Her mouth went a little dry.

Daron Hardy was young, sexy, playful, fit…and he wanted her. Wouldn't she be nuts to pass that up?

With emphasis, he stated, "So here I am. More than anxious to know what I'm up against. Should I take notes? I have a good memory if we're talking a list of one to ten, but if it's, like, one hundred rules long or anything—"

She smashed her fingers to his mouth, and damn it, that was the exact move that led her to kissing him last time. In contrast to his firm bod and sharp wit, his lips were soft.

The contact sizzled, jolting through her fingertips, her arm and straight to her core. A *starving* core. She had it bad.

So maybe she should just give in.

He probably read the indecision in her eyes because he caught her wrist and carried her hand to his chest. "Come to my place. I'll cook dinner."

It was an old habit, using sarcasm as a defense mechanism. First she said, "By cook, do you mean you'll order a pizza?" and as if that weren't bad enough, she tacked on, "Could be like a step back in time, right? I bet your apartment is decorated with band posters and black lights. Will I find another woman's underwear beneath the bed?"

His hold on her wrist loosened, then fell away. He even took a step back, his expression masked. "Actually, I'd thought about making fried chicken. And my *house* might not be up to your standards, but I left posters behind in college."

Her jaw loosened. "You have a house?" That absolutely was not envy squeezing her heart, but…she'd longed for a house forever. Then the rest of what he'd said hit. "I didn't know you went to college."

His mouth firmed and his chin jutted. "Yeah, some colleges let anyone in as long as they pay tuition."

God, she'd been insulting. Protecting herself at his expense…well, that made her a not-very-nice person. "I didn't mean it that way. I just didn't realize—"

"I have an associate degree in business," Daron explained, his brows still pulled tight. "Nothing too fancy, but it's useful now and then."

"But…you've been working here for so long—"

He shrugged. "I was in college when Coop hired me. This is a full-time job, so it put me behind a little, but I eventually finished up."

Maris remembered telling him that he didn't know her, and that was true, but did she know him any better? Curious, she offered him a cookie, took one for herself, then leaned on the counter. "Business, huh?"

He smirked. "Yeah, not like I'll use a degree here, right?"

"I didn't mean that. A business degree would probably come in handy lots of places." Heck, she wished she had one, but education hadn't been high on her list. Independence had been her basic goal.

"I could put it to use somewhere else. That was actually

the original plan. But I like it here. Actually, I *love* it here. The park suits me."

Yes, it did. Would Cooper's Charm even seem the same without Daron?

No, it would not.

Enjoying this new insight into him as a man, Maris said, "And you have a house?"

"It's small. Three bedrooms, one and a half baths, quarter-acre lot."

He called that small? To her, it was an unattainable dream.

"I figured it was an investment, right?" he continued. "Rent doesn't earn equity, but property does."

She nibbled at the edge of her cookie, feeling pretty low, before admitting, "I'd love to get a house. Right now I'm dumping everything into savings. Well, that and making improvements to this place. Eventually, I hope to buy my own home. It's just not in the cards yet." There were days, sometimes weeks, when it felt like it'd never happen.

Daron reached past her—bringing the heat of his nearness and the scent of the fresh outdoors—right past her nose as he pilfered another cookie. "You run a good business."

The *but* hung loud in the air. She felt defensive, but said, "I'm open to advice."

"No," he stated firmly, "you aren't. Not ever. Especially not from me."

True enough. Before this minute, she might have bit his face off if he'd offered an opinion, because she would have taken it as criticism.

The truth didn't set well with her, but she faced it all the same.

She'd been terrible.

It would be best to start over, and that could more easily begin with another kiss. When he started to take another bite of his cookie, she stopped him, blocking his hand, then stepped into his space, close enough that her body pressed all along his.

His mellow brown eyes widened and he went very still. "Maris?"

An actual apology stuck in her throat, but she managed to ask, "Is the dinner offer still open? Maybe tomorrow night around seven?"

With his gaze on her mouth, he nodded, followed with a fast, "Yes."

Bless the man, he was far more forgiving and flexible than she'd ever been. "Perfect. Rule number one, my work comes first." When he started to speak, she touched his chest. "Rule number two, never underestimate me—and going forward, I'll give you the same respect, I promise."

His arms looped around the small of her back. "Rule number three, always be yourself, because I like you, Maris. A lot."

She was starting to believe that he did. "These are my rules," she reminded him with a smile.

"Well, that one should be included." Without waiting, he turned his head and fit his mouth to hers in a cookie-sweet kiss that left her crowded against him, and a little carried away.

As she caught her breath, she said, "Rule number four, no sex on a first date."

His slow grin did crazy things to her insides. "I think you just made that up because you're tempted."

"Daron—" she tried to object...even if he was right.

"Hey, as long as there's a second date, I can live with number four."

Well, damn. He could live with it.

But could she?

CHAPTER NINE

Joy shivered as she cut construction paper into shapes inside the lodge. Glancing toward the window, she saw the flurries coming down, just as Daron had predicted. Ohio weather was nothing if not unpredictable. Too many times, over too many years, snow fouled up Halloween, then went away again.

She hoped this wouldn't be one of those years.

Not long after she'd picked Jack up from school the day had turned gray and gloomy. She wondered if Phoenix and Daron had finished their work.

Just then the lodge door opened and before she'd even finished turning, Chaos bolted in. Jack looked up from his task and squealed. Together, he and Chaos made a fair ruckus, reuniting like friends long separated.

Royce stomped his feet a few times, then stepped in and shut the door. His cheeks were ruddy from the cold, his dark hair mussed, and he wore a coat rather than a jacket.

He looked good enough to eat.

While Jack and Chaos greeted each other, Joy went to him. "I didn't expect you."

"Hope you don't mind us dropping in. I returned a tool to Daron and since I was here—"

"Of course I don't mind." She reached up to smooth his hair into place. "Coffee?"

He shook his head. "I just had hot chocolate at the camp store. I wanted to see if you two were free for dinner."

Her heart jumped but she tried to suppress any outward reaction. No, it wasn't alone time with him, but it was terribly sweet of him to include Jack again.

She thought of the chops she had marinating, but they'd keep. Turning to Jack, she asked, "Would you like to go to dinner with Mr. Nakirk?"

Jack cheered, and that got Chaos running in circles.

Grinning, Royce said, "Obviously, it'll be at my house since I can't leave Chaos alone. I'd planned on steaks off the grill, but it might be too cold for you."

Steaks sounded amazing. "I'll bundle up," she promised.

He stuffed his hands in his pockets, and said low, "Do you know how hard it is not to touch you?"

Warmth spread through her. "Oh, I have a guess, since I so badly want you to."

"When can we get together again?"

Thrilled that he'd sought her out to ask, she said, "It depends on how together you want to be." Before Royce could take that the wrong way, she explained, "I can eke out an hour or two most afternoons, while Jack is in school, especially now with things so slow. Any more marathons, though, I'd need to arrange for Maris to watch him again."

His mouth quirked. "It was a marathon, wasn't it? Should have tided me over for a day or two, but I swear the minute I got home, I wanted you again." With a warm smile, he murmured, "Your scent was on my sheets, but then, so was a lot of dog hair, so I had to wash them."

Joy laughed. "I think it's sweet that you let Chaos sleep with you."

"I didn't really have a choice. That first night, he damn near slept on my head. I didn't have the heart to put him out of the bed."

He'd probably cuddled the dog, she thought, knowing how good he was to Chaos. "I'm glad."

At the sound of laughter, they both looked over to see Jack darting around a table, Chaos hot on his heels.

"Good news, though. Daron suggested that I get him a doghouse, with his own cushy bed in it. It's an indoor thing that almost looks like furniture. I put it in the corner of the bedroom and added a few of his favorite toys. He seems to like it. Last night he started out with me, but middle of the night he went to his own bed."

While Jack was occupied, Joy stepped up against Royce. "So we might not need a dog sitter next time?"

"Next time," he whispered. "I like the sound of that." He, too, glanced at Jack, then stole a quick kiss. "Chaos isn't there yet, so yeah, I might still ask Daron to lend a hand. He agreed to help train Chaos, but he'll still know why I'm asking."

Joy gave that quick thought, and decided it didn't matter. Not to her, anyway. "Will it bother you for others to know?"

"Not if you're okay with it."

Always so considerate. "Thank you."

"I just remembered. The school called and they want to do a field trip to the drive-in sometime after the season ends."

"I suggested it, but I didn't know they'd made a decision." Her brain started to buzz with ideas. "I'll volunteer as a chaperone, and maybe we could do some activity for the kids while they're there. A short animated movie inside so they could see how it works."

Royce nodded. "I like it. I figured I'd give each kid a little bag of popcorn, but I don't know about drinks."

"We'll take care of it. The school and I, I mean. Let me think on it and I'll get some ideas together."

Jack skidded up next to them, and Chaos tumbled right over Joy's feet. Laughing, she bent down to stroke the dog's downy ears, and then gave her attention to Jack.

"Can me and Chaos go outside?"

The correction for his grammar was on the tip of her tongue when a memory from the past hit her. She hadn't been much older than Jack when she asked about going to the school's haunted house. Suddenly she could see her mother's face, the disapproval pinching her features. Yes, she'd gone to the school function, and the next day she had a speech tutor.

"Mom?" Jack asked, a little more uncertain.

Royce was looking at her, too, so she smiled. Actually, she had so much to smile about it was easy to do.

"I need to clean up this mess—"

"I'll help," Royce offered.

"Awww," Jack complained, clearly disappointed by a delay. "Chaos has to go."

They all turned to see the dog actively sniffing the floor. Royce quickly scooped him up. "How about I take these hoodlums outside, and you can join us as soon as you're done?"

Jack cheered, taking her agreement for granted, and ran off to grab his coat.

"Hat, too," she called to her son, pleased to see his excitement, and then to Royce, she said, "I'll only be five minutes."

"If you're done here, we could go to my place straightaway."

She looked around at her half-finished project, but there wasn't anything critical that had to be done. Actually, it felt nice to concentrate on something besides work, to have a reason to put it aside.

The dog did more squirming, so she said, "That sounds perfect. I'll finish up here, grab a warmer coat upstairs and be out before either of you can get too cold."

Two HOURS LATER, as Royce put the last few dishes in the dishwasher, Joy stood nearby drinking hot chocolate. Her nose and cheeks were no longer pink from the cold, but either way, she looked beautiful to him.

The snow had fallen steadily, accumulating two or three inches, but Joy and Jack had both stuck with him in the yard, bundled up in hats and scarves, boots and mittens, while he'd grilled steaks and potatoes.

As the weather conditions had worsened, he'd tried to talk her into going inside, especially when she started shivering. Instead, she'd scooted closer to him, soaking up the warmth of the grill. In between turning steaks, Royce had hugged her—and Jack didn't even seem to notice.

As if impervious to the cold, he and Chaos had raced the perimeter of the fenced yard, slipping and sliding in the snow.

Everything about that had felt intrinsically *right*: small talk with Joy, her nearness, the sounds of Jack's happiness and Chaos's excitement.

For once, his run-down little house had felt like a home. A happy home.

Had he been craving that without even knowing it?

Of course they'd eaten inside, and though she'd worn knee-high boots outside, Joy had them off now so that he could see her thick socks. She'd also removed Jack's snow-caked boots, and even dusted off Chaos's paws.

Going by what Daron suggested, Royce fed Chaos a cup of doggy chow while they ate at his small table.

Apparently the dog and Jack had worn each other out, because once they'd both finished, they crashed in the living room to watch a TV-edited version of *Toy Story*. Side by side on the floor, Jack, with his elbows bent, braced his head on his hands, and Chaos rolled to his back against Jack's side, occasionally snuffling against him.

"They'll both be out shortly," Joy predicted.

"Jack, maybe." Royce had his doubts about the dog. "Daron thinks Chaos needs more exercise to burn off energy."

Smiling, Joy said, "Why do you think I take Jack to the playground almost every day?"

Ha. So it worked for kids and animals alike, huh? "I'll try some walks in the morning and evening." Royce looked out the window. "That is, when the weather cooperates."

Joy bit her bottom lip, glanced in at Jack and then set her empty mug in the sink and pulled him to the side.

He saw it in her eyes, what she wanted, what she would do, and damned if he didn't react to it. As her hands slid up his chest to his shoulders, he clasped her waist and drew her body flush to his. He bent down as she tilted her face up, and they met in the middle with a kiss that started slow and easy and advanced from there. Twice they stopped, only to come right back for more. He threaded his fingers into her hair close to her scalp and fit their mouths together for a deeper, hotter taste.

His forehead to hers, Royce said, "Soon, Joy. I don't think I can last much longer."

She gazed at his mouth and nodded. "I'm sorry. I shouldn't have let that get out of hand."

He tipped her face up again. "That's not on you, babe. Not even close."

"I started things."

And she'd quickly melted against him, so Royce quirked a smile. "Okay, so it's partly your fault. If you weren't so damned sexy—"

She gave a strangled laugh.

"And so irresistible, I might be able to keep it together."

"I could say the same for you." She touched his mouth with her fingertips and sighed. "I think about you, about being with you again, far too often."

"Good to know." He smiled.

"I had no idea a fling would be so difficult to maneuver."

A fling. Well, hell, that was a sobering thought. She stared up at him with those incredible green-gold eyes full of sincerity, and called this, their time together, a fling.

It's what he'd told her he wanted. Just because he'd *maybe* changed his mind didn't mean she felt any differently.

He needed to get his thoughts in order. One thing at a time, he decided, and the first thing was a softer, gentler kiss. "I don't mean to complicate your life."

The smile came quickly, followed by a quiet laugh. "Hot

sex, a night out, a friend—trust me, those are not complications."

Still relegated as a friend? Shit. He tried not to let that bother him. "No?"

"I'd call them improvements."

For him, definitely. "Let's see what we can do about repeat performances, okay?"

"We'll make it happen," she promised. "If you find yourself with time while Jack is in school, let me know. If I have ten minutes' notice, I can be ready."

He didn't know if he could find someone—or at least someone he knew well enough to trust—to watch Chaos during the day, but he'd give it a try. Daron's time with the dog would be more toward evening, so it wouldn't interrupt his own work at the park.

Just then Jack appeared in the kitchen doorway, Chaos at his side. The boy looked first at his mom, then at Royce, who slowly stepped away so he wouldn't appear too guilty.

Curiosity had Jack's brows twitching, but all he said was, "Your phone's buzzing, Mom."

"Oh, thank you, sweetie." She brushed a hand over Jack's hair as she hurried past him, heading to the couch where she'd left her purse.

Jack stood there still studying Royce. He rubbed his nose, his mouth shifted to the side and he stared some more.

The kid was smart, no two ways around that.

"Blast," Joy said, poking her head back into the kitchen. "It was a call from Maris and I missed it. Do you mind if I take a minute to call her back?"

"No problem." Royce gestured at the table. "Jack and I will grab some dessert."

"Thanks." Joy disappeared back into the living room.

Coming forward and climbing into a chair, Jack said, "You were hugging my mom."

Yup, not much got past the kid. "Hugged her outside, too, because it was cold." Royce poured a cup of milk and got a packaged cookie from the cabinet, setting both in front of Jack.

"It's not cold in here."

Unsure what else to say, Royce shrugged. "Guess not."

"I think you just like hugging her."

Very true. Royce enjoyed talking with her, touching her, hugging her—and so much more. "You like hugging her, too, right?"

Jack said, "Yeah, but she's my mom," like maybe Royce had forgotten.

He tried a different approach. "Do you mind that I hugged her?"

"No." Then, being a sly little boy, he asked, "Does that mean I can come here and play with Chaos again?"

Oh, the workings of a five-year-old mind. Royce laughed. "Sure, if your mom's okay with it."

That seemed to solve everything, at least for Jack.

For Royce, it wasn't quite that easy.

JOY COULD HEAR the low hum of voices in the kitchen as she returned Maris's call. What did Jack think, seeing them together?

She didn't have long to ponder it because Maris answered on the first ring.

"Hey, it's Joy. Sorry I didn't get to the phone in time."

"I need your help tomorrow," Maris blurted.

"Okay." Maris didn't sound upset, like there was a problem, but something in her voice made Joy go on alert. "Whatever you need."

"I'm going to Daron's house, for dinner. And...well, it's dumb, but I want to look pretty."

"Oh my gosh!" A hundred questions buzzed through Joy's brain, but she said only, "You're *always* pretty."

"Prettier, then. Like...hair, makeup. A cute shirt?" Maris groaned. "We won't have time to shop and I don't own anything! Not even mascara. How pathetic is that?"

"It's not pathetic at all, but don't worry, I have it covered." Catching on to the excitement, Joy paced the living room. "I have everything we need, and I can stop at the store tomorrow after I drop Jack off at school."

"I don't want to put you to any trouble."

"Are you kidding? I'm already excited!" This was something Joy could do for Maris, and she could barely wait.

"I can't look like you, hon. I mean, no skirts or—"

"You look terrific in denim! I wouldn't think of changing anything like that." She could imagine a pretty shirt and softer hairstyle. "You don't need to go heavy on the makeup, either." Joy knew that sometimes a little makeup just made a woman feel good about herself and boosted her confidence. "We'll enhance things a bit. Do you have scissors?"

"Um...scissors?"

"We'll trim an inch off your hair. Only an inch, I promise." Joy didn't know if Maris had ever cut her hair, but a trim to tidy up the ends always worked wonders. "And I have a fabulous conditioner that you're going to love."

"Oh wow." Maris sounded a little dumbfounded. "Am I really doing this?"

"Having a date with Daron? About time, if you ask me."

"I told him no sex."

Joy huffed a laugh. "What? *Why?* You insisted it was good for me, but now you—"

"He's six years younger than me."

"Big deal. You're both young and healthy and that's what counts."

With a long sigh, Maris said, "I don't feel young."

"Well, you are, because you're only a year older than me and I'm young." No way could Maris argue with that logic.

"He has a *house*, Joy. Did you know that?"

Of course she did, but Maris sounded so surprised Joy asked with caution, "Didn't you?"

"No! He comes off all… I don't know. Irresponsible."

"Daron? Daron Hardy?" Joy repeated with disbelief. "We're talking about the same guy, right?" Yes, Daron liked to joke and God knew he had his fair share of female admirers, but Joy could never fault him on his sense of responsibility. "The same man who pitches in to help anyone who needs it, who keeps everything in the park working, who stays late or comes in early when something goes wrong? The same Daron who always answers his phone, smiles at everyone while working his behind off, who—"

"Ugh, enough already." Maris sucked in an audible breath. "You know what I'm talking about. He makes everything a joke."

Gently, Joy said, "It's called being happy."

Two pulse beats of time passed, then Maris muttered, "Shit."

"It's true," Joy offered, "that he teases you more than anyone else. Always has. We all realize it's because he has a thing for you, and you…well, you seem to like everyone except him."

Sounding hurt and defensive, Maris whispered, "I like him."

"But you're afraid of liking him too much?"

"I already said *shit*, right?" She groaned loudly, then said it again, a little louder. "Shit."

Joy grinned. "It'll be fine. You two will talk over dinner and work out any misunderstandings. I'll get to the camp store early tomorrow so we can make plans."

"Maybe I could have him pick me up at your place? That way you could help me spiff up and I won't have a chance to ruin it?"

"Love that idea. Consider it a date!" Smiling, she disconnected—and found Royce standing there, Chaos sitting on his foot, Jack leaning against his thigh. The three of them watched her.

Royce asked mildly, "Date?"

Though he tried to seem relaxed, resting one hand on Jack's shoulder, wariness had crept into his expression.

Silly man.

Joy could barely work out a time to see him, so he shouldn't think she'd have time—and definitely not interest—to see anyone else.

"With Maris," she specified. "For some girl stuff." Even saying it made Joy want to laugh in giddy excitement. Maris might expect big changes, but they weren't necessary. With her dark blond hair and naturally dark lashes and brows, any more than the barest makeup would be too much. Joy knew exactly what she wanted to do, the top she wanted to loan Maris and the advice she'd give before she left.

For now, though, Royce continued to watch her, so she tucked away her phone and picked up Jack's coat. Leaning toward him, speaking in a stage whisper, she stated, "Maris is going to Daron's for dinner."

The surprise she expected never came. Instead, Royce tipped back his head and groaned. "Guess that means tomorrow is out for us." When he looked at her again, he wore a lopsided grin. "Good for Daron, though."

Smiling, Joy handed Jack's coat to him and sat down on the couch to pull on her boots. "Remember, call anytime."

Jack, not understanding the significance of that, said, "Yeah, call us. We can come over to dinner again." He held Chaos's face. "You'd like that, wouldn't you, boy?"

Chaos gave an enthusiastic *yes*.

"Well, now," Royce said. "Your mom will have to let me know your favorite foods."

Jack's face lit up. "I'll eat anything!"

With a roll of her eyes, Joy said, "If only he felt that way at home."

Turning on her, Jack said, "But you cook fish."

She grabbed for him, but he squealed and ducked behind Royce, which got Chaos superpumped for a game.

Laughing, Joy said, "I *try* fish. Occasionally." With a mock frown aimed at Jack, she added, "Someone says it smells bad."

Falling to his back and sprawling out like a starfish, Jack groaned. "It's terrible!"

"Personally, I love fish." Royce scooped up Chaos before he could accidentally scratch Jack's face. The pup's paws were oversized for his body, which meant he had a lot of growing to do yet. "When fish is raw, it smells, but once it's cooked… Mmm. Delicious."

Cracking open one eye, Jack peered up at him. "I could try your fish."

"My son," Joy said. "The master manipulator."

"Tell you what." Royce knelt down beside him, Chaos still held close with one thick arm. "Each time you come to dinner, you have to agree to try something new. Deal?" He held out a hand.

Rolling to his bottom, Jack sat facing him, ready agreement tripping off his tongue. "Deal."

They shook hands.

"If you decide you like fish, we could try catching our own in the spring."

In the spring? Around Jack's enthusiastic response, which included jumping up and down, Joy wondered where they'd be in the spring. A fling couldn't extend that long, could it?

When it eventually ended, as she assumed it had to, would they remain friends? Would Royce still be a part of her son's life? Jack might be satisfied with that arrangement, but Joy couldn't imagine a time when she'd see Royce and not want him. Like now.

Royce, Jack and Chaos all tumbled around the floor, wrestling and laughing, with Royce alternately hefting Jack into the air over his head, and playfully pinning him down so Chaos could lick his face. It was an irresistible scene, hearing her son's hilarity and seeing how comfortable he was with Royce.

One that made her long for more.

It would be so easy to fall in love with Royce.

Heck, she was already halfway there.

"Wow." Maris looked in the mirror, turning her head this way and that. "Trimming off that tiny bit made a big difference."

"The conditioner helped, too." As did the way Joy blew out her hair for her, using a round brush to add some volume. "You have gorgeous hair. I know women who would pay big bucks to get those summer highlights, and yours are natural."

"Life in a sunny park," Maris said, peering closer to see

her eyes. "The mascara is nice, too. It's just enough that I look like me, but better."

Joy grinned, pleased with the results. "And the sweater?" She'd borrowed from her own closet, choosing a black, crisscross sweater with a wide V-neck. She'd bought it on clearance, then regretted the purchase when, the one time she'd worn it, it had felt too revealing, like she might actually fall out. Because Maris had a smaller bust, it fit her perfectly.

She was also shorter than Joy, so it crossed at exactly the right spot. Luckily, Maris had worn a black bra.

Paired with trim-fitting faded jeans and black boots, Maris looked amazing.

She slanted Joy a look. "Now I have boobs."

That made Joy laugh out loud. "You've always had them. You just wear boxy T-shirts and sweatshirts that make them harder to notice." She glanced at Jack, saw he was involved painting with the kit Royce had bought him. Knowing he wasn't listening, she said low, "That never slowed Daron down, though, which is why he was always teasing you."

"Yeah, well, he can't miss 'em tonight, can he?" Maris shook her head, making her hair drift back and forth over her shoulders. "It feels so different. I keep it in a ponytail so it's not in my way, but this is more feminine."

"Most women like changing up their look every now and then."

"And those boxy shirts? They're comfortable for working."

Joy turned Maris to face her. "You're not working tonight, and I'm going to give you the same advice you gave me, but maybe tempered a little. Have fun."

"Yeah, we'll see."

Joy didn't like that lack of confidence. It wasn't Maris's way. "You really do look terrific."

She nodded. "Thanks. You do great work. It's just... I'm wondering if this is all too obvious?"

"What do you mean?"

"Is Daron going to think I want to impress him? Because I *don't*. I'm doing this for me, not him."

It was a novel thing, seeing Maris struggle with uncertainty. In a way, it made her even more likable. "I vote you do it for both of you."

There was a knock at the door, and Maris blanched.

"I'll get it," Jack said, already scrambling out of his chair.

"Look out the window first," Joy reminded him. They'd arranged for Daron to meet Maris here so they could ride together to his house. Still, she wanted Jack to always be careful.

Hand to her stomach, Maris whispered, "This is a mistake."

Joy lifted her brows. Wow, Maris really was nervous. How crazy was that? Grabbing her up in a hug, Joy said, "This is *amazing*. Now put on your game face and get ready to have a well-deserved good time."

CHAPTER TEN

DARON KNEW HE needed to stop staring, but…damn. He'd been half-hard ever since he laid eyes on Maris tonight. She'd greeted him in Joy's apartment with a discernible chip on her shoulder. Her beautiful, almost bare shoulder… which led into the creamy skin of her chest and down into mouthwatering cleavage.

Maris as her usual self was tempting enough.

This was just overkill.

"How far to your house?" she asked.

"Almost there." He tried to keep it together because tonight was to show her he respected her rules, that he was a grown-ass man, and that they had more in common than she thought. "You warm enough?"

"Yes."

That curt answer didn't reassure him, especially with the way she sat huddled in the seat, her arms folded around her, her shoulders up. Since he'd picked her up, his truck hadn't completely lost the heat, but the wind outside sent tree branches dipping and dried leaves tumbling. In the space of a few hours, a cold front had moved in and it felt more like winter than fall. If they got the precipitation that the dark clouds predicted, there'd be problems at the park tomorrow.

Last he'd noticed, a few couples were in the cabins, one young man was in a tent and three RVs remained on the property. He didn't expect any of them to last much longer, especially with the weather changing.

"Here we are." His headlights danced over the front windows as he turned into the driveway. He hit the garage door opener and pulled into the single car space.

As Maris opened her seat belt, she checked out the shelving and the tools placed precisely on pegboards. "So tidy."

For some reason, it made him feel self-conscious. "Yeah, well, being organized is a necessity at the park so naturally it carries over." He got out and circled the car, but she didn't wait for him and was already out, hugging herself again, before he reached her.

"Come on." He took her elbow and led her to the two steps up into the kitchen. This was his favorite room of the house, with the bright white Shaker cabinets and black granite tops.

She looked around in something close to awe. "It's so warm."

"The slate floor is heated. Same in the bathroom. When I'm home, I prefer to go barefoot." And he was often in just his boxers. "When I remodeled things, I tried to figure out all the modern gadgets, you know?" Like a kid showing off his first car, Daron stepped over to the sink to point out the faucet. "I agonized over this beauty the most, but..." It suddenly hit him that he was being rude. "Here, let me take your coat."

"Thank you." She stripped it off and handed it to him.

As if it didn't leave her standing there looking like his hottest fantasy.

While he soaked in the sight of her, she pushed up her sleeves and tested the hands-free faucet. "Huh. That's pretty neat." She dried her hands. "Will you show me the rest?"

"Sure." It might not matter, but he wanted her to see that he was settled, that he had as much yearning for home and hearth as the next person.

A tour through the house that should have taken three minutes took twenty with Maris admiring every small detail and giving lots of oohs and aahs.

Showing her the bedrooms tested Daron. The smallest, which was *really* small, was still mostly empty. The guest room was sort of an office with a foldout bed on one wall and a desk and chair on the other, and his room...well, his room made him think about getting her on the king-size bed. Naked.

But by God he'd follow her rules if it killed him, and to that end, he led her back to the kitchen. "Something to drink? Beer, wine?"

She shrugged one shoulder. "Tea?"

"I have bottled but not fresh. Is that okay?"

"Yes." She slid her sexy behind into one of the chairs along the island bar. "So you're going to have a chicken dinner sometime tonight?"

"It's mostly done, smart-ass." He grinned as he set her drink on the counter with a paper napkin. Turning, he opened the oven and showed her the fried chicken, already cooked and keeping warm, with an oven-safe bowl of mashed potatoes beside it. "I fixed everything before I left to get you."

"Good, because I'm hungry." She closed her eyes and took a deep breath. "Mmm. Smells delicious."

For a second, Daron couldn't pull his gaze away, caught by that soft, somehow sensual expression on her face. When her lashes lifted, it jolted him back to reality and he grabbed up a pot holder to get out the food.

His hands shook. *Crazy.*

But yeah, he wanted her that much, had wanted her for too long, and now he had her here and his main goal was *not* sex.

Somehow he'd survive, but he suspected the evening would be both pleasure and torture.

Using tongs, he put the chicken on a platter. With a serving spoon he stirred the potatoes. Glancing over his shoulder at her, he said, "I had two tomatoes left on the vine. Just picked them yesterday. Give me five minutes and I'll have it on the table."

She turned to see the small four-seat table in his connected dining room. "You already set the table, too."

"For you." And only for her. "I usually eat here at the bar or on the couch watching TV."

She went quiet, too quiet, as he cut the tomatoes into thick slices. Nothing fancy, but then he wasn't a fancy cook. Yeah, he could read a cookbook and follow directions, but his tastes ran more toward down-home cooking.

"Where do you sit with your dates?"

He paused on his way to the table. Maris stayed half turned away, only her eyes slanted toward him, almost like she didn't want to face him head-on.

It pissed him off a little, her mentioning other dates.

He was here with her, and no one else mattered. He didn't think saying that would score him any points, though, so he tried to be honest. "I don't generally cook dinner for other women."

"Don't bother feeding them, huh?"

Yeah, she was out for battle. Was this another of her defensive moves? A way to make him lose interest?

No way to tell for sure, but he'd gotten her this far so he wouldn't give up easily.

"If I do," he said as he put the dishes on the table, "it's pizza or something like that." There, let her stew on that.

He walked past her, trying his damnedest not to scowl, and adjusted the playlist on his phone so muted music filled the air. "Tea okay with your dinner, or did you want something else?"

She lifted the glass like a toast. "This works."

At the table, he pulled out a chair for her and waited.

"Such a gentleman."

He locked his teeth at the way she said it, which didn't sound anywhere close to a compliment. "I have my moments."

"I like your music."

Well, that was something. "I prefer country," he told her, "but if you have another preference—"

"I don't." She listened as she chose a chicken breast. "Who is that?"

"Keith Urban, 'Parallel Line.'" He chose two legs, a heap of potatoes, then asked, "You like it?"

"It's sexy." She swayed a little in her seat. "That's what you listen to?"

Usually his music was a little rowdier, but these lyrics were perfect for their first date. "I have a variety. A little of this, a little of that. George Strait, Brad Paisley, Sam Hunt, Chuck Wicks, Carrie Underwood—"

Her head shot up, a forkful of mashed potatoes held just before her mouth. "You listen to Carrie Underwood?"

"Course." What, did she think he singled out male singers? "Some of hers are my favorites." He gave it quick thought, then said, "I'll make you a playlist. When you have a little quiet time, you can give it a listen."

Her gaze softened even more. "Okay, I'd like that. Thanks."

Daron made a mental note to get the music together right away. It'd give him a good excuse to see her again.

They managed a few peaceful minutes while they each ate. Every couple of bites, Maris made one of those sexy "Mmm" sounds that he somehow felt everywhere, most especially in inappropriate places.

"Good?" he asked, just to make conversation.

"Delicious."

At least he could do something right. "I'm glad you like it."

"I had no idea you cooked."

So she thought he sustained himself…how? On cold cereal and her cookies? "There are probably a lot of things about me you don't know."

"No kidding. Like this amazing house? I love it. When you said it was small, I wasn't sure what to expect." She got another helping of potatoes. "But there's enough room here for a whole family."

Daron almost choked on his bite of tomato. He swallowed, cleared his throat and said without thinking, "It's our first date, so let's not get ahead of ourselves."

The second she froze, he knew he'd blundered. Damn it, he wanted to relax, to be natural, *to be himself*, able to joke, but she had him on pins and needles, worrying about how to act and what to say.

So of course he said the wrong thing.

The slight narrowing of her eyes gave fair warning to her mood. "Probably our first and only date, so you have nothing to worry about, believe me." Her hand fisted in her napkin. "I shouldn't have wasted my breath on the compliments. I should have known someone like you would take them wrong."

Carefully, Daron set his fork aside. She'd been tossing barbs left and right and he'd done his best to ignore them.

No one could ignore a direct hit like that, though.

"Someone like me?" he repeated. "Tell me, Maris, what the hell does that even mean?"

Her mouth pinched, she breathed through her nose—and then she deflated with disgust. Sitting back in her seat, she muttered, "I have no idea."

"What's that?"

She gestured at him. "You're so full of charm and so… well, the opposite of serious. No matter what you're doing, it seems like you have a good time. You're…free."

That last word emerged as a whisper, diluting some of his annoyance. "Yeah, well, as you can see, I'm not the drunken frat boy you paint me to be."

"I know." Her frown seemed self-directed. "I think that bugs me most of all."

Meaning he couldn't win for losing?

Sitting back in his seat, Daron studied her, the averted gaze, the downturned mouth. Hell, he hadn't invited her here tonight to make her miserable. "I like you, Maris." That felt inadequate, so he corrected, "I *more* than like you."

Her startled gaze latched on to his. Was that fear he saw?

Yeah, he thought it might be. So did Maris fear what she felt for him? It would explain a few things.

With his heart punching against his ribs, he asked, "So what would it take?"

Her tongue slipped over her lower lip, and she asked, "What do you mean?"

"What would it take for you to give me a shot?" He saw her breath stall, her gaze dart away.

Talk to me. Tell me the problem and we can work through it.

For the longest time she looked down before picking up her fork and scooping up a bite of potatoes. "You really are a good cook. No reason to let the rest of my meal go to waste."

Of all the... Daron struggled with his frustration, but he felt like he was on to something here and he instinctively knew pushing Maris would never work. She was too independent to be verbally strong-armed, while at the same time he sensed her vulnerability. Giving her time, he followed her lead and finished eating.

When her plate was clean, she set aside her cutlery and folded her hands in her lap. Her nervous swallow seemed to signal something.

Daron gave her his complete attention.

"I grew up pretty poor." Her gaze darted to his, and away. It took her a few more seconds, and she added, "Embarrassingly poor actually."

Embarrassingly? The way she tensed, as if waiting for a reaction, put him on the spot. If he knew what she needed, he'd give it to her, but he wasn't a mind reader so he said, "I grew up middle class. Dad worked at a car plant and Mom taught grade school."

After a deep breath that seemed to ease her a little, she smiled. "That sounds really nice."

He rubbed the back of his neck. Hell, her tension had become his own. "What did your folks do?"

"Well…" Color painted her cheeks and chest.

Maris didn't do anything half-assed, not even blushing. It intrigued him, seeing that wash of color over the tops of her breasts, her neck and cheeks.

"Mama mostly read the Bible." She rushed on, anxious to explain. "She loved me a lot, she really did, but she also enjoyed praying. I think because Daddy tended to drink too much in between jobs, and he was usually in between… because of the drinking."

Hoping to acknowledge that without any overt reaction showing, Daron gave a very slight nod.

"He wasn't a drunk. I mean, not like a mean drunk who abused anyone." Using both hands, she tucked her hair behind her ears and hunched her shoulders. "Mama said he was a functioning alcoholic, and that his own parents had been mean, is why he drank so much, but…"

This was the first time Maris had ever opened up to him and as awful as the subject matter was, he considered it a step in the right direction.

The direction that would bring her closer to him.

"That's why you were poor?"

She nodded. "Mama spent most of her time in a rocking chair, sometimes reading the Bible aloud, sometimes reading it silently. My parents relied heavily on assistance, but they didn't always ask for it, so there were times that we did without dinner. All my clothes were donated hand-me-downs."

Damn. Maris deserved better. *Every* kid deserved better. Doing his utmost to keep any judgment from showing, Daron asked, "Donated from the church?"

She nodded. "And some neighbors. I used to wonder what it would be like to go to a store and just…buy what I wanted."

Daron barely kept his jaw from clenching. He saw nothing wrong with people getting help when they needed it. Hell, it was as nice for the one helping as it was for the one who got the help. But it sounded like her parents could have done a lot better.

In his mind, there was all kinds of abuse, some worse than others, and what her parents had done to her counted. A child should be cared for in *all* ways, and obviously she hadn't been.

"So, anyway," Maris said, switching tracks. "From the time I was thirteen I knew I'd be different, because I decided it."

"Different from them?" Or did she mean different from…him?

She answered in a roundabout way, saying, "I wanted to be my own boss."

"Mission accomplished," he said with a smile. "You have a hell of a business."

She nodded. "I never wanted to…to rely on anyone for anything."

"But you do so much for others." Maris was one of the most generous people he'd ever met.

She snorted. "Cookies and coffee? Big deal. I wanted to support myself, to never ask anyone for anything important."

That's why she worked so hard? Was it also why she shied away from getting involved with him? She didn't want to rely on him? "Determination is a powerful incentive."

His observation earned him a bitter laugh. "Maybe. I screwed up, though, diving straight into a job instead of getting an education." She peeked up at him. "I wanted to do that shopping, you know? And I did, but even then I was frugal. I've never bought music. We didn't have it growing up, and there's a radio in my car, so..." She shrugged. "I've *always* been frugal. I don't how to be any other way. Heck, even this sweater is Joy's, not mine."

Is that why she'd asked him to pick her up there?

Or was it that she didn't want him anywhere near her apartment? It seemed every answer with Maris led him to two more questions.

He'd be willing to bet Joy had done something with her hair, too, and all in all, it relieved him, because that meant Maris *would* accept help.

But maybe only from certain people.

Wishing he could hold her, wishing he could say a lot more but not wanting to bash her parents, Daron remarked, "College isn't for everyone."

"Maybe. But for several years it felt like I was just spinning my wheels, barely able to save any money, definitely not enough to get ahead." She looked across the table at him. "Stability is important to me."

"I can imagine." He had a few bites left on his plate, but his appetite was gone. "Where are your parents now?"

"They've both passed, died in a house fire from smoke inhalation. I gave them the best funeral I could, but it wasn't much."

No way did he want to blow this by misspeaking or interrupting, so Daron only said, "I understand."

"When I got the job at the park, I thought it'd be a part-time gig, a way to make some extra money. Then I took over Summer's End, and things kept changing, the situation grew and now…" She pressed a fist to her chest. "Summer's End is mine."

And that meant it mattered, even more than he'd ever realized. Cautiously, going for honesty and hoping it was right, Daron said, "You know everyone likes you. A lot. But the foundation of that like is a ton of respect and admiration." From him more than anyone.

"I think I resented you." She winced. "I've been an awful date and I know it, but seeing everything you've done, it just reminds me what I haven't been able to do yet."

"Our experiences are night and day." He was glad for the explanation, and the semiapologetic tone, but she needed to understand the advantages he'd had. "I'm close with my parents, always have been. They've given me things—" guidance, encouragement and, yes, the occasional loan when he was first starting out "—that your parents couldn't give you. It makes a huge difference."

"Still—"

"You might not realize it, but you're special." He meant that with all his heart. "The park wouldn't be the same without you."

Smiling a little, she played with the ends of her hair. "Are you trying to get laid?"

Grinning with her, he held up his hands. "I'm being honest, I swear." That feminine gesture with her hair was something he'd never seen her do before because she always wore it in a ponytail. Now that he'd seen it loose, the dark blond waves trailing over her shoulders and chest, he'd always know what she looked like with it down. It'd probably plague him, but in a good way.

Maris said, "It feels like we're all important to the park. We work together like a family, don't you think?"

"Yes." Though Daron didn't want her thinking of him

that way, not when he wanted a more intimate relationship. "I have this vision of me as a cranky old seventy-year-old unclogging the showers, tweaking the pump on the pool and tuning up the mowers." Folding his arms on the table, he studied her. "What about you? Do you see yourself retiring from the park?"

"That wasn't my plan in the beginning, but now, yeah, I can't imagine ever leaving." Making another topic switch, she patted her stomach. "I'd ask if you have dessert, but I'm stuffed."

"Give it a few minutes and I can get us ice cream." He hesitated, but couldn't hold back. "I'm glad you plan to stay at the park. Whatever happens with us—"

"Nothing is happening with us."

"I'm glad you'll be there."

After speaking at almost the same time, they stared at each other.

Her gaze dropped to his mouth.

It was like she'd cast out a fishing line and reeled him in. He found himself pushing back his chair, which prompted her to quickly do the same. As he circled the table, she licked her lips, her eyes tracking him—until he stopped right in front of her.

"Maris." Her name sounded like a groan, but he was dying a little here, especially with the hungry way she looked at him. "Something *is* happening. You know that, right?"

Emotion seemed to coil within her, and Daron didn't know if it was anger, or...

She grabbed him, her hands sliding over his shoulders to lock behind his neck, her body crashing against his, her mouth on his mouth, her tongue slipping past his startled lips.

Lust. That emotion was lust and he wanted to rejoice.

He turned his head for a better fit, softening the onslaught so his tongue could twine with hers, so he could taste her deeply. One hand settled low on her back, the other tangled in her silky hair.

God, he could kiss her all day and it wouldn't be enough.

Suddenly she pulled back, breathing hard, staring up at him as if dazed. "This is nuts."

"Then let's be nuts." He started to pull her close again... No, wait. Rule number four. No sex on the first date. He shook his head, hoping to clear it of the pounding need. "I mean—" He cleared his throat. "Let's be nuts enough to make out."

Maris searched his face. "Make out?"

"Yeah, you know. Neck a little. Maybe go to second base." He bobbed his eyebrows playfully, needing to lighten the sexual tension. "I can take it if you can."

She blinked once, twice—then shoved him back and turned, one hand pressed to her forehead. "No, I don't know that I can take it. I don't feel like me. I don't even look like me."

He eased up behind her the same way he would with a fractious animal. "You look amazing, but you always do." He kept his voice gentle. "Have to admit, I like seeing more of you."

"You mean my boobs."

Standing behind her, he rested his hands carefully on her rigid shoulders, his thumbs moving in slow circles over the base of her neck. "I'm always a fan of more skin, but the biggest difference is this." He nuzzled against her hair. "You have fucking amazing hair."

She turned with a purpose. "Okay, I'm convinced. I want you. You clearly want me. Let's do this."

Let's do this?

She wasn't much for romance. Or maybe that was just what she wanted him to think. He tried to sort out the ramifications of scooping her up and taking her down the hall to his bedroom.

Her cursed list of rules danced through his brain. Tonight was supposed to be about getting closer to her, period.

"Well?" she demanded.

"Um…" Damned if he did, damned if he didn't, so he opted for the long haul and said, "Rule number four, remember?"

Her eyes flared. "*You* are citing rule number four?"

"It seemed important to you."

"Rule number four," she repeated, musing. "Rule number four…"

Did she even remember the fucking rule? His shoulders bunched. "That's the one where you stated no sex."

"Thank you for reminding me." Stepping around him, she snatched up her plate and empty bottle of tea, and headed for the kitchen.

Goddammit, this was not good. "What are you doing?"

"My share of cleanup."

He grabbed his own plate and hustled after her. "You don't have to do that. Let's…talk. Maybe watch TV. I'll clean up later."

"Nope. It's time for me to go." She opened the cabinet under his sink, didn't find what she was looking for and opened another cabinet.

"Maris." He set his dishes on the counter. "Don't go."

"Where the hell is your garbage?"

Shit. Was it too late for him to agree to sex? One look at her face and he knew it most definitely was. "Son of a bitch."

Startled, she drew back. "Are you *cussing* at me?"

"No, because I would never do that—just like I wouldn't ignore *your* damn rules that said no sex." He snapped open the dishwasher and practically threw in the dishes. "Frustration is the son of a bitch. Do you know, I never walk on eggshells? I'm just me, and if that's not good enough for someone, that's their problem. But for you, I tried." He jammed in a pan, making the stupid thing fit, without even rinsing it.

"You know that's not going to come clean."

"Shows what you know. It has a pot scrubber feature." He closed the dishwasher and turned to her, arms folded. "I want to spend time with you, Maris. A quick fuck would be great—"

"I was hoping it wouldn't be all that quick."

"If that was all I wanted." She had an answer for everything. In other circumstances, he'd admire that about her. Now, it just infuriated him.

By small degrees, her features softened. "What is it you want?"

"Sex, for sure." She needed to understand how much he wanted her. "But more than that, too—and all you do is fight me." He smoothed a hand over her hair, then tipped up her chin. "It was *your* rule, honey. I'm just trying to make sure you don't regret coming here."

Her lips twitched, then bloomed into a self-deprecating smile. She snuggled in against him, not with lust this time, but with something even better, more like affection. "Can you forgive me?"

He rested his jaw against the top of her silky head and breathed in the scent of floral shampoo. He had her in his house. She was hugging him.

How could he not forgive her? "Consider it done."

"Thank you for being the reasonable one."

Not a trait she normally applied to him. "I have my moments, when something really matters." If Maris caught on that *she* mattered, she didn't say so.

"Date one, in the books." She looked up at him. "Really, Daron, I'm sorry. I don't usually unload my family history on people."

"I know and I'm honored that you told me." It made him feel a little special, too.

"I don't usually run from hot to cold in a heartbeat, either."

"It keeps me on my toes." He was so glad she wasn't slamming out, hell, he'd forgive just about anything.

"I didn't mean for any of that to happen, it just... I'm not used to being sexually frustrated, I guess. It's made me both whiny and bitchy."

He grinned at her roundabout way of admitting she wanted him. "You are not either of those things, I swear. But hey, I could tell you about sexual frustration."

Maris snorted. "Like you've ever done without."

"I've done without you, and that counts for a lot." He kissed her hard and fast, before she could protest. "Truce?"

"All right. Truce." She glanced around the kitchen. "Where do you keep your bowls? I think I want ice cream, after all."

Joy woke to the sounds of hushed voices outside her apartment, which was really odd since she lived up a flight of outside stairs. The glow of the digital clock showed it to be 6:15. Too early for visitors.

Slipping from the bed, she peeked out the window, but the angle was wrong and she couldn't see the landing from where the low voices came.

More curious than alarmed, she darted into her son's

room and found him sound asleep, sprawled sideways across his bed. Jack often ended up in that position, which made sleep tough on the nights that he had a bad dream or when he'd been sick and wanted to sleep with her.

Feet in the face, or a head in her ribs, was the norm whenever they shared a bed.

Quietly pulling Jack's door shut, she peeked into the living room. Through the curtain she saw shadows moving beneath the security light outside her door. She glanced down and saw that the door was still locked.

Should she call Coop? No, not yet. It might be a camper at the wrong door, or it could even be Coop, waiting for her to wake up because…of an emergency?

Moving more quickly now, Joy hurried into the bathroom, took a few seconds to take care of business, then pulled on a thick chenille housecoat and stepped into fuzzy slippers. She didn't dare look in the mirror as she tied the belt around her waist. If she did, she'd probably find the need to comb her hair or rinse her face…

Vanity was a stupid reason to keep anyone waiting.

Creeping now, she went back into the living room and carefully pulled aside the curtain on the window.

There on her landing, both of them bundled up in winter coats, were Royce and Daron. What in the…? Dropping the curtain, she turned the lock and pulled open the door.

Startled, they both looked at her.

Then Royce looked all over her while Daron grinned and turned his back. "I'll wait at the bottom with Coop." Holding tight to the handrail and moving cautiously, he went back down the stairs.

With Coop? Joy leaned out the door, and sure enough, Coop stood at the base of the stairs with Chaos and his own dog, Sugar. The two animals were busy sniffing each other in impolite places and wagging their tails.

"Morning," Coop called up to her.

"Good morning." Gaze back on Royce, Joy asked, "Is something wrong?"

"No, and I'm sorry that we woke you." He pressed forward, which caused her to step back and into the apartment. Royce followed, quietly closed the door, looked past her and then at her mouth.

Knowing that look oh too well, Joy backpedaled. "Nope." She put a hand to her mouth. "I haven't even brushed my teeth yet."

Smiling, Royce caught her, anyway. "Just a quick kiss," he murmured as he bent to press his chilled lips to hers, gradually tugging her into full-body contact.

Still not fully awake, she had no defenses and melted against him.

With small pecks he kissed her jaw, her neck, and nuzzled right below her ear, before he breathed, "Damn, you look incredibly hot straight from your bed."

Joy touched her hair and felt her face heating. "So... what's going on?"

"Ice storm last night." He put one more kiss to her temple and stepped back. "I found out when Chaos wanted out at the butt-crack of dawn, and I knew you'd be using those steps to get Jack to school. They're treacherous." His gaze went down her body. "By the way, the schools are on a two-hour delay."

"It's that bad?" She returned to the window to look out again. Sure enough, the outside light glinted over a layer of ice coating the front half of each step. "There's salt in the maintenance building."

"Yeah. Daron was here when I arrived, already salting the parking lot and all around the camp store."

Because he'd been worried about Maris. *Aww*, Joy thought with a small smile. She couldn't wait to hear how their evening had gone. She'd waited up as late as she could, but her car was still in the lot when she finally went to bed.

Daron's diligence this morning was more proof that he wasn't the negligent, immature person Maris wanted to believe him to be.

Royce cocked a brow. "Want to tell me what that secret little smile means?"

The smile widened into a grin as she headed into her kitchen. "Just wondering how he and Maris did last night."

"Daron's in a good mood, if that helps."

"Daron's always in a good mood." Joy got down the coffee can and filters from an upper cabinet. This time of year, Maris wouldn't arrive at the park for another hour, but Joy was willing to bet all the men would appreciate coffee since they were already up and working. While filling the carafe with water, she asked, "So why is Coop here?"

"Same as me—he was up with Sugar and realized the park would be a mess. He came out to help Daron."

"And now you're all here because of my steps?" She shook her head, touched by their consideration but feeling bad that they'd gone to so much trouble. "I would have seen the ice and been careful."

"Sure." He leaned against the cabinet beside her and pulled off his gloves. "But it's still dangerous, and you have a five-year-old to think about, plus his school bag and your purse."

She didn't admit that she'd slipped on those steps more than once. "If you guys leave the salt, I can—"

"Joy." He traced a still-cold finger over her jaw. "How

about you let us take care of it? I'm already here, Coop and Daron are already up, and we don't mind doing it. In fact, Coop has a rubber mat he's going to put at the camp store and we're thinking of running into town to buy some treads for the stairs, at least until I can do something about keeping the snow and ice off them in the first place."

Her mouth dropped open. He planned to do *what*?

Joy knew there was something she should say, some denial she could make, but her brain drew a blank.

Finally she managed, "Let the guys know I'll have coffee in five. I'll be right back," and she rushed away before Royce could reply.

CHAPTER ELEVEN

In her bedroom, Joy closed the door and, still racing, went into the bathroom to clean her teeth, brush her hair and wash her face. She looked in her closet, but everything seemed too complicated with three men waiting, so she pulled out a thick, tunic-length sweatshirt and lined tights, which she usually wore only when doing yoga…which sadly, didn't happen often enough. She pulled on socks and stepped into low boots. No makeup, but it was the best she could do on very short notice.

When she reached the kitchen again, she found Royce filling three mugs. He glanced up—and his gaze snagged on her all over again.

That particular heat in his eyes could be lethal. Feeling

as if he'd just physically stroked her, she held her breath and waited.

Voice rough, he growled, "I need to be with you again, Joy. Soon. Right this second wouldn't be soon enough."

Joy flushed with reciprocal heat. Yeah, she needed that, too. Unfortunately, it wasn't meant to be. At least, not in the next few hours.

"I... That is, Jack..." She lifted a hand toward the hall behind her. "He's sleeping, but—"

"What I need," Royce stressed, giving her a fond smile of understanding, "and what I think should happen are two different things. It's almost guaranteed that every time I see you, I'm going to want you, but you shouldn't worry that I'd take a chance on Jack walking in on us. You have my word right now that I'd never do anything to hurt that little boy."

His ebony eyes, which looked a little tired to her, shone with sincerity. "Thank you."

"Ah, honey. Don't thank me for *not* being a selfish ass, okay?"

Smiling, Joy nodded. "So, what brought that on? The sudden interest, I mean."

"You're kidding, right? Nothing sudden about it, but seeing you like that—" his gaze went over her again, his nostrils flaring slightly with a deep breath "—is enough to make me half-hard."

Of course her gaze dropped to his lap, but his coat covered his fly. She swallowed in equal parts relief and disappointment. A little self-conscious, she tugged on the thick sweatshirt. "People don't usually see me all sloppy."

"Your version of sloppy is hot." After getting down a fourth cup, Royce said, "Hope you don't mind that I made myself at home."

"I'm glad you did." When he carried two cups outside, she used the opportunity to doctor hers with a liberal amount of sugar and creamer. She needed both caffeine and a sugar jolt this morning. Her heart thumped from the exchanges with him.

He wanted her as much as she wanted him.

Better still, he truly cared about Jack's feelings. That, more than anything else, endeared Royce to her.

Endeared him and made her question her intent with this entire affair.

A few seconds later, her door opened again and, after cleaning his feet on the entry rug, Royce strolled back in. Ice crystals clung to his hair and shoulders, telling her it had started to sleet again.

If the winter weather held, it'd throw off her Halloween plans for the park—and would also negatively impact Royce's business since Halloween at the drive-in almost guaranteed a packed lot.

But not under these conditions.

She was used to the crazy Ohio weather and had adjusted plans too many times to count when snow arrived on the worst possible day. Things could flip again just as quickly, so for now, she'd hold out hope for milder weather.

Stuffing his gloves into his coat pockets, Royce went first to the coffee, took a few drinks, then turned to her. "I told you I'm handy with my hands, right?"

Oh, the things that statement brought to mind. She knew well what he could accomplish with those hands.

His grin told her he'd read her thoughts. "Besides that," he said, one brow arrogantly cocked as he approached, stopping right in front of her. "I'm good with building and repairs."

"Yes?" Joy had no idea where he was going with this, and it wasn't easy for her to think with him so near, the brisk scent of the winter storm mixing with his own delicious aroma.

He dropped his head for a moment, and when he raised it, he snared her gaze with his own. Looking far too serious, he said, "Your stairs are solid, but still dangerous. The treads and salt will help for now, but there's a better long-term solution."

"The stairs are fine," she said, already knowing her budget didn't allow for "long-term solutions."

As if she hadn't spoken, he continued. "Covering the stairs so the snow and ice never reach them is the way to go."

"Royce." She didn't like the idea of imposing on him. "You have enough to do with your own repairs."

He ignored that, too. "By the way, Coop told me to let you know he'll cover the cost. Said he should have done something about the steps ages ago, but you'd never complained so he hadn't thought about it."

Until Royce pointed it out? Joy gulped down the rest of her coffee, letting it warm her from the inside out, hoping it'd clear out the cobwebs.

Setting aside the cup, she took a step forward, until she and Royce almost touched. "Royce."

He brushed his knuckles over her cheek. "Hmm?"

"I appreciate what you're doing. I really do."

The problem was that their relationship didn't make allowances for him to do things like this. It crossed the bounds of a friend with benefits into something very different.

Didn't it?

Joy shook her head. "You shouldn't be here now, bothering with this stuff when your hands are already full."

He held out his muscular arms, palms up, fingers spread. "Do I look like I've taxed myself?"

No, he looked like a sensual offering. His coat parted, showing her a thermal shirt fitted over a broad chest.

Stay on track.

Joy cleared her throat and worked up a slight frown. "That's not the point."

"The point is that those stairs should be covered to make them safe."

Deciding to be blunt, Joy said, "I don't need you to take care of me. I've managed on my own for years now."

There was something in his eyes, something she didn't understand, before he turned away and retrieved his coffee from the counter. He kept his back to her as he sipped. "The thing is…" The words trailed away. He set the coffee aside and braced both hands on the edge of the counter.

Concerned, Joy edged closer to him. "What?" She'd never seen Royce like this, so pensive and obviously troubled. "What is it?"

Dropping his head, he laughed, but it wasn't a happy sound.

"Royce?"

Wearing a smile of irony, he turned to face her. "When I moved here, I had this grand idea of being…" He visually searched for a word. "Unencumbered."

Joy didn't know what that meant, but surely if he wanted less on his plate, he shouldn't be here this morning, offering to take on more work. "I see," she said, because it seemed like the appropriate response. "Well, then, taking on my responsibilities isn't—"

"I'm not. I *couldn't*." He ran a hand through his hair, pushing the inky strands back, then letting them fall forward again.

Could a man be any sexier? She honestly didn't think so.

"Look," he said, "I can't imagine a bigger responsibility than a child, right? That's a lifetime commitment and the bulk of it is going to fall on you no matter what. Doesn't mean others can't help a little, especially when the help is easily given."

"Caring for Jack isn't a hardship," Joy countered, "because I love him so much."

"I know, and full disclosure, it's damned appealing."

"It is?" Joy didn't entirely understand that, either. She started to say that all moms loved their children—and then she thought of her own mother and bit her lip instead. No, all mothers most definitely did not feel the same love and devotion that she had for her son. She'd cross heaven or hell, and everywhere in between, to care for Jack.

That didn't mean she wanted to take advantage of Royce.

Folding her arms, she studied him. "The thing is, our… arrangement doesn't allow for such an imposition."

As if that description of their relationship offended him, his brows twitched down.

Joy didn't know what else to call it. "Royce—"

"The last few years were nonstop. I guess I got used to staying busy."

"You're still busy."

He shook his head. "The drive-in doesn't take nearly as much time as I thought it would, and we'll be off-season in another week. I'll work on the house, but still, I feel like I'm at loose ends, like things aren't quite as I imagined them. Or maybe…" He let out a breath and said lower, "Like maybe I don't even know what the hell I want anymore."

She understood that feeling. Lately, she'd been uncertain, as well, not just for herself but for Jack, too. Any decisions she made would ultimately affect him.

Keep things as they were, and lavish all her attention on her son?

Or consider the idea of a stronger male influence, a unique bond with another person who cared for him?

That person could, or could not, be Royce. His indecisiveness now didn't necessarily mean he was looking for a more meaningful relationship with her. If she took his words at face value, he simply wanted to help because he could—as any *friend* might.

Joy tried to think of the right thing to say, something that wasn't too heavy. "You have Chaos."

His laugh this time sounded just right, making her smile with relief.

"He's a frisky little pup, but not exactly a time-sink, and not at all what I meant." Royce caught her waist and hauled her in.

Oh, how she liked that, the familiarity of his body, the comfort of their interactions.

Much, much nicer than wading through emotional questions she had no answers to.

"The point," Royce stressed, "is that I'm adjusting my expectations, and I *want* to help with your stairs. Do me a solid and say yes."

That was so ludicrous Joy stared at him. "It's doing you a favor for me to…let you help?"

He put his forehead to hers. "Yeah, something like that." Warmth filled eyes as dark as pitch, the brawny hands on her waist gave a slight squeeze and his mouth brushed hers. Close, so very close, he murmured, "Now agree, because Daron and Coop are waiting for me."

That statement hit her like a dousing of ice water. "Oh my God." How had she forgotten about them standing outside in the freezing sleet? Pushing Royce back and shooing him with her hands, she said, "Go, go. But please be careful."

"The same to you. If you decide you and Jack need to leave, text me first, okay?"

Her independent pride bristled. "For what reason?"

"So I can make sure the stairs are clear."

Umbrage lifted her chin. "You think I can't do that?"

His mouth curled. "I'm pretty sure you can do anything you set your mind to, but I meant I'd move any tools we're using."

"Oh." And...now she felt foolish. It had been a very long time since she'd checked in with anyone, but she had little resistance left so she nodded. From someone else the request might have felt intrusive, but with Royce it felt caring. "Will you also let me know if you need anything?"

"Sure." His gaze moved to the hall that led to their small bedrooms. "Will it wake Jack if we start working?"

"A Mack truck driving through here probably wouldn't wake him."

Royce grinned. "Perfect." Hesitating at the door, he looked at her over his shoulder. "Maybe if I finish in time, and Jack is still in school, Coop would keep an eye on Chaos."

His gaze was so intense, so probing, it thrilled her. "That would be perfect."

A slow appreciative smile promised heated things. "Then I can guarantee we'll finish in time."

FOR ONCE, MARIS wasn't working. It felt oddly right, sitting in a booth with her feet propped on the opposite seat, a hot coffee in hand as she waited for Joy to arrive. She used the YouTube app on her phone to listen to more country music, now that Daron had turned her on to it.

She liked it. She couldn't see herself purchasing music, not when she could put the money to something she deemed more important, but if Daron did as promised and made her a playlist, she wouldn't need to, anyway.

Why had she never thought about music before? Sometimes in her car she turned on a radio station, but not out of any deep preference. Mostly she needed to break the quiet. Being still had always been a problem for her, but there was no way to bustle around when behind the wheel. That stillness, combined with the silence, always drew her into the past.

It was never a friendly visit.

Now, thanks to Daron, she might actually find a new way to ease her troubled thoughts.

She'd made some crazy assumptions about him, like the idea that he'd gravitate to death-metal music or something equally loud and jarring. It was dumb, because that didn't really jive with his overall persona of a happy-go-lucky guy.

Pegging him as a carefree, too-young bachelor who spent every additional minute in the sack with a variety of young women who would idolize his fit bod and sexy smile was equally dumb.

Oh, she wasn't under any illusions. She figured Daron had more than his fair share of sexcapades, but it couldn't be to the degree she'd assumed, not with all the work he'd put into his house.

And the man had a garden. Before he'd driven her home, he'd shown her the rectangle of yard that, over the summer, had yielded tomatoes, green beans, squash, zucchini and carrots. He'd also shown her the coop he'd recently started building so in the spring he could get some chicks.

A stud who wanted to raise chickens and grow his own produce?

How the hell could she have ever envisioned that? It was like he'd dragged together her version of the perfect guy—short a few years of age—and rolled it all up into the perfect package.

Just for her.

He'd set down roots. He'd focused on his future.

He'd be practically self-sustaining!

When she closed her eyes, Maris could almost see him in his yard, bare feet in the lush, neatly trimmed grass, a bucket of corn in hand as he strolled along, feeding chickens in his usual summer garb of loose board shorts and a raggy tee.

The image made her mouth go dry and accelerated her pulse.

It was a nice visual, calming and peaceful, but it also sent a frisson of heat racing through her.

What would it be like to have that life?

He didn't propose marriage, she reminded herself.

If you want that life, you have to get it for yourself.

Another good one.

Maris looked out the window at the rippling surface of the lake.

There'd be no more leaving the camp store door open in welcome, not with frost everywhere. This time of year usually made her a little melancholy. She needed the liveliness of the season, the nonstop frenzy, to keep her thoughts focused away from her past, away from the feelings of hunger, of people looking down on her with pity.

This year was a little different. She felt such an incredible bond to Joy that she actually anticipated the quiet so they could visit more. Instead of her thoughts going inward to sadder times, they bloomed out, thinking of Joy's reaction to different things, wondering what her suggestions might be.

Wondering, too, how she and Royce were getting along. That made her smile. Daron had been right. Joy was falling for Royce fast and hard. She only hoped Royce felt the same.

But then, if he didn't, Joy would get through it. Her girl was a fighter clear down to her soul. A quiet, unassuming woman with a will of iron.

Damn, but Maris loved Joy's spirit.

She was busy searching for a new song when the door opened and a gust of wintery air blew in. Thinking it'd be Joy, she smiled as she looked up—and the smile froze when she found Joy's mother in the doorway instead.

Whoa. The wintery storm had nothing on that lady.

Suddenly being in the shop alone didn't feel quite so cozy.

Without standing, Maris asked, "Can I help you?"

"Where is my daughter?"

Other than a slightly red nose, the woman seemed impervious to the cold, thanks to her fur-trimmed leather coat with matching gloves.

"Who's your daughter?"

Maris's question, deliberately absurd, caused her mother's mouth to tighten. "Young lady, you know exactly who I mean. Where is she?"

Maris made a point of looking around the store. "Not here."

"I can see that."

She hadn't moved from the doorway, which Maris considered a good thing—except that she kept the door wide open. When the furnace kicked on, Maris mentally tabulated the additional cost to her electric bill.

Lazily, she dropped her feet to the floor and stood, coffee cup in hand as she headed around to the serving side of the counter. Less chance of frostbite with a little space between her and Joy's mother. "If you want to leave your name and a number, I'll tell Joy that you dropped in. But it might not be for a while." Actually, it could be any minute now. "Or not at all today."

"I demand that you give me her address."

Demand? Maris didn't mean to exacerbate the situation, but her snort of laughter probably did just that. "Go ahead," she said, full of challenge. "Demand."

Footsteps carried in, and then Daron pushed past the woman, his gaze seeking out Maris, and filling with relief when he spotted her. Keeping his gaze resolutely on her, he said, "Ah, there you are."

Maris couldn't help but smile. "Yes, here I am." It amused her how he deliberately ignored the other woman.

Pulling the stocking cap from his head, he lifted his brows in question. "Everything okay?"

Praying Daron would understand, Maris said, "This lady is looking for Joy, but I told her Joy isn't here and we don't know when to expect her. Probably not for a while, right?"

"Right," he said, quickly putting a thermos on the counter. "Fill her up and I'll be on my way."

Hoping that meant he'd warn Joy, Maris took thirty seconds to do as asked. Daron screwed the lid back on, nodded at her, said, "Ma'am," to the mother and stepped back out—thankfully pulling the door closed behind him.

Releasing a breath, Maris smiled. Daron would warn Joy and it'd be up to her if she wanted to see her mother or not.

Maris voted for not.

The driver from the previous visit stuck his head in

the door. "Are we staying?" he asked. "I'll need to park if we—"

"Wait outside," Mrs. Reed snapped, and pushed the door shut in his face. Eyes narrowed on Maris, she said, "You may give my daughter a message."

"Okay, sure." Maris refilled her own coffee, and no way in hell would she offer any to the old bat, "Shoot."

"Tell Joy that…" As if lost for the right words, she hesitated, and for only a single moment she looked almost human.

Then her narrow chin shot up. "Tell her we need to talk before she visits the attorney. It's important."

"I'll pass it along. When I see her, I mean."

"See that you do."

Because…she was an errand boy? Pretending nonchalance, Maris blew on her coffee to cool it.

There was another moment of indecisiveness, and the woman said a brisk, "Thank you."

Huh. Maris summoned a smile. "You're welcome."

Nodding, the woman turned to leave.

Wow. The second the door closed, Maris set down the coffee and slumped on the counter. Good God, how had Joy survived being raised by that churlish, rude witch? Here she'd thought her own mother was bad with her constant rocking and praying. At least she'd prayed for Maris; she'd hugged her often and always told her she loved her.

No, her mama hadn't shown that love in conventional ways, but she'd never made Maris feel *un*loved.

Pulling out her phone, Maris texted Joy. Your mother just swept out of here. Stay low for a bit.

An immediate reply showed. I'm so sorry!

It seemed clear to Maris that while her parents' lack of

initiative had made her überdriven, the cold demeanor of Joy's parents made her sympathetic.

And apologetic.

Don't be, Maris texted. *Not with me.* Want to gab soon? I have coffee to share & updates to give.

Be there in ten!

Ten minutes. Crazy how much she valued that time with Joy. She'd grown up without anyone to really talk to, to confide in. Like music, she hadn't known what she was missing.

But now she did, and she'd never take it for granted.

Not when she was dying to unload on everything that had happened last night with Daron. Being this confused wasn't a usual occurrence for Maris. Throughout her life she'd set goals, and then worked her ass off for them. The situation with Daron was a challenge she couldn't figure out, because she couldn't decide if she wanted it—wanted *him*—or not. It would be such an enormous change, and yet—

The door opened again and he strode in, his expression uneasy. "Hey, you okay?"

Now why the hell wouldn't she be? Maris was coming up with a snarky reply, just to be contrary, but he hadn't stopped walking and it struck her that he was coming right around the counter and that he apparently planned to—

Lips on lips, firm, two seconds… His warm breath caressed her cheek. Three, four, five…

He straightened and his hand went to her face. "I hated leaving you alone like that, but I figured you wanted me to warn Joy."

Maris didn't mean to, but she licked her tingling lips. "I…"

Daron took her mouth again, deeper this time, more thoroughly. As he gradually eased back, he groaned, then murmured, "Sorry. You were saying?"

Who the hell knew? Maris sure didn't.

"You're okay?"

Right. He'd come in like a hero to save her. Unacceptable.

After clearing her throat and standing a little straighter, Maris said, "I'm fine. Sharp words have never done me any damage."

"They can hurt all the same." He wrapped his hand lightly around her ponytail and slow-stroked it to the end. "I found Joy in the maintenance shed with Royce. She was worried about you, all hell-bent on charging down here to take the heat off you." He leaned down, and this time his mouth trailed over her neck. The damp heat of his lips, the touch of his tongue on sensitive skin, made her belly flip-flop in a delicious way. "I told Joy you had it under control."

See, now *that*, his confidence in her, mattered more than his macho need to protect.

"It took some convincing, because Joy feels responsible for her mother's behavior. When Royce told her he'd come along with her, she gave in and stayed put. Guess she didn't want Royce dealing with the woman, either."

"Cheers to Royce."

"Yeah. I came as soon as I saw the car. I swear when I stepped in, the store was ten degrees colder than outside. That lady is like an arctic wind, freezing everything around her."

No kidding. Maris still chilled. "If Joy had come straight here, instead of flirting with Royce, she'd have walked into that unpleasant surprise." Maris patted his shoulder and tried not to think about the rock-solid body beneath his coat and sweatshirt. "Thanks for heading her off."

"Not a problem." He grinned. "Still surprises me to see Joy with someone. She's always been…"

"Distant, I know. Having met her mother, I can understand why."

"Royce told me all about her. Sounds like a nightmare."

"That covers it." Maris tried to be casual, but having a man touch her, kiss her, didn't fall into the norm for her daily routine. "I should get back to work." Not that she actually had any work to do. Thanks to the morning ice storm, there'd been a rush on the coffee when the sun first rose, but now the few remaining campers had departed. Many promised to be back for Halloween, weather permitting.

"Yeah, me, too. With the sun out, the ice will start to melt and things can get back to normal. Weather in Ohio, right? Mild one day, winter storm the next, and right back to a typical fall."

Damn it, he could be so engaging with his casual small talk and friendly smiles. Moments like this only made her want him more.

"I'm making chili for lunch," she blurted, before the intent fully processed in her brain. *Do I have the ingredients for chili? Hope so.* "If you're hungry later—"

"Count me in." He gave her a boyish grin, then scooped her in for a hot, passionate, openmouthed kiss that made every female part of her stand up and beg for more.

When he released her, he said, "I better go before I remember that we're past rule number four now. Does chili count as a date? No, don't answer that. Let me dream a little." He kissed the tip of her nose and strode away, all sexy swagger and teasing charm.

Maris was still standing there, dazed and too warm, when Joy arrived. As she rushed in, stripping off her coat and hat, she said, "I'm so damn sorry about my mother. I owe you for helping me dodge her. Now tell me all about your date."

That effervescent enthusiasm was just what Maris needed right now, and she laughed. "Your mother wants you to call her. She's insistent that you two need to talk before you see the attorney. I say screw that, but I felt compelled to pass it along."

Nodding, Joy came behind the counter and helped herself to coffee. "Message received. Your duty is done. Now, do we need to work as we talk? Or do you have a few minutes?"

"Actually, I have all kinds of time. Let's sit."

The surprise that widened Joy's eyes and parted her lips had Maris laughing again.

Damn it, she felt pretty good today...and she knew it was because of Daron.

How scary was *that*?

TEN MINUTES LATER, Joy sat back in disbelief. Based on Maris's cheerfulness, she thought for sure she misunderstood. "So, you're saying you *didn't* sleep with him?"

"No thanks to me. I practically jumped the poor guy's body."

Joy would never have described Daron as a "poor guy," but...had Daron turned Maris down? That didn't make any sense, either. "What happened?"

"I made a giant assumption that he'd be all on board with some extracurricular activity. Not so."

"Baloney. If Daron held out, he must have had a reason.

I just don't…" Joy couldn't imagine what that reason might be. "He's chased you *forever*, it seems."

Maris pinched her mouth to the side, then sighed. "Okay, here's the worst part."

Oh no, there was a worst part? Worse than being turned down? Sympathy drew Joy closer. "Go on."

"Before I agreed to go to his house for dinner, I laid out these stupid rules—and one of them was no sex on the first date."

Oh my. When the whole point had seemed to be extra-curricular activity, Joy couldn't imagine why Maris had done that…well, except that Maris had some skewed perceptions of Daron. Maybe she'd been trying to protect herself?

If so, Joy completely got it. More and more, she felt the same way. "You said one of them? There were other rules?"

"Yup. Whole stupid list. Made up on the spot." Maris slumped back. "Most idiotic thing I've ever done."

"Let me see if I'm following. You made up these rules so he wouldn't expect sex, but then you got there and *you* wanted sex, and he…still said no?"

"He reminded me of the rule." Maris rubbed her face. "Didn't expect that one, you know? But lo and behold, the man has scruples, at least where I'm concerned. He said he was afraid I'd regret coming there and he didn't want that."

Ah. Seeing a method to Daron's madness, Joy asked softly, "What does he want?"

"More?" Maris rolled a shoulder. "At least that's what he said."

"That's so sweet." To Joy's mind, Daron's restraint showed that he cared.

"Not exactly how I'd describe it."

"You and Daron. After all this time, it's hard to believe nothing happened."

"I didn't exactly say that." As if to fortify herself, Maris finished off her coffee, plunked down the cup and stared Joy in the eyes. "We played around."

"Oh goody." Leaning forward again, Joy said, "Describe 'play around.' I need details."

Maris bit her lip in an effort to hold back her laughter, but it did no good. "He's an amazing kisser. I hadn't realized it could be like that—it's been so long since I've done anything."

"Same here, and yes, what an eye-opener, right?"

"I had no idea what I'd been missing."

Joy tipped her head, curiosity dawning. "You've never dated as far as I know, and I've known you a little more than five years. So how long are we talking?"

"Basically..." Maris winced. "Ever?"

"Ever?" Joy quickly tried to hide her shock. "Ever as in...you've never...?"

"Made out? Nope. There were a few kisses behind the bleachers at school, but they were pretty underwhelming, so they don't count." Maris dismissed the shocking confession by asking, "How could I, when I didn't date?"

"Why not?"

Rolling her shoulder, Maris said, "I didn't want anyone inside our house, and I definitely didn't want anyone meeting my parents. Heck, from one hour to the next, I was never sure if my dad would be drunk or sober, and whichever it was, you can bet the house would be full of prayers."

Sympathy nearly smothered Joy. "But...what about school dances? Parties?"

"When I only owned worn hand-me-downs? It was easier just to skip that stuff."

Joy couldn't hide her devastation.

And that prompted Maris to say, "Hey, it wasn't all that."

Sadly, Joy thought maybe it was, and in her usual way Maris chose to shrug it off.

Rather than make her more uncomfortable, Joy forced a smile. "Now I'm doubly glad you got together with Daron and had a nice time."

"It was *so* nice," Maris agreed. "Daron was pretty intense, but funny, too, and…" She glanced down at her now-empty cup.

"Hey, we're in a club, right? No secrets in the club, so spill."

Maris's gaze shifted around, ensuring no one had snuck in without her knowing. Leaning over the booth table, her hushed voice giddy with excitement, she said, "Daron Hardy looks incredibly sexy when he's turned on. Like off-the-charts sexy."

Joy grinned. "You're just now noticing how attractive he is?"

"No, I'm serious, Joy. We have lots of attractive guys around here. It's like this park is a testosterone factory and it's made me immune to man-candy. But after a lot of smooching on Daron's couch—"

"And some touching?" Joy interjected. "Please, Maris, tell me there was touching!"

"Nothing to write home about or anything, but it was a real learning experience for me." She blew out a breath. "Holy cow, he looked hot. It was all I could do not to strip naked and dare him to resist."

Joy burst out laughing. "I think it's safe to say that would've pushed him right over the edge. But hey, if you ever try it, I'll want the nitty-gritty on that, too."

"Today, back in my real life, I don't know if I should be

glad nothing else happened, or if I should arrange another date and ensure that it does."

Hand in the air, Joy said, "The answer is...second date."

"Daron's sowed his wild oats, right? But I haven't. With zip for experience, it's possible I could be a major letdown in the sack." She made a face. "Then what?"

Maris's concern struck a chord with Joy and she went still. Had Royce sowed his wild oats before moving here? Or maybe that had been part of the plan he wasn't so certain about anymore. What if he needed that freedom to get it out of his system, but she'd edged in—little boy in tow—and interrupted?

Royce was the type of kind, responsible, caring person who would think of her and Jack instead of himself when it came right down to it. But was that fair?

No, it wasn't.

Clearly, she had a lot to think about. For now, though, reassuring Maris took precedence.

Reaching over the tabletop, she took Maris's hand. "You'll have to trust me on this. Daron will *not* be disappointed. I promise."

Maris didn't seem convinced. "How do you know?"

"Because I have a little experience—granted, until very recently it was six years old, but men and women haven't changed that much. When you and Daron get together, and you will, just be honest with him. Tell him what you like and what you don't. Ask what he likes—" she bobbed her eyebrows "—or experiment around and find that out for yourself. Try not to be shy, but if you are, say so."

"Me, shy?" Maris gave her patented snort. "As if."

"You big faker." Joy folded her arms on the booth in a way that matched Maris's posture. They were close together, speaking in near-whispers even though they were in the camp store alone.

The subject seemed to require it.

"You say you're not shy," Joy accused, "and in most things I'd agree one hundred percent. But when it comes to Daron, everything is different." Saying it as a question instead of a statement, Joy added, "Maybe because how you feel about Daron is different?"

"I'm not shy, not ever," Maris insisted. "It's just that… Daron scares me a little. If I sleep with him, I know I'll be a goner." Putting her face in her hands, she groaned. "God, Joy, I'm already half in love with him."

Since Maris couldn't see her, Joy gave in to a smile. "I think that's wonderful."

Parting her fingers, Maris peeked out. "Do you, now? Well if that's true, why won't you admit you're falling in love yourself?"

Joy started to scoff, but paused as sensations thrummed to life. *Love.*

Was she?

No, she couldn't be. *Shouldn't* be. And yet…

"See what I mean?" Dropping her hands, Maris nodded. "Shakes your foundation, doesn't it? I don't know about you, but I can admit the idea makes my stomach hurt."

Yeah, Joy's stomach was starting to ache a little, too. "A fling was different enough for me."

"Tell me about it. I keep thinking of everything that could go wrong."

Automatically, before she could apply the logic to herself, Joy said, "But think of everything that could go right."

"Uh-huh." Skeptical, Maris asked, "Is that what you're doing?"

No. She was trying to reconcile herself to the fact that

she wasn't suave enough, or practical enough, to have an affair without getting emotionally involved.

But hey, this was Maris's time, so screw her own misgivings. She was here to boost her friend. "My situation is entirely different. I haven't known Royce that long, but you've been around Daron for years."

"Right. And you think that makes this any easier?" She fell silent, her eyes rounding and her jaw loosening. In an agonized whisper, she said, "Jesus, Joy, I've *watched him grow up.*"

"You did not!" That was too absurd not to laugh. "Daron came to the park as a legal and mature adult. You've watched him age a few years, but he was already a grown man." Joy laughed again at the silly argument.

"Stop that." Maris thunked her head on the tabletop. Twice. "He's only twenty-five."

"And you're only thirty-one, so stop groaning and get over the age thing already."

Ignoring that advice, Maris groaned. "I always thought he was just a handyman, that he'd eventually move on. Now I know he won't, and I don't plan to go anywhere—"

"Well, I would hope not," Joy said, startled by the idea that she could lose Maris. Or Daron for that matter. "We need to make a club rule right now—no quitters."

"Don't you get it, Joy? If I sleep with him and things don't work out, I'll still be looking at him, and probably lusting after him, for the rest of my life. We work together, for crying out loud. A day doesn't go by without us speaking to each other."

"Hmm. I see your point." At least in her own case, she and Royce didn't work together. Granted, it was a small enough town that they'd probably bump into each other now and then, but it'd be happenstance instead of a guaranteed daily occurrence. "That could definitely be uncomfortable, but I'm a big believer in honesty." *Yeah, right, then be honest about your feelings for Royce.* Joy shook that off. "I suggest you tell Daron about your concerns. Maybe he's more than ready to settle down."

"It's tragic irony that he's more settled than I am. Have you seen his house?"

Joy shook her head. She was friendly with Daron, but she'd never had any reason to see him away from the park.

"It's incredible. He's done all this work to update it and it's so...cozy. Like a real home should be. Clean and organized, but still friendly, you know?"

Knowing Daron, Joy could almost picture it. "A place to live, and a place to love?"

"It's not just a wall and floors under a roof. The man has a garden! And he's going to get chickens. And I'm..." Maris looked around at the camp store. "I'm just here, craving the security of my own home while saving every dime I can because houses cost money and debt terrifies me."

"Avoiding debt is smart." Before her emancipation from her family's wealth, Joy hadn't concerned herself with a budget of any kind. Once alone, though, that budget had taken up rent in her head and she'd fretted about it around the clock. How would she live, eat, care for the baby...?

Getting a job at Cooper's Charm that included use of the small apartment over the lodge had been a true godsend. Otherwise, where would she be? How would she and Jack have made it? She would never, ever take financial security for granted. For her, and for most other people, it was a constant concern.

Oddly pleased that she could relate to Maris's money worries, Joy prompted, "Will you tell me more about your childhood?"

"Why?"

Joy had one simple answer. "Because you're my friend and I care."

After giving it some thought, Maris shrugged. "Sure, why not?"

For the next half hour, she told Joy all about her mother's obsession with prayer for things rather than going after them herself, about her father's penchant for drinking up any money they got, the usual lack of clothes, heat and sometimes even food.

And she talked about her shame at being the neighborhood charity case, always looked at with scorn, pity or both.

"I left there as soon as I could and I haven't been back except to bury my parents." Pensive, Maris traced her fingertip around the top of her empty coffee cup. "You know what?"

The words were so softly spoken Joy worried. "What?"

"You can run away from a place, but not from what it made you feel."

Tears burned Joy's eyes. She hated that Maris was hurting, and that she was so strong she didn't lightly share that burden. "Will you promise me something?" Joy asked just as softly.

"Sure." Maris's smile flickered. "If it's something I can do, consider it done."

"Will you pretty please give Daron a chance? I know you told him about your background, but tell him how you feel about everything, okay?" In her heart, Joy knew they were right for each other. Maris just needed a nudge to let it happen.

"Hmm." Pursing her lips, Maris considered the request. And considered some more. Finally, looking Joy in the eyes, she said, "Tell you what." She stuck out her hand, as if to make a deal. "I will if you will."

CHAPTER TWELVE

I WILL IF you will.

Her promise to Maris kept replaying, over and over, in Joy's head. She had another two hours before she needed to leave to get Jack. Royce and Daron, now done with the treads, carried the tools and leftover supplies to the golf cart wagon so Daron could return them to the maintenance shed.

Knowing Royce would join her any minute, and why, had her pulse leaping and her skin tingling. She'd missed his touch. She'd especially missed his mouth.

Coop had a meeting, but Daron had volunteered to keep an eye on Chaos, and the dog now sat on the golf cart seat, panting in exuberance. From the top of her stairwell, Joy watched Royce walk around to the dog, give him a few strokes down his back, then cup his head and bend to say something to him.

Joy couldn't hear, but from the way Daron smiled the whole time, whatever Royce said must have been amusing. The dog certainly liked it; his whole furry body wiggled with his butt going opposite of his head and shoulders. He licked at Royce's face—and Royce allowed it, still speaking softly, still petting until the dog calmed again.

In such a short time Chaos looked prettier, with thicker fur, the wrap on his leg gone, and his belly full.

You could tell a lot about a man by the way he treated a stray dog. Royce's dedication to the animal was admirable.

What would he say if he knew much of her attraction to him had to do with how he'd interacted with her son and Chaos?

Joy grinned. Yes, Royce's appearance had first snagged her interest, and there was no denying he offered a very fine visual, but a troll's personality would have taken care of that in no time.

Royce was the total package, inside and out.

He spoke to Daron one last time, clapped him on the shoulder and then watched as Chaos rode away. The dog didn't look back, which seemed to satisfy Royce because he turned and headed up the stairs.

Stopping one step below her so that they were eye level, he leaned in and took her mouth in a quick kiss. "I need fifteen minutes to run home and shower, and get back here."

No way would she let him go. Joy caught a handful of his coat and said, "Or you could just shower here."

He stilled, his gaze suddenly intense, as if he saw things she hadn't said.

I will, if you will.

This one is for you, Maris. "Stay." Joy slid her hand inside his coat, feeling the warmth of his body beneath the thermal shirt. "Stay and I'll shower with you."

"Damn." Ever so lightly, his fingertips grazed her cheek. "Can't miss that, now can I?"

Until Joy heard his agreement, she hadn't acknowledged how much his answer meant to her. They both knew it was a step forward for him to be invited for a lengthier visit into her home. Others in the park would see them together and make assumptions. Daron for sure knew what they were about.

Joy didn't care, and apparently Royce didn't, either.

When he took her hand in his, it felt right. So very, very right.

He led her into the apartment. As Joy went about locking the door, she said, "It'll have to be a quick shower, because I'll need to pick up Jack at—"

His hands came around her, one open low on her stomach, the other cupping a breast while he nuzzled against the side of her neck.

"It's…it's a small shower," she whispered, barely able to speak with the way his thumb taunted her nipple through her sweatshirt.

"I'll fit." He nudged a solid erection against her backside, making her think he meant something other than the shower. "We'll just have to get really close."

They *were* getting closer, in more ways than one.

Leaning back against him, Joy gave herself over to his touch, closing her eyes and breathing deeply.

"Mmm," he murmured. "Maybe you can't wait." The hand on her stomach worked under her sweatshirt, and then into her leggings, pressing down over her mound.

Even though he'd just come in from the cold, his hand was warm, a little rough, his fingers firm as they moved over her, and then *in* her, wringing a soft moan from her throat.

So many sensations conspired against her: his mouth on her neck finding the most sensitive places to lick and suck, his big hand still kneading her breast and plying her nipple.

Lightly penetrating her, one fingertip gathered a rush of wet excitement and used it to tease her clit.

She bit her lip, braced her hands on his steely thighs and gasped for each and every breath.

"That's it," Royce murmured minutes later when she felt the release swelling within her. He readjusted his hold, wrapping his arm around her under her breasts for support.

His breath was soft near her ear, his tongue licking her skin, his fingers moving faster—

When she cried out, it embarrassed her but she couldn't do anything about it. He gathered her closer, crooning to her, encouraging her, until her legs trembled and she thought she might sink to the floor if he let her go.

"I've got you."

The soft words seemed to promise more beyond the current moment.

Or maybe that was just her being wishful.

She *did* want more. So much more. Going forward, she'd have to be careful not to pressure him.

Turning in his arms, Joy slumped against his broad chest, vaguely aware of him carrying his fingers to his mouth. Looking up, she saw his eyes close as he tasted her off his own hand.

Heart thundering, legs like noodles, she whispered his name.

His eyes opened, liquid black with desire, and he kissed her, not just any kiss but one that felt powerful and possessive.

Reaching between their bodies, Joy found his erection through his jeans. Abruptly he ended the kiss, stepping back to strip off his coat while staring at her. Next he removed his lace-up boots.

Coming to her senses, she hastened out of her coat, as well, and toed off her boots.

Royce grabbed her hand, and in no time at all, they were in the small shower, warm water cascading over them, Royce on his knees in front of her, until she came again.

By the time they got to the bed, she really was limp, sated from the fast back-to-back climaxes.

It was nice, because this time she didn't get lost in her own quest for release, which made it possible for her to watch his. The powerful way his shoulders bunched as he held himself over her, the flex of his upper body when he entered her.

The rich, almost painful pleasure that tightened his features when she gripped his ass and matched his thrusts.

No man could be more beautifully masculine than him, and watching him build to the pinnacle brought her there again, too. He drove into her one last time, pressed hard and deep and stayed that way, head tipped back, eyes squeezed closed, while he shuddered and growled out his release.

Joy kept moving against him, getting that last bit of stimulation that she needed for her final orgasm. Heaven. That's what it was.

Heaven with Royce.

Could it be that way for a lifetime?

ROYCE COULDN'T THINK of a time when he'd been this relaxed with, or this hyperaware of, a woman, of his own wants and needs, of the *rareness* in a moment.

Joy did that to him, draining away tensions, annihilating his plans…or more like realigning them to include her. Every moment with her felt special so that his instinct was to hold on to her, to not let go.

So far he'd been successful in fighting that inclination, but every time with her made it more difficult. And now, he didn't think he wanted to fight it. Not anymore.

He glanced at the clock, saw they only had half an hour left before she'd need to leave to pick up Jack, and he silently resented the narrow timeframe while also kissing her temple.

He should have been spent, but having Joy warm and soft against his side, one bare thigh over his, her hand toying with his chest hair, stirred him all over again.

Her mother's visit intruded on his thoughts, and he recalled how it had shaken her.

In so many ways he wanted to protect her.

Without a doubt he knew she'd reject that idea.

To him, to anyone who looked, she'd already proven herself to be a strong, resourceful, capable woman who could handle the world on her own terms.

Royce also knew that dealing with the outside world didn't take the same emotional toll that dealing with family did. Trying to inch his way into her confidences, he asked, "Have you called your mother yet?"

"Hmm?" Tracing idle circles on his chest, she whispered, "No. I'm not even sure that I will."

Avoidance? That didn't seem like Joy, which meant dealing with her mother was even harder for her than he'd imagined. "You don't think it's anything important?"

"She didn't call me to let me know Grams had passed. What could be more important than that?"

Good point. Her mother presented a rare form of insufferable detachment, and he should know since he'd lived with detachment for years.

But *nothing* like what Joy had suffered.

His mother had merely had other interests that took precedence. She hadn't deliberately snubbed him.

"Royce?" Joy twisted to look up at him, then tucked close again. "Do you have plans for dinner?"

"Not yet." Touched that she, too, wanted to spend more time together, he gave her a one-arm hug. "You and Jack want to go out for something? We haven't tried the pizza parlor yet, but I hear it's good."

"It is. They have incredible bread sticks." She flattened her hand against his abdomen. "But I was thinking you could eat here. With us."

As if kick-starting, his heart gave a hard thump before breaking into a gallop. How Joy posed the request was as important as the request itself. The timid way she hid against him proved that she was inviting him into her *life*, not just her home.

"Nothing fancy," she added, keeping her face down, "but I have enough pork chops, and I can easily make extra mashed potatoes."

"Thank you." To make sure she didn't retract the offer, he tugged her up on top of him and accepted. "I'd enjoy that."

Sprawled over him, her hair pouring over his shoulders, Joy smiled. "Really?"

He had to draw a slow breath before he could nod.

Her smile faded. "Is something wrong?"

"No, nothing," he promised quickly. God, she was beautiful, inside and out. Gentle, loving. Sometimes apprehensive. This had to be as unusual for her as it was for him.

One way to find out.

He threaded his fingers through the fall of her hair, letting it sift free in silky waves. "I feel like this means something." Waiting for a reaction, he cupped a hand over her cheek and watched her, wondering if she'd deny it or pretend she didn't understand.

Expression softening, Joy touched her nose to his, then gave him a sweet kiss. "Does that scare you?"

So, she didn't deny her intent to deepen their relationship. He liked that Joy was up front with him, and he understood why.

She had a lot at stake, most importantly Jack's wellbeing, which left no room for misunderstandings. Having dinner out, or even at his house, was different. Jack was away from his home. By inviting Royce to stay *here* for dinner, she took a risk on letting him further into their lives.

"Scare me? No." Actually, it felt like one hell of a gift. "A few days ago it might have." He coasted his hands down her back to her rounded bottom. He could die happy like this, Joy resting over him, his hands cuddling her sexy ass, her long hair tickling his chest. "You realize I'll have Chaos with me, right?" Joy kept her home neat and organized—and Chaos was anything but that. "You sure that's okay?"

Her smile twitched. "Chaos is also invited. Jack will be thrilled." But she wouldn't let him sideline her. "A few days ago, I wouldn't have invited you over because I was worried about Jack getting too close to you."

"I know."

"You do?"

"Sure." The care she gave Jack was an intrinsic part of her. "I was raised by a single mom, sort of."

Curious, she tilted her head. "What do you mean, sort of?"

Good question. "Mom wasn't like you."

"Like me how?" She folded her arms on his chest, clearly getting comfortable in her current position. "You said she was an artist?"

"Right, and she was wholly invested in her artwork. You know the distraction and disruption a boy can cause. Nana said I was well behaved, but I didn't have Jack's talent and it plagued my mother." He gave a short laugh. *Plagued*, now that he thought about it, was an apt word to articulate his mother's struggle. "She couldn't understand why I didn't see what she saw, how I overlooked details—details that Jack sees, by the way. That's how I recognized the artist in him."

"Not because you were an artist—but because your mother pointed out that you weren't?" She shook her head. "That's a little confusing."

It had been more so for him as a boy. He wanted to please his mother, but he could never remember all the little things she thought were obvious. Things like fingers on a hand, or branches on a tree.

Like many kids, he'd drawn people as stick figures. If he got two arms and two legs on a torso, he thought he'd done pretty darn good. Nana had agreed, but his mother had not.

"I think Mom assumed I'd be her little prodigy. Unfortunately, when she gave me paints, I stacked the tubes to build a fort. She gave me chalk and I rolled them across the floor, racing the red against the blue." Those memories both amused him and still made him a little sad. "She couldn't believe that her son would rather climb a tree than paint it."

"Where was your father?"

"He was never part of the picture. According to my mother, they had a brief fling that resulted in me. She never gave me his name, or any details beyond that. I assume he was an artist, as well, and honestly, one disappointed parent was enough."

Sympathy and understanding pinched Joy's brows, and the gold in her eyes eclipsed the green.

Royce loved her eyes. His mother would have loved them, too. No doubt they would have inspired her, they were so unique. If he had his mother's talent, he'd certainly paint them.

"Your mother told you she was disappointed?"

Joy probably couldn't imagine such a thing since she was, as he'd said, a different type of mother. "Not outright, but I could tell." Kids could *always* tell. "I didn't share her talent, and she didn't share my interests."

"Your interests?" Her curiosity sharpened. "Like what?"

"I did sports all through school." He rolled one shoulder. "Mom had no use for anything too physical, so that's where Nana came in. She rarely missed a game."

"Then I'm grateful that you had your grandmother." Joy pressed a lingering kiss to his chest, right where his heart would be. "You and your mother had a good relationship otherwise?"

"She wasn't cruel or anything, if that's what you mean. She was a dramatic, emotional, creative person…who got pregnant and had me, and did the best she could with her artist's soul." He smiled. "I remember sitting cross-legged on the floor in her studio when I was probably a year or so younger than Jack. She'd put a painting tarp beneath me so I could eat my cold cereal where she could see me. She knew I needed to be watched, but her painting was 'calling to her.'"

"Were *you* calling to her?"

"I don't remember, but if I was, I was probably asking to go outside." He looked up at the ceiling, remembering their small yard, the birds that visited one of their biggest trees, the dog two doors down that often barked... "God, she tried so hard to get me to paint, or work in clay, or even to color with crayons. I tried hard, too, but I mostly made a mess. My mother would look at my work, put the back of her hand to her forehead and lament my lack of talent. She did that a lot." He grinned, remembering. "Hell, she did everything with theatrical flair."

Joy touched the edge of his smile. "That's actually horribly sad."

Maybe. Royce didn't want to ruin their quiet time together, so he explained an upside to his youth. "Nana would step in and carry on as if I'd created a masterpiece."

"Go Nana."

Royce gave a short laugh. "She kept damn near everything I made."

"Like you kept Jack's picture?"

Yes, he'd remembered how good it felt to have his effort appreciated, but with Jack it was different, since the kid *did* have talent. "One day Jack will sell his art. I was just getting a leg up on other buyers."

Joy laughed softly, then asked, "How often did you see your grandmother?"

"She moved in with us when I was a baby. Nana said that my mother loved me too much to have me away from her, but that artists were flighty and not ideal for parenting. The 'flighty' part, she said, was our secret." Everything he remembered of his grandmother filled him with warmth. "She pretty much raised me, though my mother paid the bills."

"Your mother must have been very successful."

Royce nodded. "I used to be bitter about it. I loved her, but I resented her talent like she probably resented my lack.

Still, we made it work and then...then she got sick and required around-the-clock care."

"You put your own life on hold?"

Exactly how it had seemed. "There was no one else, definitely no one who would have understood her artistic bent. Now she's gone and..."

Laying her cheek against his chest, Joy whispered, "And you came here to be unencumbered'?"

Wishing he'd never said that to her, Royce rubbed his mouth. How could Joy ever be a burden? Wasn't possible. She brought laughter into his life, warmth and direction. All good emotions, with lots of sizzling physical need, too. Around her, he felt completely alive.

Somehow, without obvious effort, Joy had drawn him from his sad, burdened past and focused him squarely in the positive present.

When he didn't answer, she tentatively asked, "How long did she have dementia?"

"Years, with the last few being the worst. It's a disease that steadily steals from a person—memories, thoughts... the ability to function." God, he still hated thinking about it. "She started falling, each time causing more damage, until she ended up in a wheelchair—and hated it." He should have stopped there. He meant to, but the words flowed seemingly against his will. "Sometimes she hated me."

"Royce." Scooting up so she could look him in the eyes, Joy cupped her small soft hand to his jaw. "That can't be true."

"Honestly, I have no idea if it's true or not. The doctors told me that people with dementia react in different ways, some with rage, some going completely passive."

"Your mother raged?"

"I think she was understandably miserable." Saying it

aloud helped Royce believe it, to maybe start to understand it. "She had me late in life, and got the disease early. Before that, she'd been a strong person, doing as she pleased, when she pleased. Celebrated for her talent. Physically healthy, but steadily losing her independence and dignity."

Putting himself in her shoes, Royce could only imagine how he'd react. Anger might be the least of the emotions.

"I'm so sorry."

He lifted her palm to his mouth and pressed a kiss there. "She got to where she wouldn't eat, then to where she couldn't drink." His voice softened to a rasp. "She cursed me daily, but there wasn't anyone else. No other relatives. So I cared for her the best that I could."

"Because you're a good, kind person. And you were a good son." With her eyes growing misty, she said, "I'm sure it was the disease, not your mother, who said unkind things."

It wasn't easy to let Joy see him like this, a grown man baring his fucking hurt. He only told her now to explain the stupid way he'd started this relationship, the absurd boundaries he'd set.

Because now he wanted more. From her. *With* her.

It relieved him when Joy settled down against his chest again, no longer looking at him, quiet but still very much with him.

"Mom never forgot her painting." For some reason, stroking Joy's hair made it easier to talk. "I changed jobs so I could be with her more, and I made sure she always had her art supplies at hand."

"What did you do for a living?"

"Mobile sawmiller." He briefly explained that to her, and doing so made him miss it. He'd always enjoyed working with his hands, being outdoors and later repurposing the wood. "I took only the jobs I wanted, and since I worked on my own timetable I could arrange for the occasional caretaker to stay with Mom while I was away."

"Did she do well with the caretaker?"

He gave a short laugh. "She despised anyone I hired, no matter how kind or qualified, so before leaving for a job, I'd set her up in her studio, getting her wheelchair arranged just right with a canvas in front of her. It was best for the caregivers to be there in case of an emergency, but otherwise they'd leave her be and let her paint." He thought about that, again seeing his frail mother, lost to her own little world where only her painting existed. "There were times she could barely hold a brush, but her eye for color and light never faded. Her talent was a fundamental part of her, or so the doctor said. One day I'd like to show her work to Jack. It might inspire him."

"That would be nice," Joy replied softly, "but I thought she sold her art."

"She did. There were several galleries who bought her, and toward the end, before the disease worsened, her paintings had tripled in value." Even now, gallery owners asked about his personal collection. "Through the years she gave me different pieces for my birthday, Christmas. Sometimes just because." He couldn't bear to look at them right now, but neither would he part with them. Not ever.

"Really?" Excitement brought Joy to her elbows again. "What a special gift that would be. Can you tell me about some of the paintings?"

Why not? As the minutes ticked past, talking about his mother and her obsession became easier. "The tree I most enjoyed climbing? She painted me in it." A memory rekindled and he laughed. "Mother told me every day not to climb that tree, that I'd fall and break something, but I always did, anyway. I'd sit on this big branch and let my feet dangle. Sometimes I'd find a caterpillar in the leaves, or a bird would land nearby and I'd sit real still so I wouldn't scare it. That's what she painted. Me in torn jeans straddling a branch, my bare dirty feet dangling and a blue bird looking at me from a different branch."

Joy smiled. "I can't wait to see it."

He let out a breath. "Honestly, it's an amazing piece. You can almost feel the heat of the summer day when you look at it."

"What else?" Joy asked, and there was something in her eyes, a spark that turned them more gold than green.

Thinking about it, Royce said, "She did a massive painting of me at eight years old, sleeping on top of my covers. Another of my toy race cars lined up on a shelf. All you can see of me is my forearm, and a grubby little hand arranging the cars."

"Royce," Joy whispered, holding his face in both her hands. "Can't you see that your mother was trying to show you her love?"

Joy's tone arrested him, making him still. "What do you mean?"

"Your mother sounds very unique, but she noticed the same things about you that I see in Jack. His favorite toys mean more to me, because I know what they mean to him. When he's sleeping, he's so peaceful and sweet, my heart melts. And you in your favorite tree? The forbidden place you so often snuck off to?" Joy sniffed, her eyes glassy with emotion. "That's how she pictured you, happy and free, following your heart, doing what you enjoyed most."

The truth started to sink in. "Since I couldn't do what she enjoyed?"

Smile trembling, she nodded. "Yes."

Jesus. Suddenly he knew Joy was right. *How the hell had he missed it?*

His heart seemed to fill his chest and he ran a hand through his hair, giving it a slight tug. "That painting of me in the tree was one of the last she completed. Hell, I was a grown man when she did it, but it was still crazy accurate…"

"Right down to the dirty feet?"

Emotion squeezed a laugh from his constricted throat. "Yes. Being barefoot gave me better traction to climb."

Even ill and struggling, his mother had painted *him* when he was happiest. Why hadn't he realized it before?

No, she might not have shown her love in conventional ways, but she'd shared it in the way that was best known to her.

Through her art.

"You know," Royce said, ready to unearth the work, "I think I'll get out some of her smaller pieces to show Jack. Do you think he'd like that?"

"I know he would." Joy sat up and this time there was no hiding the tears in her eyes.

It sent emotion welling in him, too. He teased his fingers lightly up her arm, enjoying the warmth and silk of her skin. "Don't cry, babe."

Swallowing heavily, Joy dashed a hand over her eyes. "I'm not."

He sat up beside her. Voice a little too gruff, he said, "Thank you for listening." He kissed her shoulder. "And for seeing things I didn't."

"Sometimes when we're too close to a situation, the obvious is out of reach." She leaned into him, but only for a second, and then she stood, beautifully bare.

Too bad they were out of time.

As she reached for her panties, she shared a wobbly smile. "Dinner is at six."

A WEEK PASSED as quickly as a single day when you enjoyed every moment as much as Royce did.

With Chaos repeatedly tugging on his boot laces, pulling them loose as he growled and shook his head, Royce looked around at the park. After closing out the drive-in late last night, he should have been tired. Yet here he stood, just outside the supply building with Coop and Baxter, his shoulder braced against the metal wall.

He couldn't seem to stay away.

Being closer to Joy for any reason was worth less sleep. And besides, he enjoyed helping out the guys.

Over the past several days, the weather had decided to cooperate, warming up for the Halloween weekend. The temps had gradually climbed each day so that now, by late afternoon, they reached the lower sixties. The mornings were still cold, but with all the sunshine it wasn't too uncomfortable. No rain or sleet in the forecast.

Perfect, beautiful fall weather, at a perfect, beautiful location.

"The cover you made for the stairs looks great." Coop stacked a few more things on a wagon, then bent to scratch at Chaos's ear.

The dog reared back, wiggling butt in the air, and pounced on Coop's hand, grabbing his sleeve and tugging. Laughing, Coop freed his coat and stood again.

"I should have it finished up soon," Royce said. He'd worked on it nearly every day, and with Daron's help, they'd completed the majority of the project. Joy wouldn't have to worry about the elements causing problems on the steps this winter. A slanted roof protected the stairs from precipitation, and partially enclosed sides kept snow or sleet from blowing in.

"Speaking of Daron," Baxter said, "is he with Maris again?"

"That's where he's spent every free minute for the past week," Coop said with a grin. "Looks like he's finally worn her down."

"I'm happy for him," Baxter said. "But am I the only one to notice she's offering fewer cookies these days?"

Royce laughed. Either Maris was too busy to bake, or Daron ate her offerings before anyone else could get to them.

"Speaking of new developments..." Baxter lifted his brows at Royce.

Yeah, he'd spent some part of each day visiting Joy. It warmed him, remembering Jack's excitement the first night he'd shared their dinner.

Joy was a terrific cook, the atmosphere was relaxed and Jack had repeatedly beamed at him. Guests in the apartment, for any reason, rarely happened.

"No denials from me," Royce said. "You can probably expect to see me often."

"We appreciate you pitching in." Coop looked around at the busy park. "Halloween weekend is always huge."

"My pleasure." Literally. "Like Daron, I'm happy to have a reason to hang around."

"As if you need an excuse," Coop said.

Everyone knew Joy was enticement enough.

"And to think," Baxter said, "we all warned you off, saying she wouldn't be interested."

"Whatever you did, I approve." Coop stared out toward the lake. "She smiles more now."

Royce felt honored to be the first man Joy had shown interest in since having Jack. After that first dinner in her apartment, they'd just naturally fallen into a pattern.

On the first sunny day they'd hung out at the playground after school with Royce pushing Jack on the swing or standing ready to catch him while he climbed on the jungle gym. Joy stayed bundled up on the bench, drinking hot chocolate and taking lots of pictures with her phone.

Another day, he'd brought the food to them and they'd made use of the picnic table and the warmth of the sunshine down by the beach. They'd all worn coats and stocking hats, and they'd laughed a lot watching Chaos chase the water along the shoreline. After the meal, Jack had predictably used a stick to draw in the wet sand.

An artist, Royce well knew, utilized every opportunity. When Chaos ruined it with his paw prints, Jack just laughed and had an impromptu game of chase with the dog.

What really warmed Royce was the way Joy praised everything her son did, from how fast he ran, to questions he asked, to his gentleness with Chaos. She was just the most amazing mother, and though he'd never thought about that as an asset for a woman he dated, he had to admit he liked it a lot.

Twice that week, he and Joy had slipped away in the afternoon for some horizontal alone time. Royce would have been happier with twice *a day*, but he understood and accepted the limitations.

She'd already made numerous allowances for him, and based off what everyone had told him, that was an aberration of the best sort.

It felt good to be accepted, not at all the burden he'd thought a relationship would be. Total opposite, in fact.

"There's Daron now." Baxter nodded toward Maris's store.

From where they stood on a slight rise, they could just make out Daron's progress. It looked like he planned to jog past the pond, the lodge, numerous campsites and the playground.

If the trees were green instead of bare, they wouldn't have had such a clear view. On this particular Saturday, the park was already packed with RVs and fifth-wheel campers ready to celebrate Halloween. Women and men went all out decorating their areas with Halloween lights, signs, animated characters and more. Joy was already in the lodge, setting up the kid-friendly haunted house.

"Huh," Royce said, seeing Maris call out to Daron, which had him turning back. "Guess he forgot something."

They all grinned.

When Daron reached Maris, she spoke to him, then he grabbed her up and twirled her in a circle before kissing her with enthusiasm.

Baxter laughed. "He's relentless."

Coop grinned. "I'd say he's getting encouragement in that regard."

"Shame on you guys," said a female voice. "Clucking like a bunch of hens."

Royce turned to see Coop's wife, Phoenix, coming to them arm in arm with her pregnant sister, Ridley.

The two women had similar blue eyes, but very different personalities. Even while obviously pregnant, Ridley came off as innately sensual whereas Phoenix was all understated sweetness.

"Maybe they're jealous," Ridley said, giving Baxter a lazy smile. "Because they're old married men now."

"Who are you calling old?" Baxter scooped her up,

which made her squawk, and disappeared with her into the supply building.

Phoenix rolled her eyes. "Every time she provokes him, he uses it as an excuse to act like a newlywed."

Royce had a feeling that's why Ridley did it.

Sliding an arm around his wife, Coop asked, "Now who's jealous?"

Phoenix's cheeks warmed and her smile bloomed. "I have you, Cooper, so I have no reason, ever, to be jealous of anyone."

So in love, Royce thought, seeing the way Coop and Phoenix looked at each other, how openly they shared their affection.

Damn it, *he* might be the jealous one.

Then Phoenix said to him, "Ridley and I are going down to help Joy decorate."

"Looks like a big job. I'm sure she'll appreciate it."

"Maris wanted to help, too, but she can barely keep the coffeepots full, plus she's trying to stock up on cookies."

"Maris and Joy are close now," Royce said. "Almost like you and Ridley."

"They do act very sisterly," Phoenix agreed. "Except they get along better than Ridley and I do." She raised her voice. "Since my sister is always sneaking off to dark places with her husband."

"Mind your own business," Ridley shouted back.

They all heard Baxter laughing.

Wearing a grin, Phoenix shook her head. "I might as well head on down. See you guys later."

Coop gave her a quick kiss and hug, and seconds later Ridley came scurrying out, her hair a little mussed, one hand pressed to the small of her back, grouching as she hustled toward her sister, "Wait up, already. Pregnant lady waddling through."

Baxter reemerged, a smug smile in place. He yelled to his wife, "You don't waddle."

"Bite me!" she called back, making Baxter's smile widen.

Just then Daron joined them. He was more windblown than usual, his hat on crooked, his grin stretched from ear to ear. Whatever Maris had told him, Daron liked it. "Did I miss anything?"

Royce laughed. The three men were really nothing alike, except that they were each so obviously in love. Pretty sure he was headed in the same direction.

Kneeling, Royce wrestled his leather lace from the dog and noticed it was considerably shorter now. Apparently Chaos had won that particular battle.

He handed the dog a small rawhide chew from his pocket, and tied the laces the best he could.

Glad that he'd come by to help with the Halloween setup, Royce said, "There's never a dull moment here at the park." He lifted Chaos. "I like it."

"We know what you like," Baxter drawled. "And it isn't the fine scenery."

"True enough." Royce shrugged. "But the scenery is nice, too."

CHAPTER THIRTEEN

Joy was surprised when shortly before the haunted house would open Maris burst in. All around her, black lights blinked and gray gauze hung in atmospheric tatters.

As Maris made a beeline for Joy, darting around the yarn-web obstacle course, the hanging pool noodle maze and the tableful of creepy cupcakes, she did her best to hold a smile at bay.

The second their gazes met, Maris gave up. Grinning hugely, she grabbed Joy and pulled her toward the kitchen. "I need two minutes."

"I'll give you twenty." Which was exactly how long she had before she'd need to open the doors and welcome in the kids. Luckily, she had everything ready to go. "What's up? Why are you smiling like that?"

Furtive, Maris glanced around to ensure they were alone.

"No one's here," Joy assured her. "Ridley and Phoenix left a few minutes ago to get dressed in their costumes." The two women would help hand out snacks and supervise activities. "Jack is busy making a glow-in-the-dark ghoul." Joy had warned him not to make it too scary, but given the gleam in his eyes, she wasn't sure what to expect.

Maris sucked in a big breath, then blurted, "I've decided it's time for me to hold up my end of the bargain."

Joy didn't follow. "Your bargain for...?"

Flagging a hand between them, Maris reminded, "I will, if you will? Do you recall that promise? Well, you and Royce have been living it up all week—and don't deny it!"

"I wouldn't," Joy said, allowing her own smile. Normally she'd have given Maris a daily update, but with them both now in relationships, and all the activity at the park, they'd barely had time for chatting. "It's been wonderful. *He's* wonderful."

"I'm glad for you. And see? You've inspired me." Nodding to emphasize that, Maris said, "Tonight's the night. For Daron and me, I mean. Oh God, did I just say that out loud?" Bouncing on the balls of her feet, she shook her hands, her nervousness palpable. "Joy, I'm so anxious I'm about to go nuts."

Laughing, Joy said, "What? Why?"

"Daron is a terrible tease. He's had me on pins and needles all week. The man is diabolical with the way he kisses me, knowing it'll obliterate my concentration. How could I keep holding him off?"

"I'm surprised you've managed this long." Joy shook her head. She hadn't understood Maris's restraint, so how could Daron? "It's going to be wonderful, you'll see."

"But what if I suck?" Maris went still, her eyes widening. "Wait. Let me rephrase that. What if I'm lousy at this? I'm…" She threw up her hands. "I'm *worse* than a virgin, because I'm *thirty-one*."

"Let's put that on T-shirts," Joy said, holding up her fingers to make a square, as if to frame the saying. "'Worse Than a Virgin.' I like it. It's catchy."

Maris shoved her shoulder. "Be serious, will you?"

Laughing, Joy said, "Okay, okay. Here I am, dead serious." She tempered her smile, but only a little. "You, Maris Kennedy, are one of the strongest, most capable people I know. I admire that about you. So you aren't superexperienced? So what?"

"Daron *is* superexperienced."

"That doesn't mean he won't be nervous. Know what he's probably worried about? Disappointing you. After he's spent all this time winning you over, the stakes are higher than ever for him." Joy halted Maris's automatic denial with a raised palm. "I know what you're doing, Maris. You're used to attacking problems, but, hon, Daron isn't a problem."

"God," she groaned, covering her eyes. "He's the worst problem ever."

"Only because you care so much about him." When Maris lowered her hands, Joy cocked a brow. "You do, right?"

"I don't want to," Maris grumbled.

"But you do, anyway. Be brave and admit it."

"Only to you." Dropping back against the wall, eyes closed, Maris deliberately clunked her head. Twice.

Joy waited.

Peeking one eye open, Maris asked, "Any advice?" Her mouth twisted. "I mean, since you appear to be happily burning up the sheets with Royce and all that."

SISTERS OF SUMMER'S END   265

"As a matter of fact..." Joy leaned into the doorway to make sure Jack was still in his seat.

He wasn't, and her heart almost stopped, especially when she saw the open door. "Jack!" Already striding out of the kitchen, she called his name again. *"Jack."*

He stepped into the doorway. "Mr. Nakirk is here, Mom."

Joy strode over to him, each step echoed by the hammering of her heart. "Jack Lee, you know better than to open that door without me."

Royce stepped in. "My fault. I poked my head in, saw you were, um—" he glanced at Maris, who had stepped up to her side "—busy talking and decided to wait a few minutes more. But Jack saw me."

That didn't matter. "Under *no* circumstances," Joy stressed, "is he to open that door without asking me first." Strangers filled the park. That was bad enough, but add in the visits from her mother and her worry was totally legit.

Embarrassed, Jack cast a glance at Royce, then at Maris, before ducking his face in shame. Voice small, he whispered, "Sorry, Mom."

Damn it, now she'd hurt her son's feelings. Hand to her forehead, she turned to Maris. "I need—"

"Totally get it. I need to head back to the diner, anyway."

"No!" She didn't want to let Maris down. "I only need one minute. Wait. Please."

As if to console her, Maris patted her shoulder. "Okay, sure."

With a hundred awful scenarios winging through her head, Joy knelt down. "Jack, honey. I need you to know how dangerous it could be to—"

"I saw Mr. Nakirk, Mom," he said, his voice subdued but stubborn. "I knew it was him."

"I know. And I understand why that seemed perfectly

fine to you. Can you also understand why I would worry? I didn't see you, so I didn't know you were with him. All I knew was that my son wasn't where he should be." Her heart continued to gallop.

"I answered soon as you called me."

Mouth firming, Joy drew back. "We've talked about this before, Jack. With so many people coming and going, I need to know where you are. *Always*. No exceptions. No excuses."

Shoulders hunched, he nodded.

Joy stroked back his hair. "Tell me you understand, Jack."

"I understand."

"Jack." She lifted his chin. "I need your promise, honey."

He cast another look toward Royce.

Royce surprised her by putting his hand on Jack's shoulder. "I don't want your mom to worry, so I'm going to promise, too."

Wide-eyed, Jack looked up at him. "You are?"

"Absolutely. I should have told her right away that you were with me. I was thoughtless and for that I'm sorry." His gaze shifted to Joy. "I promise, in the future, I will always let you know."

Awed, Jack nodded. "Me, too. I promise, Mom."

Royce patted his shoulder. "We don't want to upset her, do we?"

Slipping his arms around her neck, Jack squeezed her. "Sorry, Mom. I promise I won't worry you again."

A lump of emotion clogged her throat. Joy seriously doubted Jack could keep that promise, but for now, it was good enough. She returned his hug while smiling at Royce. She silently mouthed, *Thank you.*

He nodded, then helped her up. "How about Jack shows

me around the haunted house while you and Maris finish your conversation?"

Without waiting for her permission, Jack slipped his hand into Royce's. "We have peeled grapes in gelatin," he said in excitement. "They feel like eyeballs! And gummy worms in crushed cookies that look like dirt, and…"

His chattering voice faded as he dragged Royce to the food section.

Joy stared after them, seeing more than just her son with Royce. She saw a future, she saw a family. She saw…love.

Until Maris slipped her arm around her. Dry with irony, Maris said, "Yeah, no one will ever guess how you feel."

Oh Lord. She'd been gazing after them like a lovesick fool.

"Come on," Maris said, urging her along. "I need to get back to the diner, and you need to get it together because a slew of costumed kids are arriving in three, two, one…"

"I'm sorry," Joy said. "I just—"

"Panicked. Big-time. I know. Totally understandable." In the kitchen, Maris grabbed a cup of punch and pressed it into Joy's hand. "I don't suppose you have anything good to slip in that?"

Joy laughed, knowing neither of them would spike a drink while responsible for entertaining children. "Sadly, no." She sipped, then set the cup aside. "I'm fine now, so let's get back to you and Daron."

"Advice. Right." Maris braced herself. "Quick, lay it on me."

"I already told you this once. Trust Daron. Tell him your concerns and everything will be fine."

"Yeah, sure." Maris scrunched up her face. "How would that conversation go? *Sorry, Daron, but I'm clueless so you have to do all the work.*" She rolled her eyes. "I don't want to look that dumb."

"You mean inferior, and that's just silly because you won't." Knowing she was out of time, Joy took her hands. "I can promise you, Daron won't be judging you, and you won't be judging him. Just enjoy yourself."

"Okay." Maris puffed up. "Enjoyment. Should be a piece of cake."

It would be, if Maris stopped overanalyzing it. That wasn't likely to happen, unless… "Best advice? Get Daron naked first."

Maris's eyes flared wide. "Okay, I'm with you so far."

"Once he's naked, you'll have the upper hand, right? Start with that and then improvise as you go along."

"See, this is why I came to you." Maris offered her a high five. "I think I'll nominate you as prez of our club."

"Only if we get to wear the Worse Than a Virgin shirts."

They were both still laughing when Phoenix and Ridley slipped in. Phoenix made a beautiful fairy, and Ridley made a nicely rounded jack-o'-lantern.

Royce ducked and darted through the hanging pool noodles, a laughing Jack slung over his shoulder.

These people, Joy thought, looking at each of them. Oh, these wonderful, friendly, warm people.

She adored them all so much.

As she headed in to get the party started, she said to Maris, "Soon as you can tomorrow, I want to know how it went."

"Guaranteed." Maris shrugged. "You're the only one I have to tell."

If things progressed as Joy suspected they would, Maris would soon have Daron as a confidant, too. But for now, Joy relished that singular closeness.

She faced the room, and announced, "Let them in. We're ready!"

Maris paused in his kitchen, looking uncharacteristically timid. Daron wondered at it—and then an awesome, incredible, boner-inspiring thought occurred.

Maybe she was ready to put him out of his misery.

The second he thought it, he couldn't unthink it, and it probably showed in the hot way he looked at her. It felt like he'd wanted her forever, and in fact, it had been years.

Earlier at the park she'd initiated their public display, which indicated she was ready to accept their relationship, instead of still denying him. He'd been plenty pleased by that, but this? The chance for more?

His heart started pumping hard. "Maris?"

She took off her corduroy coat—a coat that had to be a decade old—and laid it over a stool at the island. "One of these days Joy and I are going to shop together and grab lunch. I'll probably get a new coat." She wrinkled her nose. "The thing is, I've never been shopping with another woman. Never turned it into an adventure, you know? Joy assures me it'll be fun."

"I'm sure she's right." Daron did his utmost to look casual, while fighting the urge to kiss her.

After shoving her phone into the back pocket of her jeans, Maris put her purse on top. Nothing unusual in that since the stool had become her unofficial coat and purse tree over the past week.

Shifting, she asked, "Do you feel bad that we're not at the drive-in supporting Royce on his last night?"

"Not even a little." Not if it meant he'd finally get to have Maris. He took a few steps toward her, unable to pull his gaze from her eyes. "You seem different." He cleared the gravelly lust from his throat. "Want to tell me what's up?"

"Besides you?" she asked, nodding at the erection behind the zipper of his jeans.

Without hesitation, he said, "Yeah, besides me." He wouldn't deny wanting her, wouldn't deny he reacted strongly to her.

She'd moved near enough to touch, so Daron drifted his fingertips over her cheek. Because she still looked nervous, he teased, "Want to make out?"

Maris nodded. "Yes." Yet when he reached for her, she held him off and said, "Get naked."

Trying to reconcile what she'd said and what she really wanted, Daron blinked. He rubbed his mouth, at a loss, then looked around at his house. They stood halfway between the kitchen and the dining room. "Here?"

Her mouth twitched. "Just like that? I ask and you'll do it?"

"Pretty sure there isn't anything I wouldn't do for you, Maris."

She sucked in a breath. "Wow. Way to make me feel powerful."

He couldn't stop touching her skin. Maris was so soft and warm he was dying to feel her all over. "I'd rather make you feel hot."

"Yeah, okay." She snagged his hand and dragged him down the hallway to his bedroom. "You can strip in here." She put her phone on the nightstand, sat down on the side of the mattress and gestured. "Go ahead."

It was all Daron could do not to laugh. No one would accuse him of being modest, but he'd never stripped on command before.

"Whatever the lady wants." Toeing off his shoes, he pushed them aside, then bent and tugged off his socks. Probably going a little too fast—which he'd blame on burning lust—he straightened and peeled his sweatshirt off over his head.

Licking her lips, Maris nodded her approval. "You're gorgeous."

"You've seen me without my shirt before."

"Often," she replied. "You like to flaunt your bod all over the place."

"Er..." That sounded like a complaint. "You realize we work at a casual resort and it gets hot in the summer, right?"

She snorted. "You wouldn't pare down so often if you didn't look so damn good."

He looked *so damn good*? Nice.

Appreciating her assessment, Daron brought his hands to the snap of his jeans.

"Wait!"

If he didn't let his dick free soon, it'd break the zipper.

Maris pretended to grasp the air with her hands. "Lemme."

"You want to open my pants?"

She nodded fast. "Yup. Bring your sexy self over here."

"Yeah, all right." Crazy that *he* now felt uncertain. "Go easy, though, okay? I don't want to—" Her small hand squeezed him through the denim and he sucked in a breath...that ended with a broken groan as her small, strong hand worked over him. Through his teeth, he said, "That's probably not a good idea."

"Let's find out." By slow degrees, she eased down the zipper, making it a form of torturous foreplay. Once the jeans were opened, she wedged her hand inside to stroke him again, this time with only his boxers in the way.

Every muscle in his body clenched. "You're killing me, babe."

"Killing myself a little, too," she murmured, then she surprised him by leaning in and brushing her nose over the line of hair leading down from his navel. "Mmm, you smell good."

Daron put his head back and concentrated on control. Wasn't easy, not with Maris's breath on his stomach, her lips on his hip, all while her fingers toyed with his erection.

Abruptly releasing him, she said, "Off with the rest."

The husky note in her voice pleased him. Hoping to get things going, Daron shoved out of his jeans and boxers as fast as he could, all the while watching Maris.

Her delicate nostrils flared and color bloomed on her cheeks. "You're big."

"Average actually."

"No," Maris whispered, the words strained. "There's nothing average about you."

"Tell you what." He leaned in to take her elbows and gently tugged her to her feet. "Let's even things up a bit, okay?"

Swallowing audibly, she nodded. "Fair warning—I haven't done this in a really long time."

Daron wondered *how* long. Since he'd known her, Maris had never dated or even hinted interest in a guy. She'd broken that long dry spell with him and he was determined to ensure she enjoyed every second.

"It'll be fine," he promised, while dipping down to her throat, trailing his lips over her skin, up to her jaw and to the delicate shell of her ear. In the barest-there whisper, he breathed, "Leave everything to me."

"Joy was right," she gasped.

Um… Daron paused, pulling back to see her. "Right about what?"

"This is easier with you naked. She promised it would be."

Yeah, that didn't make a bit of sense, but at the moment Daron didn't care enough to ask her to explain. Instead, he returned to her throat again, opening his mouth against her just the way he knew she liked it. On her own, she stepped up against him, her hands going to his bare back.

Within a single minute, she frantically touched him everywhere, up to his shoulders, down his spine to his ass. Taking that as an invitation, Daron reciprocated, and soon they were both breathing hard and fast.

He fingered the hem of her thick sweatshirt. "Let's get this off, okay?"

Nodding, she tried to wrestle out of it, but got it twisted up with the T-shirt she wore underneath.

"Let me help." He eased each arm out first, then pulled it and her T-shirt up and over her head, leaving her with frazzled hair, a deep blush and a plain bra.

He was busy taking her in, loving the curves of her body, when Maris thrust up her chin. "I don't own any lingerie."

Pulling his gaze from her sweet body to her face, he smiled. "If you think this—" he gestured at her bare skin "—isn't sexy as hell, you're wrong."

She looked down at her beige bra and quirked a disbelieving brow.

"It's you, Maris." Clearly she didn't get how madly in love he was. "I don't care what your bra looks like, as long as you're willing to take it off."

Humor, and relief, curved her mouth. "You're the hot shot. You get it off me."

"Yes, ma'am." Reaching out, he opened the front closure with a flick of his fingers.

"Wow." She blinked down at her bra. "You are good."

He wanted to give a joking reply, but couldn't manage it. Gently, he parted the cups and revealed her bare breasts.

Beautiful. He'd always assumed the tawny glow of her

skin was sunshine, but now he knew she carried that subtle glow everywhere.

And it made him nuts.

He brushed the bra straps off her shoulders and pulled her up against him for a kiss meant to rattle her as much as she'd rattled him. He coaxed her lips to part, licked over the edge of her teeth, then deeper into her mouth, feeling both possessive and starved for more.

When she tangled her fingers in his hair, Daron slipped his hands down to open the snap of her hip-hugging jeans. He pushed them down to her knees at the same time he eased her onto the bed. His heart thundered and any finesse he possessed abandoned him.

This was Maris, and he'd finally have her.

Even while she struggled to kick her jeans off the rest of the way, he couldn't stop kissing her. Her tongue played against his, her breasts pressed to his chest as she wiggled and contorted—and then finally they were both naked.

Daron was so hard that he actually hurt with need, but he also wanted to taste her all over—and did.

Encouraging him with little gasps and mewls and soft moans, Maris relished his mouth on her breasts, arching when he drew on her nipples. When he slipped his fingers between her thighs, over her sex, then in her, she clutched at him and rocked her hips.

"Daron," she gasped.

She was so tight, as tight as a virgin, and he nearly lost it.

Against her stomach, he murmured, "I have a rubber."

"Good." Her hold on his hair was almost painful.

He left her long enough to grab the protection from the nightstand drawer and roll it on. Maris hadn't moved a muscle, but her dark eyes tracked him.

The second he finished, she held out her arms to him.

He went to her, and she feasted on his mouth as Daron struggled to rein himself in. When she hooked a leg over his hips, he lost the battle and reached down between them to guide himself in.

Eyes heavy and hair tangled, Maris bit her lip.

"Easy," Daron whispered, pressing into her in slow degrees.

She breathed harder, hooked her other leg around him and lifted her hips to take all of him.

They both groaned. Undone by her urgency, Daron put his forehead to hers. "Christ, you're tight."

"And you're big."

He choked on a laugh. If she wanted to think that, he wouldn't debate it with her. No, he was too busy concentrating on giving her a few moments to adjust.

"Daron?"

At her husky whisper, he lifted his head and met her smoldering gaze.

She kissed him and said, *"Move."*

God, he loved her bossy ways. "Yes, ma'am." He stared into her eyes as he began slowly thrusting.

Her heels pressed into his back, her fingertips dug into his shoulders and she squeezed his cock while making those low, sexy sounds.

They moved together, the rhythm accelerating, him going deeper, her squeezing harder.

When he knew he was losing the battle to hold back, he scooped a hand under her bottom, tilted her up—and she cried out a long, charged, ragged release.

Yup, that did him in.

Daron let himself go, loving the moment, loving *her*.

And hoping like hell he could turn it into forever.

MARIS SHIFTED ON the bed, her skin finally cooling, her heartbeat slowing.

The tingling sensations remained, almost as if little sparks continued to ignite in select places.

She was pretty sure that was as good as sex could get, because she didn't think she could survive anything more intense.

Daron had rolled to her side, but kept her close, one leg resting over hers, his fingers idly combing through her hair.

What now? She should probably open her eyes.

Should she also ask him to take her home?

"Stay with me," he whispered.

Startled that he seemed to have read her mind, Maris turned her head and whispered back, "What?"

"Stay the night." His hand coasted down to cup around her breast, his thumb idly playing over her nipple—and making her squirm. "Stay."

Coming up on an elbow, she looked around. Their clothes were scattered over the floor and the blankets were off the foot of the bed.

Daron was wonderfully naked, and every inch of him was enough to fill a lifetime of fantasies.

"Do you need to do something with that?" She nodded at his now flagging penis and the spent rubber.

"Yeah, I do." He stared into her eyes, his gaze probing. "Will you stay?"

The thought of getting dressed and going back out in the cold didn't appeal to her at all, whereas the idea of sleeping with Daron...yeah, that definitely enticed. "I've never stayed the night with anyone."

"Then show me I'm special and stay."

He *was* special. Why was she still fighting it? Stubbornness, probably.

"What if I snore?"

"It'll be adorable."

Snorting over that nonsense, she warned, "I'll need to be at the store early."

A wide grin made him even more handsome. "No problem." He bounded up from the bed, gave her a firm, quick kiss and headed for the bathroom.

"I don't have a toothbrush," she called after him, a little flustered at how quickly they'd moved from sex to an overnight visit.

Bare-assed and not the least bit reticent, he said, "Feel free to use mine."

Dropping back to the mattress, Maris laughed. A second later she decided she wanted a quick shower.

It turned into a long shower...because Daron joined her.

Then they were both hungry so they ate PB&J sandwiches on the couch while watching an old horror movie. She did use his toothbrush, and he helped her straighten the blankets before they both got into the bed.

Before Daron could reach for her, Maris grabbed her phone.

Brows lifting, Daron asked, "Everything okay?"

"Yup. I just need a second." Pulling up Joy in her contacts, she texted, He sealed the deal.

She knew Joy was at the drive-in still, so she didn't expect a reply—

What deal are we talking about?

Grinning, Maris replied, Followed your advice & I'm officially hooked.

Yay! Knew you would be. ☺

Yes, Joy had been quite certain. Staying the night but will let you know when I'm home. ☺ Details tomorrow.

Joy replied with Whoo hoo! Can't wait.

Funny, because Maris couldn't wait, either. It was such a novel thing to have someone close to share her excitement, to celebrate with her, to talk about the most private parts of her life.

She hesitated, swallowed nervously…but it felt right, so she texted, Luv ya.

There was a pause, then three hearts came across the screen, followed by, Luv u, too!

When Maris grinned, Daron asked, "Should I be jealous?"

"If you want to be jealous of Joy, sure. Knock yourself out."

"You're texting Joy…now?"

She set the phone on the nightstand and turned toward him. Oh, but he looked incredibly delicious. How had she resisted him for so long?

Teasing, Maris said, "We tell each other *everything*."

"Is that right?" Tugging the blankets away again, Daron loomed over her. "Guess I better make sure it's all bragging without any complaints."

Maris was about to assure him—but then his mouth was on hers, his hands on her body, and she decided to let him have his way.

AFTER THE BACK-TO-BACK Halloween kid movies ended, Royce breathed a sigh of…relief? They'd wrapped up with a bang, a full lot and a great many happy customers. He'd lost track of the popcorns and hot dogs they'd sold, and the candy counter was now almost empty.

He had big plans for the off-season, and for reopening

in the spring, but for now, he'd get some downtime—which meant more opportunity to further his relationship with Joy.

He was in the back, wrapping up a few things, when through the open doorway he saw them come into the concession stand.

Jack slumped against his mother's hip, looking more asleep than awake. Two nights of movies was clearly throwing him off his schedule, especially after the earlier Halloween festivities in the park.

Jack and Joy, along with most of the families, had segued directly to his drive-in. More than a few of the kids still wore their costumes.

Jack had changed into sweats; Royce suspected he'd be sleeping in them. He thought of Joy trying to get a sluggish five-year-old up the outside steps and to his bed, and more than anything, Royce wished he could be there to help. He liked the idea of carrying Jack up and tucking him in.

He especially liked the idea of being alone with Joy afterward.

"I'll be right there," he told her.

"We were just going to say goodbye." She steered Jack one step toward the door.

"Hold up. I only need a minute."

Joy smiled. "All right, if you're sure we're not interrupting."

"Never." Even while Royce had fought it, even while *she'd* fought it, both Joy and Jack had become priorities for him in a very short time.

Earlier today, when he'd slung Jack over his shoulder and the kid had called him Mr. Nakirk...that was the moment Royce knew he needed the formalities to end.

Jack was more important to him than that, and he wanted to be more important to him, too.

Since he hoped Joy would take down the barriers, he'd start encouraging her tonight.

Headlights repeatedly flashed against the windows of the concession as cars pulled away from the theater. Only one of his employees remained. Cindi, who'd just turned twenty, had proven herself more than capable of locking down the premises.

Giving her a set of keys for the cases, Royce said, "I'll be right back."

"Take your time. I can handle this."

"Thanks." Royce walked over to where Joy and Jack waited by the door. Joy had to be tired, too, and here he was, keeping her out. "Thanks for coming in." He lifted Jack so the little boy could rest against his shoulder, then took Joy's hand. "Come on."

"Where are we going?"

"I want to tell you something." *And I'm dying to kiss you.*

Her smile flickered with curiosity. "Okay, but it will have to be quick. Jack needs his bed."

Around a huge yawn, Jack said, "I'm not tired."

"Well," Joy teased, "I am."

As he led them to the back room, Royce asked, "The haunted house was a success?"

"Some girl spilled the food," Jack voluntarily mumbled. "Then a boy fell and ripped his costume and cried for, like, *forever.*"

Joy smoothed his hair. "Ridley got a headache and Phoenix walked her home early, but it was fun."

Royce laughed. "Sounds like a rockin' good time."

"Yeah," Jack said, his head lolling.

He knew the second Jack nodded off, his little body going boneless against him.

"Uh-oh," Joy said. "He's out. Now you'll have to carry him to my car."

"Not a problem." Royce leaned his cheek against Jack's crown, giving him a small hug. How would Joy get him up to bed? Hopefully she wouldn't try to carry him.

"You're good with him," she said, her voice softer than he'd ever heard it.

Leaning forward, Royce pressed his mouth to hers in a brief but tender caress. As he drew back, he said, "About Jack…" Unsure how to lead into the topic, he hesitated.

The gentleness left her, and her eyes turned wary. "What about him?"

Disliking that look, the one that said she still didn't completely trust him, Royce stated, "I'd like Jack to call me by name."

"You—" Joy blinked, the wariness replaced by surprise. "You want him to call you Royce?"

"He talks about Coop and Baxter, Phoenix and Ridley, Daron and Maris… I'm the only *Mr.* in the group and—" he sounded like a kid himself, complaining about being left out. But what the hell? Left out was exactly how he felt "—I want to be part of that group. His group. I am, right? So the Mr. thing has to go."

He saw it in her expression, the knowledge that this was another big step, a signal that they were getting serious.

He was here for the long haul.

"This area is now my home," Royce explained. "I don't want to feel like an outsider." Shit, that sounded lame. "Especially not with you or Jack."

A smile flickered over her lips, one of happiness, maybe understanding. "You're right, of course. I'm sorry I hadn't thought of it before now."

Jack surprised them both by mumbling, "I wanna call him Royce, too. He's my friend."

They both looked at him, at his angelic little face that showed no signs of being awake.

"Are you faking?" Royce asked, rubbing his hand up and down Jack's narrow back.

No answer. Jack just snuggled in and let out a sigh.

The grin caught Royce by surprise, and without thinking about it, he gave Jack another slight hug. "Will you be able to get him up to bed?"

"He cooperates." Joy watched him with a soft expression he couldn't quite read, but enjoyed all the same. "Like a little sleepwalker, he puts one foot in front of the other and I just steer. Brushing his teeth is out, though. He cleaned them the best he could in the car with a bottle of water and a travel toothbrush."

Damn. Again, she surprised him. "You planned for everything, didn't you?" And here he'd thought he had a lot of details on his mind.

"I've been bringing Jack to the drive-in for Halloween since he was two. We've learned a few shortcuts."

Royce tangled his free hand in her hair. "You should win Mom of the Year."

With a husky laugh, she said, "Right along with every other mother who's doing the best she can." She stepped into him, tilting up to kiss him one more time before saying, "It's past time for us to go."

Royce would have a few minutes more before he could lock up the drive-in, but he carried Jack out and got him buckled in his booster seat in the back. By then, everyone else had left the lot and the screen was dark.

A cool breeze stirred the night air.

Tonight, with Joy, it felt like possibilities.

"Want to get together tomorrow?" So that she wouldn't think he meant only for sex—though he'd certainly be there in a hot minute if she wanted him to—Royce added, "I'm free whenever. We could do dinner again. My house or yours, or I could take you and Jack out." He wanted time with her. Hell, he needed it.

Joy touched his arm. "Hopefully we'll all sleep in a little, and then I need to take down the haunted house and get the rec center in order. I'm free after that, though. Oh, and Monday I have…errands. So after tomorrow, it'll probably be Tuesday before I'm available again."

It hit Royce that he didn't know what Joy did in the off-season. He'd been so wrapped up in his own business, his own needs, he hadn't thought to ask.

"Tuesday," he said. "When Jack's in school, you and I should talk."

Solemn, she nodded. "Agreed."

"Tomorrow, though, I'll help you with the cleanup."

"Royce—"

He touched a fingertip to her mouth. "I want to." He wanted to be with her, regardless of what they did.

For a moment, she simply stared at him, those green-gold eyes hiding all sorts of secrets. Then she smiled and nodded.

Accepting him. Accepting *them*.

Another step forward. At this rate, he'd have their relationship settled in no time.

CHAPTER FOURTEEN

TINTED FLOOR-TO-CEILING windows softened the afternoon sunshine of a blustery but bright Monday. Inside the conference room, the overall mood was edgy and grim. Joy didn't care. She wouldn't allow herself to care.

Spine straight, shoulders back, she sat in a leather chair facing the attorney at the end of a long teakwood table. Her mother and father flanked her, her father's posture guarded but not unfriendly. Her mother's, however, screamed of disapproval.

I expected nothing else, Joy reminded herself. *What she thinks no longer matters. It hasn't mattered for six. Long. Years.*

Ms. Barbara Wickham, a very nice woman in her mid-sixties, went over details about little divisions of property, photos, jewelry and furnishings. The bulk, of course, went to Joy's father as Grams's only child, but she did bequeath respectable settlements to dear friends, her caretaker and her house staff. A few keepsakes would go to Joy, and the kindness of the gesture touched her. One of the items was a whimsical glass elephant that Joy had often admired as a child. That Grams remembered meant the world to her

Unfortunately, since her grandmother's estate was sizable, it took quite a bit of time to cover everything and Joy began watching the clock. At this rate, she'd be cutting it close to get back on time to get Jack from school.

Before the attorney could finish going over a few other details, her mother's clipped voice interrupted. "I want to know your intentions."

Ms. Wickham paused and glanced at her, a frown in place.

But of course Cara Reed wasn't speaking to the attorney. Her icy gaze was leveled on Joy.

Sighing, Joy pretended her mother wasn't there. *Not an easy feat.* She had a limited amount of time to get this done and still get back in time to pick up Jack from school. Arguing with, debating or even acknowledging her mother's eternal animosity wasn't worth the effort, or the wasted time.

Cara Vivien Reed wasn't easily deterred. Never had been. Once, so very long ago, Joy had admired that about her mother, how she would stick to her principles no matter what.

Now Joy had a difficult time even thinking of the stubbornness as a principle of any sort.

Flattening a hand on the table, her mother said low, "What do you plan to do, Joy? And who was that man with you at the trailer park?"

"RV resort," Joy corrected, before she could stop herself. Damn it, why did she let her mother provoke her? But even as she thought it, she added, "You disowned me, remember? My plans, my life, are my own."

Her mother straightened in a snap, creases forming at either side of her mouth. "Disowned means you don't inherit."

Joy nodded at the attorney. "If that's so, I have no idea why I'm here." Honestly, she was more curious than anything else. She'd already heard the phenomenal assets bequeathed to her parents, who were already wealthy. Now they were more so. The numbers hadn't fazed them, and they meant absolutely nothing to Joy.

"Family dissension," Ms. Wickham stated, "may or may not be an influence. So if I may continue?"

Whoa. Score one for strong women. Joy barely suppressed a smile at the attorney's calm and professional tone. "Yes, please do."

"Wait." Her father shifted.

Joy felt him staring at her, and though she didn't trust her own judgment, she thought his gaze felt…concerned.

For her mother, or for Joy?

It was impossible to tell.

Her father had always deferred to her mother. No, he'd never been unkind to her. Just the opposite.

But she remembered him as often busy, involved in travel, and for the most part he'd left the parenting decisions to her mother. Joy loved him, yet she'd never shared a special bond of any sort.

Voice gruff, he said, "I have a question, if I may."

After a brief hesitation, the attorney deferred to Joy. "Ms. Lee?"

She really wanted to get this over with, but couldn't remain immune to the expression on her father's face and in his eyes.

Eyes that, she realized, had aged a lot in the years she'd been gone.

"If you have the time, Ms. Wickham, then I can also spare an extra minute or two." Joy almost winced; she'd sounded as cutting as her mother. Softening her tone, she said, "Go on, Daddy."

Her father's mouth firmed, not in anger but almost as if he was suppressing strong emotion. "How are you?"

Oh. Oh, that's what he wanted to ask? The inquiry sounded so genuine Joy's heart began to thaw. Not a good thing under the circumstances. She needed to keep up her guard.

She needed to end this bitter reunion as quickly as possible, before she crumpled.

Leaning forward, her father said, "Tell me, honey. How have you been? Are you well?"

"I am, yes," she said slowly, touched by the warmth in his gaze. "I'm doing quite well."

He studied her face for only a moment, and his mouth softened. Sitting back, he said, "Good. I so often wondered…"

Her mother cleared her throat. Loudly. *"Wallace—"*

With a single look he shut her down. "We're here for a reason, Cara. Allow me to get to it."

For a reason? An inheritance, only that and nothing more, Joy reminded herself.

So why did it suddenly feel like more?

The urge to run had her breathing faster, yet pride kept her in her seat.

He smiled at Joy. Toying with a pen on the table, he asked, "How did you…?" He clutched the pen. "Joy, honey, how did you…?" Again he faded out. "I see your necklace is gone."

The necklace? Joy's fingers automatically reached to her throat, then fell away because there was nothing there to touch. Not for years had she thought about the gift given to her on her thirteenth birthday. A gift she'd cherished for so very long.

All of the jewelry she'd parted with had gone to a greater cause than sentiment. Namely: survival. "I sold it, along with the rest of my jewelry. Is that what you're asking?"

"Sold?" he repeated with a stricken expression.

"Pawned actually." Talking about it dredged up the desperation she'd felt back then. It shored up her resolve…and sharpened her tone. "I learned all about pawning jewelry for cash."

"Dear God," her mother whispered, equal parts horrified and dismayed.

Her dad looked so old suddenly, older than his seventy years.

On the other side of her, her mother remained silent… and almost worried?

Why not tell them? She could sum up her life in only a few short sentences. "If you recall, I left with my clothes, my jewelry and a few of my personal possessions." Fortunately, that included a limited savings account, though it hadn't taken her very far. "Without a job, I knew I'd run out of funds pretty quickly, so I sold the jewelry and then looked for work that would allow me to be both a mother and an employee. The park was perfect for me because…" Did she really want her mother to know where she lived, as well as where she worked?

Yes. Because it no longer mattered. Never again would she allow her mother to intimidate or bully her.

"My job at the park came with a modest apartment. That's where I've raised Jack."

"You sold...everything."

The disbelief in her mother's tone had her turning to face her head-on. "What exactly did you think I would do?"

Cara's head snapped up and her eyes glinted. "I thought you would *return*."

Without Jack. That's what she meant, whether she said it or not, and it infuriated Joy. She felt her temper unwinding, control slipping away—

"Jack," her father repeated, savoring the name and interrupting the flare of hostility. "My grandson."

Reluctantly, Joy broke her gaze from her mother's and turned back to her dad. "Yes, you have a grandson. He's an absolutely beautiful, brilliant, *kind* little boy." Love for Jack blocked all other emotions, allowing her an authentic smile. "He's also a talented artist."

"Did he get that from his *father*?" her mother asked.

Joy laughed. "No. I'm pretty sure Vaughn wasn't into painting." How absurd. Vaughn had been into sex, cars and parties—in that order.

Her father sat forward. "Is Vaughn out of the picture?"

"Completely." At her father's questioning frown, Joy assured him, "He made it clear before Jack was ever born that he had zero interest in a child." Much as her mother had. "I haven't seen him since the divorce."

"Hmm." Wallace Reed looked at the attorney, then back to Joy. "We should legally ensure it stays that way."

"No," Joy said gently. "I'm sorry, but there is no *we*. *I* care for Jack. *I* ensure his safety. And *I* alone make the decisions that are best for him." She'd keep it that way, come hell or high water.

It was odd, but something like pride curved her father's

mouth, lifting the lines that age had carved into his features. "You always were strong-willed."

"Me?" Joy said, unsure how that description applied to her.

Her mother snorted. It was such a rude sound, so uncouth, that it not only startled Joy and her father, it startled her mother, too. The hilarious look on Cara's face caused another laugh to escape Joy. The laugh might have been part nerves, but was largely hilarity.

Her father tried and failed to suppress his own chuckle.

Cara cleared her throat and murmured haughtily, "Excuse me." Then, with a frown, she asked, "Could we get down to business now, instead of all the idle chatter?"

Her father checked his watch, and tried for a compromise. "Maybe we should finish this on another day."

For him, that would be no problem. For Joy, it'd be a major inconvenience. She thought of her life, of the changes she'd made, not only since her parents had made their preferences known, but lately.

With Maris as a sister of her heart.

With Royce as a lover *and* a friend.

With a home at the park where she cared for people, and they cared for her.

She said to her father, "Today is good for me." To the attorney, she asked, "Do they need to be here for the rest?"

"Actually... I've already explained the details to them, so there's no reason for them to remain. I can update them on the decision later."

Joy wasn't sure what that meant. What decision? *Whose* decision?

Whatever the explanation, Joy preferred that her parents go. Not because of the heart pangs caused by proximity to them. Not because hurt ruled her. No, she realized her life was currently so full she had new defenses, new emotions, to counter the old.

Happiness to repel the sadness.

She'd already had that with Jack. Never, ever would she regret the choices she'd made. But now the contentment was bigger, richer, brighter.

She'd gone from a flashlight in the dark, carefully picking her way toward the future, to the full illuminating scope of the sun.

Now, thanks to those additional changes, she had the ability to forgive. Not that either of her parents had asked for forgiveness; it was just that, for her own sake, it made sense to shrug off the depressing weight of resentment.

"We're not leaving."

Joy tipped her head at her mother's militant stance. Clearly, she wouldn't budge. Was it worth a debate? No, not really.

"Fine." Standing, Joy moved down the table, aware of her mother's gaze burning against her. She took the seat to the immediate right of Ms. Wickham. "If you would continue?"

"It's easy," her mother stated. "Reconcile with your family, and you inherit."

Ah, so it was as she'd suspected. There were strings attached...and that meant her business here was done.

To Ms. Wickham, Joy said, "In that case, I should be going. Thank you for your time."

"You will not leave yet." Cara cleared her throat. "Not until I've finished."

Joy tried to keep her back to her mother, but it proved impossible. No matter what, she was her mother and deserved some respect. Inhaling a deep, bracing breath, Joy swiveled on the seat and lifted one brow.

Hands clasped before her, chin elevated, her mother

said, "If you return to your family, we'll...double the in-heritance."

Double her... *"What?"* A slap couldn't have confounded Joy more.

Her father seemed equally surprised. "Cara—"

"It's time for you to return home," her mother said. "End the rebellion. Move away from the trailer park—"

"It's an RV park!" Without thinking it through, Joy found herself on her feet again. "But FYI, Mom, there is nothing wrong with living in a trailer park. They're good, close communities for kids. Small homes are wonderful, too. Even an *apartment* is terrific when the people who live there make it a home." Since Joy lived in an apartment, she felt compelled to make the point. "There's nothing wrong with working for a living, and staying within your means." Arms out, she said, "There's nothing wrong with my life."

"Except that you have no family."

"You're wrong. The people I work with are my family."

Slashing a hand through the air, Cara said, "But you don't have to work."

Fist to her heart, Joy assured her, "I *enjoy* my work. I enjoy where I live and I enjoy the people there, too." How dare her mother try to buy her? Did she honestly think it'd be that easy? That Joy would throw away everything that mattered to her just to have a pampered life? "Actually, I love each and every one of them." She lifted her chin to match her mother's expression. "And I especially love my son."

Shooting to her feet, Cara stepped forward, her tone nearly shrill, to insist, "Since you kept him, we have a right to know him!"

Ice ran through Joy's veins. "You have *no* rights, not

when it comes to Jack." Somehow they were now toe-to-toe. "Not since you discarded us both."

Oh damn. That just sort of dropped out there, hostile and filled with hurt. It gave away far too much, things Joy would prefer her mother never know.

They stared at each other.

As if this particular battle had taken all their strength, they each breathed heavily.

Slowly, her mother pulled her dignity around her like a cloak. "You were a spoiled, ungrateful child, refusing our advice, and for all your bragging about the wonders of your new life, I can see that hasn't changed." With that parting remark her mother turned and left the room, closing the door quietly behind her.

Joy was still troubled a half hour later when Ms. Wickham finished explaining the details of her inheritance. It was…well, she refused to call it life-altering, because she refused to alter her life.

Her grandmother, in her misguided way, had hoped to put them all back together by offering two choices. Joy could have a nice inheritance, enough to upgrade to a newer car, or add a comfortable cushion to her bank account, no strings attached.

Or, *with* strings—maybe more like chains—she would be given enough to purchase a house with cash, to ensure a higher education for Jack, to never again have to worry over a budget.

All she needed to do was make amends with her parents.

Easy to say, not so easy to do.

With the second choice, she'd be able to give Jack things she couldn't before. But at what risk?

Her son was a sweet, caring child in part because she hadn't spoiled him.

He's an artist, and art supplies cost money. I could give him an art tutor, or send him to classes...

Again, Joy mentally shook her head. Jack was still only five, for crying out loud. Despite Royce's assurances and Jack's obvious inclinations, no one knew who they were at such a young age. Why, Jack could turn to a sport, or music. Favorites changed as people matured.

And those things cost money, too.

While Joy struggled with the stipulations of the inheritance, her father remained silent at the end of the table. He hadn't joined her mother in the outer area and Joy wondered if they'd decided together that one of them would remain with her. Maybe her father wanted to give Cara time to cool down.

Or maybe he wanted to spend more time with Joy.

Feeling very uncertain, she glanced at him.

The second their eyes met he smiled, the same warm, indulgent smile she remembered as a little girl, a teenager and a young woman. She'd missed it.

Ms. Wickham stood. "I have a phone conference in a few minutes. This room is free for another hour, so take your time deciding."

Joy shook her hand and thanked her.

Once the attorney had gone, her father stood, as well. "I can't tell, honey." He didn't yet approach her. "Are you pleased with the money, or upset?"

Good question. "I'm...numb?" She truly couldn't decipher her own mood. "I don't know what to do." If she had Royce here, or Maris, or *both*, they could help her decide.

No, she corrected herself, *this is not their problem*. But it'd be nice to have a sounding board at least. Someone she truly trusted.

Gruff, trying to give her a nudge, her father said, "It should be an easy choice."

"It's not." Seeing the hurt on his face caused her to hurt, as well. "Try to understand, Daddy. Jack and I have a nice, comfortable life. That kind of money...it could change everything."

"It's not such a staggering amount as all that."

Not to him. Not to a man who had never lived on an inflexible budget.

Very seriously, he said, "Your mother meant it, you know. We will happily double that amount."

Joy twisted her mouth. "Until she said it, you knew nothing about it."

He nodded. "That happens a lot actually. But I don't disagree with the idea. Just think, you could buy a house for you and Jack." He held up a hand. "I know you said you like your apartment. I wasn't suggesting you leave it. Only offering ideas for your future. For Jack's future."

Hearing her father say Jack's name brought home all the ramifications. "I can't drag my son into that life."

"That life?" He looked down at the table, and when he lifted his gaze, she saw a touch of anger in his eyes. "I tried to give you everything you needed or wanted. Did I spoil you? Yes. Not because I didn't care, but because I did. Were we the best parents?" He shook his head. "I'm not sure perfect parents exist."

"You disowned me, Daddy." She loved him, yes. God help her, she loved her mother, too—if she didn't, none of this would be so difficult—but she wouldn't let him delude himself. "I never asked for perfection, but to be told to toe the line or else? That if I had my child, I would no longer be *your* child?"

His mouth firmed and he looked away.

No, her father hadn't said those words, but neither had he gone against her mother's wishes. "You sent me away, alone and pregnant, very unprepared to deal with life. How can you call that love?"

"It was misguided, I agree, but we were so worried for you. Vaughn was never a good person, certainly never good enough for you. We feared how he might destroy you."

"And instead it was my parents who almost did that."

He flinched, his breath catching before he regained control. "Your mother thought it would shake you up, that you'd come to your senses and return to her."

"Minus my baby?" Joy could barely get those words out of her constricting throat. All of this—rehashing the past, seeing her parents, having to defend her position all over again—wore on her.

"As I said, it was misguided. Worse than misguided, it was wrong, but it *was* a decision made from love. How could a future child who we didn't know ever compare with what we felt for you?"

More importantly, Joy wondered, how could they make her feel so all alone if they really did care?

"You think you won't make mistakes but you will." Hands in his pockets, her father gave her a sad smile. "Different mistakes, sure. But would you want them to damage your relationship with your child for life? Or would you hope that your son would forgive you, that he'd understand you meant well."

Had her mother meant well? It was hard to imagine.

Before Joy could reply, he added with heartfelt emotion, "Would you want Jack to understand that you were doing the best you could with what you knew of life, and your own experiences?"

Was this his way of saying her mother hadn't known any other way to deal with the situation? Did that make it excusable? "She tried to control me," Joy stated, tears burning her eyes. "It was my decision, and she tried to insist on making it for me."

"Yes, she did." With the briefest of smiles, her father whispered, "But instead of giving in, you countered Cara's bluff and managed just fine on your own."

Had she? Joy recalled that day, how devastated she'd felt, how scared. With her voice emerging small and wounded, Joy said, "It didn't feel like a bluff."

"I'm sure it didn't. Cara might not have realized it was when she spoke it. She was so relieved that Vaughn was out of the picture. We both were. But a baby could have caused long-term ties—" His jaw worked as he sought more explanations. "Honestly, we were afraid if Vaughn stuck around he'd drag you down with him."

"If I'd let him, yes." Joy couldn't deny that. "If only you'd trusted me."

"You chose Vaughn," he reminded her, his own eyes suspiciously red. "How was I supposed to trust you when I still don't understand why you hooked up with that bum in the first place?"

Because Joy didn't understand it, either, she couldn't explain. She couldn't recall ever feeling a great love for Vaughn.

Not like the things she felt for Royce.

She closed her eyes. With Royce, everything was bigger, stronger, richer and deeper than any emotion that had driven her to Vaughn. Mostly, she'd gone to Vaughn because...

Her eyes popped open with the realization. "He was the first thing you denied me."

Her father's bushy, graying brows scrunched together. "What?"

"You gave me everything, no matter how extravagant. Then I wanted Vaughn, and you and Mother both flatly denied me." Oh God, this didn't speak well of her decision making at all. With a self-deprecating laugh, she admitted, "It's just this second occurred to me that I never learned how to cope with *no*."

He blinked at her, and then scowled. "Should we have given our blessing to that bum?"

"Of course not." What an amazing, *awful* realization. "You're right that I was spoiled."

"Your mother said that, not me."

"But you were thinking it, too," she pointed out, her heart starting to lighten a little, "and neither of you were wrong. I was also horribly immature. The truth is, I really could have ruined my life."

"You didn't," he insisted, belatedly affronted on her behalf.

"No. My life only expanded, showing me new challenges and teaching me things about myself that I never knew." She was a stronger person now, her priorities in proper alignment. "Jack is a blessing. In every conceivable way, he's made my life wonderful."

"I can see that." He edged toward her, that slight smile in place again. "You might have been slow to mature, but you've made up for it."

"Having a baby will do that for you, teach you what's really important and show you what you can do, instead of what you can't." Because it was necessary. Because Jack depended on her. Her throat tightened. "With Jack, I've learned who I truly am."

His tone softened, went husky. "I'm proud of you, Joy."

Hearing it felt wonderful, she could admit that now, but was the sentiment too little, too late? Could she and her parents ever repair all the damage? She glanced at her mother outside the office, and it didn't seem possible.

"If you think about it," her father said, "if you go over everything we've discussed here today, you'll see that we were all a little to blame for this current situation."

Yes, Joy acknowledged that she did have blame, at least as much as her parents. "That's fair—though I'm not sure it can change anything."

Her father stopped before her. He looked so solemn, so grave, it surprised her when he said, "You're as beautiful as I remember."

"Daddy." She shook her head. "I was never beautiful."

"You are." He clasped her shoulder for a gentle squeeze. "Regardless of whatever decision you make here today, if you find it in your heart, I'd like to meet my grandson."

Joy had gotten so used to the idea of them not being in Jack's life, she almost gave an automatic *no*.

At the last second, she caught herself. Something this important deserved more than a gut reaction. She needed to consider everything. And she'd also talk with Maris and Royce before she came to a decision. Not so they could make the choices for her, but because they cared and could possibly help her weigh possibilities.

Through her friendship with Maris she'd learned the value of talking out a problem. She'd never again underestimate the value of caring friends.

Her father prompted her, asking, "What do you think?"

Gently, she replied, "I need some time."

Disappointed, he nodded. "On your terms, okay? No pressure at all."

"Mother might not agree with that."

"Your mother might surprise you."

Feeling a bit like she'd landed in an alternate universe, Joy struggled with saying goodbye. "Before you go, can I ask you something?"

Her father nodded. "Anything, always."

Except for while I was disowned? No, she wouldn't allow herself to keep harping on that. As they'd both concluded, there was plenty of blame to go around. "Why now? Jack is five—he'll be six before too much longer. Why reach out to me now? Why start caring about him now? Is this new concern really only spurred by Grams's death?"

It was her father's turn to take his time mulling over his answer. Finally he sighed. "I'm seventy, Joy, ten years older than your mother. Not a young man." His smile faltered. "My mother lived to the ripe old age of ninety-two, but look how incapacitated she was. From one day to the next, everything changed. It's made me think about life. Pretty sure it's done the same for your mother. We've wasted too many years already. I don't want to waste a single minute more." He took both her shoulders in his hands. "None of us are guaranteed tomorrow, and regrets are a son of a bitch. I know, because I have plenty of them."

Going on instinct, Joy embraced him.

After a second of surprise, he hugged her back, his arms folding tight around her just the way she remembered before the years of animosity had pulled them apart.

He seemed in no hurry to let her go, and honestly, other than the tears clinging to her lashes, she enjoyed the embrace.

In her ear, he whispered, "Your mother is a stubborn woman, but you're more so."

Taking that as an insult, she stiffened, but still he hugged her, and she didn't like the idea of forcing him away. "Daddy—"

"All I'm saying is that you're stubborn enough, *strong* enough, to keep her in line. That is, if you decide to come around." He patted her shoulder and finally let some space between them. "She's not a young woman anymore, either. Think about that."

Joy saw the sheen of tears in his eyes, and it broke her heart. "Okay," she promised. "I will."

He touched her face. "What I said about regrets is true, and no one, not even you, gets to avoid them." He kissed her forehead and walked out to join his wife.

Leaving Joy alone with her confusion...and new regrets.

Through the open door she saw her mother glance at her, her posture and bearing just as unforgiving, yet there was something else in her eyes.

Did she dare believe it was...hope?

Joy had yet to decide when her parents left.

It was a relief when the attorney returned because it gave her a new focus.

When she explained that she wanted to wait until she had time to consider things, Ms. Wickham was very understanding.

"Give me a call when you've made up your mind and I'll fit you in."

Glad that at least the attorney didn't press her, Joy said, "Thank you."

"No thanks needed." In an impetuous move, Wickham reached out to pat Joy's hand. "It's what your grandmother wanted, for you to be treated with care, respect and pa-

tience. I was with her a long time, so I would never dis-
honor her wishes."

Bless Grams. Though Joy hadn't seen her for years, she
missed her now that she was gone. Regrets…yes, she had
them. Already too many to tally.

With a glance at the clock—and a swift kick of panic—
Joy realized she'd waited too long. Bidding Ms. Wickham
goodbye, she hustled out of the building without an ounce
of decorum.

Gray clouds covered the sun and it felt as though winter had returned once again. Shivering, Joy pulled her coat
around her, unlocked her car and slid behind the wheel.

As long as she didn't hit any traffic, she'd make it home
just in time.

All went well for the first hour of her drive, and that
freed up her mind to dwell on her parents.

A mistake apparently, because as she drove through a
more rural area where pine trees lined the road, a deer
jumped in front of her and she reacted…badly.

Swerving and braking, her heart in her throat, Joy nar-
rowly missed the beautiful animal, but the action sent her
car in a slight spin. With a white-knuckle grip on the wheel,
she felt the rear of the car punt hard against a rock on the
side of the road with teeth-jarring impact.

Thank God her airbags didn't deploy.

Finally stopped, her heart punching like mad, she struggled to catch her breath.

Turning her head to the side she spotted the white tail
of the deer—probably a buck, judging by his impressive
rack—as he disappeared into the woods.

She dropped her head to the steering wheel.

Too much, all of it. Overwhelmed, buried in tension, she
nearly let the tears free. A slow, deep breath brought them

under control, but didn't stop the shaking in her hands. At least she was more off the road than on it.

After checking that no one else was around, she opened her door and stepped out. The car seemed intact…until she circled the back and found a shredded tire.

Gentle snowflakes began to float on the brisk air, the clouds thickening.

Numb, Joy got back in the car, locked the doors and turned on her blinkers.

Then she sat there, trying to decide what to do. She definitely wouldn't make it home in time, so her first priority was Jack.

When she dug out her cell phone, she saw that, being here on the long stretch of wooded road, she had only a few bars.

Worse, her battery was nearly dead.

She didn't have a way to recharge. That awful realization leveled her after she dug through her purse and found that she'd somehow left the cord behind.

Frustrated, despondent and more than a little panicked, she called Maris before the damn thing died completely. It took several heart-stopping tries before she finally got reception.

On the first ring, thank God, Maris said, "Hey, how'd it go?"

With no time to waste, Joy said, "Maris, I have to rush through this. I'm so sorry but can you get Jack? I have a flat and there's no way I'll—"

"Whoa. Slow down."

"I can't! My phone is about to die."

"Yes," Maris affirmed, "I'll get Jack. Don't worry about that. Are you near an exit?"

"No, I'm in the middle of nowhere." She stated the highway and the last exit she'd passed.

"Do you know how to change a tire?" Maris asked.

Squeezing her eyes shut, Joy shook her head, and admitted, "No."

"Well, I do," Maris informed her, "so just stay put. I'll grab the squirt and come to you, okay?"

"I can't ask you to do that."

"Actually, you're right. I have a better idea." Maris drew a breath. "This is a call for Royce."

No. Calling Royce would make her a burden, after all.

"*Yes.* Please. Let me call him for you."

Since her phone was dying, Joy rushed to say, "Could you just call a garage or something instead?"

"Sorry, but no garage is going to drive out to you."

The battery icon on her phone turned red. Danger zone. Dying any second. "My phone is almost gone!"

"I got this," Maris said fast. "Sit tight! Help is on its way."

"Maris—"

"Thanks, hon. You just gave me an excuse to get hold of Daron."

For a single heartbeat, that gave Joy pause. "You need an excuse?"

"Well, I can't let him know how much I'm starting to care, now can I?"

Before Joy could reply, the phone blinked off.

Gone. Kaput. Never before had she realized what a lifeline her phone could be. The tall trees left her in shadows and she shivered, both from the cold and a bone-deep dread. She was at least forty minutes from home.

Carefully, going very slowly, she put the car in Drive and rolled farther off the road in case it started to get icy.

The last thing she needed was to get sideswiped by an out of control driver.

Like herself.

Groaning, Joy dropped her head back against the seat. Should she attempt to change the tire herself? One peek out the window at the glistening sleet and the trees casting long shadows, and she opted against it.

First thing tomorrow she'd buy an extra cord for her phone and leave it in the car. The second thing she'd do is order Triple A.

And the third…? She'd have to make a decision about the inheritance.

Honestly, she'd rather learn to change a tire.

CHAPTER FIFTEEN

ROYCE AND CHAOS arrived at Summer's End in time to see Daron stomping snow from his feet on the stoop. He noticed Daron's scowl and wondered at it. Usually Daron personified a happy-go-lucky guy. These days, especially, he was all smiles.

His new romance with Maris had done that to him.

"Hey," Royce said, wondering what had turned Daron's mood.

Glancing up, Daron saw him and asked, "You on camp store duty, too?"

Having no idea what that meant, Royce shook his head. "I was just going to grab a coffee while I wait for Joy to get home."

After a long pause, Daron chuckled and bent to give

Chaos some attention. "I have a feeling your master is in the dark."

As if he understood, Chaos barked and turned a circle, getting wrapped in his leash.

"In the dark about what?" Royce asked.

Opening the door with a flourish, Daron gestured for them to go in. "Let's talk inside."

They brought in with them a gust of cold air that sprinkled snow over the floor. It worried Royce that Joy was driving in the nasty weather, even just to the school and back, but he held that concern in check. She'd gotten along just fine without his input for a very long time.

"Maris?" Daron called.

She poked her head out from the back. "Oh good, you're here." Then her gaze went to Royce and Chaos, and she frowned, too. "You called him?"

Daron crossed his heart. "Nope. He just showed up."

"Oh." Speculative, Maris bounced her gaze back and forth, then said, "I guess you should clue him in while I get these cookies on a plate. Then I need to roll."

"Yes, ma'am. Whatever you say, ma'am."

Maris shot him another look, but didn't say anything before disappearing around back.

Holding the dog to check his feet for snow, Royce asked, "What the hell's going on?"

Daron went behind the counter to pour two coffees. "Long story short, Joy left town to meet with her grandmother's lawyer after dropping Jack off at school. Apparently the place is better than a few hours away. She had a mishap coming back and she needs Maris to pick up Jack."

Royce's heart slammed against his ribs. "She's all right?"

He must have hugged Chaos a little too tightly because the dog wiggled.

"She's fine." Daron slid a coffee over to him.

Royce drew a breath, unleashed Chaos and set him on his feet.

The dog immediately attacked Royce's shoelaces, and he was worried enough that he didn't even mind. "So what's up, then? What mishap?" Had something gone wrong at the meeting? Had Joy's mother shown up and upset her?

"Joy's on the side of the road with a flat. Relax," he said when Royce tensed again. "She dodged a deer and must've hit something that damaged the tire. Maris will pick up Jack and then head out to help Joy."

Royce didn't even realize that Joy was going out of town. The meeting was today? He remembered her saying she'd be busy…but he'd decided to try his luck, anyway. He could always find an excuse for being at the park. "Why the hell didn't she call me?"

"That's between you and Joy," Daron said with a roll of a shoulder. "All I know is that when I offered to go after Joy instead, Maris almost bit my head off. Said she could damn well change a tire without my help, and that, besides, I couldn't get the squirt. So…" He spread his hands. "Here I am, ready to watch an empty store."

Fuming inside, Royce jerked out his phone and called Joy. No answer. What the hell did that mean?

"Er, Maris mentioned that Joy's phone had died in mid-conversation."

Son of a bitch. So she was stranded on the side of the road, in the cold and snow, with no way to call anyone? What if something else happened?

Bothered in part by the fact that Joy hadn't called *him* instead of Maris, Royce rounded the counter and headed toward the back. Chaos barked and charged after him.

Startled, Daron followed, too. "Royce—"

He found Maris pulling on her coat, fragrant cookies cooling on a rack beside her. "Where is she?"

When Chaos started sniffing the air, Maris broke off a piece and offered it to the dog. "Who?"

"Don't do that," Royce said, doing his best to keep his tone calm and noncombative.

"Cookies will hurt Chaos?"

Yeah, a sugary diet wasn't what the dog needed, but it wasn't what he meant. "Don't act like you have no idea who I'm talking about." With emphasis, he asked, "Where is Joy?"

Maris glanced behind Royce at Daron, then back again. "For some reason, Joy didn't want to bother you."

He took that on the chin. Yes, he'd told her he wanted to stay unencumbered, but come on. They'd talked about it, he'd explained—and they were supposed to be well past that now.

Why the hell hadn't he told her that he wanted a more committed relationship? He couldn't remember. "Tell me where she is and I'll go get her while you get Jack."

"I'm not sure that's what Joy wants."

"It is," Royce assured her. "She just thinks it's not what I want."

Arms crossed and hip jutting out, Maris asked, "But you do?"

"Yes." He wanted to take care of her and Jack, to be there for her—and he wanted her care and attention in return.

"Think maybe you ought to tell Joy that?"

"We were going to talk on Tuesday, but tonight will be better."

"Nah," Maris said, relaxing enough to get a purse off a hook. "Stick with tomorrow. I have a feeling she did enough talking today. She'll need time to chill."

"Tell me where she is. You can get Jack, I'll go get her, and I'll let her do all the chilling she needs."

Daron backed him up, saying, "I'll watch Chaos for you. Jack will love seeing him."

Royce nodded. "Thanks." In his mind, it made perfect sense.

"I don't know," Maris said, hedging.

"Come on," Daron urged. "Cut the man a break."

She frowned at him. "Because I never cut *you* any?"

Typical of Daron, he grinned, and sidled over to loop his arms around her. "I'm spending time with you, so I'm not in a complaining mood."

"It could be a win-win," Royce said, hoping Maris would agree. "You'll save Jack from the drive in the cold. You know he'd rather hang here and play with Chaos and Daron."

"Fine." Disengaging from Daron, Maris explained where Joy's car was, going into extra detail since Royce wasn't from the area. "It's going to take you more than a half hour to get to her, but I'll feel better knowing you'll reach her sooner than I could, since I need to get Jack first."

Royce pulled her into a hug of his own. "Thanks. Tell Jack not to worry."

"Do you have a phone cord with you?"

"Yup. Keep one in my car."

"Great. Have Joy let me know when she's on her way back."

"Will do." Royce knelt to give Chaos some extra attention. "Stay here with Daron."

Chaos turned a circle, barked and tried to get at his laces again.

Smiling, Royce handed the dog a chew that would hopefully keep him and his puppy teeth busy for a while. "Be good."

When he started away, Maris stayed him with a hand on his coat. "You do know how to change a tire, don't you?"

Daron started laughing, then couldn't stop, even when Maris gave him a push.

On his way out, Royce assured her, "Piece of cake."

And just before he got out of range, he heard Daron say, "You do love busting balls, don't you?"

Royce grinned as he jogged to his car. Maris and Daron made a fun pair. He had a feeling they'd be teasing each other fifty years from now.

It was a nice thought.

His humor ended when he thought about Joy alone on the road with a steady snowfall. There wasn't much accumulation yet, the flurries mostly a nuisance, but the longer he drove, the more slick spots he found on the road.

Forty minutes later, after fearing he'd missed her, he finally spotted her car, blinkers on, at the opposite side of the old highway.

Soon as he could, he made a U-turn and came back to her. She recognized him and stepped out before he'd gotten into Park.

Collar and shoulders up, snow collecting on her hair, she greeted him with an apology. "Royce, I'm so sorry. I told Maris not to call you! I wanted her to try a garage or something."

He met her with a kiss…and a pounding heart full of realization.

Damn it, he wasn't falling in love.

He was already there.

Her chilled lips softened under his and Royce fought not

to deepen the kiss, to pull away instead. Touching his nose to hers, he growled, "I want to be number one on your list."

She blinked up at him. "Number one?"

Yeah, throwing that out there hadn't been the smoothest move. He didn't want her to think he placed himself above Jack, so he clarified. "When something comes up. When you need someone." He brushed snowflakes away from her hair. "Especially when you need a helping hand. I want to be the person you think to call first."

It crushed him when her eyes went glassy and she swallowed heavily. "I'm sorry—"

"Please stop saying that, honey." Royce kissed her again, light and easy. "Please."

That earned a choked laugh and a shaky nod. "Okay. May I say thank you?"

"Not for this." It dawned on him that her nose was cherry red and her car wasn't running. "You turned it off?" She had to be freezing.

"On top of causing a flat and forgetting my phone cord, I didn't think to fill her up before leaving."

He hated the embarrassed, guilty note in her tone. God knew she'd carried an emotional burden when it came to her mother. It was enough to throw off anyone. "Deer take everyone by surprise, so the flat isn't on you."

"I still should have been better prepared."

"Pretty sure you had other things on your mind. Come on." He led her to his car and got her inside. "Stay warm in here while I get the tire changed, okay? Then I'll see if you have enough gas to make it to the next station."

"I think I will. That's why I turned off the engine, to conserve fuel."

"Good thinking." He moved his mouth over hers one last time before saying, "Maris wants to hear from you, so feel free to use my charger." He pointed out the white cord dangling from his dash.

She jumped on it like it was salvation. "Thank goodness. It's crazy how lost I felt without my phone."

He never wanted her to feel that way again, not if he could help it. "Sit tight. This won't take too long."

WHILE ROYCE CHANGED the tire, Joy texted Maris. You got Jack okay?

Yup. Playing with Daron & Chaos.

Thank you for doing this.

You're not mad about Royce? ☺

Joy laughed at the smiley face that somehow managed to look hopeful. Not mad. Grateful, she texted back.

::High five::

So...you & Daron?

I'm flippin' addicted.

Joy could almost hear Maris's voice. Yay!

Catch up when you get here. Don't worry!

Joy replied with a thumbs-up emoji.
No, she wouldn't worry about Jack...but she couldn't

keep her thoughts from veering to the big decisions that loomed ahead.

What she needed was a distraction, so she leaned forward to watch Royce. In the headlight beams from his car, she saw him working the jack. A minute later he sat back on his haunches, frowned, then stood and went to the back of his own car.

He returned carrying a funny-looking tool. If she had any lady-balls at all, she'd get out there with him to observe the whole process.

But seriously, why should they both get cold and snow-covered?

Not that he looked cold. He just looked very masculine and actually...sexy.

One day when it wasn't snowing and freezing cold, she'd ask him to teach her how to change a tire, so she could truly be self-sufficient. Didn't have to be today, though.

Not when she'd already learned more than she'd expected.

JOY'S EMERGENCY SPARE was a joke and he didn't trust it, so Royce followed close behind her as she drove to the next exit where they found a gas station and she filled the tank. Luckily, the gas attendant also knew a nearby place to get a tire.

Once they arrived there a few minutes later, he'd tried to convince Joy to get a complimentary cup of hot chocolate while he dealt with everything.

Apparently allowing him to change the tire was as far as she'd go in relying on him.

At least for now.

He watched her as she ordered the tire for her car, saw her nod at the technician and ask how long it would take.

Royce wanted to know how the meeting with her parents had gone, but didn't want to ask her in the tire station, not when she already looked so very fragile.

Whatever had happened, it had taken its toll on her.

Getting each of them a hot chocolate, they went to a small waiting room with a plastic-covered couch and a television turned low.

Joy first used her phone, talking quickly with Maris, explaining their progress and giving a guess on when they'd return before sinking into the seat. She smiled when he handed her the chocolate. "Mmm, thank you."

Royce watched her sip, and saw that her hands were shaking. "Have you eaten?"

"Not since breakfast, but Maris says food will be waiting when we get to the camp store. Coop and Phoenix dropped in, too, so Chaos is playing with their dog, Sugar, and Jack is…"

Her voice faded off.

"Jack is what?" he asked gently.

"Having the time of his life." Her smile trembled, and she swallowed heavily. "They really are family to him, you know? I don't think I totally grasped it before, but a lot of things are clearer to me now."

What she felt for him—was that clear, too? Royce hoped so.

She sipped the cocoa again, holding the foam cup in both hands. "I know you don't want to hear it, but I'm grateful for you, for this." She gestured at the station. "Thank you for coming out in this weather, for changing my tire and… and waiting here with me."

"Here with you is where I want to be. I mean that. You and Jack are both important to me."

She gave him another heartbreaking smile. "Maris said

that Phoenix and Coop brought down a big pot of stew. They thought Baxter and Ridley would be joining them, but Ridley is miserable with a cold so she stayed home with Baxter pampering her."

Royce let her switch topics without complaint. There'd be plenty of time for him to tell her how much she meant to him. "My guess is that Baxter is good at pampering."

"He adores Ridley, so I'm sure you're right. With her pregnant, he's especially attentive—too much so, Ridley sometimes complains, but I can tell she loves it."

"Because she loves him."

Eyes averted, Joy nodded. "Maris baked bread to go with the stew while Daron looked over the dogs and Jack." Her next smile was a little more carefree. "She said that Jack tried to sketch Daron with the dogs, but the dogs didn't cooperate."

"That's where a photograph can come in handy." Royce wouldn't mind showing Jack how to use photography to help him capture a moving object. Because his mother had done her best to train him, Royce could even explain the technique of showing motion. He couldn't execute it, but he could describe it.

"Maris said Daron tried to corral them—and lost, and it was so funny she heard Jack laughing all the way in the kitchen."

Royce was enjoying the intimate chat so much he almost regretted it when the technician came into the waiting room a while later to let Joy know her car was done.

By the time they got out of there and drove the rest of the way to Cooper's Charm, the sun had set and the security lights were on. Joy parked in her usual spot near her apartment, so Royce parked beside her.

Hand in hand, each of them silent, they walked down

to Summer's End. The wind off the lake was extra chilly, but it also felt clean and crisp.

"I want to talk," Joy whispered.

His gut clenched at the way she said that with such dark foreboding. "All right."

Briefly resting her head on his shoulder, she added, "I want to see Jack first, though. Are you in a rush?"

He'd sit up all night with her if that's what she needed. "I'm here as long as you want me." If she wanted him for the rest of her life, he wouldn't mind at all.

The second they stepped inside, Jack looked up from his seat on the floor with the dogs. "Mom!" He ran to greet Joy with an enthusiastic hug, both dogs chasing and yapping at his heels. Talking ninety miles a minute, Jack told her about his awesome day, which, typical of little kids, didn't include any worry for his mother who'd been stuck on the side of the road with a flat.

While Jack chattered on, Royce scooped up Chaos and accepted his adoration, including lots of tongue swipes and wiggling.

Because Sugar was caught up in Chaos's enthusiasm, Royce gave Coop's dog some attention, too.

Even while stroking the dogs, Royce noticed that Joy clutched Jack a little tighter, a little longer, than usual.

He met Coop's gaze and knew others had noticed, as well.

These people cared about Joy. As she'd said, they were family, closer family than her own could currently claim.

As casual as he could, Coop said, "Glad you're both back. No problems?"

Knowing Maris had surely updated everyone, Royce said only, "None at all, except we're both hungry." The stew did sound good, but it was Joy he worried about. She needed to eat and she wouldn't appreciate being singled out.

Maris, who'd been sitting with Phoenix and Coop, her gaze fixed on Joy, stood with her empty bowl. "Grab seats and get comfortable. I'll bring it out to you."

Daron called Jack over, saying, "Now that Sugar knows a few tricks, let's see if we can teach Chaos."

Excited by the prospect, Jack squirmed out of his mother's arms and was off again in a flash. Sugar followed, which meant Chaos was frantic to do the same. Smiling, Royce put the dog back on his feet and watched him scamper away.

"It's nice," Joy whispered, "seeing Jack so animated."

"He's a happy, healthy, well-adjusted boy." Because she was such an amazing mom.

Her breath shuddered in. "Yes. He really is."

Sensing there were emotions at play that he didn't understand, Royce put his arm around her. "Let's grab a seat."

It spoke volumes to her exhaustion that she allowed him to lead her away. Before she slid into a booth, he helped her out of her coat, and removed his own. While watching Jack, she rubbed her cold hands together. They were in the seating area with her son, Daron and Maris, Coop and Phoenix, but because they'd sat apart they had a touch of privacy.

With his pinky, Royce eased back a tendril of hair, tucking it behind her ear. Her cheeks and nose were pink from the cold, her lips chapped, her mascara a little smudged. And she was the most beautiful woman he'd ever seen. "You okay?"

She nodded, but then murmured, "My grandmother left me a sizable inheritance."

It was more her inflection than the words that gave him pause. "Oh?"

Maris coasted in with a tray holding two bowls of stew, hot slices of bread with a bowl of butter and glasses of tea. She kept her gaze trained on Joy. Probably for the same reason Royce had difficulty looking away.

She saw Joy's vulnerability.

"Dig in while it's hot," Maris said with false brightness. "There's more if you want it."

Joy had already picked up her spoon when she said, "I'm famished, but I didn't mean to have you waiting on me."

"Don't piss me off, Joy." Maris gave her a brief but fierce hug. "If our situations were reversed, you'd do the same."

"I would try," Joy said, "but you're really good at making people feel pampered."

Maris preened comically. "It's my calling. Now eat."

"It smells delicious." Louder so that Phoenix would hear, Joy said, "Thank you for the stew. I didn't have time to eat today and this will be perfect."

Phoenix turned in her seat to see her. "My pleasure. Hope you enjoy it."

Joy took a bite, and said, "Mmm. Nirvana."

With a smile, Phoenix nodded and turned back to her husband.

Holding the now-empty tray, Maris hesitated. "Everything go okay?"

"Overall, yes." Joy sighed. "I had a few surprises at the meeting. Good ones, I guess."

"You aren't sure?" Maris asked.

Joy shook her head. "Want to get together in the morning? Right now I'm beat, but I can update you then."

"Club meetings start directly after school drop-off."

Royce had no idea what that meant, but Joy laughed. "I'll be there." She reached out to take her friend's hand. "Everything went okay with you?"

"Jack is a doll."

"Uh-huh," Joy said knowingly. "But I meant with Daron. We haven't talked much this week, not since…you know."

Royce was starting to feel like an interloper, but he liked seeing Joy like this, teasing a friend. "Maybe I should—"

Maris waved him back into his seat, then glanced at Daron. "He's good with Jack. And animals. And people in general, so yeah, other than him being too freaking perfect, everything is great." Her gaze went to Royce, which prompted him to show a lot of interest in his stew. He couldn't quite suppress his smile, though.

"Tomorrow," Maris said. "We have a lot of catching up to do."

"Or," Royce offered, "I could find somewhere else to be for a few minutes."

Maris patted his shoulder. "If we got started, it'd take longer than that and you two need to eat." She winked at Joy and rejoined Phoenix and Coop.

Royce waited, but when Joy didn't say anything, he prompted, "You got an inheritance?"

"With a stipulation." Holding a warm hunk of fresh buttered bread, she added with a strange detachment, "All I'd need to do is reunite with my family."

A bribe? Was that the reason for her upset? "By sizable, you mean…?"

"Half a mil." Her mouth pinched as she stated that astronomical sum. "My mother said she'd double it if I moved back."

His lungs seemed to empty of air. Royce couldn't take it in. Joy would be financially set? And her mother wanted her to move back, as in…*leave the park*?

Well, obviously a million dollars would give her better options than being a recreation director at an RV resort.

Where did that leave them?

Misunderstanding his expression, Joy shook her head. "Believe me, that's chump change for my family. I have no idea why my grandmother decided to use it as a lure, though I'm certain she meant well."

"Joy…" Tension gathered at the base of his skull. He wanted to hold her tight and ask her not to go, but had he missed his chance? Would it even be right to put her in that spot now?

"If I return to them," Joy said, "they'd probably expect me to live by their standards, their rules."

That would make her miserable. Royce tried to sound neutral when he asked, "Can you do that?"

"No. Definitely not."

He didn't feel relief, because regardless of what Joy said, he sensed her indecision. He couldn't remark on it, so instead he sat quietly, his thoughts in turmoil as they ate.

Would he really lose her—on the very day he realized that he loved her?

JOY LITERALLY DEVOURED the food. Few people knew it, but she ate more when stressed, and tonight she felt more stressed than she had since before Jack was born.

No, she couldn't live with her parents' expectations. But was it fair to keep them from Jack? Was her father right? Could she control the situation to somehow have the best of both worlds?

If she reconciled with them—and honestly, she already had with her father—she could offer Jack the best of schools. He'd receive, in moderation, all the luxuries she'd grown up with, the things she'd been accustomed to and had taken for granted.

The things she better understood now.

Yet they were poor replacements for love and affection, attention and guidance.

Would Jack grow to resent her later in life when he learned what he could have had, what she'd deliberately kept from him?

Worse, would access to those things change him?

Joy shook her head, more to shake off the old disturbing memories of who she used to be, more than in any type of denial.

Royce sat back, and it felt like a retreat, as if he'd pulled away. "What will you do?"

There was something in his low voice, something she didn't understand. "I'm going to refuse."

"Are you sure that's wise?"

The gruff sound she made was part hurt, more disbelief. Speaking in a hushed whisper, she asked, "You think I should expose Jack to people who would hand him the world while not caring about him, about who he is as a person? Without any love?"

"Is that what it would be?"

"Yes." She hadn't meant to raise her voice, and now the others looked at her with concern. Joy swallowed, trying to clear the anger and hurt from her throat. Anger directed not at Royce, but at the situation. "I'm sorry."

"Don't be."

Of course he said that. He was so damn nice all the time, and she was…a mess. One little hiccup in her life and she was ready to fall apart.

Yeah, she was such an independent woman.

She wasn't fooling anyone, least of all her mother.

Her eyes grew damp, forcing her to blink fast and take deep breaths. Her lips trembled, and no matter how she tried to control herself, Joy knew she was losing the battle with her emotions.

On a gulping breath, she choked, "I can't cry here. Not where Jack will see me."

"Come on." Royce stood, gently catching her elbow and drawing her up.

If he hugged her now, she'd lose it. She'd already fought it off for so long any sign of sympathy would turn her into a sobbing mess in seconds.

"Outside," he whispered. "We'll walk along the shore."

She nodded, hating herself for relying on him again, but also immeasurably grateful that he'd save her from humiliating herself.

He said to Jack, "We'll be right back."

Jack was so busy teaching Chaos to sit he didn't even reply.

Royce snagged their coats, and she was aware of him passing a significant look with Maris. By now she knew what that meant. Her friend would keep an eye on Jack, probably with help from Daron, who didn't seem in any hurry to leave.

Damn it. The tears welled over and slid down her face.

As they stepped outside, she slapped them away, her breath catching, her throat squeezing tight.

Gruff, as if he did a little struggling of his own, Royce said, "It's cold. Let me help you with your coat." As she buttoned it up, he pulled on his own, and then steered her well away from the camp store.

Frosty air, prickly with sleet, pelted her face, making the tears sting.

Near a tree, Royce turned her and pulled up her collar, then wrapped her muffler around her throat. While she pulled on her gloves, he glanced out at the stars twinkling on the rough surface of the lake.

"I'm sorry," Joy said, knowing it was a weak refrain. "It's been such a long day."

Shielding her body from the wind with his own, he cupped her face with hands somehow still warm. His thumbs brushed away the tears she couldn't seem to stop, and then he kissed them away, his mouth gentle as it touched each cheek, her forehead and her lips.

She thought she might be able to get it together...until he folded her close, those big, strong arms secure around her, holding her tight, rocking slightly.

Emotion pounded against her restraint and the dam burst. The first sob was horrible, a wounded animal sound that should have embarrassed her more than it did, but God, she hurt too much to care.

"Joy," he whispered.

"I'm sorry," she sobbed again, unable to hold back as six years of grief overflowed, prompting his arms to tighten even more.

He tucked his face close to her, saying softly, "It's okay, sweetheart." His hand petted her hair, then his fingers tunneled in and he held her close.

Giving her permission to cry.

How had she gotten so lucky to meet this amazing man? To have him in her life, as either a lover or a friend, was a true blessing.

Yards away, she heard the camp store door open as conversation spilled out. The soft glow of light barely reached them before it all faded away again.

"Just Coop and Phoenix," Royce told her. "Maris and Daron are still with Jack."

Horrified by the idea of what her face must look like, she hiccupped a breath. "I don't have a tissue."

She felt his mouth warm against her temple. "Want to use the hem of my shirt?"

"God, no." She probably had mascara everywhere, and she didn't even want to think about her nose.

"How about this?" He offered her a knit glove, then retracted it. "Oh wait. Napkins. I grabbed them for Chaos's paws the other day, but then didn't need them."

Joy took one, mopped her eyes, blew her nose and stuffed it into her pocket. "I forgot about Chaos."

"The dog is fine."

"But I'm keeping you out here in the cold..."

"Joy." He brought her back against his chest. "As long as you're warm enough, I'm happy to be with you. Take all the time you need."

This man. He was the finest, nicest, most caring person she'd ever met.

Today she'd been offered a huge sum of money, but she didn't want it. Her parents offered her reconciliation, but she wasn't sure she could accept it.

What she wanted was Royce. On a more permanent basis. Was that fair, to project her neediness on him?

No, most definitely not.

"I shouldn't be unloading on you."

His thumb brushed her face just under her eye, maybe removing a tear. "I want to be that person for you, remember? You can trust me, Joy. With whatever you're feeling or thinking."

Damn it, she almost welled up again. To hold it at bay, she related everything that had happened at the attorney's office, including her father's revelations.

"He thinks it was a big misunderstanding?"

Royce asked it with honest curiosity and no accusation. "No, but he says we were all to blame—and he's right. I never should have been with Vaughn in the first place."

"If you hadn't gone against their wishes, you wouldn't have Jack now. That means it wasn't a mistake, right? Not in any way."

So very true. Why couldn't her parents see it that way? "I can't imagine my life without Jack, so obviously I wouldn't change a thing, but Vaughn *was* a terrible person."

"In the scheme of things, it's a blip on the radar."

Joy almost laughed. See, *this* was why she'd wanted to talk with him and Maris. She'd known they could add perspective that would lighten her load, make her feel less like a spoiled screwup and more like a regularly flawed human. "A blip, huh?"

He nodded. "I'd like to see anyone who gets through life without tripping a few times."

"Including my parents?"

"There's a blip, and then there's a deliberate explosion."

Joy managed a small wobbly smile. "They are incredibly outrageous, especially my mother."

He smoothed her hair. "And no matter what, she's still your mom."

Joy nodded. "I see their side of it now. They thought having Vaughn's child would keep Vaughn hanging around and they... Dad said they were afraid for me."

"And yet they let you go?"

"Thinking I'd relent." She shook her head hard. "It doesn't excuse them. Disowning me financially would have been one thing, but they cut me out entirely. Mom said I wasn't her daughter anymore and my father didn't correct her. Nothing excuses that."

"Or makes up for all the hurt?"

So, so much hurt. "Is it fair to keep Jack from them?" Before Royce could reply, she said, "My father thinks I can take charge and allow the relationship on my terms."

"He's right there," Royce agreed. "You're an incredibly strong woman, and the love you have for Jack would always protect him."

His faith buoyed her. "I don't feel strong."

"You are. I see it, and so does everyone else who cares about you." He tipped up her chin. "We're always our own worst enemies. Try not to be so hard on yourself."

Because she wanted it to be true, Joy nodded. "I think... I *hope* you're right. I'd always do my best for Jack." The problem was *how* to protect him—or would she actually hurt him by forbidding contact with his grandparents? "If I only reconciled with my parents, I would inherit from my grandmother and I wouldn't be obliged to them."

Royce loosened his hold on her. "It's a lot of money to pass up."

"Yes, but I have zero interest in being manipulated." More than most people, Joy knew the insignificance of money when compared to things of real value. "I don't know what to do. The inheritance would be nice obviously." Even if she only put in the bank, it would be security for the future. For *Jack's* future. "It's been so long since I heard from them, I easily convinced myself that it was the right thing, that they didn't care about him, anyway. Now my dad says I was wrong and that they care very much. Have I been selfish by not seeking them out?"

"It's not selfish to do the best you can for your child, especially since your best was pretty damn good. No one could ever doubt your devotion to Jack."

She appreciated the sentiment, but devotion didn't always equal wise decisions. A gust of wind blew her hair into her face and she shivered. She'd kept Royce outside in the cold long enough. "Thank you for listening, for understanding, and for the pep talk."

He took another step back and his smile seemed strained. "So you'll get in touch with your folks and call a truce?"

What an assumption he'd made! It was such a big decision she didn't plan to rush it. "I didn't say that." The sleet increased, stinging in intensity. "It's getting late. I should get Jack home. It's past time for his bath."

Nodding, Royce asked, "You feel better now?"

Her smile went crooked and she swiped her gloves under her eyes. "People talk about a 'good cry' and how you should let it out. For me, though, crying always stuffs up my nose and makes my eyes swell so bad I look like a miserable troll."

"You're beautiful."

That made her laugh it was so absurd. "Maybe the darkness helps hide me."

"I see you just fine."

Oh, what that husky voice did to her. She hugged his arm, loving his strength, needing his sense of humor. "I do feel better, not as pent-up, but I regret sobbing all over you."

"Hey, no regrets." He closed his hand over hers when she held his arm. "Not with me."

Joy wondered about their relationship. Everything had changed recently—too many things, really—and she needed to sort it out one emotion at a time.

Royce walked with her the few yards to the camp store. "I meant what I said. If you need me for anything, I'll be there."

Something in the way he said that made her think she'd have to reach out to him…because he wouldn't be in touch? No, she was just emotional and too tired to think straight.

Leaning into his shoulder, so big and solid, she nodded. "One more favor?" Scrunching her nose, she said, "I'm such a mess… I don't want to step in there for Daron and Maris to see. Will you get Jack for me?"

"You want to stand out here in the cold?"

Actually, the cold was preferable to the embarrassment she'd feel. "Do you mind?"

Royce kissed her ever so gently, and said, "We'll be back out in one minute."

CHAPTER SIXTEEN

AFTER JACK HAD a lingering, playful bubble bath, a bedtime snack and had brushed his teeth, Joy lounged in his bed to read him a story. She wanted, *needed*, her usual routine with her son to ground her after all the surreal happenings of the day.

Few things could calm her turbulent thoughts and fill her with peace like cuddling with Jack.

With her shoulders propped against the headboard, only the bedside lamp on, he rested beside her, smelling little-boy-sweet.

Beneath her fingers, his hair was soft and cool. He listened intently while she finished reading aloud *Hecate the Bandicoot*, by Janet Little. It was one of Jack's favorites, in part because the illustrations fascinated him, but he always felt sorry for the bandicoot.

Honestly, so did Joy.

"If I had a bandicoot," Jack said, "I wouldn't make it take a bath."

Joy grinned. "Most people wouldn't bathe a bandicoot, and from what I understand, most bandicoots are too small to want to eat a human. They're more like a big mouse."

He tipped up his face, his eyes filled with curiosity. "Can you show me?"

"All right." Joy picked up her phone and did a search.

For a long time, Jack studied the images she found, then peeked up at her again and asked, "Could I get a bandicoot?"

"They're wild animals, honey. Not pets."

"Could I get a mouse, then?"

How in the world had they gone from reading to requests for a mouse? "Do you think Chaos would like that?" She stroked his hair again, comforted by the warmth of him. "He might get jealous."

Giving that some thought, Jack shrugged. "Yeah, probably." Abruptly he sat up and crossed his legs on the bed. "Maybe Chaos would like a friend, though."

Joy gave a silent groan. She knew this particular look on Jack's face. He wouldn't give up easily. "You're his friend," Joy pointed out.

One eye narrowed in calculation. "Bet he'd like a dog friend, though."

"Jack…" They'd been through this before, and she'd repeatedly pointed out how difficult it would be to have a pet in the apartment. Every time she had to refuse him, she felt guilty.

"I know," he mumbled, his tone melancholy. "We don't have enough room."

No, they didn't—but now she might have the opportunity to change that. Maybe this was the perfect time to see what Jack thought about moving.

Joy reached for his small hand, tangling her fingers with his. "You know, I was thinking…" She needed to word this just right so that she didn't worry him.

His earnest little face scrunched up. "Something wrong, Mom?"

"No, sweetie. No." She tugged him close, snuggling him against her side, wishing every moment of motherhood could be as easy as a hug.

"You sure?" he asked, pushing back to study her face. "You look funny."

She could imagine how funny she looked with her puffy eyes and blotchy cheeks. The devastation from tears stuck with her for hours. Luckily, Jack had believed her excuse of having a cold. But add to that her confusion over the day's dilemmas, and "funny" was probably a nice way to describe her ravaged appearance.

Joy pasted on a reassuring smile. "I was just wondering how you'd feel about living somewhere else."

Dark eyes going wide, he froze. "I don't want to live anywhere else." Looking around, he said, "We live *here*. My stuff is here."

She hadn't expected that immediate rejection of the idea. "We could take your stuff to a house. A bigger place." A place where she could get him a dog of his own.

"A house like Royce's?"

Pleased with his interest, she nodded. "Yes—"

He started bouncing up and down. "We could live with Royce!"

What? Good grief, she'd botched this horribly. "No, sweetie, that's not what I meant! I meant a house *like* his. Not…not *his* house."

The bouncing stopped. "But I like his house," Jack mulishly insisted, his brows down in confusion. "I like his yard and I *love* Chaos. If we lived with Royce, Chaos could be my dog."

"I love Chaos, too," Joy said. *And I especially love Royce.* Oops, had she just admitted that to herself?

Yes, she loved him. If she'd had any doubts, his gentle understanding today would have settled it. Poor Royce. Loving him meant she'd opened up to him completely, to the point of sobbing against his shoulder. Even with Maris, she'd be horrified by that emotional display. With Royce, she couldn't control herself—and no longer wanted to.

She loved him more than she knew was possible. That meant she wanted to share everything with him, her difficult past and his. Together, it felt like they could deal with it all.

Jack gave one insistent bounce that jostled her. "Let's live in Royce's house and Chaos can be our dog."

"Jack—"

"If we had Royce's yard," he continued, "we could get Chaos a dog friend."

"I doubt Royce wants another dog." He wouldn't have a dog now if Chaos hadn't shown up when he did. Trying to be upbeat, Joy said, "Let's think about a different house, okay?"

Jack's chin went stubborn and his mouth pinched. "I like Maris, too. And Coop and Baxter and Ridley and Daron and Phoenix. My playground is *here*. Sugar is here."

Funny that he considered the playground his own, even when other campers brought their kids to play. Joy understood, because she felt the same. The park was home in a way few places could ever be.

She smiled at him. "Everyone here is our family and nothing would change that. We would still work here."

"You work here, Mom. Not me."

"You help a lot," she pointed out.

He crossed his arms with decisive attitude. "I don't want to move."

"What if—"

"I don't want to move," he repeated stubbornly, and his bottom lip quivered.

Well…that decided that, didn't it? She'd done enough crying today for both of them. She wouldn't have Jack going to sleep upset.

"Then we won't move," Joy promised, giving his shoulder a gentle squeeze. "I just wanted to see how you felt about it."

"I want to live with Royce, or I want to live here." Worried now, he asked, "Okay?"

Only one of those choices was currently possible, so… "Got it," Joy said, keeping her tone light. "We'll stay here." She tickled his ribs until he lost his frown and squealed, then she hugged him tight, kissed his forehead and tucked him under the covers. "I love you bunches and bunches, Jack."

He yawned widely, pulled up the covers and said, "Love you, too, Mom."

Joy stayed near the door, watching him to make sure he'd be able to sleep. When his breathing deepened and his face relaxed, she eased away. New tears stung her eyes, but they were tears of gratitude, recognition of her blessings.

No matter what happened tomorrow, she'd deal with it.

And as Royce had said, she would always protect her son.

"So how'd it go?" Maris asked the second Joy walked into the camp store the next morning.

"Oh no you don't. I want to hear more about you and Daron first." As Joy peeled off her coat, she said, "I have a feeling I've missed a lot in the past week. Time for some catch-up!"

Though Joy wore her usual makeup, her eyes were still a little puffy, evidence of her tears the night before. It broke Maris's heart.

Maybe, she thought, it'd be easier for Joy to ease into the subject of her parents and the meeting if they chatted about other things first. That worked for Maris, since she was nearly bursting to share the wonder that was Daron.

"First order of business," Maris said. "We never let another week go by without a Summer's End club meeting."

Agreeing, Joy made a checkmark in the air. "Even if we only talk by phone."

Maris nodded. "Even if we're each getting nonstop orgasms."

"Whoa! Back her up." Making a rewind gesture with her finger, Joy asked, "You're getting nonstop orgasms?"

"I meant you."

"Oh." With a pout of disappointment, Joy said, "Yeah."

So little enthusiasm. Stifling a laugh, Maris said casually, "And me."

That earned a squeal. "You and Daron? Seriously?"

Maris couldn't hold back her grin. "Oh my God, Joy, he's a certified stud. If I'd been wearing socks, he'd have knocked them off."

Joy cheered, honestly, truly happy for her. It made Maris laugh, too. Who knew great sex made the perfect excuse for a celebration?

"I knew you were seeing him all week. Everyone knew,"

Joy said. "I'm surprised no one took bets on how it'd turn out. FYI, we were all rooting for you guys as a couple."

Maris wasn't sure where things would go, but she was pretty damned satisfied about it. "Halloween puts a kink in communication, with everyone being so busy."

Putting her hands on her hips, Joy said, "I can't believe you weren't here Sunday to give me a report."

Maris shrugged. "Actually, we spent Sunday in bed."

"Ah, well, then you're forgiven."

"I should have texted, but I thought I'd tell you in person yesterday, after you finished your meeting—"

"And I got that stupid flat tire." Shaking her head, Joy headed straight for the coffeepot. "I'm so glad you two are finally on the right track."

"What exactly do you consider the right track?" Following her, Maris warmed up her own cup.

After inhaling the steam from her coffee and taking a cautious sip, Joy hooked her arm through Maris's and led her to a booth. "Sex is a good start."

"Daron would agree with you there."

"Of course he would," Joy said with good humor. "And you?"

Maris grinned. "I'm loving it."

Joy asked softly, "Are you loving Daron, too?"

Why not tell her? It felt absolutely wonderful to be able to share, so Maris admitted, "Pretty much, yeah." Saying it aloud made it all too real, prompting Maris to squeeze her eyes shut and groan.

"You need to tell him," Joy said.

Admitting it to Joy was one thing, saying it to Daron would be entirely different. "Why should I do that?"

"Because once you tell him, I'm sure he'll tell you, and then you can get on with a life together."

"Listen to you." Maris sipped her coffee, a little afraid to think too much of the future. "Have you told Royce how *you* feel?"

"Well…"

Of course she hadn't. Maris could tell by the look on her face. Lifting a brow, Maris suggested, "Maybe you should follow your own advice."

"Honestly…" Joy hesitated, then sighed. "I think the timing is off. I've got all this stuff going on with my parents and I don't want to tackle too many things at once."

"I don't think you'd need to tackle Royce, but okay. Let's talk about the other first." Maris set aside her coffee. "What happened with your folks?"

Joy winced. "Are you sure you want to hear this? Wouldn't it be more fun to just talk about sex?"

No doubt. There were a lot of delicious details Maris wanted to share. *Later.* "We'll get to that," she promised. "But how are you? I've been worried all night, so give over."

Sighing, Joy shared the whole awful story.

Wow. Maris had a hell of a time not reacting. She had to keep reminding herself that these were Joy's parents, and whatever strife they had going on right now, their relationship could change. Sounded like that's what her parents wanted.

And if they did reconcile, Maris didn't want to be on the outs with Joy for stating her mind. In the long run, it'd be for the best if Joy found some form of peace with her mother and father—as long as they treated her better.

At least this morning, Joy seemed more like herself. Seeing the tears in her eyes last night had left Maris feeling so helpless. She would have liked to go to battle for Joy, but she knew Joy well enough to know she wanted to fight the toughest battles herself.

"Were you able to sleep?" Maris asked, once Joy wound down. She knew sleep was Mother Nature's way of calming disordered thoughts and easing a troubled heart.

"It took me a little while, but I did finally doze off." Her brows tweaked down even as she smiled. "I'm a terrible crier. My head gets congested and my eyes swell horribly."

"They're a *little* puffy," Maris admitted. "But I wouldn't worry about it." God knew Joy had other, more important things to concern her. "What will you do?"

"The big question, right?" Joy shook her head. "I'm not sure, but at least today I'm not so weepy. Yesterday it all just piled up, and God, you don't know how much I hated getting all emotional." She quirked her mouth to the side and confessed, "I cried on Royce."

"He's a big boy. He can take it."

She laughed. "He was so understanding, Maris. Every time I turn around, there's something else to love about him."

"Know what I think? You should settle this stuff with Royce before you make any decisions on your parents. That way, you'll have Royce's support." He could help share the burden with her. Joy had been alone long enough.

Staring down at her coffee, Joy whispered, "It would be nice to deal with this stuff during the day, and then come home to Royce at night."

"Well, then?"

"I think he needs to make that move first, you know? I can't go to him and say, 'Hey, guess what, Jack and I want to keep you so how about we shift into a more permanent, committed relationship?'"

"That's what you want *me* to do!"

"Because it's just you, and you're a catch. Don't forget, I come with a little boy."

Maris said, "Jack is a bonus. Everyone adores him."

Gratitude put a smile on Joy's face, but then she pointed out, "There are my parents to deal with, too."

With a feigned groan, Maris said, "Look at it this way. If Royce accepts them, you'll know he loves you an awful lot."

They both laughed.

Oh, it was so nice to do this, to take problems and lessen their impact just by sharing.

Idly tracing a permanent stain on the booth top, Maris said, "Know how I realized I loved Daron?"

"Seeing him naked?"

They both fell into another fit of giggles. Maris said, "Can't deny that helped. He's pretty scrumptious. The thing is, I looked around at his house and it's everything I ever wanted. The perfect home. Cozy and clean, nicely decorated and comfortable."

Carefully, Joy said, "I know that's important to you."

True. "But as much as I love that house, I know I'd want Daron even if he didn't have it. If tomorrow he had to sell it and live in his car, I'd still want him. Crazy, right?"

Joy reached over and took her hand. "That's *love*."

"Probably," Maris agreed, meeting Joy's gaze. "Because I'd still love you and Jack if you lived in a cardboard box."

Their smiles faded. Joy drew in a shuddering breath. "I'm so glad we're friends."

Nodding, Maris tamped down the surge of emotion. "Actually, I wouldn't let you live in a cardboard box. I'd move you and the squirt in with me."

Joy sniffled. "Stop or you'll have me crying when I swore I wouldn't do that today." She drew a slow breath, sipped her coffee and then dabbed at her eyes. With a wicked grin, she said, "Besides, you'll be living with Daron in his gorgeous house and we'll just be coming over for dinner now and then."

As if to ensure that would happen, they lifted their coffee cups in a toast. Bringing the conversation back around, Maris promised, "I'll talk to Daron soon. When will you talk to Royce?"

"If he calls…" Joy fidgeted. "Usually he does, just to say good morning. I haven't heard from him today, though."

"Huh." Doing her best to hide her frown, Maris suggested, "Maybe he got busy."

"Maybe." Joy hesitated. "I talked to Jack last night about the idea of getting a house of our own."

Maris choked on her coffee. As she struggled to catch her breath, Joy half stood and passed her a napkin. Waving her back, Maris managed to gasp, "You're moving? Leaving the park?"

Quickly, Joy said, "No. I mean, if I ever got a house, it'd be near here and I'd still keep my job. But Jack didn't want to hear about it."

"I agree with Jack!" Damn it, she and Joy had just become the best of friends. Selfish or not, no way did she want her moving. "How would we have coffee in the mornings? What would happen to the club?"

Joy laughed. "A club of two."

That made Maris scowl. "Small clubs are the best kind."

"Maris," she said softly with a touch of censure. "Maybe you don't realize what a difference this has made for me." Joy gestured to encompass the camp store and everything beyond it. "I cherish our friendship. You have to believe that. I grew up alone. My parents were always traveling and the house staff wasn't interested in listening to a kid. When I went to my parents, they gave me things. Just that. Lots of things. Having someone to talk to, someone who really listens, that means the world to me. *You* mean the world to me. Trust me when I say I'm not going anywhere."

Damn it, now Maris was on the verge of tears, and she never cried. Fighting back the emotion, she nodded in agreement. "I couldn't talk to my dad because he was usually drunk or sleeping off a drunk. If my mom knew something was bothering me, she prayed about it." Maris gave a sad smile. "She meant well, but hearing verses from the Bible isn't the same as someone just hearing me." She swallowed heavily and met Joy's gaze. "You hear me, Joy. You always have."

With a shaky smile and glistening eyes, Joy lifted her cup for another toast. "To sisters," she whispered.

"To sisters." Maris clinked her cup to hers. To keep from getting too maudlin, she asked, "So...what are you thinking?"

"That I need more time to consider everything."

"But you talked to Jack about moving. That sounds like you're leaning toward accepting your mother's offer."

"The extra money? No." Joy shook her head. "I couldn't do that. It would destroy me to be under her thumb."

Well, thank God.

"Plus that would require I move back near them. I love everyone here as if they were actual family, because in my heart they are. *You* are. Even if someday I buy a house, and it wouldn't be any time soon, I won't ever actually *leave*."

Feeling the same, Maris again lifted her cup. "To our family here at the park."

"To each of them," Joy seconded.

After sealing that vow with a drink, Maris said, "Okay, so I just thought of something." Determined now, she leaned forward. "If you don't mind me jumping in with ideas, I mean."

"Of course not. I was hoping you would," Joy admitted.

"The lure from your grandmother…it doesn't have to be all or nothing, right?"

Joy shook her head. "Basically, I just need to reconcile with them. Accept them back into my life. Be friendly."

"That goes both ways, right?"

"Yes. The attorney said Grams trusted that if I accepted the stipulation, I'd do my best to get along with them. There isn't a time limit or set of rules. My mother tacked on that part about moving back to the area. That wasn't in Grams's offer."

"So you'll give them a chance." As Maris spoke, the plan took shape. "That doesn't mean they own you."

"No, but they are determined to meet Jack."

"Sure, but you'll call the shots, not them. So invite them here to the park, on your turf. Like you said, this is home. We're your people. Make them come to you."

Joy sat back, mulling over the idea.

"Hell," Maris said, getting enthused by the idea, "bring them here, to Summer's End. We'll make sure the others join us. Safety in numbers and all that. I promise not to botch the coffee."

Intrigued, Joy paused, but then shook her head. "No. Absolutely not. I couldn't subject all of you to that drama."

"You said it yourself, we're your family," Maris argued. "Look at it this way. If anything happens that could upset Jack, one of us can take off with him. Daron can get him outside to play with the dogs, or I can lead him back to the kitchen for cookies. It's a surefire way to introduce them, on *your* terms, where *you* control everything."

Joy put a hand to her mouth, then nodded. "It would probably be easier for Jack that way, too, instead of taking him to their house where everything is unfamiliar." She gave Maris a look. "Going back there might even intimidate me, it's been so long."

"Then it's settled." Saying it was so might help to convince Joy. "We'll do it here. You'll have fulfilled your part of the inheritance specification, and you can just stuff the money in the bank and carry on as usual until you've decided what it is you want and what is best for Jack."

Shaking her head on a small laugh, Joy said, "You make it sound so easy."

"Take out the emotion," Maris said, "and it is."

With her thoughts showing on her face, Joy frowned. "I want you to know, a little cash won't change me."

Maris hooted. "Only someone who came from money would call that windfall a 'little cash.' But yeah, I get your point. You're you, we're friends and the club is intact. So we're all set?"

Joy bit her lip, then looked around as if considering it. "This would be a good time for it. We don't have any campers."

"Just your family." Maris put a hand over her heart, making it a vow. "Your park family."

"You're sure the others wouldn't mind?"

"What part of 'family' are you not getting?" Maris took her hand, understanding her worry, her hesitation. "I have a feeling your folks will get it together—I mean, who couldn't love Jack? That kid is all personality. But you may as well hedge your bets as much as you can."

Gratitude brightened Joy's eyes and she nodded. "Yes." After squeezing Maris's hand, she got up and circled the booth, drawing Maris up for a hug. "It will be absolutely perfect. Thank you—for everything."

It took some getting used to, the demonstrative affec-

LORI FOSTER

tion, but Maris liked it. She squeezed Joy tight, and before she could let her go Daron opened the door and stepped in.

He almost tripped over his feet, he stalled so abruptly when he saw them. "Um…"

"Come on in," Maris told him over Joy's shoulder, opening an arm to him.

Cautiously, he edged forward—but when Joy held out an arm, too, he grinned hugely and grabbed them both up for a three-way hug. "What are we celebrating?"

Hiding her face against his shoulder, Maris said, "Well, for one thing, I've decided I love you."

A sudden silence fell before he went rigid and tried to pull back.

Neither lady let him go. For her part, Joy was laughing too hard to do anything but cling to him.

Maris asked her, "Was it unfair for me to blurt it out there like that?"

"Whatever works," Joy replied, and she hugged them both more.

Maris grinned. Having Joy near made it easier, and at least now she'd gotten it over with. No reason to dread it. It was all out in the open now.

"You should probably say something," Joy told him.

Yes, he should, Maris agreed, before she died of false expectations.

"Did she…?" Daron floundered, bent his head to Maris, and asked, "Did you…?"

"She did," Joy confirmed, snickering in glee.

Maris decided that was better than Joy's upset any day. Glad that she could lighten her mood, she leaned into Daron, loving them both, feeling so very grateful for the turn her life had taken. "I did," Maris repeated.

Daron struggled against her, then barked, "Damn it, woman, let me loose."

Both ladies released him, stepping back to stare at him, at each other, then back at Daron.

Maris swallowed heavily. He didn't sound pleased.

After tugging at his sweatshirt, Daron pulled off his hat to run his hand over his hair, exhaled a big breath and said, "Now."

Crossing her arms, prepared for anything, Maris asked, "Now *what*?"

"Now I can do this." He hauled her in and took her mouth in a kiss so scorching hot she forgot Joy was still there until she heard her clear her throat.

"I think this is my cue to go."

"Or," Daron said, smiling down at Maris as he kept her draped back over his arm, "you can stay and hear me tell this lady how crazy she's made me."

"I agree you're a little nuts," Maris said, her tone deadpan.

"I've been waiting on you for years." He kissed her again, quick but thorough. "Marry me?"

Marriage? Just like that? She glanced at Joy.

Grinning ear to ear, Joy said, "I'm going now so you two can talk, but Maris, I expect—"

"Full report later," Maris promised, before pulling Daron back into a kiss.

Marriage. Yes, she liked that idea.

Because she loved Daron.

What the hell had taken her so long to accept it?

Once the door closed behind Joy, she ended the kiss and straightened, but kept Daron close. Fingering the lapel of his coat, she asked, "You love me?"

"Have forever, but man, you're a tough nut to crack."

She punched his shoulder.

Laughing, he squeezed her close so she couldn't strike him again. "You're also gorgeous, funny, smart, sexy as hell, and yes, I love you so damn much."

Maris threw herself against him, loving the strength in his arms, the heat of his body, the way he made her feel. "How did I resist you for so long?"

"I don't know. Never could figure it out." His hand went down to her behind, fondling her. "How soon?"

Tilting back, Maris asked, "How soon what?"

"How soon can you move in?" He brushed his lips over her throat, his voice dropping to a growl. "How soon can we get married?"

When she didn't answer, he raised up to see her. "Maris? Say yes."

Her heart seemed to fill her chest, beating heavily, pumping happiness into every inch of her being. "You know, I was used to being alone. I had no plans to date, much less... everything else. But you wouldn't leave me alone."

"I couldn't," he said, his tone and expression serious. "We're meant to be together."

She believed that now. And oh, this was so much better than what she'd planned for herself. Spending the night in Daron's bed, waking to him in the morning, having dinner together, arguing and laughing—it was the stuff of dreams.

Thank God Joy had convinced her to give him a chance. "Could I just get used to loving you for a little while longer?"

"You'll get used to it a lot quicker if you're with me." He smoothed his hand down her ponytail, then cupped her face. "God, babe, after waiting so damn long, I don't want to spend another single night without you."

The last of her resistance faded away. "Same," she whispered, a little broken up over the reality of loving him so very much.

She didn't know if he wanted a big wedding or small, or what his family would think, and none of it mattered.

Whatever Daron wanted was fine, as long as he wanted her.

THE REST OF Tuesday came and went, Wednesday also, and Joy didn't hear from Royce. She had so many things she wanted to say to him, so many things she wanted to share, but she hesitated to seek him out.

He'd relocated to free up his life and what had she done?

She'd unloaded her problems on him, and that was so unfair. No matter how desperately she missed him, she wouldn't do it again. Neither would she put him on the spot by asking him if their relationship was over.

But oh, it was so very difficult. In a short time she'd gotten used to him being in her life, and every second of every day she felt the void.

The closest she came to caving on her resolve to leave Royce be was when Jack asked about him. Her son missed him as much as Joy did, and she didn't know what to tell him.

On Thursday, with a full tank, a phone charger and new confidence, Joy met with Ms. Wickham and her parents.

Though she did so kindly, it felt good to refuse her mother's money. She explained that she wouldn't leave the park any time soon, and if she ever did, she wouldn't relocate to the same area as her parents.

Her mother wouldn't look at her so Joy couldn't gauge her reaction, but her father was visibly disappointed.

Hoping to ease them both, she said, "I've thought about it, and if you still want to meet Jack, I can arrange that."

That announcement changed her father's expression, carving a smile into his face. "Did you hear that, Cara? We'll get to meet our grandson."

Cara sat prim and proper in her chair, her hands clasped over her purse, her expression somehow stoic. She still wouldn't look at Joy, but her profile spoke volumes.

Was she fighting tears? Joy couldn't be sure, but it seemed so.

"Mother?" Joy asked gently.

Cara straightened and cleared her throat. "You will both come to dinner next—"

"No."

Her brows snapped down. "What do you mean? You just agreed we would meet him."

"And you may." It was strange, but instead of the familiar hurt, Joy felt a measure of…pity. What Royce had said was true: Cara was her own worst enemy. She'd let her rigid pride cost her so much.

Joy wouldn't contribute to that. She'd do her part to make things easier, but with Jack's welfare uppermost in her mind. "You're both invited to Summer's End. My friend Maris will host us."

Clearly appalled, Cara's mouth worked before she could find her voice. "You want us to *dine* there?"

Joy continued as if it wasn't a big deal for Cara Vivien and Wallace Barkley Reed to have dinner in an RV park diner. "It's one of Jack's favorite places. He'll be more at ease there." And who knew? Maybe they, too, would fall in love with the area. Joy wasn't sure how they could resist.

Ms. Wickham beamed at her. "This is excellent. A perfect solution."

"It's no such thing," her mother snapped.

"Cara," Wallace warned. He turned to Joy. "What day and time? We'll be there."

"First," Joy said, her gaze direct on her mother, "I need you both to understand that this is an assessment period."

Eyes narrowed, her mother glared. "What does that mean?"

"If either of you say anything to upset Jack, or hurt his feelings in any way, I won't give you a second chance." She turned to the attorney. "And if that negates my inheritance, I'm fine with that."

"It won't," her father said, reaching out to take her hand. "All that your grandmother wanted was for you to give us a chance, and that's what you're doing."

"How do you know that?" Before now, Joy hadn't thought to wonder too much about her grandmother's motivation. She'd always loved Joy, always treated her kindly, but she hadn't interfered in family matters.

"I asked her to," Cara stated, her chin up. "And before you say I manipulated things, I'll freely admit that I did. You have stubbornly withheld our grandson and—"

"Mom," Joy said evenly, unwilling to engage in more anger, "you never asked to meet him."

"I shouldn't have to!"

Joy felt like she'd learned many things over the last six years, most of it valuable, some of it commonsense practice, but some of the lessons had been on what *not* to do. This, she decided, was one more lesson to learn.

Pride couldn't replace love. Stubbornness was downright destructive. And never, ever would she let either one keep her from those who meant the most to her.

Smiling toward Ms. Wickham, she said, "I should be going." She stood and pulled on her coat. Her father also pushed to his feet.

Her mother sat in stony silence…and then she seemed to burst. "We're not monsters."

Startled, Joy turned to her.

"We wouldn't do anything to upset our own grandson."

Realizing that she'd hurt her mother without meaning to, Joy nodded. "I only meant that he's a little boy with a child's vulnerability. He knows nothing about the reason for our…disagreements. I expect you to keep it that way." She couldn't even begin to imagine how Jack would feel if he knew the truth.

When he was older, he might understand their reasoning, and that it hadn't been about him at all, not really. Their actions were because of Vaughn, and Joy's bad decisions.

But he didn't need to hear about it now.

Her mother's mouth tightened, then she gave one sharp nod.

Her father smiled. "Of course we wouldn't say anything. That's all better forgotten."

Joy knew she'd never forget, but she was willing to forgive. Going on tiptoe, she kissed her father's cheek. "I'll be in touch to let you know what day will be best."

Hugging her, he whispered in her ear, "Thank you."

Joy turned to her mother…and impulsively dropped a hand on her shoulder. "See you soon, Mom."

Cara's hand came up to cover hers, her grip firm for a heartbeat, then she nodded.

Well. That was something, right? A fragile beginning— which was better than a yawning void.

Joy felt better about things already.

Now to prepare Jack.

She got home in time to get him from school, and although it was cold, she walked with him to the playground.

Just for fun, she proved that she did, in fact, fit on the

slide, even though she'd told him she was too big. Jack loved it.

Side by side on the swings, they talked about his day in school. Joy let him scamper over the jungle gym even though Royce wasn't there to catch him. She did her best, but she knew if he dropped, they'd both go down.

Later, as they walked to the apartment, Joy said, "There are some people I want you to meet."

Finding a pinecone, Jack picked it up to study it closely. "Who?"

"Actually, it's your grandmother and grandfather."

Scrunching up his nose, he looked at her. "I have those?"

Joy straightened his stocking hat to cover his red ears, letting her hand linger on his cheek. "Yes. They're my mother and father and I haven't seen them for a long time, but now we've talked and they want to meet you. What do you think of that?"

Shrugging, he turned his gaze down to his feet. "Do I have a dad, too?"

The question rocked her for a moment. Carefully, she chose her words. "You have a father, but he didn't want to stay with me."

"Did he want to stay with me?"

"Oh, honey, he's never met you or I'm sure he would have. You're pretty darned terrific."

"Will I meet him some day, too?"

Joy paused to squeeze his shoulder. "I don't know where he is now. I haven't seen him since long before you were born."

"I don't want to." He peered up at her. "Will I have to meet him, too?"

"No, you don't." Thank God. Worried, Joy asked, "Do you mind meeting your grandmother and grandfather?"

He turned the pinecone over in his hand. "How come you haven't seen them?"

Joy leaned back against a tree and stared toward the lake. How to explain something so complicated to a little boy? "We had an argument. I was stubborn, and my mother was stubborn, but I think we're making up now."

He leaned against her side, his hand catching her coat pocket to hang on as he swayed a little this way and that. "What did you argue about?"

"Silly things." She tried a smile and failed. "Dumb things." Joy crouched down to his level. "Maris invited them to the camp store. You can meet them there. What do you think?"

"Will you be there?"

"Yes." She caught his face between her hands. "I'll be right next to you. Plus everyone else will be there, too. Daron, Coop and Phoenix, Baxter and Ridley. It'll be like a party."

"With cake?"

Joy choked. "I will definitely get a cake. What kind do you want?"

"Chocolate."

"Done." Hoping it'd be that easy, Joy smiled. "I'll make sure there's a lot of icing, okay?"

He pretended a great interest in his shoes. "Will Royce be there?"

Shoot. Definitely not easy.

Joy's heart beat a little too fast. "I don't know, honey."

"Will you ask him?"

The thought of approaching Royce when he might not be interested made her mouth go dry, but for Jack, to make this introduction to his grandparents easier, she'd do it. "Of course I will."

"Promise?"

"Promise." And if Royce said no?

She couldn't imagine him doing that. He'd always been so great with Jack. No matter where their relationship now stood, she believed he cared about Jack.

Joy thought of all the time she'd wasted with her parents. With Grams. Yes, she'd wanted Royce to come to her, but did it really matter?

No, not in the larger scheme of things.

So why not tell him how she felt? Clearing the air now would make it easier if they saw each other in the future. He'd still be free to stay or go, but she wouldn't let miscommunication on her part cause her another sleepless night.

"Mom? Do you think they'll like me?"

"I think they're going to adore you."

Jack looked away. "Will I like them?"

Now that was the big question. "I hope so, but you can take your time getting to know them, and then we'll see." Joy kissed his forehead. "How about we go get dinner? You can help me make mac and cheese."

"Mac and cheese," he cheered, excited in his special little-boy way.

"Pan-fried hamburgers, too."

More cheers. Joy grinned as she watched him. She'd deliberately chosen his favorites for today.

He'd taken her news well. The only thing that could have made it better was if Royce and Chaos were joining them for dinner.

Tonight…and for the rest of their lives.

CHAPTER SEVENTEEN

FROM THE SUPPLY BUILDING, Royce saw Joy and Jack leaving the playground. As he'd watched them play, he'd badly wanted to join in. So had Chaos. The dog whined now as he saw them walking away.

The effort to hold back had Royce locking his teeth. God, he missed them both and it had only been a couple of days. He and Chaos had both gotten used to their company, and without it the days dragged.

"You're an idiot, dude."

Drawn from his thoughts, he turned to Daron. "Go screw yourself." Daron had been heckling him since he got to the park. Royce was starting to think it was the only reason Daron had asked for his help.

Shaking his head, Daron said, "Whatever. I'm too happy

to let you bring me down with your sad-sack attitude. But," he added, "you could think about poor Chaos."

They both looked at the dog, who had just gone after Royce's laces. When he realized he was busted, he released the now-wet, untied laces, flattened his ears and sat back, his big dark eyes apologetic.

Sighing, Royce dug a dog treat from his pocket.

"You realize you're rewarding him for doing the wrong thing."

"You said to give him something else to chew on."

Daron laughed. "It's a timing issue. You should give him something else *before* he attacks your shoes."

Royce blew out a breath. Today it seemed that everything amused Daron, and Royce knew why. He and Maris were officially engaged.

They deserved to be happy. "Why exactly did you ask for my help?"

"Good question, since all you've done is moon after Joy and Jack." Daron hefted another bag of salt and put it on a pallet.

Rolling his eyes, Royce looped Chaos's leash over the door handle and then went over to finish up for Daron. "There's not enough work here to need two grown men to do it."

"Eh, maybe. I took pity on you, though. Joy told Maris she hadn't heard from you, and Maris told me, and we're all trying to figure out why the hell you're sabotaging yourself."

Frustrated with the situation, Royce wondered what else Joy had said.

Did she miss him?

Was she excited about regaining family ties?

Royce worried for her, but he kept telling himself it

would be better now because Joy was stronger, more independent. A woman to be reckoned with. She wouldn't take any shit from anyone, and she sure as hell wouldn't let anyone insult Jack.

Joy would own that situation, one hundred percent.

Daron stood in front of him, arms crossed, one brow cocked. "There you go again, wallowing in misery. What's up with you, man?"

Instead of answering that question, Royce said, "Come here. I want to show you something."

They walked out to his work truck and Royce lowered the back gate.

"What's this?" Daron asked.

"Before I moved here, I was a mobile sawmiller. I paid a driver to bring my trailer to me, along with some of my equipment. I was waiting for them to arrive and now that they have, I made something. For Maris, I mean."

Daron ran his hand over the highly polished plank of wood, then over the live edge. "This is beautiful. What do you mean it's for Maris?"

"I saw her working on the booth tops one day. They have a few stains and stuff… I thought I'd offer to replace the old tops. These would make the camp store more rustic, but they'd look great, don't you think?"

"I think you'll blow her mind." Daron bolted up into the truck bed to take another look. "This is a work of art."

Royce grinned. "My mother was an artist, but I never had the talent—except with wood." Maybe he'd shared more common ground with his mother than he'd realized. "I put two pieces together to make it wide enough. This is just a sample. I'd take measurements before doing any more, but I've missed working with my hands, so…" He'd missed Joy, too, so damn much. He'd needed a way to occupy his time and woodworking had always been a balm to his troubled thoughts.

Daron shook his head in awe. "She has ten booths. You know that, right?"

"There are more than enough trees between the drive-in property and the park to cover that. Some of the trees need to come down, anyway."

"Amazing." He met Royce's gaze with a grin. "I volunteer to help in whatever way you need. Just let me know when you're ready."

"Great." At least he'd accomplished one good thing, then. Royce nodded. "Thanks."

"Hey, man, thank *you*. Maris is going to flip." He hopped back out of the truck and headed for the supply building. "You know how much she loves that store."

Yes, he did. "Glad I can do something to repay her." For all the coffees, the meals and her friendship.

"You know what'd really make Maris happy? For you to get your head out of your ass and go see Joy."

Yeah, it kept coming back to that. Royce took Chaos's leash and followed Daron into the building. While the dog sniffed around, Royce decided it wouldn't hurt to explain things. "You know Joy is going to make up with her parents."

"Maybe." Daron glanced at him. "So what?"

Damned if Royce knew how to articulate it. "She comes from wealth and privilege."

Suddenly Maris was there, rudely shouldering her way in around him. "What does her background matter?"

Without waiting for an answer, she grabbed Daron for a lusty smooch. "Hey, babe. Miss me?"

"Every second," Daron said.

Great. Just what Royce didn't need to see: nauseating

happiness. "I should go," he said. "Let you two do—" he looked at them, all clutched together "—whatever you plan to do."

"Not until you explain," Maris said, turning to pin him in her gaze. "Joy is going through hell right now and you decide to bail? Don't you think she deserves better?"

Every muscle clenched in pain. "What do you mean, she's going through hell?" Yes, she'd been upset Monday night, but the entire day had gone wrong for her. By the end of their visit, she'd pretty much decided to reunite with her parents.

Plus he'd asked her to call him if she needed anything. She hadn't.

"Hello," Maris said. "You met her mother. Would you be happy to deal with the Arctic Circle?"

Incredibly bothered by the idea of Joy still upset, Royce murmured, "Joy can handle her."

"Yup. My girl is badass. But she shouldn't have to do it alone."

No, she shouldn't. Tension gathered in his neck. "If she wanted my help, she'd have asked me."

"If you care," Maris shot back, "she shouldn't have to ask."

If he cared? Jesus, he loved her. "I didn't want to impose."

Daron choked, and gave him a pitying look.

He was starting to think he needed the pity. "All that money didn't faze her," he said defensively. Yes, Royce's own mother had made a nice living off her art, but she hadn't been wealthy. He knew nothing about a lifestyle where half a million dollars was chump change. "Know why it didn't faze her?" Maris asked, her tone sharp. "Because the money doesn't matter to her."

"Case in point," Royce barked back. "Who the hell doesn't care about that kind of cash?"

Shaking her head, Maris turned away. "You don't know half what you think you know."

"Maris," Daron said, chiding. "Let up a little. The guy's suffering, if you can't tell."

She stopped, drew a breath and nodded. "Okay, fine." She turned to Royce again. "Why. Are you. Not. *With her?*"

Instead of answering, Royce asked a question of his own. "Are you saying she turned down the inheritance?"

"Nope. But you'd already know that if you were talking to her."

Of course she hadn't. The money would go a long way toward taking care of Jack, securing his future, giving him things she couldn't give him before. Things Royce would never be able to give either of them. "I just settled in here, Maris. If she's moving back with her family—"

"Are you for real? Acknowledging her folks and moving in with them are two very different things. Joy's happy here. She wants no part of that world."

Okay...wait. How could she take the inheritance and not be a part of it all? Confused, Royce said, "It's *her* world. She was born to it."

"So what? I came from poverty. My folks took handouts for food, hand-me-downs for clothes, and they didn't mind us being the neighborhood charity case—but you don't see me embracing it still."

That stopped Royce cold. Maris's family had been poor?

He couldn't imagine the proud, independent woman standing before him forced to live that way. He glanced at Daron and got his nod.

Shit. "I'm sorry."

"Don't be," she said with a shrug. "Made me who I am, and Daron likes me."

"I *love* you," Daron corrected. "Because, rich or poor, you're amazing."

Maris patted his cheek. "See, Daron gets it."

Yeah, he did. And they were so damn *happy*.

Wishing it could be that easy, Royce said, "This is different."

"No, it's not. Joy is the same. Her situation remains the same. You're the only one making it different."

Daron gave him another look. "She's not wrong, man."

Royce's heart suddenly pounded, his breath going shallow. As if to back them up, Chaos barked, turned a circle and stared at him. "No," he admitted. "Maris isn't wrong."

God, he'd let Joy down. He'd been so busy trying to second-guess things, assuming he couldn't fit into her rich lifestyle, he'd really screwed up. No matter what, Joy was a beautiful person, and he loved her.

That was the only thing that mattered.

Lifting Chaos into his arms, he said, "Thanks, Maris."

"You're welcome."

Royce turned on his heel to walk away.

"Are you going to her?" Maris asked.

"Yes."

"Great. Give her my love," Maris sang after him, her tone rich with satisfaction.

Yeah, he would—right after he gave her his own.

STANDING AT THE STOVE, Joy moved the hamburgers to a plate, making sure to keep Jack's away from the onions she loved. He'd helped her with the mac and cheese, and he'd chosen applesauce as an additional side dish, whereas Joy would have a salad.

They were ready to eat when the knock sounded on her door. Jack started to dart away from the table, but she said, "No, I'll get it," which at least slowed him down a little.

It might be Maris. Joy had made an extra hamburger just in case. But regardless, she didn't allow Jack to answer the door without her.

As she went to the window to peek out, he stuck close to her side.

It wasn't Maris.

Royce stood there, his expression stern. Maybe worried. He held Chaos in his arms, and at least the dog looked excited.

"Is it Royce?" Jack asked, his tone hopeful. "It's Royce, isn't it?"

Her smile felt a little sad. Jack had really missed seeing him the last few days. She'd planned to contact Royce later tonight, hoping she'd have a handle on things before Jack saw him again.

Now here he was, and she had no idea where they stood.

"Mo-om," Jack complained, tugging at her shirt.

"Yes, it's Royce." She hesitated, wondering what to expect.

Jack squealed, bouncing with excitement. "Open the door, Mom!"

"All right. Hold your horses." Laughing, she opened the locks and, trying to be casual, greeted Royce. "Hi."

Jack ducked in front of her. "Royce!" He grabbed him around the legs, still bouncing, making Royce brace his feet apart or topple.

"What a welcome." Shifting the dog to one arm, Royce hefted Jack up with the other to bring him eye level. Grinning, he asked, "Did you miss me?"

"We did, didn't we, Mom?"

When Royce's dark-eyed gaze touched on her face, Joy avoided answering by stepping back. "Come on in."

"You can have dinner with us," Jack offered. "I helped cook it, didn't I, Mom?"

"Yes."

Royce hugged Jack close. "Bet it's perfect, then." Chaos was whining and wiggling, so Royce bent to lower both boy and dog to the floor.

No matter how many times they'd visited, Chaos always did an immediate inspection of the apartment. Nose to the floor, looking much like a furry vacuum cleaner, he began his excited tour.

"Jack," Joy said, "why don't you close the bedroom and bathroom doors so we don't have to worry about Chaos getting into anything?"

"Okay. C'mon, Chaos." They took off in a run together.

Normally Joy would have reminded him to come right back for dinner, but instead she looked at Royce. "Is everything okay?"

"No." He inhaled, filling his lungs, then slowly let out a breath. "I mean, I hope it is."

Joy tipped her head, confused but starting to feel as hopeful as Jack.

"Screw it." Royce brought her in close and bent his head to hers.

His lips brushed over her mouth, once, twice, opened just a little so his tongue could tease her bottom lip…and she felt herself turn to putty.

She'd missed him so very much.

"Joy?" he whispered.

She heard longing and apology in the way he said her name, and it did her in.

"I'm sorry." He feathered kisses against her cheek, over

to her ear. "So damn sorry. God, I was an ass and now that I've realized it, I just…"

Hands to his chest, she looked up at him. "You just what?"

"I want to make it right."

Jack came flying back in, saw them together and slammed his brakes. "Whoa."

Chaos looked around in confusion, wondering why everyone had gone so quiet.

Flustered, Joy started to retreat, but Royce didn't let her go. "Do you mind if I talk to your mom for just a minute?"

Jack blinked at each of them in turn. "Are you going to stay for dinner?"

Royce looked to Joy, and she said, "There's enough if you're not too hungry."

"Yes," he said immediately, "I'd love to stay."

"Okay, then you can kiss her." Jack watched, making Joy snicker.

"Um…" Royce shifted. "How about you show Chaos your room again instead?"

Skeptical, Jack said, "All right. But I'll be right back."

"Don't let him chew anything," Royce called after him.

They watched boy and dog disappear down the short hall.

The second Jack's door closed, Royce framed her face in his hands. "I love you."

The declaration took her breath away.

"Who knows when he might come charging back in here," Royce explained, "and I needed you to know."

Trying to fill her lungs, Joy gasped. "I… You took me by surprise."

"It took me by surprise, too. But it's true." He pressed

a firm kiss to her mouth and said again, "I love you, and I love Jack, too."

She steepled her hands over her mouth, suddenly overwhelmed. "Royce—"

"Just so you know, the money has nothing to do with it."

That made her blink. "What do you mean?"

He shook his head. "The money *does* matter. Hell, the idea of you inheriting that much spooked me. I thought it would change everything. Where you lived, *how* you lived."

That's why he'd acted so funny?

"I just meant that it's yours. Yours and Jack's. I want nothing to do with it."

"Never, not once, did I think the money would be a draw for you." But then, neither had she known that it would turn him away. Thinking about it now, she could see how disconcerting her cavalier attitude about a million dollars would be.

"Good." Royce cupped her shoulders in his hands. "Whatever you have going on with your parents, we'll figure it out. Maris said you had no interest in moving, but if you did, I'd fix up the house and sell it. I want you to know that. I wouldn't expect you to pass on better options—"

Laughing, a little giddy with happiness, Joy put her fingers over his mouth. "Better options than you? Not possible." She opened her hand against his jaw. "I'm in love with you, too, Royce. But I'm not moving away from the area. This is home."

She saw the relief that stole the worry from his gaze, the way his big shoulders loosened. He crushed her close, lifting her off her feet to spin her in a circle, then setting her back again. After a big exhale, he admitted on a laugh, "I'm glad, because I like it here. I just need you to know that I could be happy anywhere, as long as I'm with you, and I'm sorry I didn't tell you that sooner."

That meant the world to her. "I was going to call you tonight, after Jack went to bed. I had it all planned, everything I'd say. Mostly that I loved you." Beneath her palm on his chest, she felt the steady thumping of his heart. "I was a little nervous about it, so thank you for telling me first."

"Maris was ready to kick my ass if I didn't." He grinned. "She and Daron—hell, everyone at the park apparently—knew I was making dumb assumptions." Royce put his forehead to hers. "I'm sorry I put us both through that."

She didn't yet know where their relationship was headed, but he loved her and that was a good start. "Before Jack returns, you should know that I turned down my mother's money. That was always a given. I'm ready to work with her, to try to have a peaceful future together, but that's as far as it goes."

He smiled. "Sounds like a generous compromise to me."

"I gave it a lot of thought." Talks with Maris had helped. "The bulk of the inheritance from my grandmother will go into a trust fund for Jack, with me as trustee so I can ensure that when he turns eighteen, he doesn't blow through it."

"No crazy fast cars?"

She grinned with him. "Exactly. He'll have options for college, trade school or an art academy if he's still into that when he's older."

"He will be," Royce said with assurance. "I'd bet on it." He ran his hand over her hair, tucked it back and traced her lips. "I want a future with you, Joy."

Those words did more to brighten her than any amount of money ever could. Smiling, her eyes a little misty, she nodded. "I want that, too."

Jack crept in this time. "I'm getting hungry," he said as a bold hint, his gaze scrutinizing them both.

Accepting that details for their future would have to wait, Joy got another plate and served the food while Royce helped with drinks.

Thankfully, Chaos found a comfortable spot by the window and curled up to nap.

She'd gotten her very first bite in her mouth when Jack announced, "I have a grandma and grandpa."

Keeping his tone neutral, Royce replied, "I heard about that."

"Maris is going to have a party so I can meet them. Mom's getting me a cake."

"That sounds nice," Royce said.

He shrugged and glanced at Joy. Sotto voce, he asked, "Did you invite him, Mom?"

She bit back her smile. "I was going to call him tonight, but since he's here, you can invite him yourself."

Shy now, Jack muttered, "Will you come to the party?"

"Wild horses couldn't keep me away."

"Really?" Grinning, Jack said, "We'll all be there, right?"

Royce nodded. "Are you excited to meet your grandparents?"

Pushing his fork through his applesauce, his gaze on his plate, Jack said, "I'd rather have a dad." He cast a coy glance at Royce to gauge his reaction.

"Jack," Joy said softly. "I explained—"

"He's not here," Jack insisted in a burst, rushing out with, "Maybe Royce could be my dad?"

Clearly stunned, Royce dropped back in his seat, his fork suspended, his gaze locked on Jack.

Uncertain now, Jack whispered, "Would that be okay?"

Without a word, Royce nodded, swallowed heavily and then finally, *finally*, he smiled. "That would be incredible. Thank you."

Jack grinned. "For real?"

"No matter what, I'd love to be your dad."

He looked at Joy. "I'd also love to marry your mother."

Joy covered her trembling mouth. That was the most roundabout proposal she could imagine, but she loved it just the same.

Jack turned to her. "Will you, Mom?"

Smiling, Royce set aside his fork and said softly, "I love you, Joy. You love me. We both love Jack."

Jack grinned.

"Will you marry me?"

Nodding hard and laughing, Joy said, "Yes."

"Yes?" Jack asked, wanting it confirmed.

"Yes," they both repeated.

And Jack whooped so loudly he woke Chaos.

FOR THE FIRST TIME, of what Royce hoped would be many, he helped tuck Jack into bed.

"Will you be here in the morning when I wake up?" Jack asked.

"No." Royce wouldn't ask to stay the night until after he and Joy married. It was an old-fashioned idea, but Jack had enough new ideas to deal with right now. Royce didn't want to throw too much at him at one time. "I can come back over before you go to school, though."

"Okay." Jack hugged a stuffed dinosaur and turned on his side. In a hushed whisper, he asked, "When can I call you Dad?"

Unsure how to answer that, Royce deferred to Joy.

She smoothed Jack's hair. "Whenever you want to, honey."

His sleepy eyes grew heavy and he yawned. "Okay." Snuggling into his pillow, he grinned. "Good night, Mom..." He peeked one eye open. "And Dad."

Royce knew he'd never grow tired of hearing that. "Good night."

Joy took his hand and led him from the room. On the couch, she leaned against him, both of them quiet for a moment. Finally she said, "What a week it's been."

"I'm so damn sorry I made it worse."

"All in all, I think you made up for it. Jack loves you very much."

Every time he heard it, Royce liked it more. "I feel the same about him." He pulled her closer, saying, "He's such a happy kid, I'm surprised he missed having a dad."

"He didn't," Joy whispered, "until he met you."

"Then we're even. Kids are the biggest commitment of all, and I didn't think I wanted anything to do with them— until I met him."

She smiled, and pulled out her phone. "I only need a second."

Amused, Royce shook his head. "I'm not going anywhere."

Holding the phone so he could read the screen, Joy texted, Royce proposed.

A mere two seconds passed before a fist emoji appeared, along with the word YES!

"Maris?" he asked, already knowing it was.

"Yes." She put her head on his shoulder. "We share everything." She replied, Details tomorrow. Luv u & thx.

Luv u 2 & welcome!

Grinning, Joy set the phone aside. "She's with Daron. Otherwise, she'd be demanding details right now."

"They're happy."

"Very."

Royce cupped her face, turning it up for a soft kiss. *Soft*, because he would not get carried away.

They visited for another hour or so. Joy told him everything that had happened with her parents, and they made plans. Plans for tomorrow, next week and next year.

It was the start of a lifetime.

ROYCE THOUGHT HE felt the tension more than Joy did. She presented a perfect picture of poise and serenity as she introduced Jack to her parents.

It never ceased to amaze him how she could pull it together for her son.

Music played in the background and their friends, friends that were more like family, chatted casually to each other to help make the moment less conspicuous for Jack.

Even Sugar and Chaos contributed by yapping at each other from the corner where they played.

It bothered Royce to see Jack so subdued. Since he'd known him, Jack had gotten chattier, more playful—and more affectionate. He hugged freely, sometimes even crawling into Royce's lap.

Yet today, in these circumstances, Jack had reverted to a very quiet, withdrawn little boy.

Standing protectively close, Royce put a hand on his small shoulder.

Jack looked at his mom first, then to Royce, before screwing his mouth to the side and taking a step forward.

He held out his hand, just as Royce had shown him.

Pride burned in Royce's chest. No doubt knowing exactly what he felt, Joy leaned into his side. He loved her so damn much that the urge to shelter her from this made his muscles clench.

And then tears sprang into Cara Reed's eyes.

Happy, emotional tears, Royce could tell, and that show of feeling humanized her more than anything else could have.

He and Joy shared a look of surprise.

Wallace grinned, accepting Jack's hand and then holding on gently.

Once Cara had fished out a tissue and dabbed at her eyes, she drew a steadying breath. With a smile that looked rusty, she said, "I'm your grandmother, Jack."

"I know," Jack said, sounding a little in awe. "Mom told me."

Wallace's grin widened. "Would you like to sit down and get acquainted?"

Jack glanced back at Joy again.

She said, "I'll be right here with you."

Next, Jack turned to Royce. "You, too?"

I'd like to see someone stop me. "You bet. We've got a booth right here." Royce gestured for Cara and Wallace to take one seat, and then Joy slid in opposite them, Jack in the middle, and Royce on the aisle side.

Sandwiched between them, Jack regained his precocious personality. Going to his knees, he studied both people. "I have Mom's ears."

At that announcement, Cara lifted her brows. "Hmm, perhaps you do." Gently, she reached out to touch his face. "Actually, you look very much like your mother when she was a little girl."

"I do?"

Wallace nodded. "You really do."

Jack scrunched his nose as he considered that. "Mom's hair is different."

"It wasn't when she was five," Cara said. "In fact, her hair stayed as light as yours until she was nine or ten. Her eyes were different, though. They were always that beautiful golden green shade. She got them from my mother."

Jack leaned closer to her, much as he had done to Royce when they'd met. "You have the same eyes."

Pleased, Cara preened. "Yes, I do. They're not as bright anymore, but oh, when I was young they were pretty."

As if she'd never heard her mother say such a thing, Joy blinked and her lips parted.

Wallace chimed in. "They're still very pretty, don't you think, Jack?"

Jack took in Cara's eyes the way only a young artist would. "They are. I could draw them if you want."

Wallace looked pleased. "Your mother said you're an artist?"

Rubbing his ear, showing a modicum of humility, Jack nodded. "Dad says I'm good, but that I'll keep getting better as long as I practice."

Gazes shot his way. Royce met them without flinching. They needed to know he was a part of Joy's life now. Never again would she have to face them alone.

Cara frowned at Joy. "I thought you said—"

"We're getting married," Joy stated. "We only recently decided and haven't set any definite plans yet."

As if to challenge any questions, Jack lounged back against Royce. "He's my dad *now*, though. Ain't that right, Mom? I don't have to wait."

"Absolutely right," Royce said.

Joy nodded with a smile.

Wallace studied them both. "Your mother and I would be happy to have a wedding for you."

Dread washed over Royce, but he manned up and stayed silent. If Joy agreed to some big fancy shindig, he'd muster through it.

"Thank you, but we'll handle it," Joy said. "We'll likely have the wedding here."

"Here?" Wallace gave a dubious glance around the camp store.

"In the lodge actually," Joy explained. "I've helped organize other weddings there." She shared a tranquil smile. "I *am* the recreation director, after all."

Cara's face had gone stiff and now remained that way.

Until Joy added, "We'd be pleased if you wanted to attend."

From that point, everything changed. He had a feeling Cara was on her best behavior for both Jack and Joy. Royce sat back and took it in, relieved for Joy because he knew a truce with her family would make her life easier.

Wallace had questions for Royce, too. It made sense that a father would be curious about his daughter's future husband. Cara's questions were a little more intrusive, and yet Joy had a way of curbing her tendencies by introducing people at the park.

When Maris joined them, Royce excused himself and let her have his seat. He stayed close—keeping vigil with Daron, who'd come with Maris.

Not that either of the ladies needed them.

They made a great team, finishing each other's sentences, playing off conversational topics, laughing at jokes no one but them understood.

Daron glanced at Royce, saying low, "Looks like we'll be sort of related."

With a meaningful glance at Cara and Wallace, Royce nodded. Voice low, he murmured, "Welcome to the family."

They both laughed, and soon everyone was there, crowded around that single booth.

Family newly reunited.

Friends who'd become family.

A future he'd never expected—that was better than anything he'd ever known to hope for.

* * * * *

Read on for a sneak peek at New York Times *bestselling author Lori Foster's next novel,* The Somerset Girls, *about two sisters who couldn't be more different, the familial ties that bind—sometimes a little too closely—and a brand-new love that's just where you least expect it.*

CHAPTER ONE

A REFRESHING SHOWER, ice cream and the book she was reading.

As Autumn Somerset got the unhappy pigs into the back of her truck, she repeatedly recited the awards that awaited her at the end of her day.

A day that should have ended...oh, about three hours ago.

As a designer, she'd wrapped up appointments promptly at five o'clock. Yes, she'd been thinking about that tub of carrot-cake ice cream in her fridge even then. In fact, she'd thought about it since it had arrived a few days ago. Being a dedicated member of an ice-cream club had its perks, like new flavors every month. Her efforts at healthier eating meant she only consumed ice cream on Mondays, Wednesdays, Fridays and holidays.

True, every so often she created a holiday all her own. Like Cleaned the Kitchen Day. Or Completed a Job Day.

Or Mother Didn't Insult Me Day. That particular holiday earned her two scoops.

This being a Monday, she didn't even need a fake holiday.

"Sure do appreciate it, Autumn."

Forcing her mouth into a polite smile, Autumn turned to the man who had, over the past two years, gotten several pets that he then no longer wanted. *Ass*, she thought in her head, but what she said was, "It's no problem at all, Ralph."

"Got that first pig thinking it'd be small, ya know? Like a dog."

"Yes, I know." He'd thought he was getting a miniature pig—then he'd found out differently.

"Got the second one to keep it company, but that first one outgrew it in no time—"

"I do understand." And, damn it, she wanted her ice cream. If she had to converse, she'd rather do it with the pigs that were now squealing inside the cage of the truck. "I have to get going so I can get them settled." Trying for a speck of diplomacy, she suggested, "You should really think about gifts other than pets, don't you think? Perhaps your kids would like a nice swing set? I could design one for you."

"Can't afford that."

Smile locked in place, she volunteered her sister without pause. "Ember and I will help with that, okay? But only if you promise me, no more animals."

His face lit up.

Good. One job down. She'd tackle Ember next.

At least her sister loved animals as much as she did—which, honestly, might be the only thing they had in common other than blood.

By the time she got the pigs to the farm, it was after nine o'clock. Pavlov, their six-year-old redbone coonhound, met her in the yard, jumping around the truck in excitement. Because she lived on a farm, Pavlov didn't have to be locked in the house while she was away. The doggy door let him in when he wanted—to her side of the house, her sister's, or their parents' separate residence—but more often than not he preferred to visit with a cow or mule or even a turkey.

"Hey, buddy. Miss me?"

Too busy seeing what new friends she'd brought home, Pavlov paid her no attention. Never had a dog been so taken with other animals.

"Anxious to meet, huh?" While Pavlov bounded around, jumping into the truck and then out again, she set the pigs loose in the wide-open pen.

He barked in excitement.

Noses to the ground and already rooting through their new digs, the pigs moved forward. "I present Matilda and Olivia."

Pavlov, aptly named, went into the pen, too, only because the gate was open. With the sun splashing crimson across the sky, she waited, arms folded over the wooden post, while they got acquainted. It warmed her heart to see the pigs so happy. The smaller of the two ran circles as he explored the area. The biggest one found the shade and then rolled around, wallowing in freedom.

How often had Ralph even had them outside? She'd taken them from the basement, poor babies. Yes, they'd been fed and had straw to lie on, but it wasn't the same. Farm animals needed fresh air and sunshine.

Here, at the Fresh Start Farm, they'd get that…and more.

"You're home now, babies." Stepping into the pen, too, Autumn found a grassy spot to sit and spent another half hour lavishing love, scratches and hugs on the affectionate animals.

Finally, as the sun sank behind the trees and mosquitoes filled the air, she headed in. All it took to get Pavlov to come along was to open the gate again.

The dog walked through every open door, every single time. That, in part, accounted for his name.

Because he'd jumped into the truck bed, she took her time driving the short distance, going gently over ruts and small hills so she wouldn't jostle him too much, and then parked on the gravel lot behind the sprawling farmhouse. Porch lights had automatically flicked on.

"Race you in," she told Pavlov and then took off running. Ears flopping, he gave chase and they hit the door together, her laughing and him barking.

Unfortunately, after getting two steps into the foyer, she found Ember waiting on her.

"About time!" Ember stood from the couch, where she'd been flipping through a design magazine. "Where have you been, anyway? It's late. And ewww, Autumn, you reek."

"Nice to see you, too." Putting the shower on the back burner, she made a beeline to her kitchen sink, where she washed her hands and arms up to her elbows.

Pavlov ate the food she put into his dish like he hadn't been fed in a month, which was just his way, then drank noisily, splashing water everywhere. Finally, with slobbering chops, he greeted Ember.

Laughing, Ember said, "You are such a pig, Pavlov."

Speaking of pigs…

As Pavlov headed into the living room and his big pillow bed, Ember shook her head. "I take it he's sleeping with you tonight?"

Pavlov varied his routine, sometimes staying at her side of the house, sometimes Ember's, and sometimes even with her parents or their hired man, Mike. "Looks like."

"That dog is so fickle."

"He loves us all." Ignoring the reason for her sister's visit, Autumn took the ice cream from the freezer.

"Is that going to be your dinner?"

Unwilling to debate her eating habits, Autumn pointed a spoon at her. "I volunteered you today."

With a groan, Ember flopped into a chair at the table. She, at least, looked fresh and pretty in a sundress and cute sandals. Her dark hair, much like Autumn's but with reddish streaks supplied by a salon, didn't look frazzled and wasn't soaked in sweat.

No matter what Ember did, she never seemed to sweat. If she hadn't been her sister, Autumn might dislike her on principle alone.

"Ralph gave us two pigs, one miniature—maybe—and one definitely not. I just got them settled, thus the lovely aroma you noted."

"What a jerk! Two dogs, a cat, ducks and now pigs? What part of 'not animal-friendly' is he not getting?"

Luckily they'd found good forever homes for the dogs and cat. It was a little tougher with the farm animals, since they didn't want them turned into food. "That's why I volunteered you. I promised him we'd build a swing set for his kids, *if* he'd stop getting animals."

Skewing her gloss-covered mouth to the side in thought, Ember frowned, then gave a decisive nod. "I should have enough scrap wood to make something nice. Good thinking. You draw it up and then help me put it together, and you've got a deal." She offered her palm.

Autumn high-fived her. "It's a genius plan, thought of spur-of-the-moment, but only if it actually works." More often than not, they agreed on most everything when it came to saving animals. They were well suited to run the animal rescue together.

The rest of life? Not so much.

Using that as a perfect segue, Ember gave her a sideways look. "Speaking of genius plans—"

Autumn froze. Ember's plans were always proof positive that they led very different lives.

"—guess who's in town?"

Shrugging, Autumn shoved a big bite of ice cream into her mouth. She had a feeling she'd need it.

Looking like a magician about to perform an amazing trick, Ember announced, "Tash Ducker."

The ice cream stuck halfway down her throat. Disbelieving, suffering a mix of dread and curiosity, Autumn choked. When she finally got her breath, she asked, "Tash is back?"

Many years ago—sixteen, to be exact—she'd had a ridiculous crush on him. Two grades above her in high school, and oh-so gorgeous, she'd gotten severely tongue-tied whenever he looked her way. Even after they'd graduated, she couldn't seem to look at him without going mute. Once he'd finished college, he'd moved away and she hadn't seen him since.

Going into self-survival mode, a necessity with her family, Autumn replied, "Huh" with as much nonchalance as she could muster. To further that lie of disinterest, she asked, "What'd you do today? I tried to call you about the pigs, but you didn't answer."

"Now that I know it was about pigs, I'm glad." Ember

flashed the smile that made all the local guys stupid. "Actually, I had a date and didn't want to be interrupted. I figured whatever it was, you could handle it."

That answer, given far too often, took some of the delight from the ice cream. "So...what if it had been an emergency?"

"You didn't leave a message." One eyebrow lifted. "I assume you would if it was life or death?"

"Meaning you'll only answer my calls if someone is dying?"

"Meaning," Ember stressed, "that just because you don't date doesn't mean I shouldn't. Besides, I'd already checked in on Mom and Dad."

Well, that was something. Hopeful that Ember wouldn't start in on her lack of a social life, Autumn nodded her gratitude.

"They needed groceries, and I swung by to get their stuff on my way home."

"Thanks." A few years ago, their dad had suffered a debilitating stroke, leaving him largely dependent on the care of others. Ten years older than Tracy, their sixty-year-old mother, Flynn Somerset still had his wit, but not the use of one arm and one leg.

Together, she and Ember had built their parents a small house on the forty acres left to them by their grandparents. It made helping them easier and more convenient, plus Autumn liked that she could get to them in minutes if anything came up.

As a designer, she'd fashioned the house for her father's disability, making everything wheelchair-accessible and putting all handles and light switches lower, so he could reach them. The walk-in tub and shower made bathing so much easier. An open floor plan kept the home airy and filled with light, and made it possible to see their dad from almost every room.

Ember, who'd learned carpentry from him, had overseen the construction...and they'd only butted heads a few times in the decision-making process. When it came to design, Autumn insisted on having her way.

That wasn't something that happened very often.

Their parents loved the end result because they still had their independence, but weren't really alone.

The old farmhouse had been divided into a duplex with Autumn living one side, Ember on the other. One interior door allowed them to visit without going back outside.

Ember used the door quite often, always on the presumption that Autumn had nothing "good" going on.

True enough.

However, Autumn never dared to intrude because Ember was the opposite, meaning she always indulged in the good stuff—aka, man candy.

"That's where I saw him, by the way. At the grocery."

Avoiding eye contact, Autumn asked, "Mom and Dad are all settled now?"

"Yup." With a knowing smile, Ember said, "But hey, you're changing the subject. Want to tell me why?"

"I wasn't," she lied. Everyone knew lying to one's little sister wasn't a sin. Heck, it barely counted at all. "You mentioned them so I thought I'd—"

"Avoid talking about Tash?" Ember didn't bother to hide her amusement.

Oh, how that sisterly laugh annoyed her—enough that she gave up any pretense of disinterest.

Whispering, because seriously, this was nerve-racking, Autumn asked, "You're sure it was him?"

Just as quietly, Ember leaned in and replied, *"Yes."*

With just a tiny bit of evil hope, Autumn asked, "How's he look?" By now he could be balding. Maybe he'd picked up a beer belly. Lost his studliness altogether. She was thirty-two, so that made him thirty-four. Plenty old enough for him to have drastically changed.

Ember leaned even closer. "He's even hotter now."

Deflated, Autumn sat back in her seat. "Figures." Tucking back into her ice cream, she tried to picture him a decade older, but failed. In her mind, he looked the very same. Young, healthy, energetic…and disinterested in her. "Did he say why he's back?"

Deflecting, Ember rolled a shoulder. "He's moved here for good."

Hmm. What was her sister up to? "Settling here with his wife?" That'd maybe make sense.

"He's not married."

Okay, so she wasn't married, either. She knew her reasons. But what were his? "You know that how?"

"I talked with him. In fact, we talked about you."

Lord. The ice cream must have numbed her brain, because she couldn't think of a single thing to say. Left eye twitching, she stared at Ember instead.

"I have a plan."

After pushing back her chair in haste, Autumn put space between herself and whatever nonsense her sister contrived. With a definitive *"No,"* she headed for the sink. *Whatever it is, ten times no.* After rinsing her bowl, she stuck it in the dishwasher and tried to make a strategic retreat to the shower. "Later."

Ember jumped into her path. Wearing an expression of extreme disappointment, she shook her head. "Just look at you, Autumn."

"That's a little hard to do."

"You know what I mean. You've given up and just don't care anymore. The good news is that I can fix it."

It? They'd had this conversation too many times. Truthfully, she'd never cared that much about the things Ember obsessed over, like makeup, hairstyles and the trendiest clothes.

Crossing her arms under her boobs, Autumn said, "You mean me. You want to fix *me*."

Damn it, she was the *it*.

Rather than deny it, Ember pinched the air. "Just a tiny bit. Like..." She looked at Autumn with obvious disapproval, and lamented dramatically, "Your *hair*. I'm not sure if that started out as a ponytail or what, but now it's just a mess."

"I loaded and unloaded pigs." She pointed at Ember. "By myself, if you'll recall, since you refused to answer the phone."

"I'm very glad you saved them from Ralph. That's one thing we don't need to work on—your compassion."

Hallelujah. She had an asset.

"But those clothes? I'm the builder, you're the designer, but you dress like you work—"

"On a farm? With *pigs*?"

"That was later and you know it. This afternoon, you met with clients."

Autumn shrugged.

"You should wear pretty dresses that flatter your figure, not pants that look like they came from the back of Grandma's closet."

A slow inhale didn't help. True, she was something of a visual mess. Inside, she mostly had it together. And, damn it, she liked herself. So she dressed for her own comfort?

Big deal. Everyone else could bite it. "How about you don't dissect me, and I won't dissect you?"

Ember gave a small flinch. "I don't mean to be insulting—"

God save her if she ever did mean it. Every time Ember or their mother got started, her stomach hurt. She hated that she didn't measure up, and biting back sarcasm only made it worse.

"Autumn, stop that." Ember started to draw her in for a hug, then sniffed the air and changed to giving her a small shake instead. "It's just that you're pretty and you practically hide it. It wouldn't take much to really make you stand out—and as an incentive I already…" She drew a breath as if to gird herself.

For Autumn's ire. Meaning it had to be bad.

"What?" Alarm chased circles in her gut. "Ember, what did you do?"

"You have an appointment with Tash tomorrow."

Good thing she had a wall beside her, because Autumn collapsed against it. "You didn't."

"Did." In a rush now, Ember explained, "He needs a designer, Autumn, and you know you're the best around!"

She had compassion and design skill. Hey, the compliments were piling up.

"Forget that crazy crush you had on him—"

"It was eons ago!" Heat bloomed in Autumn's face. She hated to be reminded of her most awkward years. "Of course, I've forgotten it. Maybe *you've* forgotten that I was even engaged after that."

It was the wrong thing to bring up. Ember's expression softened. "I know. Neither of us will ever forget that."

Autumn threw up her hands. "No one died, so stop looking so grim."

"You haven't dated since then."

"Choice," she emphasized. "There's no one here who interests me, that's all." *Liar, liar, pants on fire*. Sure, some guys asked, but everyone here remembered her engagement and certain assumptions came with that, making everything superawkward. "Let's forget all my past failures, okay? I'm over them, I swear."

"Great." Satisfied, Ember beamed at her. "Then it's no problem to meet with Tash, right?"

It was a massive problem, but how could she explain that after swearing it wasn't? She could only think of one excuse. "The thing is, you don't set my schedule. I already had my day booked."

Dismissing that, Ember waved a hand. "I looked at our joint calendar and, um, rearranged a few things."

Of all the intrusive, pushy, over-the-top... Straightening, Autumn squared her shoulders. "Rearrange them *back*."

"Can't." Turning, Ember headed for the shared door. "Tash is expecting you at six."

"I finish work at five!"

"Yeah, see, that's how I rearranged. Added another hour for ya. If you come straight home, I'll have a tiny bit of time to work on your appearance before you have to head to his place on the other side of the lake." She gave an airy wave. "Tomorrow, if any emergencies come up, I promise to answer the phone to leave you free and clear."

"That must mean you don't have a date."

Ember shared a slow smile. "No, but you do." And with that, she closed the door.

Feeling militant and more than a little irate, Autumn walked over and flipped the lock, then yelled through the door, "I can get myself ready, by the way! I don't need help."

A loud "Ha!" came right back to her.

They needed more insulation in the walls, and thicker doors, obviously.

Frustration amplified the discomfort of her sweaty clothes and clammy skin. Honestly, she could put up with the idiocy of the Ralphs of the world every day for the rest of her life, and it'd be easier than dealing with her family.

She really, like very badly, wanted to reopen the door and somehow intrude into Ember's life. But Ember would probably just laugh and go about her business.

Few things ever got to her. In almost every scenario, she was the life of the party, the fun girl, the one in demand.

Only one time had she ever seen her sister truly leveled, and she never wanted to go through that again.

They both had their father's coloring, with dark hair and blue eyes, but Ember had also inherited their mother's fun-loving ways.

Autumn had her mother's plump build.

She knew this because for most of her life, her mother had pointed it out.

Give Ember a break. She's a free spirit, like me. But, oh, Autumn, you poor dear, you got my big bones.

Yay. Lucky her.

Maybe she could add that info to all her social media.

Favorite movie: *A Perfect Getaway.*

Favorite music: anything by Kid Rock.

Outstanding feature: big bones.

As she walked away, she thought, *Biggest flaw: lets my family boss me around.*

Right there, in the hallway leading to the bathroom, she stalled. No, she did not have to let them do that. For a while now, she'd been working on being more assertive. Largely without success, but hey, that didn't mean she should give up.

So was it a bad thing to meet an old classmate who needed design work? No. Not if she didn't make it weird.

Would she do it under Ember's terms? Absolutely not.

She would get herself ready. She'd be professional but comfortable. By God, she had nothing to prove to her sister or to Tash.

And if Ember didn't like it, too bad.

Autumn wouldn't let it bother her.

With that decision made, she got moving again. She wanted that long-awaited shower, a comfy spot in the bed, and then she'd read.

Pavlov followed her, staying in the bathroom with her while she showered, and then he lumbered into the bed beside her as she began reading the newest title from Karen Rose. She did love a scary romantic-suspense storyline, with an evil madman and smart characters. In fact, she got so engrossed in the lives of the characters, she forgot all about her sister and hunky guys from the past and her stupid big bones.

Not until midnight rolled around did she call it quits and close the book. Not an easy thing to do, but the alarm would go off early and she had a full day—a day that would now run extra late thanks to her sister.

Tash Ducker. Her heart beat a little faster. Would he remember her? Would he see all the ways she'd changed?

Would he *like* those changes?

Autumn groaned. Maybe she'd let her sister give her just a few pointers, after all.

"You're already messing up your hair."

Putting away her dishes after a fast bowl of soup, Autumn said, "That's why I usually put it in a ponytail. Any type of hairdo just falls apart."

Tucking, smoothing and rearranging, Ember said, "If you'd let me use some hair spray…"

Shouldering away her sister's busy fingers, Autumn explained, "Hair spray gets all gummy when I sweat."

"Maybe you could try not sweating?"

Incredulous, she closed the dishwasher with a little more force than necessary and spun to face Ember. "Yeah, why don't you invent a way for me to do that? We'll sell it and make enough to save all the animals."

"Don't be sarcastic."

Why not? Her sarcasm was almost as top-notch as her compassion. When Ember pulled a tube of something from her pocket, Autumn scowled. "Now what?"

"It's just lip gloss. It won't kill you."

"I don't like it. It tastes bad."

"It does not."

"Does if you lick it…and I can't seem to keep from doing that."

Rolling her eyes, Ember gave up and put away the shiny pink gloss. "Fine. Maybe you can make the 'naked mouth look' work for you."

A rap at the screen door drew their attention and Mike, their handyman, farmhand, do-everything guy-in-residence grinned. His shaggy blond hair should have been cut weeks ago, and working in the sun had left him a little too tanned…in a most appealing way.

All in all, he looked scrumptious—but better than his stellar appearance? He did great work with the animals, never complained, accepted living in the loft apartment over the barn and was always around when they needed him.

He winked at Autumn. "A naked mouth works for most

men. Don't let Ember tell you otherwise. And for the record, I think that stuff tastes bad, too."

Ember's eyes flared, then narrowed dangerously.

Uh-oh. Autumn hurried to the door and opened it. "Mike. What's up?"

"I was going to ask you that."

"Oh." She gestured lamely. "I just have this appointment in a bit and Ember wanted to practice sprucing me up and—"

Hands in his pockets, he smiled and entered. "I meant with our new members, the pigs. When did they arrive? You left too early this morning for me to ask you about them."

Mentally slapping her own head, Autumn laughed. "Right. Matilda and Olivia."

He went right past their names. "You do look great, though—but then, you always do."

Resisting the urge to stick out her tongue at Ember, Autumn said smugly, "Why, thank you."

"Her scalp sweats."

Horrified, she gasped at Ember's bald statement.

"Everyone sweats." Indifferent, Mike shrugged, then took a jab. "Unless it's different for princesses?"

Eyes narrowed at her sister, Autumn said, "I certainly wouldn't know."

"Most of us wouldn't." Ignoring Ember now, Mike asked, "Anything special you want done with the pigs? I saw that you fed them this morning before leaving, and I fed them the usual in the afternoon and evening. I've already visited with them plenty, too, and let them play under the sprinkler for a while during the hottest part of the afternoon. Is there anything else?"

God love the man, he'd silenced Ember so easily, she could almost kiss him. Well, except that he might misunderstand the gesture of gratitude. She adored Mike, but there wasn't a speck of chemistry between them.

He and Ember, however... Different story.

Autumn went over the special diet she'd come up with for the pigs, and the area of the farm where she wanted them to get a little more freedom. "I have everything written down for you." She snatched up the paper on the counter. "Most important, though, is that I want them to feel loved in their new surroundings."

"Gave 'em lots of love," he assured her. "They're already settling in."

"Thank you. Seriously. You always go above and beyond."

"It's a wonderful place you've created here."

Ember folded her arms. "She didn't do it on her own, you know."

"Few people can feel really good about their jobs, but I do." Mike glanced at Ember, his gaze warming...and then he dismissed her. "If you don't need anything else, I figured I'd head into town for a bit. Tracy and Flynn mentioned the diner's chocolate lava cake, so I promised to bring back two slices with me."

Guilt made her frown. "Mom and Dad shouldn't impose on you...but wow, that does sound good."

His smile came big and easy. "It's not a problem. Your folks keep me entertained."

She could guess what that meant. "Mom gave you another sculpture, didn't she?" Her mother unintentionally made sexually suggestive sculptures that left Ember and Autumn red-faced more often than not. What should be one thing always ended up looking like something altogether different.

"I had to build a special bookcase to hold them all."

Winking, he headed for the door, and just before he stepped out, he added, "I'll bring some cake back for you, too."

Once the door closed behind him, Ember drifted toward it, looked out, then huffed. "He didn't offer me cake."

Autumn figured he wanted to offer her sister something altogether different. "Maybe if you were nicer to him…?"

"I'm nice to everyone." Turning back with a grin, she said, "Next time we shear the sheep, I'm going to offer to give him a trim, too."

"I like his hair longer." It curled against his neck, but didn't quite touch his big shoulders.

"Because you, sister dear, are into the messy look." Giving her a critical once-over, Ember nodded. "You know, Mike is right. You do look nice without a lot of makeup."

"Dad calls makeup war paint."

"Dad enjoys harassing Mom."

"And Mom enjoys the attention."

Ember hesitated, then released a long breath. "I'm sorry about mentioning your sweaty head."

Good God, Ember made her sound like the Niagara Falls of perspiration. "I'm often outside measuring stuff, you know." A lot of her design work was specifically geared toward kids' rooms and play areas, but she also created outdoor living spaces, man caves, she sheds, converted garages and more.

"I work outside, too," Ember pointed out.

"But you would never admit to sweating."

"Very true." She smoothed a long hank of Autumn's hair, then let her hand linger on her shoulder. "Anyway, I'm sorry. It was a stupid thing to say. Mike makes me… I don't know. Mean?" Liking that word, she nodded. "He makes me mean, but I should save all my meanness for him, not you."

Of all the ridiculous things! "He's an amazing employee. Why would you be mean to him?"

"He ignores me."

Autumn snorted. "No, he doesn't."

"He treats me the same as the animals. Or—" she wrinkled her nose "—Mom and Dad. It's disturbing." Ember flagged a hand. "He jokes with you, like you two are close pals, and I'm just a shadow hanging around."

Sudden comprehension widened Autumn's eyes. "You want him to be interested."

Ember sniffed, doing her best to look unaffected. "Maybe a little, but I shouldn't have insulted you to get it."

Especially since that tactic had backfired. Still a little amazed, Autumn said, "So you—"

"At least the jeans fit you instead of being all baggy." She tugged on a belt loop, almost pulling Autumn off her feet. "And I like your shirt. That's a good color for you."

Glancing down at her own chest, Autumn admired the bright tangerine hue. Personally, she thought it added color to her cheeks. "It's nice, right?"

"Very." With a glance at the clock, Ember urged her toward the door. "If you don't leave now, you might be stuck behind the train and then you'll be late."

Since Tash was on the other side of the lake, and it didn't make sense to take the boat then walk several blocks, she'd have to drive around and that meant crossing the railroad tracks.

"Well, shoot." She snatched up her big satchel of design materials, her portfolio, so she could show her previous projects, and slung the strap of her loaded purse over her shoulder.

Ember surprised her by kissing her cheek. "Go get him."

"Get the *job*, you mean." This trip—nice shirt and all—

wasn't about anything else. But she had to admit, having Ember's approval of her overall look gave her added confidence. "I'll see what he wants first."

Bobbing her eyebrows, Ember grinned.

"Stop that." Fighting a laugh at her sister's antics, Autumn shoved open the door and hurried to her truck, aware of Ember standing there smiling like a sap…and looking like she knew a secret.

Don't miss The Somerset Girls *by* New York Times
bestselling author Lori Foster!

Read on for a bonus novella, **When We First Met,**
*the prequel to debut author Cara Bastone's
heart-warming Forever Yours series, about
two neighbors who believe they are looking for
different things in love...until they realize what
they were looking for all along is right across the hall.*

WHEN WE FIRST MET

Cara Bastone

CHAPTER ONE

CAT LAFIEVRE WAS not a loser. But she sure had been losing a lot lately.

She flopped onto the couch in her small but comfortable apartment. The morning sun was just starting to creep across her floor. That was the main reason she was glad to live in the tallest building in the neighborhood; the rest of Brooklyn didn't block her sunshine.

At the beginning of the school year, she'd been convinced that this would be the best year ever. Everything had been coming up aces.

She'd had a miraculous stroke of luck and been given a class of only twenty students, unheard of in her school district, where the class sizes tended into the midtwenties.

Her dad's health was finally back on track after his heart

attack two years ago and she no longer felt obligated to take the five-hour train ride every weekend just to help her mom.

And she'd officially gotten over Sid.

Life was good.

But then, as it was wont to do, life decided to kick her in the ass.

Every few weeks, like clockwork, she'd gotten transfer students assigned to her classroom until she had a whopping twenty-nine students. The entire school was growing in population, more than the district had planned for, so the budget for supplies (already minuscule) was even less than it normally was. Which meant Cat was going out of pocket for a huge portion of the supplies she needed to teach her lessons.

Then, during Christmas break, Cat had walked into the grocery store around the corner from her parents' house and come face-to-face with Sid getting frisky with one of her oldest friends in the ice cream aisle. She wasn't Cat's *best* friend, but she was definitely someone that Cat had assumed would be a lifelong friend. And now things between them were just…weird.

And then the kicker. On Valentine's Day, her folks had been out for a romantic dinner (so cute) when her Pops had had a second heart attack (devastating). It was less serious than the first one had been, but still not good. Cat and her two sisters had divvied up the weekends, and she'd found herself schlepping up to Ithaca every third weekend.

She'd coasted to the end of the school year on fumes. She was lonely, exhausted and basically paying the public school system for the privilege of working.

Luckily for her, she knew exactly what she needed.

A fling.

A good old-fashioned love-'em-and-leave-'em-rose-between-the-teeth-handprint-against-the-window-condensation fling.

She wanted heat with some handsome man who promised her literally nothing. She wanted a few nights of mindless distraction, uncommitted companionship, something to fondly reminisce about on her eventual deathbed.

And she knew exactly who could give it to her: her neighbor Jared, who smoldered like he was constantly filming a cologne ad. He was gorgeous, a little ridiculous and apparently very good at sex.

Cat knew this because Clare, who lived a few floors down, had hooked up with him a year before when he was on a break with his girlfriend. Cat had asked Clare if it would be awkward if they slept with the same man and Clare had just laughed. "Trust me," she'd told Cat, "Jared is not that kind of man."

Now, Jared was apparently single again and Cat was looking for the right moment. She thought she'd found it a few months ago when Jared had invited her to a party at his house, but she'd gotten caught up in a great conversation with his roommate and the opportunity had passed her by. She didn't count that as a fail though, because Quentin, the roommate, was so cute. He'd been attentive and funny and seemed genuinely interested in the things she was saying. She'd left that party hoping that she'd made a new friend, but ever since that promising start, it seemed like he was avoiding her.

But wait! Cat's head popped up from the couch cushion like a prairie dog. She heard a door open in the hallway. Either that was Jared (time to flirt) or it was Quentin (time to friend). She slid on her flip-flops and raced to her front door.

QUENTIN FOSTER'S ROOMMATE was a prize idiot. The fact that Jared was also Quentin's first cousin did absolutely nothing to redeem him.

Quentin could not believe that he was looking down at the same pair of red-bottomed high heels neatly lined up next to the front door of his apartment again. It had been months, *months* since Jared had last hooked up with Lara. She'd finally stopped dropping by unexpectedly, wearing trench coats with suspiciously bare legs, frowning in disappointment when Quentin inevitably answered the door instead of Jared. She'd even returned the engagement ring that had at one point been Jared's mother's. It had been a blissful three months of radio silence.

Quentin had just begun to dare to dream that the rest of his life might just be Lara-less.

And now, on this rainy June Monday, here he was staring down at Lara's Louboutins once again. He grimaced over his shoulder at Jared's closed bedroom door. Technically it was 8:15 a.m. and technically that meant that Jared should be getting ready for work. But they were twenty-six years old and Quentin wasn't Jared's babysitter. And he sure as hell wasn't going to knock on any door that might be answered by Lara. He preferred his eyes un-scratched out.

His next few weeks were either going to be marked by Lara in his home every single second of the day, bogarting the remote control, filling his refrigerator with raw-juice smoothies he wasn't allowed to drink and taking forty-five-minute showers, or by his cousin's mopey whirlpool of misery after they broke up for the umpteenth time.

There was never any middle ground when it came to Jared and Lara.

Hearing footsteps from inside Jared's room and fearing a run-in with the dreaded Lara, Quentin hastily scuttled out of his apartment. He pulled the door closed, safely ensconced in the hallway of his building.

"Pssst!" came a whisper from across the hall as he juggled his thermos of coffee in one hand and his bag in the other. He suppressed a sigh. He knew exactly who was "pssst"-ing him and frankly, he wasn't sure he had the energy this morning. He knew, without a doubt, that if he turned around, he was going to see Cat LeFievre standing across the hall in her doorway in a pair of indecently short shorts.

It wasn't the shorts he had a problem with—heck, he had fever dreams about those shorts—it was the woman currently occupying said shorts who he'd been actively trying to avoid for the last few months.

Knowing that keeping his back to her for any longer was just going to be weird, Quentin finished locking his door and turned around. He didn't quite prevent his eyes from swooping down the length of her legs.

Not only was she in the shorts, she was also—God help him—eating a Popsicle.

During the school year, five days a week she wore demure, professional clothing to the elementary school where she worked. But on the weekends? On the weekends she liked to, as he'd once heard her say, "channel Aphrodite." Which basically meant that she drank red wine, ate dark chocolate and wore as little clothing as legally possible.

For the first time in his life Quentin found himself dreading the summertime. Because starting this very day, Ms. LeFievre was officially on summer break, and there would be no break from her hotness.

"Hey, Quentin," she said, leaning against the doorjamb and biting off the end of her Popsicle. She was still whispering, her eyes on the door Quentin had just closed.

"Hey, Cat."

Her big brown eyes flicked to his for the first time since he'd turned around. "Did your superhot roomie leave for work yet?"

Quentin suppressed yet another sigh.

"I was thinking," she continued in a low voice, "that I might try to synchronize our exits today, maybe walk him to the train."

See, this, *this right here*, was exactly why Jared was an absolute numbskull. Because if he opened his eyes just the tiniest bit, he could have Cat LaFievre on a silver platter, Popsicle and all. Instead he was in there, tangled up in the sheets with a woman who'd once thrown a gyro at his head because he sat on the remote and changed the channel in the middle of a TV show she was watching.

Instead of acknowledging that Cat had the hots for his dummy of a cousin, Quentin chose to shift the subject. "Where are you off to so early in the morning? I thought you were on summer break?"

She contracted into herself, one hand on her heart and her eyes squinched closed, the Popsicle lolling dangerously in her fingers. "Oh, my God. That sounds so good it hurts. Say it again, big boy."

Quentin pinched his lips together but couldn't keep his cheeks from rising. She was so ridiculous. He didn't resist the urge to play. Leaning forward, he lifted one eyebrow and used his deepest, sexiest voice. "Summer break," he crooned.

She shivered theatrically. "That's the stuff."

He couldn't help but laugh.

Smiling right back at him, she finished off the Popsicle and cracked the stick in two. "Yup. Officially on break. I was gonna head out to Fort Tilden beach this morning before the crowds descend."

"How do you get out there?" He adjusted the strap on his messenger bag and cocked his head to the side, his interest piqued.

"The train to a shuttle bus, it's not—oh, I see what you're doing."

He flushed. "What?"

"You're totally pretending to have a normal conversation with a neighbor but actually you're nerding out. Don't think I've forgotten about your public-transportation obsession." She ticktocked her finger back and forth and gave him a knowing look.

He flushed even more, which he knew was painfully obvious on his complexion. He had coppery hair and pale skin. Even the slightest blush and he was roughly the same hue as a can of coke. "It's not an obsession," he insisted, fiddling with his messenger bag again. "It's my *job*."

"Uh-huh. Says the guy with a train set in his bedroom."

Aaaand here they were, back to the reason he'd been attempting to avoid her for the last three months.

Because after the last breakup with Lara, Jared had unilaterally decided that he was going to throw a party and invite all the hotties he knew. The hottie from across the hall had been absolutely no exception. Quentin had had the befuddling experience of coming home from work and discovering no less than twenty-two beautiful women in his apartment.

A little overwhelmed, he'd been quite relieved to find himself in a friendly chat with his cute across-the-hall neighbor. "Just call me Cat. Catherine sounds like somebody who went down with the Titanic," she'd told him.

Half an hour later, he'd been downright stoked to be

chatting with her. She was whip-smart and funny. Her features were small, a ski-jump nose and a rosebud mouth, but she had this way of animating her entire body when she talked that made her presence expand and fill any space that she was occupying. She had lots of wild brown hair that had tumbled over her shoulders that night. She'd worn a big, slouchy sweater, tight jeans and mismatched socks.

They'd covered the basic subjects quickly. Where she was from—Ithaca—and where he was from—Sleepy Hollow. She'd briefly enacted headless-horseman-ing his head off when he'd told her that detail. And they'd quickly plunged on to more interesting topics. What she'd been for Halloween that year—Doc from *Back to the Future*—and the most ridiculous reason a kid ever gave for not turning in homework to her—apparently Santa took it as evidence for his "nice" file.

Quentin remembered every word of their conversation from that night.

When she'd asked to see his bedroom, his hands had started sweating.

Once, at a buddy's bachelor party—the one after which Lara had briefly dumped Jared for attending—Quentin had placed a random bet at a roulette table. He'd watched in blank, stunned amazement as his number came up and he won $1,650. That moment with Cat had been exactly the same feeling.

He wasn't altogether unfortunate when it came to women. But he was quiet and often a little shy and had only recently figured out that a short beard made his jaw look more defined. He'd gone on a few semi-successful dates over the last few months. But even so, he was plenty nervous escorting the cutest girl at the party toward his bedroom. It wasn't something that happened very often to him.

He'd left the door open, stood to the side and shoved his hands in his pockets. Cat had come in to the room and immediately started touching stuff. She trailed a fingertip over his textbooks, bounced a few times on one corner of his bed, checked the view from his window. And then she'd turned and spotted the antique Lionel train set that was set up along the back edge of his dresser.

"You have a train set? That's so *cute*."

His stomach sank as she crossed the room to inspect it. *Cute* was a word with so many different connotations. When he'd inwardly labelled her as the cutest girl at the party, the connotation was that he'd very much like to make her breakfast after she slept over. When she looked at his train set and called him cute, he feared the connotation was that she'd like to watch a rom-com with him while they sat on opposite sides of the couch. Her version of cute had a distinctly nonsexual bent to it.

"Um. Yeah. I'm an urban planner, like I mentioned before. My specific area of interest is public transportation. I just graduated from NYU last year." He didn't usually mention his prestigious alma mater, but he felt a need to legitimize—in any possible way—the presence of the toy train in his room. "I guess it's always been an interest of mine." He cleared his throat. "My grandfather was a train conductor for Amtrak. We had a love of trains in common."

"Wow. That's so sweet."

He was still trying to figure out if *sweet* was any better than *cute* when she'd come up beside him and peeked out his bedroom door toward the living room. Her face fell. "Shoot," she'd muttered. "Guess I missed my chance!"

Quentin had followed her eye line across the party to where Jared was leading one of his more shapely coworkers into his bedroom, then firmly closing the door behind them.

Understanding conked Quentin over the head with all the subtlety of a nine iron.

Cat had come to the party with her eye on his cousin.

"Oh."

"I meant to finally make my move on your sexy room-mate but you distracted me with your hot takes on breakfast sausage!" she'd playfully accused Quentin.

They had, in fact, spent a good deal of time debating whether flat or round breakfast sausage was better.

They'd chatted a few more minutes after that before Quentin told her that he was tired and she took the hint. He'd locked himself into his room that night feeling pretty stupid and deflated.

They'd run into one another in the hallway a few times since then, but as she always found a way to ask about Jared, Quentin had started trying to avoid her.

Jared was tall and good-looking. He had this sort of dark-haired vampire thing going on. He always looked to Quentin like he'd spent the night crying over his own poetry, but apparently women were into it. With or without Lara in his life, Jared didn't need Quentin as a wingman. He could pull pretty much any woman he had his eye on.

"Ah, right," Quentin finally said, standing across the hall from her, responding to her comment about his train set. "Well." He cleared his throat. "Gotta get to work. Have fun at the beach."

"Hold on a sec and I'll head down with you!" she chirped.

"Gotta run!" he said over his shoulder and took the stairs two at a time.

CHAPTER TWO

THE THURSDAY MORNING after she'd run into Quentin in the hallway, Cat tossed her gym bag over her shoulder and headed out. By the middle of (the blessedly glorious) summer break, she would be able to sleep in. But less than a week in, she was still naturally waking up early and searching for things to fill her days with, which was why she loved New York City. There was literally always something to do. She'd gone to the beach the last few mornings, but not today. Today she was working out.

But first, pie.

This neighborhood had a pie shop that was famous citywide. It was a cute little establishment with long, wooden communal tables and myriad pies in sparkly glass cases. There were more kinds of pie than Cat had ever even heard of before she'd first become a patron. They had the classics, of course: apple, cherry, pecan. But then there were also chocolate chess pies and salty honey streusels, black oat pies with crust as thick as the September issue of *Vogue*.

It was a dangerous, dangerous heaven.

In the two years that Cat had lived in this neighborhood, she'd seen plenty of employees come and go through the pie shop, and almost every single one of them quit a few pants sizes larger than when they'd been hired. Cat herself attributed her soft belly and more than a handful of ass to their lemon custard pie. She didn't mind. She considered every pound a worthy trade for the ambrosia they were selling.

She was just polishing off her slice of pie, standing at the counter in the window of the shop, when she looked up and saw Jared and Quentin walking by, chatting to one another. Quentin was wheeling a bike as they walked, and they paused at the corner, obviously about to part ways.

Here was her chance!

Cat tossed her plate and bolted out the door, but she wasn't three steps toward them when they waved at one another and Jared headed off in the direction of the train and Quentin started putting his bike helmet on.

Dang! She'd wanted to catch them together because Quentin was easier to talk to than Jared and if she chatted with both of them maybe Jared would see how charming she was. But it was not to be. Should she follow Jared and risk some more of their slightly awkward conversation that they'd occasionally had when they'd run into one another in the laundry room? Or should she catch up with Quentin?

"Hey, Quentin!" she said, coming up beside him on the street corner.

"Cat! Hi." He was surprised to see her. "Um, on your way to the train?"

"Yup, just stopped by the pie shop for a morning slice."

He laughed. "You say that like a slice of pie for break-fast is a perfectly normal thing."

"Isn't it?"

He laughed again and then spied her gym bag over her shoulder. "So, slice of pie and then you go work out?"

He looked cute this morning in his slacks and button-down, carefully put together for work. His coppery hair, usually very neat, was messy from where he'd put his bike helmet on and then slid it off when they'd started talking. He wasn't as tall as Jared was, but something about seeing Quentin out in the world, standing next to this man-sized bike, made Cat realize that he was bigger than she'd thought he was. He was wide in the shoulders and probably six or seven inches taller than she was.

"Pretty much, yeah."

"Which gym do you belong to?"

"Oh, I don't. I don't really work out in the traditional sense. I'm headed to a pole-dancing class."

He went instantly, adorably, pink in the cheeks. He was obviously trying to school his features into a placid look. "I...didn't know they offered those kinds of classes."

"Oh, sure. They're really popular. The dance studio where I take them offers them all day. I'll take the nine and then probably stay for the ten o'clock as well."

Now he couldn't stop his eyebrows from raising even higher. "There's something slightly, um, incongruous about a 9:00 a.m. pole-dancing class, no?"

Cat burst out laughing. "Totally. It's kind of like taking a biology course at eleven o'clock on a Saturday night. Just doesn't quite fit the aesthetic."

Silence descended for a moment while he scratched at

the back of his neck, obviously searching for something to say.

"You, uh, been doing it long?"

She leaned in, wanting to make him blush again for some reason. "Are you asking if I'm any good?" She waggled her eyebrows.

"No! God." He did that cute thing he sometimes did when he was flustered where he dragged a hand down his face as if he were trying to wipe away any evidence of whatever embarrassed expression wanted to make a home there. "I was just making conversation."

"To answer the question you didn't ask, no, I'm not any good. It's really freaking hard and I'm still pretty much trying to figure out how to slide around the pole without getting major pole burn."

"Pole burn," he repeated dimly. He looked a little dazed.

Deciding to cut him some slack, Cat changed the subject. "I've never seen you ride before."

She often rode her bike to and from the elementary school where she worked a few neighborhoods south, and she was pretty sure she knew all the bike riders in their building because there was one big room in the basement where they all locked their bikes. She'd never seen Quentin down there before.

"I don't really," he confessed. "I'm doing it for work right now."

"What do you mean?"

"Well, I'm working with the city on reconfiguring the bike lanes in a few key places and we needed some more hands-on experience to really be able to answer the questions we have."

"That's so cool!"

"In theory. In practice I'm hoarse by the time I get to work because I've been screaming for half an hour."

Cat laughed again. "What, you're not a fan of cars side-swiping you and pedestrians with strollers jumping into your path and the doors of parked cars swinging open to smash you into the pavement?"

He groaned. "I'll be glad when I can just take the train again like a normal New Yorker. Bikers have a death wish."

"Your roommate is the craziest biker I've ever seen, did you know that? I watched him cut off a semitruck on Third Ave. Like it was no big deal. Just *zoom*, weaving in and out of traffic."

He blinked at her for a second and Cat realized that she was grinning at him like a crazy person. He was so easy to talk to. She could have stood on that corner and chatted with him for another hour. But he was putting his helmet on, straightening his bag over his shoulder.

"Well, I don't want to make you late for your, uh, class," he said after a second.

"Right. Those poles won't slide around themselves."

He was decidedly pink again. "Uh-huh."

"It was nice to run into you, Quentin," she said. "Twice in one week."

He suddenly looked uncomfortable. "Right."

Was it her or was he backing away from her?

"Maybe we should do it again," she suggested. "On purpose? Hang out, I mean. I don't have many friends in the building."

"Right," he repeated. "Sure. Okay. See you later." He waved at her and hopped on his bike.

For someone who claimed to hate being on a bike, he certainly looked natural on one. He'd done that one-leg-swing thing to get on and now merged smoothly with traffic.

It was the second time in a week that he'd pretty much run away from her. Maybe she'd have to do something about that.

CHAPTER THREE

THE FOLLOWING SATURDAY night Quentin was sniffing at a container of questionably old Chinese food when someone knocked on his door. He chucked the food into the trash on his way past and tugged his door open.

"Hey, Quent— *Mamma mia.*" Cat was standing on the other side of the door in tight jeans and a shirt roughly the size of a handkerchief. Her brown hair was wild around her shoulders the way it had been the night of the party at his house. Her big brown eyes were popping with some sort of magical makeup trick and Quentin couldn't help but notice that she was looking him up and down.

"What?" he asked, looking down at himself, checking for spills of some kind.

"I've never seen you in jeans and a T-shirt before," she

said, her face melting into an expression he wasn't sure how to interpret. "You're always in your work clothes."

"Saturday," he said by way of explanation.

"Yes. Exactly," she replied, a smile splitting her face. "It is Saturday. Which is exactly why I'm knocking on your door right now."

"What's up?"

"Well, you know Clare from two floors down?"

He didn't but she didn't seem to register the shake of his head. She barreled on.

"She and I were gonna head out to the Jarhouse tonight to see that storytelling show they do there, but she just bailed and I'm already all dolled up."

Dancing eyebrows accompanied her big smile and he just stared back at her until it dawned on him. "Oh. Are you asking me to go with you?"

"I don't wanna walk by myself. I'll buy you a drink if you play my bodyguard on the walk there?"

He inwardly sighed. He should have known better than to think, even for a second, that she was asking him on a date. He was the "cute" guy who still kept toys in his bedroom. Not exactly date material. But he didn't blame her for wanting someone to walk her to the bar. They lived in a slightly skeevy part of the Gowanus neighborhood of Brooklyn. Half a mile over and you were in ritzy Park Slope. But in this area, the blocks were long and dark at night; most of the buildings were warehouses, not residences. The Jarhouse was the place to be on a Saturday night, but walking there alone could definitely be nerve-racking.

"Sure, lemme just grab my wallet."

He was back from his room in a second and glancing over at her as he locked his apartment door. He couldn't help but meet her smile with one of his own. She was one of those people whose smile you felt all the way down to your toes.

"So," Quentin said as they started the few-block walk to the venue, "what've you been doing on your summer break?"

"Let's see… I've been to the beach a bunch already. I'm also trying to catch up on all the movies I missed over the school year. And I've been brunching pretty hard."

He laughed. "You make it sound like a contact sport."

"The way I brunch? It kind of is. I'm like 'pitcher of mimosas before I start flipping tables!'"

"I hope you're not drinking those pitchers all by yourself."

She laughed. "No. Trust me, I'm a lightweight. I don't really drink that much at all. I've been told I'm kind of a party all on my own."

He could definitely understand why someone would say that to her. She sort of sparkled under the circles of the streetlights they passed, the orange light catching on the curves of her dark hair, the rise of her cheekbones, the white flash of her teeth. She skipped along to keep up with his long strides, and as she'd attached her keys to her belt loop with a carabiner, each step she took jingled.

"You do sort of have a one-man-band thing going on," he told her, hiding his smile and tucking his hands into his pockets.

She laughed and nudged his side with a pointy elbow. "I'm deciding to take that as a compliment."

"Good."

When they got to the Jarhouse, she scampered forward and grabbed the door before he could.

"After you," he said, stepping back so that she'd go in first.

"No, no," she insisted. "You performed your body-guarding duties admirably—at least allow me to hold the door for you."

He reached over her head and grabbed the door. "My mom would kick my ass if I didn't hold the door for you."

"It's nice to be out with a gentleman." She grinned up at him and ducked inside.

He was grateful for the dimly lit bar because he was pretty sure he was blushing again as he followed Cat inside. Music played over the sound system and people were milling around and ordering drinks in the front room. In the back room, they would be charged a cover for the storytelling show that would start in half an hour or so.

"Let's get a drink!"

"You want to grab seats for the show?" Quentin asked, speaking at the same time as Cat.

"Oh." She leaned back to catch his eye. "Are you staying for the show? I thought you were just staying for one drink."

He reached up and flattened his hair down with the palm of his hand. "Um, I thought I would stay. If I'm invited, I mean."

She jumped forward and squeezed his arm above the elbow. "You're invited!" she said immediately. "I'm so stoked you want to stay! I just figured that I was disrupting your Saturday night." Squinting her eyes, she cocked her head to one side and brought her hands to her hips. "I kind of get the feeling sometimes that I annoy you or something, so I didn't want to assume that you were gonna spend the whole evening with me."

Instead of standing there, gaping like a dope, he nodded toward the bar and led her through the crowd. With the same kind of magical serendipity that had won Quentin $1,650 in Atlantic City, two people vacated their bar stools right as they approached the bar. Quentin and Cat plunked into the seats and the bartender waved at them from the other side of the bar, saying she'd be over in a second.

"What do you mean you think you annoy me?"

She shrugged and gave him a much smaller smile than usual. "I thought we'd gotten along so well that night we first hung out, at the party at your house. I had such a good time that I was pretty sure we were gonna end up being really good friends. But then I got the feeling that you were avoiding me. We never really hung out again even though I sort of tried to make it happen."

He thought guiltily of the times she'd offered to walk him to the train or caught up to him in the lobby for a quick chat. He'd dodged her almost every time.

"I know I can be a lot for some people," she continued, but he jumped right in to stop her.

"You're not a lot," he insisted. He'd been standoffish on purpose, to protect himself from thinking she was even cuter than he already did. But he could see now that it had sent the wrong signals. He didn't want her to disparage herself. "You're…just the right amount."

He twisted his face at how awkward that sounded, barely resisting the urge to face palm.

But she laughed delightedly and nudged him with that pointy elbow again. "Thanks. You certainly have a way with compliments."

"Can I help you?" The bartender leaned her elbows on the bar, flipping her long braided hair back over her shoulder. Suddenly she bent toward Quentin, squinting her eyes. "Wait…"

"Sylvie?" Quentin exclaimed. He hadn't recognized her

from afar, but now he realized that he was staring at a woman he'd gone to elementary school with. She'd moved in early high school and he hadn't seen her for probably ten years.

"Quentin? Wow!" Sylvie grinned and leaned over the bar to pull him into a hug.

As Quentin hugged her back, he looked over her shoulder and saw three different men scowling at him over their drinks. When he released Sylvie and sat back on his stool, he realized that she'd become a very attractive woman in the years since they'd last seen one another. He remembered her as having been awkwardly tall, with a really bad short haircut and lots of dark eye makeup that was always smudging. But the Sylvie of today had gracefully aged into her height, her body rounding into curves and her natural beauty needing no embellishments.

"It's been so long," he said, and then winced when he was needled by an elbow he was becoming very familiar with. "Oh. Sylvie, this is my neighbor Cat. Cat, this is my friend Sylvie. We grew up together in Sleepy Hollow."

"Old friends!" Cat exclaimed happily, looking back and forth between the two of them. "That's so cool. I'm…not really in touch with anyone I grew up with, except for my sisters."

Sylvie gave Quentin a chagrined smile. "I wouldn't exactly say we were friends."

It was true. Quentin would never have said it aloud to her, but for some reason he and Sylvie had never quite clicked. She'd always been nervous and quiet around him. He opened his mouth, unsure of what to say next, when Sylvie cut him off.

"I always had way too big of a crush on Quentin to be his friend."

His mouth clapped closed with a hollow *thunk*. He stared at Sylvie. "Oh. I— Really?"

He wasn't sure why but something about his delivery made both women laugh.

"Really," she said with a smile. She drummed her hands on the bar top. "All right, what can I get you guys?"

They ordered and Sylvie brought their drinks with a wink before moving off to help other customers.

"Wow," Cat said after a second. Quentin could feel her eyes on the side of his face.

"What?" he asked, turning toward her as he sipped his beer.

"I think she short-circuited you."

"I mean…" Quentin said as he flattened his hair yet again. He searched for something to say. Something witty. Something un-dorky.

He came up with absolutely nothing and that made Cat laugh even more. "Hasn't anyone ever told you they had a crush on you before?" she asked.

"Um. No."

Cat's big brown eyes widened in surprise. "Really? I find that hard to believe."

Again, Quentin was struck dumb. This really wasn't his night for elocution.

"Ooh!" Cat said, tugging at his elbow. "I think the show is starting. We can come back afterward so you can get lover girl's digits."

There was too much there to respond to, so Quentin just let himself get tugged along into the back room of the bar.

Two hours later he and Cat were walking home side by side. They'd stopped by the bar to say goodbye on their way out and now Sylvie's phone number tingled Quentin's fingertips where he touched the napkin in his pocket. But it wasn't Sylvie he was thinking about as they crossed a bridge over the Gowanus Canal, the water an inky, noxious stripe below them. It was the woman walking beside him that drew his thoughts.

Cat reminded him of clementines in the height of their season. The brightest, zingiest fruit he could think of. He didn't want to simplify her down into just her positive attributes. Of course she was—like all people—a complicated amalgamation of hidden puzzle pieces and gardens of melancholia, he was sure of it. But her general vibe was phosphorescent, tart, addictive, a little overwhelming.

He wanted more.

His stomach sank as he realized how much more he wanted. Exactly what he'd been worried about happening had. His crush was more than just a lit match. It had matured into glowing coals simmering in the pit of his gut, sucking the oxygen out of the air, waiting for him to fan it into flame. It wouldn't take much more for him to be a certified goner.

"So, you gonna ask her out?" Cat asked.

Quentin's heart skipped because he'd been thinking of just that: how to ask Cat out. But Cat wasn't talking about herself; she was talking about Sylvie.

"I'm...not sure."

"Why not? She was gorge. And obviously into you."

He laughed. "You really think she was into me? She talked about her crush in the past tense."

Cat pursed her lips and ducked her chin, her eyes telling him he was a naive fool. "Are you kidding me? That woman practically suffocated you with her cleavage and then told you she'd always had a crush on you *in front of me*. That's girl-speak for *'come and get it, daddy-o.'*" Cat mimed twirling a long cat tail behind her back, tipping an imaginary top hat.

Once again, he was laughing. "I'm not sure what *that's* supposed to be, but I think you're confusing my life with, like, an old-timey cartoon or something."

She laughed too. "I'm just sayin', I think you're missing an opportunity there."

"Actually…" Quentin said as he slowed his pace so that he could steal a few extra moments with her. His heart beat hollowly in his chest, like a stone clanging in an old tin pail. "It's not her that I'm thinking about asking—"

"Ohmygawd," Cat squeaked, grabbing Quentin's arm and jumping halfway behind him. "It's him!"

They'd just rounded the corner toward their building and standing on the sidewalk in front of the entrance was Jared, talking to someone through the open window of a cab. A moment later, beautiful blonde Lara unfolded herself from the cab, an overnight bag over one shoulder.

Quentin groaned. Jared had sworn on his—still-living—mother's grave that the thing with Lara last weekend had been a one-off. That they weren't getting back together. Yet, here she was, obviously about to spend the night again.

"I can't believe this," Quentin muttered, grunting when Cat bodily hustled him back behind the side of their building so that they could peek around and spy on Jared.

"Who is that chick?" Cat said, peering around the corner at the couple.

"Jared's ex. Or maybe Jared's current. It's hard to keep track with Jared and Lara. They're pretty messy."

"Dang!" Cat stood up straight and snapped her fingers. "I'm always behind the eight ball with this guy."

His heart somewhere in the general vicinity of his socks,

Quentin stepped back and surveyed her. "You're really into him, huh?"

Cat shrugged. "He's stupid hot. And kind of funny. We run into one another around the building every once in a while."

"So." Quentin cleared his throat. "Why not ask him out?"

"I'm too chicken," Cat answered in a tone that indicated the answer should have been obvious. She turned to Quentin and his stomach dropped further at the bummed expression on her face. "And now he apparently has a girlfriend again."

"Or not." Looking up, Quentin watched in amazement as Jared leaned down and reopened the cab door, one hand on Lara's lower back.

"Oh, my gosh!" Cat squeaked. "He's sending her home!"

Never in his life did Quentin think that he'd actually be conflicted about the banishment of Lara.

They both watched in silence as Lara whirled on Jared, fire in her eyes. She said something that neither of them could quite make out, but the venom in her tone was unmistakable. As cold as ice, she reached forward and plucked Jared's phone from his hand. Quentin's jaw dropped as he watched Lara pitch the phone to the pavement and then bring the heel of her Louboutin down on the screen. A smirk on her face, she whipped back around and slid into the cab.

Quentin and Cat shrank into the shadows as her cab drove off down the street.

"Holy smokes," Cat muttered. "That was crazy."

They both peeked back around the corner, but Jared had disappeared into the building.

"That's nothing when it comes to Lara. A few years

ago, she slashed all the tires of his car only to find out that it wasn't his car."

"What?"

"Yeah. And the kicker was that she couldn't afford to buy the owner new tires so Jared paid."

"Wow. Either he's a total pushover or he's really sweet." Quentin kept his mouth shut.

"How long have they been together?" Cat asked.

"On and off since high school. We've all known each other since grade school." They started a slow stroll toward the building.

"I'm detecting in your tone that you really don't like her."

Quentin sighed. "As you can see, she's kind of a... difficult person. But I wouldn't really have a problem with her if I didn't have to live with Jared. It's just too much Lara in my life."

"What do you mean *have* to live with Jared?" Cat asked as he held open the door for their building for her. She scampered forward and pressed the elevator button.

"He's my cousin, did you know that?"

"Oh!" She brightened immediately, like someone had flicked on a lamp inside her. "I didn't know! That's cool."

"Yeah. We were really close growing up." He rolled back on his heels after they stepped onto the elevator, debating how much to divulge. "It's kind of a long story, but I lived with him and his mom, my aunt Sarah, in middle school and high school. So, when Jared and I moved to the city for school, it was kind of a given that he and I would be roommates. He's been in and out of work for a few years so my place is a really reliable situation for him and... Yeah. I can't exactly tell him that his girlfriend can't come over, you know?"

"Wow."

"Anyways, things are better—calmer—when he and Lara are on the outs."

She was quiet as they walked down the hall together, his shoulder brushing up against her hair. When they got to their opposing doors, Cat turned slowly to look up at him and he knew what she was going to ask before she even said a word.

He could see it in her big, lovely eyes.

"You think if they're really broken up, there's any way you could introduce me and him? I mean, we've already met, but is there a way that you could get us to hang out together or something?"

Shit.

This was, literally, exactly what he'd been trying to avoid. But there she was, looking up at him with those maple-syrup eyes swimming with hope, her bottom lip caught between her teeth, and he just couldn't say no.

"Ah. Sure. Maybe. Yeah. I guess I could do that. But I can't promise to make it romantic or anything. Jared isn't exactly a romantic guy."

Once again, she brightened like a lamp had flicked on. And then she was up on her toes, one hand on his arm and her lips at his cheek. "Oh, man, Quentin, you're the absolute *best*. Thank you, thank you, thank you!"

She dropped back down and threw her hands in the air, letting out a little squeak of delight.

He laughed a little, even though there was a pit in his gut that seemed to be getting wider and wider with each passing second.

"Maybe sometime this week?" she asked. "It doesn't have to be anything fancy. I could just come over and hang out when he'll be there too?"

"Sure." He cleared his throat. "Yeah. I'll come knock on your door."

She unlocked her door and then backed up into her apartment, her solemn eyes on his and one finger twirling into a point. "Seriously, Quentin. The best."

And then her door closed and he was alone in the hallway.

CHAPTER FOUR

CAT PROPPED THE laundry room door open with her hip and attempted to heave her thousand-pound laundry basket onto the nearest counter. Alas, gravity won that particular battle and she found herself tipping sideways, almost ass over applecart.

"I gotcha," said a deep voice to her left, and then the heavy load in Cat's arms was suddenly gone and she was free to catch herself against the counter.

"Thanks, Quentin!" she chirped once she saw who it was. "That was a close one."

"You almost met your maker." He set her laundry basket down and slid over a few feet to where he was folding his whites.

"I never understood that phrase. I'm like, I know my own mother. I've already met my maker."

He laughed. "I think people are referring to God when they say that."

"Ohhhhh. I get it! They're talking about the *cosmic maker*." She made her voice deep and swirled her hands around in the air.

"So, in your mind God sounds like the genie from *Aladdin* when he does the 'phenomenal cosmic power' bit?"

They both burst out laughing. "I guess? Jeez. What does that even say about me?" She finished loading her laundry into the washer and grimaced. "Oh, crap."

"What?"

"I forgot my detergent all the way upstairs."

"You can use mine," he offered, nodding his head to where the big red bottle sat on top of another set of washers.

"What does yours smell like?" she asked, doing something that only made sense because she didn't give it any sort of lingering thought and stepped behind him, burying her nose in the fabric of his shirt between his two shoulder blades.

He didn't even break pace in his folding. "Did you just smell me?"

"I did."

And he smelled freaking amazing. Cat had no idea what his laundry detergent smelled like. All her frisky brain had registered was man pheromones (very delicious). He smelled like a snow leopard stalking through a stand of icy pines. That made zero sense, but it was the best she could do. He'd discombobulated her with his man scent.

She wordlessly took some of his detergent and turned around to see him smiling to himself.

"What's that smile for?"

"Nothing," he said with a shake of his head. "You're funny."

She tossed the detergent into the washer and recapped the bottle. "How so?"

"Well, for starters you just washed all your laundry in one load, without separating. Who does that?"

She turned and hoisted herself onto the counter where he was folding laundry. "I'm a wild animal, Quentin. Thoroughly undomesticated. Pass those over, I'll help fold."

He gave her a look but handed over a pile of undershirts.

"No tighty-whities to fold?" She batted her eyelashes.

He just rolled his eyes, biting back a smile. It was fun how easy he was to amuse. She considered that an excellent trait.

"Can I ask you something?" he asked after a quiet minute of companionable folding.

"Anything."

"What exactly is it about my cousin?"

"What do you mean?" she asked.

"What is it about him that has you hiding around corners and trying to time your walk to the train with him?"

"Oh." She thought for a second. Jared's appeal could be neatly summed up by that one cartoon cat whose tongue rolls out of his mouth and down the stairs. But Quentin likely wanted an answer more nuanced than that. So, Cat thought of a better way to put it. "He looks like he lives inside an advertisement for expensive watches. I used to think it was a cologne ad. But nope, his aesthetic is definitely top-of-the-line watches."

Quentin laughed. *"What?"*

"You know, he's all toned forearms and broody stares. One look at him and you feel like you're on a hardwood speedboat sipping a martini at sunset. In black-and-white. You know, like a Rolex ad."

"So, basically, he's hot."

Cat nodded vigorously. "Absolutely smoking."

Quentin snapped the wrinkles out of a dress shirt. "And that's what you're looking for? Martinis and forearms?"

He was facing away from her while he carefully folded the shirt. His coppery hair was longer than when she'd first met him, just starting to curl at the ends. She'd spent so little time with him, but already he was so familiar to her. Something about his presence was calming. He was like warm sun on a comfy couch. He was where she wanted to be.

Quentin made it easy to want to explain her story. "I guess," she said. "I mean, that's not *always* what I was looking for. But I dated this guy, Sid, for a long time and things were good with him. We were happy together for a while. And then it all just sort of faded away and fell apart." She reached for more clothes to fold for something to do with her hands. "The breakup itself wasn't that bad, but it was right around the time my dad had a heart attack, and the whole thing just kind of kicked me when I was down."

She stared off into the distance for a second.

"Anyways." She sighed. "I guess what I really want is just someone who can show me a good time."

"Who really cares about you," Quentin said at the same time.

"Oh," he said with a little smile and a shake of his head. "Sorry, I shouldn't have assumed I knew what you were gonna say."

"That's okay."

His laundry dinged and he went to switch it over to the dryer. Cat stared at his back for a moment. Her thoughts were caught in the spiderweb of what he'd just said. *Someone who really cares about you.*

It was something to think about, that when Quentin heard her story, he'd assumed that she would go looking for connection with someone. Was that what he would have done?

Was that what he was looking for?

"HEY, I THINK I'M gonna invite our neighbor over to watch with us," Quentin said to Jared the next Tuesday.

After a lot of consideration, he'd decided to find a way for Cat to hang out with Jared. For one, he'd told her he'd do it and he hated going back on his word. Even though it was a nightmare to think of her becoming one of Jared's casual hookups, he thought there was something kind of condescending about trying to intervene. He didn't think that Jared and Cat would be good together, but that wasn't for him to decide. That was for Cat to decide. He had a crush on her, but that didn't mean he was allowed to screw around in her dating life. Besides, if she got to know Jared better and still wanted to hook up with him, then Quentin figured that he and Cat probably weren't right for one another in the first place.

So this was him, sticking to his stupid principles on a Tuesday night, trying not to crack a molar as he ground his teeth.

"Huh?" Jared looked up from where he was stirring pasta on the stove.

"Our neighbor Cat, across the hall."

"Who has a cat across the hall? When Lara wanted me to get that pet hedgehog you told me this was a no-pets building."

"Jared," Quentin said with a laugh, dragging a hand

down his face. "Look alive over there. First of all, this *is* a no-pets building. Second of all, you can't have a hedgehog in New York City. It's illegal. Third, I'm talking about our neighbor whose name is Cat. I'm gonna invite her over to watch the movie."

"Oh. Sure." Jared turned back toward the pasta and stirred listlessly.

Quentin had seen Jared mope like this every single time he and Lara had broken up. But it didn't feel good to see his cousin hurt. "Are you sure you're all right, man?"

"Yeah. I'll be fine. But it's just really over this time," Jared said hollowly.

That was what he'd said last time as well, but Quentin didn't want to be an asshole by bringing it up. "What makes you say that?"

"Because she smashed my phone." Jared sighed as he dumped the pasta into a colander to drain. "She knows I don't have the money to get a new one right away. Which means that when she smashed it, she knew she wouldn't be able to reach me for a while. She's never done that before. Usually when we break up she's blowing up my phone like crazy for weeks."

Quentin cleared his throat. "Maybe it's better this way. A clean break. It's harder to get a fresh start if you're always in communication with each other, you know?"

"A fresh start? I haven't had one of those since we started dating sophomore year."

Quentin got a sudden flash of the person Lara had been in high school. Chipper and smiley. She'd always had a temper but she'd been…happier. Quentin remembered the way her high ponytails used to bounce when she'd gallop down the hallway to jump into Jared's arms. When he considered the person she'd been then versus the person she was now, it seemed highly probable that Jared wasn't any better for Lara than she was for him.

"Do you want to be with her or do you want to break up?" Quentin asked point blank.

Jared sagged as he slid a plate of pasta across the counter to Quentin. His head lolled to one side, a defeated look on his face. "Neither. But, you know, I guess breaking up is the closest to what I want."

"Then you have to stick to it, man. It's not fair to either of you to drag this out. Both of you deserve to move on." Quentin scooped the salad that he'd made onto Jared's plate and watched his cousin's face carefully. It wasn't often that he inserted himself into anyone's life, and the feeling was distinctly uncomfortable.

"Maybe you're right," Jared said after a long moment. "If you were going to try for a fresh start, how would you go about it?"

Quentin, not having had very many relationships to "fresh start" his way out of, racked his brain for healthy suggestions. "Hmm. Join a rec league for soccer? Meet some new people? You always said you wanted to get a short story published. You could work on that. Or, I don't know, maybe date?"

"Ding ding ding!" Jared sang, pointing across the counter toward Quentin. "We have a winner. I'll go on some dates. I could definitely stand to get laid."

In Quentin's eyes, Jared got laid plenty, in or out of his relationship with Lara. He should know; they shared a bedroom wall. "That's not exactly what I—"

"I'll go out and meet somebody. Somebody amazing. You know, Lara was always so serious about her nine-to-five. Maybe I need to be with someone more…" He snapped his fingers, searching for the word. "Artsy. Yeah. Someone really creative. You know, like one of those girls who lives in an artists' loft and wears overalls with paint smeared on them." Jared was really starting to perk up now that he was a man with a plan.

"Oh. Yeah. One of *those* girls," Quentin said drily. Only Jared would actually believe those girls existed outside of rom-coms written by men.

"Yeah," Jared said, obviously warming to his genius idea. "Gotta get back out there. Can't keep a good man down. Fish in the sea, et cetera, et cetera."

"Uh-huh."

Jared was practically inhaling his food now. "This is good," he decided. "This'll be a good thing. I'll do a little mambo Italiano and recalibrate my world view."

"I...don't even know what that means," Quentin said with a laugh.

"Well, that's *your* problem, Q. You need to learn how to get messy every once in a while. Life is better when it's a little bit rocky." He scraped the last of his pasta sauce off his plate with the side of his fork. "Why do you think I've dated Lara for this long?"

Quentin opened his mouth but clapped it closed when he couldn't think of a response. "Huh."

"Trust me, man," Jared said, clearing his plate away. "The smoothest road is the most boring one."

CHAPTER FIVE

CAT TUGGED HER door open with a toothy smile on her face. She'd just checked the peephole and seen Quentin knocking.

"Hi!"

"Wow" was his answer, his eyebrows up in his hairline. "You're looking very…green."

"Oh, right. I didn't think I was going to have any visitors. Come on in while I wash the mask off."

She waved him into her apartment and scampered into the bathroom to wash the avocado and seaweed mask off her face. She looked down at her yoga pants and T-shirt and considered changing her clothes. But after all, it was just Quentin; she could be comfortable around him.

When she went back into her living room, he was bent down, reading the titles on her bookshelf.

"You really like romance novels," he observed.

"The finest form of escapism, as far as I'm concerned. It's like a vacation in book form. And since I'm a public school teacher, those are the only kinds of vacations I can afford."

"I get that," he said, straightening up. "The escapism thing, I mean. I'm pretty into fantasy novels for the same reason." He winced. "Dang. Probably shouldn't have mentioned that. Now you're going to think I'm an even bigger nerd than you already do."

Cat cocked her head in confusion. "Have I ever called you a nerd?"

He blinked at her for a second. "No, but with the train set and everything... I just assumed." He cleared his throat. "Anyways, I came over to invite you to watch a movie with me and Jared. You said you wanted help getting to know him. So, yeah. Come on over."

He backed up toward the door but Cat's mind was still on the whole nerd thing. He thought that she thought that he was a nerd. Why? It bothered her that she'd made him feel that way, because she really didn't think that about him. He was cool and interesting and fun. And, looking at him now in his joggers and V-neck T-shirt, he looked casually cool.

Actually, if she were being honest, he looked handsome. She hadn't really thought that before now, because he didn't have that knock-you-in-the-teeth sort of prettiness that Jared had, but Quentin was definitely handsome. He had broad, even features, a good strong jaw and blue eyes the color of a quilt that had been washed a thousand times. Faded, friendly, warm.

"Cat, are you coming?"

"Oh." She shook her head a little to break her reverie. She'd been daydreaming about Quentin when she should have been getting ready to see Jared. "Right. Just gimme a second and I'll change."

"Why?" Quentin asked, his head cocked to the side.

Cat looked down at her attire. "Because I'm in yoga pants and a T-shirt."

"You don't have to change." Quentin, pink in the cheeks, dragged a hand over the top of his head, straightening his coppery hair. "Trust me, guys like yoga pants."

He held her eyes for half a second longer than she expected and something in his expression made her stomach swoop. "Oh. Okay."

Feeling a little flustered, she followed Quentin into his apartment.

"Hey, Jared, we're ready to watch whenever you are!" Quentin called. He waited a second, and when he didn't hear anything, he headed toward Jared's room. A moment later he came back out, a confused expression on his face. "That's so weird. He was just here."

"He's not here?" She should probably feel disappointed that her hookup was thwarted once again, but she was just happy that she got to spend some time with Quentin.

"I guess he went out?" Quentin scratched at his head. "Sorry for the false alarm."

"That's okay. What're we watching?"

"You're gonna stay?"

"Yeah! A movie sounds good." She made herself comfy on his couch, pulling an afghan down to cover her legs and fluffing one of the couch pillows behind her.

"Um. Okay. You want popcorn or something? Or let's see… I have pretzels and some muffins."

"Yes to all," she said happily, picking up the remote and flipping through the channels. This was shaping up to be a really fun night.

He laughed. "You want all of it?"

She turned and put one arm along the back of the couch, eyeing him where he stood in the kitchen. "I'm starving. I haven't had dinner yet."

"Oh. Okay. Why don't you choose something for us to watch? Anything is fine with me."

A few minutes later Cat was blinking down at a tray of food being set on her lap. There was a heated-up bowl of spaghetti and meatballs, a little plate of salad and a slice of thick brown bread. A glass of icy lemonade sat in the corner, condensation dripping down the side.

She looked up at Quentin in surprise. "You made me dinner."

"It's just leftovers. Nothing special. If you're still hungry afterward you can have the popcorn and pretzels. But I figured someone who regularly eats pie for breakfast could stand to eat a nice round meal every now and then."

She stared down at the tray again. "I don't remember the last time someone made me dinner. You even gave me lemonade. That's my favorite drink."

"I know. It's what you ordered at the bar the other night."

Thinking of the bar made Cat think of Quentin's friend Sylvie. It made her think of the napkin Sylvie had written her phone number on for Quentin. Where was that napkin now? Had Quentin called the number yet? Would Quentin make a tray of leftovers for Sylvie too?

"So, what are we watching?" Quentin asked, settling on the other side of the couch.

Cat felt strange, nervous and not sure why, but she wasn't going to let it ruin her night. *"Star Wars."*

"Really?" His head was cocked, a funny little smile making his eyes sparkle in surprise.

"What's wrong with *Star Wars*?" she asked.

"Absolutely nothing. I just thought for sure you'd have chosen a rom-com."

"Because of all the romance novels?"

"Um. Yeah." He looked away.

"And…" she prompted, reaching across the couch with one socked foot and prodding him in the thigh.

"And what?" He still wasn't looking at her.

"And what's the other reason you thought I'd choose a rom-com? There's something you're not saying out loud. Come on!"

She prodded him again with her foot and this time he caught her by the arch, trapping her foot against his leg and preventing her from poking at him. When he turned to look at her, those friendly blue eyes had a spark lighting them from within. Nerves? Or was it something else?

"Remember that night we first talked? The party?" he asked.

"Sure."

"When you were in my room you called me 'cute.'"

"I remember." It hadn't made her blush then, so why was the memory of it making her blush now?

"And to me—I don't know—the tone of your voice or something, it indicated that the kind of 'cute' you were talking about was the kind that watches girlie movies with you on the other end of the couch."

"Oh." She was all turned around now, like a ship in foggy weather. She wasn't sure what exactly he was saying and what exactly he wasn't saying.

His thumb suddenly stroked hard against the arch of her foot, loosening a muscle that she hadn't realized was tight.

She swallowed down a gasp, her bottom lip getting caught between her teeth.

"Was I right?" he asked in a low voice, his eyes still on hers.

"Oh," she repeated, still trying to regain her bearings. "I...don't know. I wasn't thinking about it that hard." She cleared her throat and narrowed her eyes playfully at him. "You should know me well enough by now to know that sometimes I just say stuff."

"Right." His hand released her foot but his eyes stayed on hers. "You should eat while it's still warm."

He turned to get the movie started and Cat took the opportunity to gather herself a little bit. She took a deep breath and started in on the meal, the familiar opening credits rolling.

When she was finished with her food, Quentin wordlessly relieved her of the tray and came back a minute later with two bowls of ice cream.

She glanced over as he sat and was startled by the pang of disappointment she felt when he was just as far away as he'd been at the beginning of the movie. *The kind of cute that watches rom-coms at the other end of the couch.* What did that even mean?

"Do you want some blanket?" she heard herself ask, scooting toward him, her ice cream in one hand and the blanket in the other. "The ice cream must be making you cold."

"Sure." He pulled his half of the blanket over his lap, his eyes on the side of her face as she stared rigidly at the screen. She'd seen this movie a hundred and two times and for the life of her she couldn't have explained what was happening on screen.

Why was she sweating? Jeez. There was still a foot of space between them, but every little movement he made caught her attention. When he set his empty bowl on the coffee table and leaned back, she held her breath. When one long arm lifted up and rested on the back of the couch, she swore her heart got stuck on the downbeat. This was crazy. This was Quentin. Her friend Quentin! She should not be acting like such a basket case!

What *had* she meant when she'd called him cute? She'd been having so much fun with him it had just popped out. *Girlie movies on the other end of the couch.* Maybe he was right and she had really been unintentionally calling him…nonsexual? Yeesh. Nobody wanted to be thought of that way. Even by their friends.

Cat paused the movie, the trash compactor ten feet from squeezing Luke and Leia and Han into Spam. She kicked her knee onto the couch between them as she turned to face him.

"Quentin—"

BAMBAMBAM.

She jumped six inches into the air as someone attempted to take the front door off the hinges with their fist.

"Holy hell!" Cat stared at the door as the incredibly loud pounding happened again.

"I'll go see who it is," Quentin said into her ear. It was only then that Cat realized she'd jumped straight into his lap. Her heart pounded like a sprinter running stairs. Quentin's hands gently touched her hips and she slid off of him.

She watched him walk to the door, her eyes wide, one hand on her chest, unsure if she was feeling this way because of the unexpected visitor or because she'd just been sitting in Quentin's lap.

He looked through the peephole and rested his forehead against the wooden door for a moment. He took a deep breath and swung the door open. "Hi, Lara."

"Hi, Quentin," said the stunning woman who Cat had seen smash Jared's phone last weekend.

"Jared's not here," Quentin told her.

She pushed past him into the apartment, taking her high heels off and lining them up beside the door. Cat couldn't help but notice that the woman had a gorgeous pedicure. Actually, she was kind of objectively perfect in every way. Long, trim figure, not a hair out of place. She sort of looked like the kind of woman who would betray James Bond and turn out to be the evil genius at the end of the movie.

"Thanks," she said, glancing at Cat.

"Oh, my gosh. Did I say that out loud?" Cat asked the room.

"Yes," Quentin replied, looking like he was having a very hard time keeping a straight face.

"Where is he, then?" the woman, Lara, asked Quentin.

"I have no idea. He had dinner and then left."

"I assume he hasn't gotten a replacement phone yet?" Lara asked, injecting a fair amount of haughtiness into her tone, but something in her eyes spoke of regret. Embarrassment.

"Not yet." Quentin must have seen the look in her eyes as well because he spoke gently.

"Okay, well. Can I just wait here for him to get back, then?" Lara's hands went up to her hair, back to her hips, then just fell at her sides. She did not seem like a woman who was very accustomed to asking for permission.

Quentin's eyes flicked to Cat and Cat nodded her head.

"Sure."

"You want some ice cream?" Cat offered. "We just had some."

"No...thank you." The second half of the sentence was

delayed enough to imply that that was another thing she wasn't very accustomed to.

"You're offering up my ice cream?" Quentin muttered with a half smile as he plopped down on the couch again, this time close enough for his shoulder to brush Cat's.

"Oh." She laughed. "Apparently. I guess in my mind, your ice cream is my ice cream?"

"It's like the opposite of *mi casa es su casa*." He laughed. *"'Oh, you thought that was yours? Nah. It's mine.'"*

She face palmed. "I told you I was a lot." He bumped her shoulder with his. "And I told you. You're not a lot. You're the perfect amount."

"You two are cute," Lara said softly from where she sat in the armchair at the other end of the couch.

"Thanks!"

"Oh, no, we're not—" Quentin and Cat spoke at the same time but he cut himself off and looked down at her. "Did you say, 'Thanks'?"

"Uh—" For the second time that night, a noise at the door cut her off. All three of them turned and looked at the front door as the sound of a key scrabbling around for the lock sounded clearly through the room. On screen, the walls of the trash compactor still bore down on the cast.

The door burst open and in stumbled Jared and a woman who appeared to be sucker-fished to his face.

Jared's hands were tangled in her hair as he turned her to the door, pushing her up against it, lifting her so that her combat boots dangled on either side of his hips.

"Dude!" Quentin said, standing up from the couch and glancing toward Lara.

Lara's face was white as she slowly stood up, her eyes glued to the amorous couple.

"Dude!" Quentin called again when his first attempt

failed at getting his cousin to stop dry-humping in the living room. "JA-RED."

Jared looked back over his shoulder after Quentin called his name and did an almost comical double-take. His eyes were bleary and his lips swollen, his mussed hair tumbling over his forehead. He blinked at his ex-girlfriend.

Slowly, the woman he was kissing slid back down to her feet and peeked around Jared's body, her face a grimace of chagrin once she realized she had an audience. Then recognition dawned over her face and she buried her face in her hands.

"Sylvie?" Cat gasped.

"So," Quentin said as he rocked back on his heels. "I guess you went to the Jarhouse to pick up girls and you ran into Sylvie, huh?"

"Sylvie Peters?" Lara said, her hands on her hips, looking back and forth between Jared and Sylvie. "From middle school?"

"Oh, my gosh." Cat—horrified—peeked through her fingers. "I can't believe you all went to middle school together. This is— Wow. This is really something."

She glanced at Lara again and saw a very familiar expression on her face. Just like that, Cat was back in the ice cream aisle, watching her ex-boyfriend suck the lips off her oldest friend. Even when a relationship was officially over, this wasn't necessarily something you wanted to walk in on.

The drama was just heating up. The color was quickly returning to Lara's face. Cat did not want to stick around and see just how red those cheeks were going to get.

Cat twisted on her toes and pecked Quentin on the cheek. "I'm gonna go. I'll let you all, um, figure this out."

She bolted toward the door, reaching for the door handle. "Um. Sorry," Cat said as she danced one way and Jared and

Sylvie danced the other. Nothing was more awkward than that let's-get-past-one-another shuffle.

She drew a deep breath as she stepped into the hall. She'd never felt that trash-compactor scene quite so viscerally before.

"Cat," Quentin said as he joined her in the hallway, pulling the door closed behind him. "Sorry about the…mess."

She laughed. "It's totally fine. I just thought that I didn't need to be there, in everyone's business. I'm not exactly a key player in that drama."

"Me either."

"Well," Cat ribbed him. "It's your drama a little bit. Jared *did* kinda steal your girl. I guess Sylvie had a crush on your cousin too."

She expected him to laugh but his face just kind of shut down. "They usually do," Quentin muttered. "Ah, look, Cat, have a good night, okay? See you around."

He turned and stepped back into his apartment.

Cat watched the door close, her eyebrows pulled down. "See you around?" she mouthed.

CHAPTER SIX

LUCKILY SYLVIE WAS not interested in any drama because she apologetically skedaddled about three minutes after Cat did. Lara and Jared disappeared into his room while Quentin cleaned up the kitchen and ignored the television that was still paused on Star Wars.

He wanted to go over to the couch and plunk down and press Play and have Cat sitting there beside him again. Wouldn't it be great to rewind to an hour ago when the two of them had been inching closer and closer on the couch? Wouldn't it be great if the reason she'd come over tonight had been to watch a movie with *him*? And not as a way to make a play for his cousin?

The memory of Cat's face when she'd seen Jared making out with Sylvie flashed in Quentin's mind. She'd looked…

Well, he actually couldn't name the emotion that had been stamped across her features. But she had not looked happy at all. And she could not have left any faster than she had. Quentin had thought that Cat just had the hots for Jared. But now he was left to wonder if maybe she had real feelings for him.

Quentin gave up scrubbing the sink and strode over to the couch. Sinking into the cushions, he let his head tip back so he could stare at the old water stain on the ceiling. He thought he'd long ago become immune to girls preferring Jared over him.

Apparently it could still hurt.

Suddenly, he felt the way he had as a teenager when he'd gone to live with Jared and Aunt Sarah. Quentin had been the child of a divorce so brutal that after his mom had finally gained full custody of him, she'd dropped him off at her sister's so she could take a "well-earned vacation." A month turned into two into six into a year into two years, and then there was Quentin, graduating high school with only Aunt Sarah in the bleachers.

Jared had been good-looking and popular and everyone always wanted a piece of him. Quentin had been the designated driver who hadn't wanted to screw anything up with Aunt Sarah.

He understood why the girls had flocked to his cousin, but still, it would've been really nice if things with Cat had been a different story.

The door to Jared's room opened and Quentin straightened, surprised to see Lara walking out by herself. She was red around the eyes, but she was otherwise the same walking perfection that she always was.

She balanced one hand on the wall by the door and

started wiggling into her Louboutins. "You gonna miss me, Quentin?"

He looked at her in surprise. "You're...not coming back?"

When they'd disappeared into Jared's room together, he'd expected to have to sleep with a pillow over his ears to block out the sounds of their reunion.

She dropped her eyes. "Yup."

He looked at Jared's closed door and then back at Lara. "You're not getting back together?"

"Nope. That's not why I came over tonight." She sighed and leaned against the wall, checking her manicure. "I actually came over to apologize to him. I haven't been on my best behavior lately. This has been an absolutely terrible few years for me." She gave him a wry smile. "Perhaps you've noticed."

He was hesitant to agree, but he couldn't lie to her. "Uh, there's been a few indicators."

She chuckled, but sobered quickly. "I'm not going to try to justify my behavior. But just know there's been reasons for it. Some of them Jared-related and some of them not."

He cleared his throat. "Everybody's got their stuff."

Her eyes flicked up to Quentin's. "I came to apologize to Jared, but while I'm at it, I probably owe you one too."

This was a curveball. Quentin rose up. "For what?"

She laughed and sauntered over to the couch, her heels clicking with each step. "Oh, please. We both know I've not exactly been a treat these last few years."

She collapsed onto the couch, landing in a heap.

Quentin lowered himself to the other side of the couch, his eyes on her, trying to gauge her mood.

She rolled her head to catch his eye. "We used to be friends," she said, almost accusatorially.

For the second time that night, the image of Lara in high school flashed across Quentin's memory. It was strange because he hadn't thought about that time in their lives in years. "Yeah. We had freshman algebra together," he reminisced.

"You and I were friends before Jared and I had even really gotten to know one another. The first time I came over to your all's house, it was to hang with you, not Jared."

"That's right." How had he forgotten that?

"We used to hang out, the three of us."

"Yeah." Quentin scratched at his stubble.

"But then a few years ago, you just completely stopped wanting to be around us. What was up with that?" She sat up a little bit, smoothing her hair back.

Quentin chose his words carefully. "It was harder once me and Jared lived together. It seemed like you two were fighting a lot and there was nowhere for me to get a break from it."

"I get that," she said quietly. "Jared and I were going through a lot of stuff. Both together and separately. And I guess our fights did get a little more…bombastic. But it was more than that. Even when things were good with us, it was like you could barely stand to be around us."

Quentin wasn't sure what to say to that, so he just scratched at his stubble again.

"Have you ever wondered why that is?" Lara asked.

He shrugged.

"I have a theory," she said.

He laughed. "Of course you do. All right, let's hear it, then."

"The higher the stakes got for me and Jared, the farther away you got."

"What do you mean?"

She crossed her legs. "I mean that when Jared and I were just two silly high schoolers, you didn't have to take our relationship seriously. But when we stayed together, in college and after, you started to get nervous. The more we gave up to be together, the more intense things got, the more you pulled away."

Was that true? The thought was unwieldy, but it also sort of fit.

"You know you have to risk things to actually be in a relationship, right?" Lara asked.

Quentin laughed. "Actually, Jared said something like that to me tonight as well. He said that the smoothest road is the most boring one."

"He's right. But I'm not saying you should go completely off-road like Jared and I did either."

"You literally threw a gyro at his head once."

She winced. "Low point."

He raised an eyebrow and she laughed, chagrined.

"Okay, okay," she grumbled. "*One* of the low points."

Lara stood and brushed off her immaculate skirt. "Look, we used to be friends, and when I walk out that door, we're likely not going to see one another very much anymore, so let me just make a point. You're awesome and funny and cool and shouldn't compare yourself to Jared. It's apples and oranges. In a good way. I've wondered for years why you never seriously date anybody. And I'm not pretending to understand your issues here, but if it's because Jared and I made being with somebody look really bad, well, I just want to say that risking things—even, like, dignity—is worth it to be able to really connect with someone. It really is."

He frowned at Lara. Maybe he hadn't been as good at melting into the background as he'd once given himself credit for. She kinda had him pegged.

"Do you get what I'm saying, Quentin?" She pointed toward the front door. "That girl likes you. She does. It's as clear as day. She flirted with you on the couch. She kissed your cheek when she left. Don't argue with me." She turned that pointer finger back toward him. "I know what you're gonna say. You're gonna make some argument as to why I'm wrong and you're right, but guess what? You're wrong. Listen and listen close. Sometimes all we see in ourselves are our worst failures, all the thoughts we're not proud of, all the mistakes, all of our worst moments. And that makes us think that anyone who cares about us just doesn't have the full story yet."

He blinked at her. "I... Wow."

"Am I checking any boxes for you?" She took a step toward the door and paused. "If there's anything I've learned in this whole mess—" she nodded in the direction of Jared's room "—it's that sometimes you just have to listen to the people who care about you when they tell you you're great. So, why don't you give her a chance to tell you that you're great? And when she does, listen."

She turned toward the door.

"Lara." He stood up.

Lara froze, one hand on the doorknob.

"I'm sorry about all this," Quentin said, and truly meant it.

She sagged at the shoulders and pulled the door open with a sigh. "Oh, me too. But someday I'm sure I'll look back and think of this whole thing as a learning experience. Or something trite like that."

He watched as she closed the door without saying goodbye. He stood there and listened to those fancy shoes click down the hallway.

CAT DECIDED MANNERS were not as important as her immediate need for pie. Instead of waiting for the barista at the pie shop to bring out the freshly washed forks, Cat just stood at the counter by the window and picked up her pie in one hand, taking a bite out of the end like it was a slice of pizza.

The zingy-sweet lemon custard was almost, *almost* enough to lift her spirits. She'd been down ever since what Cat privately referred to as the Lara Sylvie Trash Compactor Debacle.

Well, to be specific, she'd been down ever since Quentin had given her the brush-off right after the Lara Sylvie Trash Compactor Debacle.

Cat really didn't understand. She'd thought she and Quentin were getting along so well. Actually, she'd thought there might have even been a spark there.

But it had been four days since he'd told her he'd see her around. So, apparently she'd misidentified the aforementioned spark.

Sigh. More pie.

She was most of the way through her first slice and already contemplating a second.

"So, what's good here?" asked a deep voice from behind her.

Cat whirled to see Quentin standing there, hands in his pockets, his expression both open and solemn.

"Pie," she blurted around a mouthful. "Pie is what's good here."

"Right." He did that adorable blushing thing and looked at the ground for a moment. His chest expanded and he looked back up at her. "I didn't come for the pie, actually. I was hoping to see you here."

She swallowed and cocked her head to one side. "You

came to the pie shop to see me instead of knocking on my door?"

"I wanted to talk to you, but coming to your apartment felt like—I don't know—an ambush or something."

"Okay." Her stomach turned upside down. Was he here to tell her he didn't want to hang out anymore? Hadn't the "see you around" been sufficient? She finished off the last of her pie with a flourish, hoping to summon some gusto. "Shoot."

He cleared his throat. "Take a walk with me?"

"Sure."

They took a right out of the pie shop, away from the trains, and wound away from the industrial part of the neighborhood. The warehouses gave way to brownstones with crooked sidewalks and cast-iron lampposts in the front yards.

"I'm just gonna say it," Quentin said as they walked side by side, his shoulder brushing against her hair.

"Okay." She braced herself.

"I think you're the funniest...most interesting...prettiest..."

Oh. Cat stopped walking. This was not the direction she'd been expecting this conversation to go. He turned to face her. An older couple walking a weenie dog scooted past them but Quentin and Cat just stared at one another.

"I have a crush on you," Quentin continued after a moment. "In case that wasn't clear."

Those friendly blue eyes of his were a perfect combination of nerves and determination. Cat's stomach went upside down again, but this time it felt good.

"Look," he said, flattening his hair down with one hand. "I know you have a thing for my cousin. And that's historically been sort of a sore spot for me. Because of the way we grew up, I always compared his life to mine. Like I said before, it's a long story. But I think that's made me be kind of closed off to you. Which I don't want to be. Because—you know—the crush."

His cheeks were pink and his coppery hair was getting messier and messier each time he attempted to flatten it. Cat would've given anything for a series of portraits of him, exactly as he looked right at that moment. She'd never have to google puppy videos ever again when she got sad. All she'd have to do was look at those photos of Quentin and feel her heart float away on a hot-air balloon.

"I guess," he continued, "I just wanted to tell you how I feel. You said that what you're looking for is a good time." He spread his hands out to the side. "I'm a good time. Also, I care about you. I don't know if that disqualifies me from the running. But I guess I just wanted to…see?" He groaned and flattened his hair again. "Man, I am really not good at this."

She covered her face with her hands just to give herself a second to think. But she found she didn't even need it. She was laughing as she pulled her hands away. "I don't," she told him.

Quentin's brows came down. "You don't what?"

"Have a thing for your cousin."

His eyebrows popped up. "Oh. Really?"

"Yeah. I *tried* to have a thing for your cousin. But, you know, when I wanted to become a teacher, I went to school, got my degree and certificate and applied to, like, twenty jobs. When I wanted to help my mom take care of my dad, I took the train home every weekend. When I wanted to learn to pole dance, I found a studio and went the next day. When I want pie, I eat pie. But when I tried to hook up with your cousin…" She stepped forward and nudged one of his feet with the toe of her sandal. "I just kept hanging out with you."

He cracked into a grin and Cat almost laughed with delight at how much it changed his face. He was absolutely shining. His eyes were crinkled at the corners, his teeth white and just a little crooked. He was perfect.

"I thought you were gonna tell me that you didn't want to be friends anymore," she said, nudging his foot again.

His smile faded a little bit. "I might have said that, because I'm generally really good at protecting myself. But I got some good advice lately. It was about risk. And connection. And yeah. Here I am."

Cat had a hundred questions. A million. She looked up into his handsome face and couldn't wait to ask every single one of them. She couldn't wait to know him better.

A raindrop landed on his forehead and they both looked with confusion at the sky.

"When did those clouds roll in?" he asked.

"I think it happened when we were gazing goofily into one another's eyes."

That heart-zapping grin of his was back. "Wanna gaze goofily into one another's eyes indoors somewhere?"

"Yes!"

They speed-walked back to their building but didn't beat the rain. Her shirt was stuck to her skin and her jean shorts felt like they'd shrunk two sizes. She couldn't help but notice that his T-shirt clung to what seemed to be some very nicely shaped back muscles.

"Hubba hubba," she said, tracing his biceps as they stood in their hallway, dripping from the rain.

He laughed. "You're ridiculous."

"I'm melting, is what I am."

CARA BASTONE

"At the risk of sounding presumptuous," he said, "your place or mine?"

Cat took him by the hand and unlocked her door, dragging him inside her apartment. Her breath caught at how warm and strong his hand felt.

She kicked the door closed behind her. "Want a towel?"

"Sure—oomph!" He staggered back in surprise when she jumped forward into his arms, her hands linking behind his neck and her legs around his waist. Those warm, strong hands of his found their way to her ass, holding her steady.

"Hi," he said, blinking at her from four inches away.

"Hi," she said back, her smile so big her cheeks ached. "The towels are in the back closet."

"Okay." He turned and carried her to the linen closet and she couldn't stop smiling. He scrabbled for a second at the closet door, but apparently couldn't open it and hold on to her at the same time, so after a brief struggle, simply gave up, pressing her back into the closed door and leaning into her. "I can't get the towels."

"Dang," she said in mock disappointment. "I guess we'll just have to find some other way to warm up."

"I guess we will," he agreed solemnly, his eyes on her mouth.

The blue of his eyes was even more devastating at point-blank range. She couldn't begin to explain why that friendly color was just so freaking sexy. Faded blue, not piercing or even intense. Just perfect.

His eyes bounced from her gaze to her mouth. He leaned in and Cat inhaled hard, her eyes falling closed. He smelled like his familiar detergent. Mint toothpaste and warm weather. His nose touched hers, his wet hair sliding against her forehead. And then his mouth, warm and sure, closed over hers.

EPILOGUE

Ten years later

QUENTIN JUMPED TO the side to avoid the chattering herd of elementary schoolers that careened through the hall to make it to class before the first bell. It was the first day back from summer vacation and he had to smile at the joyous, puppy-like reunions taking place left and right.

He weaved through the hallway until he stood outside Cat's classroom, the same one he'd helped her move into a few years ago.

A dad and his son blocked the doorway as the kid poked his head around the doorjamb.

"She's not here yet," the kid hissed to his dad, something akin to panic in his eyes.

She was a flower in the sun, water on a hot pan, that first gasp of breath after a second too long underwater. He held her firmly pinned between the wall and the broad line of his body. When his tongue swept against hers, Cat knew this was the kind of kiss she'd feel for days, weeks. This kiss was going to have aftershocks.

"Holy smokes," she gasped, rolling her face to the side to take a gulp of much-needed air.

"Yeah," he half laughed, half panted. "Holy smokes."

She narrowed her eyes and brushed her nose against his. "You're going to leave a mark, aren't you?"

"We can only hope," he said. And kissed her again.

"Matty, she's gonna be here. I promise. We checked the class listings. You're both in Ms. Foster's class."

Hearing that, a little electric zing of energy zipped through Quentin from his feet to his ears. Every once in a while—even after all this time—it just really got him, that Cat shared his last name. He'd never expected her to give up her name. LaFievre. He'd been thrilled and honored when she'd decided to hyphenate after they got married. She went by Ms. Foster in the classroom, and at first she'd told him it was because it was easier for the kids to remember. But a few years ago she'd confessed that she liked hearing his last name over and over all day. That every time she got called Ms. Foster, she thought of him.

"Joy!" the little boy called as a girl with two long black braids came scampering up to the doorway.

"Hi, Matty!"

The little boy took her by the hand and tugged her into the classroom, all first-day fears apparently promptly forgotten.

"Oh, thank God," the dad muttered, scrubbing a hand over his face. "That was a near-death experience."

Quentin chuckled and caught the dad's eye. "You were worried? You seemed so calm."

"*Seemed* being the operative word there. I find parenting to be, like, ninety percent bluster. But if Joy had been switched to another class… Man, I am not above bribing somebody."

Quentin laughed and held out his hand. "Quentin."

"Sebastian." They shook hands. "Which one's yours?"

"The one with the long curly hair and the big silver earrings."

Sebastian squinted into the classroom and then his face broke into a smile. "You're Ms. Foster's husband?"

"Yup."

"Nice to meet you, man."

"You too. I'm just gonna deliver the lunch she forgot this morning."

They nodded goodbye and Quentin looked back just in time to see Sebastian taking one last peek into the classroom, checking to see his son safe and happy at his seat.

And then Cat was bounding up to Quentin, going up onto her tiptoes to kiss his cheek. "Q! What are you doing here?"

She looked beautiful today, as she always did. Something about her just really rang Quentin's bell. Her hair was just as wild as when they'd first met, though now there were silvery threads running through it. It was a premature gray, as she was still in her mid-thirties, but instead of freaking out, she'd started naming each new silver hair, delighted with each and every one. "They're my badges of honor, Quentin," she'd insisted.

Had he mentioned that he really dug his wife? Because he pretty much thought she was the greatest of all time. The number one.

He held up her sack lunch to answer her question and the brilliant smile he got in return was definitely worth the schlep over to school.

"Thanks!"

Something over Cat's shoulder caught Quentin's eye and he couldn't help but chuckle as he watched Matty do a pretty spot-on chipmunk impression that had Joy laughing hard. He thought of the rapport between Matty and his dad. The obvious ease. The obvious love.

Quentin and Cat had kicked the having-children can down the road a few times. But Quentin was starting to see it on the horizon again, waiting for them in the middle of the road. And this time? It didn't seem so scary. This time it actually sounded pretty good.

"What's got you smiling like that?" Cat asked him, nudging him in the side with that poky little elbow he'd come to love so much.

"Nothing," he said, pulling her into a hug. "Possibility."

"What kind of possibility?" she asked through comically suspicious eyes.

He shrugged. "Family possibility."

Her eyes widened and then she broke into her signature grin. She knew how complicated his family situation was. She knew every in and out of what it had taken to get him here, to this moment. All the work, all the emotion, all the love. It would be scary for a man like him to stare down the barrel of a family of his own.

But it wasn't. Not with Cat.

Whatever route he took, all train tracks led back to her.

* * * * *

Don't miss Just a Heartbeat Away, *Cara Bastone's full-length debut, available July 2020 wherever HQN Books and ebooks are sold.*

www.HQNBooks.com

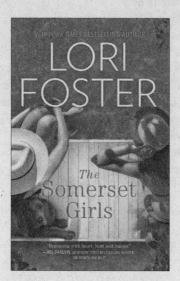